THE SYLPH

EDITED AND WITH
AN INTRODUCTION BY
JONATHAN GROSS

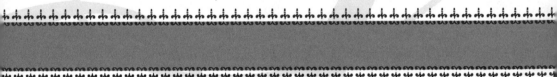

The Sylph

GEORGIANA, DUCHESS OF DEVONSHIRE

a novel

NORTHWESTERN
UNIVERSITY PRESS
EVANSTON, ILLINOIS

Northwestern University Press
www.nupress.northwestern.edu

Printed in the United States of America

10 9 8 7 6 5 4 3 2 1

LIBRARY OF CONGRESS CATALOGING–IN–PUBLICATION DATA

Devonshire, Georgiana Spencer Cavendish, Duchess of,
    1757–1806.
    The sylph : a novel / Georgiana, Duchess of Devonshire ;
edited and with an introduction by Jonathan Gross.
        p. cm.
    Originally published: London: T. Lowndes, 1779.
    Includes bibliographical references.
    ISBN-13: 978-0-8101-2229-1 (pbk. : alk. paper)
    ISBN-10: 0-8101-2229-4 (pbk. : alk. paper)
    1. Guardian angels—Fiction. 2. Welsh—England—
Fiction. I. Gross, Jonathan David, 1962– II. Title.
PR3409.D46S95 2007
823.6—dc22

                                              2007017821

∞ The paper used in this publication meets the minimum re-
quirements of the American National Standard for Information
Sciences—Permanence of Paper for Printed Library Materials,
ANSI Z39.48-1992.

For Sue Betz

CONTENTS

NOTE ON THE TEXT

I have chosen the first 1779 London edition of *The Sylph* for the text of this edition because it had the fewest mechanical errors; it is taken from the Harvard University microfilm (Spencer, Georgiana, Duchess of Devonshire, *The Sylph,* London: T. Lowndes, 1779). There were three editions of *The Sylph* in 1779: a first London edition by T. Lowndes, a second London edition by T. Lowndes, and a first Dublin edition by S. Price et al. All three editions differ in font size, layout, and punctuation. I consulted the first London edition at the Newberry Library as well as the Harvard University microfilm noted above, the first Dublin edition on microfilm at the University of Chicago, and the second London edition in the University of Chicago Special Collections.

The first edition of this novel and subsequent editions that year contain many internal inconsistencies in italics, paragraph breaks, punctuation, capitalization, and spelling of general words and of character names. To achieve internal consistency and to make the text more accessible to today's reader, this edition has been edited to modernize usage, while retaining the spellings and flavor of the original. My thanks to Jessica Paumier of Northwestern University Press for her assistance.

I am pleased to acknowledge Darren Trongcau, Frank De Constanza, Gregory Chavez, and other members of my 1999 bibliography class at DePaul University who created an early edition of the novel as a class assignment. Darren deserves particular mention for his painstaking proofreading and his role as general editor for that assignment. Shannon Siggeman and Peter Stein assisted with bibliographical and historical research.

My special thanks to the University Research Council of DePaul University for financial support.

EDITOR'S INTRODUCTION

"The private (for secret it never was) history of Devonshire House would be curious and amusing as a scandalous chronicle—an exhibition of vice in its most refined and attractive form, full of grace, dignity, and splendour, but I fancy full of misery and sorrow also," Charles Greville wrote.[1] *The Sylph* is a novel that draws heavily upon the "misery and sorrow" that attended Lady Georgiana's life at Devonshire House. The *Gentleman's Magazine* said it showed "too great a knowledge of the ton, and of the worst, though perhaps highest part of the world." Hester Thrale called it "an obscene Novel,"[2] but other reviewers were more positive. "There is ingenuity in the plan of this novel, and a sufficient variety of events, but several improbabilities in the subordinate circumstances," the *Critical Review* wrote. William Enfield of the *Monthly Review* noted that "this story has the uncommon merit of some originality in its plan; the story is agreeably related; and many good moral reflections are suggested in the course of the narrative."[3]

Lady Georgiana never publicly acknowledged that she wrote *The Sylph*, for it would have been unthinkable for an aristocratic woman to do so, especially considering the negative account of her marriage to the duke and her unflattering portrait of her close friend, Lady Melbourne. The novel itself contains internal evidence of her authorship, however: references to the "radishes" with which the Duchess of D—— adorned her hair, to the Spencer name, and to fashionable innovations in hair and dress. "When challenged in public Georgiana refused to comment," Amanda Foreman notes, "but it became common knowledge that she had admitted the truth in private."[4] A receipt at the British Library suggests that Thomas Hookham paid Sophia Briscoe for *The Sylph*. Though Briscoe may have served as middleperson between Lady Georgiana and her publisher, it is unlikely that Briscoe wrote the novel. The author's allusions in both *Emma*, Lady Georgiana's first work, and *The Sylph* distinguish them sharply from Sophia Briscoe's *The Fine Lady* and *Miss Melmoth*. *The Sylph* contains a few quotations identical to those in *Emma*. Other allusions to similar writers—Nicholas Rowe, Fanny Greville, Alexander Pope, and Matthew Prior—suggest the same person wrote both works. "A close reading . . . shows it is Georgiana's voice we are hearing," Brian Masters notes.[5] Finally, a Dublin edition of *Emma* published in 1787 lists the anonymous writer as "author of *The Sylph*."

Georgiana, Duchess of Devonshire, wrote many plays and poems. The two novels attributed to her, *Emma; or, The Unfortunate Attachment* and *The Sylph*, were published in 1773 and 1779, respectively. Georgiana's life was only beginning to unfold when she wrote the sentimental and somewhat contrived epistolary novel *Emma*. By the time she finished *The Sylph*, her ideas were more fully formed. She had married in 1774. A year later, she was consoling her friend Anne Damer after Damer's debt-ridden and dandified husband shot himself in a tavern. Lady Georgiana drew on these events, as well as her gambling addiction, to write her novel. Three years later, she began her extraordinarily close friendship with Elizabeth Foster. Other life-altering events followed: she helped Charles James Fox win election to Parliament; witnessed a secret wedding between Maria Fitzherbert and the Prince of Wales; had an illegitimate child by Charles Grey; toured the continent for two years with her mother, Bess, and her sister; underwent a series of excruciatingly painful eye operations; retreated from the public gaze; and died in 1806, a stranger to her own family, her best friend having effectively usurped her position as wife to the Duke of Devonshire. How did all this happen to a woman who, according to the prince, was the "best natured and best bred woman in England"?[6]

Lady Georgiana's Life

Georgiana was born on June 7, 1757, the daughter of Lord John Spencer and Lady Spencer. John Spencer became Baron Spencer Althorp in 1761, then Viscount Althorp, and finally Earl Spencer in 1765.[7] His wife, Lady Spencer, was a woman of strong religious convictions, bordering on fanaticism, though she shunned metaphysics and controversy. "Christianity as taught in the Gospel has nothing formidable in it," Lady Spencer wrote. "The end and design of it is not to sour but to sweeten life."[8] But Lady

Spencer was a formidable woman. She rose early, at five thirty in the morning, dressed, said her prayers, and read some passages from the Bible. She dined at three, had supper at nine, and went to bed by ten. While following this strict regimen, she found time for amusements including gambling, a vice that became hard to break. "I have known the Poyntzes [Lady Spencer's birth family] in the nursery," George Granville noted, "the Bible on the table, the cards in the drawer."[9]

There were five children born to this family: Georgiana, George (1758), Harriet (1761), Charlotte (1765), and Louise (1769), but the latter two died as infants. In 1772, the family went on a grand tour of Europe to help Lord and Lady Spencer recover from their deaths. "You know the perhaps uncommon tenderness I have for my children," Lady Spencer explained to Thea Cowper.[10] Frequent trips to the continent as well as an increasing religious fanaticism helped Lady Spencer stave off depression. During the tour in 1772, Lady Georgiana traveled from Calais to Brussels and Spa, taking part in a boar hunt with her sister in Liege. She slept with a blanket on the floor and visited the gallows. "Papa says it is foolish and superstitious to be afraid of seeing dead bodies," Harriet reported in her diary.[11] Despite Harriet's account of their hardships, Lord Spencer, who boasted a weekly income of seven hundred pounds, traveled in style. In Paris,[12] Lord Spencer gave a ball on Marie Antoinette's birthday[13] that lasted until six in the morning. Amid this dissipation, Georgiana's parents nevertheless taught their children the importance of religious tolerance, especially between Catholics and Protestants. In April 1773, the family visited the convent of Saint-Cyr, returning to England in June of that year. Despite her best efforts at repentance and religious instruction, however, Lady Spencer still found "a mixture of Vanity and false humility about me that is detestable."[14]

While her sister, Harriet, kept a diary of their travels, Georgiana wrote her first novel, *Emma; or, The Unfortunate Attachment*, which appeared anonymously in 1773. Lady Georgiana was well equipped to write her novel at so young an age. Some of her rivals, Maria Falconer for example, were likewise only thirteen or fourteen. Jane Austen was a tender sixteen when she wrote *Love and Friendship*. Lady Georgiana's own juvenile work went into four editions and included an illustration, the latter of which was rare for that time. It is not known how the young girl arranged for publication with

Thomas Lowndes, but she came from a family connected to the publishing world. Her mother, an amateur musician, served as patron to Laurence Sterne and enjoyed the company of Samuel Johnson. Lady Georgiana was also highly educated, displaying her erudition with a light hand. She learned drawing from the royal drawing master, John Greese; music from composer Thomas Linley (father-in-law to playwright Richard Sheridan); and writing from Sir William Jones; as well as French, Latin, Italian, dancing, and horsemanship.

On June 7, 1774, Lady Georgiana married the fifth Duke of Devonshire. In some ways, this arranged marriage came about naturally, since the duke had visited Althorp as early as 1765, when he was sixteen and Lady Georgiana was eight. Her husband's great wealth warrants some explanation, for to learn about his ancestors is to understand key passages in England's history. The story begins with Sir William Cavendish, an advisor to Henry VIII, who played a key role in the dissolution of the monasteries. He married Elizabeth Hardwick, Countess of Shrewsbury (or Bess, as she was called), one of the most celebrated women of the sixteenth century after Queen Elizabeth. Of Bess's four marriages, this was the only one to produce any children, so she left William Cavendish almost all of the property she had acquired from her three other marriages.[15] Bess's first surviving son, William Cavendish, inherited Chatsworth, Hardwick, and Oldcotes, all in Derbyshire. Cavendish became a baron in 1605 and the Earl of Devonshire in 1618. The second earl was a student of Thomas Hobbes's and the third a fellow of the Royal Society in 1663. Most famous of all was the fourth earl. He supported the Exclusion Bill (which limited the monarchy to Protestants), inviting the Prince of Orange to assume the English throne. For his bravery in playing a pivotal role in the Revolution of 1688,[16] William III made the fourth earl, William Cavendish, Duke of Devonshire in 1694. During the eighteenth century, the second and third dukes acquired more property while the fourth became prime minister for six months in 1756.[17] He married the Earl of Burlington's daughter. By the time the fourth duke died in 1764, his property included Chatsworth in Derbyshire and Devonshire House in London, as well as five other homes: Lismore Castle in Ireland, Hardwick House and Bolton Abbey in Yorkshire, and Chiswick House and Burlington House in London.[18] All of this property as well as the enormous responsibility for its upkeep passed to the fifth duke, the fourth duke's sixteen-year-old son, William,[19] who would marry Georgiana Spencer.

"Constitutional apathy formed his distinguishing characteristic," Nathaniel Wraxall, the diplomat, noted of Lady Georgiana's future husband.[20] He rarely attended the opera, played the piano with indifference, and shunned the waltz. "His Grace is an amiable and respectable character, but *dancing is not his forte*,"[21] one newspaper observed. He liked nothing more than playing whist and faro at Brooks until four in the morning and returning to a meal of cold mackerel. "To be sure the jewell *has not been well polished*," observed Mary Delany, a diarist who wrote six volumes of letters as well as an autobiography. She knew the Spencers as far back as 1754 and so was in a good position to judge.[22] "I wd not marry him," Mary Hamilton noted in her diary, "it is a pity he is not more ostensibly agreeable, dear charming lady Georgiana will not be well matched."[23]

The duke's cultivated eccentricity concealed a profound knowledge of classical languages and Shakespeare as well as sound political judgment. At Brooks, a prominent social club in London, his opinions about literature were regarded as final. Despite these talents, he shunned the political spotlight during the Regency crisis and did not participate in Lord Grenville's alliance of Charles James Fox's supporters and those of former Prime Minister Lord Sidmouth (dubbed the "Ministry of All the Talents"), much to his wife's dismay. He had an almost pathological reserve, preferring the company of his dogs to close relations. Other members of the family were, by turns, shy, intellectual, and adventurous. The fourth Duke's brother, Lord John Cavendish, served as Chair of the Exchequer. George Cavendish wrote *The Life and Death of Cardinal Wolsey*, a landmark Tudor biography. Thomas Cavendish became a well-known navigator. Henry Cavendish was a well-respected astronomer, mathematician, and geologist and an admirer of the duke's multitalented wife.[24]

Georgiana Spencer also came from a distinguished family. Her father had been knighted by Henry VIII and made Baronet Althorp in 1508. The earldom of Sunderland came into the family in 1643, staying with them for ninety years until absorbed into the dukedom of Marlborough in 1733. Lady Georgiana's grandfather was John Spencer, the favorite grandson of Sarah, the Duchess of Marlborough, from whom he inherited Althorp in Northamptonshire and Spencer House in London. The Blenheim estates went to Spencer's older brothers and sisters. At the death of his sister, Spencer also inherited Wimbledon Park, under the condition that he not accept office under the Crown. However, much of the monetary portion of that fortune would be gambled away by Georgiana's parents. When her father died in 1783, his widow had to live on a restricted income, mortified by the debts they had accumulated.

Georgiana's father had married Margaret Georgiana Poyntz, daughter of Stephen Poyntz, in 1755. Poyntz was the son of an upholsterer. Despite his modest family origins, Stephen Poyntz became tutor to George I's son, the Duke of Cumberland, and then a Privy Councillor. His friendship with the Duke of Devonshire's family became his daughter's greatest contribution to her marriage to John Spencer.[25] The Poyntzes had raised Margaret and their other children to be little courtiers, a quality passed on to their grandchildren, Georgiana and Henrietta Frances (hereafter referred to as Harriet). Georgiana's mother and father were friendly with the French court, especially Marie Antoinette and the Duchess de Polignac, a lifelong and sometimes jealous friend of Lady Georgiana's.

Shortly after their marriage, Lady Georgiana was presented at St. James, where she was well received by George III and Queen Charlotte. At their home in Chatsworth, Lady Georgiana learned to keep public days, when the duke and duchess welcomed clergymen, attorneys, and their families to their home. Painful at first, this social custom, like others, became something at which the duchess excelled. Nevertheless, Lady Georgiana also became increasingly aware of the social pressures that attended her position as the duke's wife. The rules were counterintuitive, even soul-killing, for they included showing little to no affection to her husband in public. Shortly before being presented at court, for example, Lady Georgiana sat on her husband's lap and put her arms around his neck. Brutally, he broke the embrace, quickly rose, and left the room. All this occurred while her mother and sister watched. Afterward Lady Spencer wrote letters admonishing her daughter to do her best to please her husband.[26] "Does he seem pleased and satisfied with you, and do you ever pass any part of the day together in riding, walking, reading or musick?" Lady Spencer asked in one letter.[27]

Despite Lady Spencer's best efforts, Lady Georgiana grew increasingly distant from her husband. The process may well have begun when the young bride learned that Charlotte Spencer, who happened to have the same last name as his wife's family, was carrying the fifth duke's child when he married Lady Georgiana. This type of sexual promiscuity was as prevalent in Lady Georgiana's world as the double standard. The third Duke of Richmond had three daughters by his housekeeper, Mrs. Bennet. Of Lady Melbourne's six children, only the first was fathered by her husband with any certainty. When they had affairs, most aristocratic women did so after they provided a male heir, thus giving the first-born son exclusive right to the family estate. Primogeniture, as this system was called, restricted the marital prospects of all other members of the family. Many an English novel treats the injustice of it, but in 1775, one played by the rules, or not at all. Lady Georgiana broke one of the unwritten ones: discretion. Demoralized by years of compromises with her truculent husband, she indulged in a public affair with Charles Grey after the birth of her son, Hart.

In January 1775, the duke and duchess moved to London and Devonshire House. Lady Georgiana delighted the society she met in London. With her fair hair, sparkling eyes, and tall stature, she impressed a number of men, including David Garrick. "Were I five and twenty I could go mad about her," Garrick wrote to Henry Bate. "As I am past five and fifty I would only suffer martyrdom for her."[28] Mrs. Delany praised her "*kindness embellished by politeness.*"[29] Wraxall found that she diffused "a nameless charm over existence."[30] Lady Georgiana uses the phrase "animated nature" to describe her heroine in *The Sylph*, but this term was obviously first applied to Georgiana, who once posed for a painting by Maria Cosway in which she was depicted as the goddess Diana, bursting through clouds. And Georgiana cherished a compliment she once received from a drunken Irishman who asked if he could light his pipe by the fire of her beautiful eyes.[31]

Before her marriage, Melbourne and Carlton House were the central attractions for the leaders of the Whigs. After her marriage, Lady Georgiana became the most fashionable woman in London. Lady Melbourne soon befriended the duchess and included in their circle of intimacy the sculptress Anne Damer. Some of Lady Melbourne's friends were slightly disreputable, and Lady Spencer, Lady Georgiana's mother, worried about her daughter's connection with them. Damer's husband, John (the prototype for *The Sylph*'s Lord Stanley), shot himself dead at the Bedford Arms in Covent Garden on August 15, 1775, when he was overcome by gambling debts. Anne Damer was ordered from Milton Abbey, blamed by her father-in-law for his son's demise. Depicted in a novel, *Marriage,* by Susan Ferrier, as a mannish woman who cross-dresses, Anne Damer certainly led a life apart, although there is no evidence that Damer wrote her only novel, *Belmour,* in 1802, to conceal her sexual preference. She came to live on Craven Street, behind Lady Melbourne's home, and enjoyed a remarkably productive career as a neoclassical sculptress, producing, among other works, busts of Napoleon, Charles James Fox (presented to Catherine the Great), and her close friend Lady Melbourne. Damer commissioned a painting of herself and her two friends titled *Witches Round the Cauldron,* which gives some idea of the trouble these women courted. On the back of the canvas there appears a short poem referring to the "witchcraft" of the eyes depicted.

Despite her social success, even the status-conscious Lady Melbourne had to admit that Devonshire House was grander than her own residence at Whitehall, with an art collection that could not be matched. The marble and alabaster staircase led to a library and to works by Titian, Tintoretto, Van Dyck, and Rubens.

Within this magnificent home, Lady Georgiana found her affectionate nature crushed by the duke's icy demeanor and sought to escape. She took refuge in cultivating French fashions in England, gambling, and dissipation. "The pretty Duchess of Devonshire . . . dines at seven, summer as well as winter, goes to bed at three, and lies in bed till four: she has hysteric fits in the morning, and dances in the evening," Lady Sarah Lennox observed.[32] Despite an allowance of four thousand pounds a year, Lady Georgiana found herself in significant debt by 1776.[33] She owed sixteen hundred pounds to tradesmen, which, as William Combe later pointed out, did not sit well with her political views and hard-won populism.

In August 1777, Lady Georgiana met Charles James Fox at Chatsworth. Like Georgiana, he had a weakness for gambling, having spent a fortune of two hundred fifty thousand pounds by the time they met. Fox had attended Eton and then Hertford College, Oxford, for two years. At seventeen, he traveled to Paris and Italy. He spent sixteen thousand pounds in ten days in Naples and traveled from Paris to Lyons to buy several silk waistcoats. He once smashed his father's gold watch just to see what it looked like broken, and his doting father did not stop him. Upon his death in 1774, Fox's father left him twenty thousand pounds cash, estates in Sheppey and Thanet, and the estate of Kingsgate. His father's brother Stephen (Charles James Fox's uncle) left him a sinecure worth twenty-three hundred pounds a year in 1775. He spent it all. Lady Georgiana's daughter, Harriet (or Harry-O, as she was called), noted that "with his superior talents and abilities, he is with all the nature and simplicity of a child."[34]

In *The Sylph*, Lady Georgiana mocks French fashions and ridicules Lord Stanley as a fop. She never reconciled this with the fact that Charles James Fox, the man she most admired, led the macaronis in outlandish conduct. "The term 'macaroni' was coined to describe the fashionable young fops of the 1770s who wore exaggerated clothes about town," Amanda Foreman observes.[35] There was a Macaroni Club, which distinguished itself by preferring foreign, especially Italian, food and employing foreign terms. In June 1770, the *Oxford Magazine* noted, "There is indeed a kind of animal, neither male nor female, a thing of the neuter gender, lately started up amongst us. It is called a Macaroni. It talks without meaning, it smiles without pleasantry, it eats without appetite, it rides without exercise, it wenches without passion."[36] Both Lady Georgiana's husband, who posed for Pompeo Batoni, and Fox emulated the manners of Italian men.

With his swarthy appearance and corpulent frame, Fox was an unlikely candidate for this delicate species. Friends called Fox "the Brow" because both eyebrows seemed permanently connected. For days, he would wrap himself in a winding cloth, barely bathing between bouts of gambling and dissipation. At other moments, he affected an interest in fashion. Fox imported blue hair powder from Paris, used cosmetics extensively, and wore hats with feathers, red heels on his shoes, and frilly lace, velvet, and brocade. In the House of Commons, he donned the buff and blue worn by George Washington's army. As Camus wrote of the dandies of another era, Fox signaled his political views by the clothes he chose to wear.

But Fox was also a genius. By age twenty-eight, he had been in Parliament nine years. He served as Junior Lord of the Admiralty at twenty-one and was then Junior Lord of the Treasury. At a time when Edmund Burke quoted *Macbeth* to explain the Regency crisis and Sheridan wrote speeches for the Prince of Wales with one hand and dramas with another, Fox was the standard of eloquence, possessing erudition in five languages. He could fill the House of Commons. "He seems to have the particular talent of knowing more about what he is saying and with less pains than anyone else," Lady

Georgiana observed.[37] Perhaps the emphasis should have been on "seems." In her diary, she noted that the "virtues and foibles of Mr. Fox, the comprehensive mind, undaunted genius, and unabating kindness, which added to the most unaffected simplicity, constitute his Character, but we may also trace what has told alas, so much against him; a contempt for even necessary expedients, a great imprudence in conversation; and a fear, which in him is superior to every thing of seeming to yield what he thinks right to the bias of public opinion."[38]

At the time Charles James Fox met Georgiana, she had already cultivated a few eccentricities of her own. The Devonshires had developed their own accent, calling yellow "yaller," gold "goold," and Rome "Room." *Spoil* rhymed with *mile*, and London was called "Lonnon." "Cucumber" was "cowcumber"; "china" was "chayna." Her late hours and skimpy wardrobe inspired satires by the sanctimonious William Combe, who wrote "A Letter to Her Grace the Duchess of Devonshire" and "The Duchess of Devonshire's Cow," poems admonishing her to set an example for her social class.[39] More impressively, Georgiana drew the attention of Richard Sheridan, whose *School for Scandal* satirized the circle he longed to enter.[40] His play, attended by the Devonshire House circle on opening night, May 8, 1777, was dedicated to Anne Crewe, whom Sheridan described, later in life, as "the handsomest of the set."[41] She hosted a salon on Grosvenor Street and was a rival to Lady Georgiana in the fashionable world, but they all attended the play together. Sheridan playfully ridiculed the conversation, gambling, and obsession with fashion prevalent in the Devonshire House set. Some of the best *bon mots*, however, come from the philosophical Lady Melbourne, dubbed "the Thorn" by her acquaintances for her sharp tongue. She resembled Sheridan's Lady Sneerwell, who states, "There's no possibility of being witty without a little ill-nature."[42] Lady Melbourne's cynical view of marriage is also recalled by Lady Teazdale, Sheridan's heroine, who informs her husband that "women of fashion in London are accountable to nobody after they are married."[43] Both Lady Melbourne and Lady Teazdale hail from the provinces and quickly learn to gain the upper hand over their husbands, who seriously underestimate their abilities.

Lady Georgiana had a softer side than her friend Lady Melbourne. She made her mark on the beau monde not by outtalking her rivals, as the Thorn did, but by outdressing them. Though she helped invent the Spencer bonnet, muslin gown, and various and sundry hats, Lady Georgiana is perhaps best remembered for the high hairstyles she helped popularize. Following her example, women began decorating their hair with roses, acorns, turnips, and potatoes. They wore not one, two, or six feathers, but eleven. "The three *most* elevated plumes of feathers are the Duchess of Devonshire, Lady Mary Somerset, and Lady Harriet Stanhope,"[44] one woman recorded in her diary. Lady Georgiana finally defeated her rivals by wearing an ostrich feather four feet high, which she acquired from Lord Stormont. Sheridan mocked the fashion in *A Trip to Scarborough* (1777):

> No heads of old too high for feathered state.
> Hindered the fair to pass the lowest gate.
> A church to enter now they must be bent,
> If ever they should try th'experiment.[45]

As Sheridan's play predicted, soon women not only "bent" to enter church but sat on the floors of their carriages in order to be transported to and from their fashionable evening engagements. Even Lady Georgiana acknowledges this extreme fashion in *The Sylph*, when Lady Stanley observes, "A head might burn for an hour without damaging the genuine part of it."

Lady Georgiana's frivolous concern with fashion reflected the personality of a woman with more sensibility than sense. She paid a high price for this. "Life is a comedy to those who think, a tragedy to those who feel," Lady Melbourne wrote, quoting La Bruyere.[46] Lady Georgiana fell into the latter category. Sheridan must have understood this when he asked Lady Georgiana to compose the music for a song, "I Have a Silent Sorrow Here," that appeared in one of his plays; the work was a success on both sides of the Atlantic.[47] Georgiana's response to feeling in literature, as in music, is also evident in her copy of *La Nouvelle Héloïse* at Chatsworth, which has several passages underlined by her own pen: "Sens-tu combien un coeur languissant est tender, et combien la tristesse sait fermenter l'amour?" ("Can you feel how tender a heart is that languishes, and how sadness knows how to inspire love?").[48] At the end of her life, she followed the strategy of Rousseau in his *Confessions*, believing "tout comprendre est tout pardonner." She wrote a note to exculpate herself with her grandchildren: "Before you condemn me, remember that at seventeen, I was a toast, a beauty, and a Duchess, and wholly neglected by my husband."[49]

The Sylph was most likely written in Derby, England, during April 1778, when Lady Georgiana underwent a spiritual crisis and self-reckoning, the results of which can be clearly seen in her novel.[50] At this time, Lady Georgiana wrote to her mother, "I have the strongest sense of having many things to repent of and my heart is determined to mend."[51] Once in Derby, her plan was to take Holy Communion, which was not often given in the eighteenth century. Georgiana's letters to her mother show that religious self-study formed an important counterpoint to her bouts of giddy dissipation. Lady Georgiana's voice in the novel is thus complex, since she imported (often from Paris) many of the fashionable vices she criticized. "The hurry I live in here distracts me," she confessed in a 1778 letter to her closest friend, Mary Graham. "When I first came into the world the novelty of the scene made me like everything but my heart now feels only an emptiness in the *beau monde* which cannot be filled."[52] In October 1774, shortly after her marriage, Georgiana wrote another letter, which may have lingered in her mind when she chose the novel's title: "I should be very happy if I could borrow some friendly Sylph (if any are so kind as to hover about Hardwick) and a pair of wings that I might pay you now and then a visit."[53]

Many details of Lady Georgiana's life resemble motifs in her novel: the passion for gambling, the influence of bad acquaintances, and the lure of dissipation. Lady Besford recalls Lady Melbourne; Maria Finch, Lady Georgiana's sister, Harriet. More striking are the incidents the novel records: Lord Stanley's horrific suicide evokes John Damer's. Maria Maynard's visit to Edward Grenville's military camp anticipates Lady Georgiana's visit to Coxheath in June 1778. Like Maria, Georgiana also lived in camp, accompanied by a maid. Maria insists on fighting alongside her husband, an exaggeration of Lady Georgiana's female military corps at Coxheath, the members of which wore a modified version of a man's riding coat over a close-fitting dress.[54] Lady Georgiana's attention-getting behavior annoyed her husband, who took his revenge by having an affair with Lady Jersey that June. Many of these events, though not the last, found their way into revisions of her novel, begun in April.

Though the novel reveals Lady Georgiana's sense of loneliness and despair, matters were soon to change. In 1782, Lady Georgiana traveled to Bath with her husband and met a person more helpful (at least initially) than the one she had imagined in her novel. Elizabeth Foster, or Bess, as she came to be called, appealed to Georgiana because of her frailty and helplessness. Trapped in a loveless marriage and struggling to conceive a child, Georgiana found in her close friend an immediate confidante. All three of them spent a memorable summer together in Plympton in June 1782. During this time, the stolid Duke of Devonshire, with the more conniving Elizabeth Foster, quietly orchestrated the eighteenth century's most famous example of a ménage à trois. They referred to each other by nicknames: Racky (Bess, who had a recurring cough), Canis (the duke, who loved dogs), and the Rat (Georgiana, for reasons which escape us, but the nickname came to fit the unflattering role she would play in the threesome). In some ways, Bess was a more experienced (if absentee) mother than Georgiana, having given birth to two sons, Frederick in 1777 and Augustus, born at Ickworth, in 1780, before being deprived of custody by her unpredictable and vindictive husband. Lady Elizabeth Foster played the role of victim as well as that of the comforting and corrupting mother-replacement for Georgiana, who demanded Foster's exclusive attention.

Georgiana's mother distrusted Bess from the beginning, both for her ingratiating, manipulative ways and for the Hervey blood she inherited from her father. The Herveys were a deeply eccentric family, one of whom was parodied as the bisexual "Sporus" in Pope's verse. "Once a week, he ate an apple and took emetics every day," an observer wrote of Lady Bess's father.[55] Without telling his family, he rented their St. James Square house for seven hundred pounds a year and spent the money in Europe while forcing his daughter to live on three hundred pounds a year. "Blasphemy was the puddle in which he washed away his Episcopal Protestantism," Walpole wrote acidly of Hervey, calling him a "mitred Proteus."[56]

When tongues began to wag about Bess's continual presence with the Devonshires and the possibility of her affair with the duke, she was given the responsibility of governess to Charlotte Williams (the duke's illegitimate daughter) and sent to travel Europe in December 1782.[57] Lady Spencer had much to do with Bess's departure, but Foster had already played a crucial role in the life of the Devonshires, unbeknownst to Lady Spencer. She helped Georgiana conceive her first child, who would be born the next year (1783), by keeping her from bouts of self-destructive behavior. In 1783, Bess wrote tearful letters from Paris, Nice, and Naples, complaining of her loneliness. She reminded the Devonshires of her role as spiritual midwife to them—"Kiss *our* child for me," she wrote—and her longing to be reunited with her sons.[58] "Oh my dear dear children, had I them with me I think I should find a resting-place."[59] Lady Georgiana embraced such vulnerability. So close had Lady Georgiana and Bess become that a jealous Duchess de Polignac, who prized her friendship with Lady Georgiana and noticed the extensive correspondence between London and Paris, helped circulate rumors that Lady Georgiana and Bess were a lesbian couple. "Who has any right to know how long or how tenderly we love one another!" Bess protested. "Why are excuses to be made for its sharpness and its fervency . . . Why is our union to be profaned by having a lie told about it?" she asked.[60]

After Lady Georgiana's first child was safely delivered in July 1783, when Bess was on the continent, Lady Georgiana returned to the fray of exhibitionist politics. Observing her talent as a populist organizer at Coxheath, in 1778, Charles James Fox asked her to canvass on his behalf in Westminster. Along with her sister, Harriet, and the Duchess of Portland (a relative of her husband's), Georgiana played a crucial role in getting Fox elected. The election hinged in part on the Prince of Wales's hostility toward his father. Fox, Sheridan, and others courted the prince's company, while the staid George III, or Farmer George as he was known, resented them for corrupting his son. As radical Whigs, Fox and his consort were determined to wrest executive power from the king, and they made use of the Devonshire House circle to help them do so. Fox won a seat in Parliament, a Pyrrhic victory, since he also earned the enmity of George III and Queen Charlotte in the process.

Georgiana's tactics for getting Fox elected were controversial. She allegedly kissed butchers, a charge she vehemently denied, and drove potential voters to the polls in her own carriage. She paid exorbitantly for ordinary items in a local London shop, thereby gaining votes for her favorite candidate. One Cockney elector wrote of her with approval: "Lord, sir, it was a fine sight to see a grand lady come right smack to us hardworking mortals, with a hand held out, and a 'master, how-dye-do.'"[61] Others were less impressed:

> I had rather kiss my Moll than she,
> With all her paint and finery;
> What's a Duchess more than a Woman?[62]

Alarmed by the duchess's campaigning tactics, William Pitt began proceedings charging Lady Georgiana with election fraud and enlisted the Duchess of Gordon to organize support for the Tories.

Campaigning so vigorously for Fox and dancing at public events with the Prince of Wales, Georgiana exceeded the rules of propriety. Soon she was accused of having relationships with both men.[63] Caricaturists depicted Lady Georgiana suckling a fox, implying a romantic liaison between the two. "You do not think that I, as a woman, ever was, could be, or am in love with Charles Fox," Lady Georgiana wrote.[64] Circumstantial evidence suggests that Georgiana did become romantically involved with Fox,[65] perhaps at a weak moment, but romantic attraction was not her motive in campaigning for him. She longed for an active role in political life that Georgian England was not prepared to offer a woman.

After the election came to a close in April 1784, Lady Georgiana helped the Prince of Wales through a romantic crisis. That July he staged a false suicide attempt to convince the reluctant Catholic widow Maria Fitzherbert to marry him. She had good reasons for her reluctance. The Act of Settlement forbade a monarch from marrying outside the Protestant faith. More pointedly, the 1774 Royal Marriages Act left the Prince Regent's choice of wife to the king. Maria Fitzherbert arrived at Devonshire House on that day in July, requesting that Lady Georgiana, the prince's close friend, accompany her. Upon arriving at Carlton House, they found the prince covered in blood, though the wound was superficial. "They told me the Prince had run himself through the body and missed his heart by the breadth of a nail," she later remembered. "If P had died they might all [Keates, the surgeon, Bouverie] have been tried for their lives."[66] Lady Georgiana was furious about the prince's manipulative behavior. At the same time, Lady Georgiana lent the prince one of her rings, which he then placed on Fitzherbert's fourth finger. The hastily conducted marriage ceremony was not binding, but the incident had the dubious merit of drawing Lady Georgiana even closer to the unstable Prince of Wales. After the suicide attempt, when Georgiana became pregnant with her second child, the prince visited her three or four times a day to discuss his ongoing affair with Maria Fitzherbert. Many assumed that he was the father of Georgiana's second child, further compromising Lady Georgiana's reputation and earning her the wrath of Fitzherbert.

Fitzherbert was not the only one annoyed by the duchess's ability to attract attention. Feeling estranged by his wife's flamboyant conduct during Fox's election and the prince's marriage, the duke reunited with Bess, who had returned to England in August 1784. When Bess departed again for Europe in January 1785,[67] she was pregnant with the duke's child (Lady Georgiana also became pregnant at this time). Foster gave birth to Caroline St. Jules on the island of Ischia[68] and returned to England in July 1786. In 1787, she bore another child by the duke, though she remained envious of Lady Georgiana's established position as Whig grandee.

At this time, Lady Georgiana had two children but no male heirs, a serious problem given her position. Her husband's attraction to Elizabeth Foster, along with Lady Georgiana's fertility problems and gambling debts, threatened to undermine her position as duchess. Her anxiety about these matters led her to plunge further into a life of gambling. A few years later she did give birth to a son and heir named Hart, whom many considered to be Foster's rather than her own, but the blow to her self-esteem and self-respect had already been struck. On the evening that Lady Georgiana went into labor, Lady Foster visited the opera in Paris to dispel rumors that she had given birth herself.

Lady Georgiana believed her husband would forgive her debt once she provided him with a male heir. He did so, but not without imposing on his nervous wife a carefully calibrated system of emotional blackmail. As a woman who used her charm to gain favors, Lady Georgiana brought this on herself in part. Helpless financially—she could not work for a living—she lived in a world of barter. For example, in 1787 she accumulated debts with the banker Thomas Coutts, promising to introduce his daughters to French society in exchange for loans. He played along with her for a while, but eventually embarrassed her by going to her husband for repayment. Later that year, when Coutts failed her, Georgiana borrowed from the French banker Comte Perregaux and the French finance minister Charles Alexandre de Calonne, delaying payment to both as she had to Coutts. She sold a watch to pay her debts, then tried to buy it back after she won at the gaming table. Trading on her charm, she would play the helpless female, procuring a six-thousand-pound loan from the Duke of Bedford or a two-thousand-pound loan from the Prince of Wales. The Duke of Bedford refused to speak to her after she defaulted on a loan she had interpreted as a gift, but she could never understand his hostility. When her daughter came out in 1800, Lady Georgiana tried to marry her to the thirty-five-year-old Bedford. He became engaged to the Tory Duchess of Gordon's daughter instead—a double snub, for this highly influential landholder was now lost to the Whigs.

Disturbed by her daughter's gambling addiction, Lady Spencer confessed to having set a bad example, which Georgiana had "but too faithfully imitated."[69] After one year of marriage, Georgiana had owed money which her husband quickly paid, but the problem persisted. Moneylenders such as Howard and Gibbs advanced her sums at exorbitant interest. The following year a game Lady Georgiana's father had played was fashionable once more. "The . . . amusement which engrosses everybody who lives in what is called the pleasurable world is Pharo," George Selwyn wrote in 1781.[70] The game came to England from France, where it was popular in the court of Louis XIV. It was played with a pack of fifty-two cards, a banker, and punters. During the 1784 election, Lady Georgiana confessed to Elizabeth Foster that she had "a very, very large debt. I never had courage to own it, and try'd to win it at play, by which means it became immense and was grown (I have not the courage to write the sum, but will tell you when I see you), many, many, many thousands."[71] In May 1787, Georgiana and Harriet joined a consortium behind a new faro bank, which included the Prince of Wales and the Duke of Rutland. "The duchess is in debt to all the banks she has ever been connected with," Daniel Pulteney wrote in 1787.[72] Four years later, Georgiana was practically arrested with Harriet for betting on numbers in a lottery office behind the opera. A sneering Horace Walpole wrote to Mary Berry on March 5, 1791, informing her, "Two of our first ladies, sisters, have descended into the *basse cour* of the [Exchange] Alley with Jews and brokers, and waddled out with a large loss of feathers, though not so inconsiderable as was said—yet twenty-three thousand makes a great gap in pin money."[73]

Gambling could make women sexually vulnerable to their creditors, as *The Sylph* suggests, but Lady Georgiana seems to have escaped this humiliation. In 1783, she fell in love with the talented orator and future prime minister Charles Grey, but she did not allow herself to act on her passion until she had delivered a male heir in 1790. Remaining more or less faithful to her husband for eighteen years, she had a child by Grey in 1792. The duke forced Lady Georgiana to choose between her children and Grey. She chose her children, and Grey never forgave her. During her exile, for the duke had not forgiven her entirely, Lady Georgiana sent letters to Lady Melbourne for "Black," her code name for Grey, but he rarely answered, or did so in anger. While abroad to deliver Grey's baby, Lady Georgiana wrote a letter in her own blood to each of her children, declaring her undying devotion to them. More publicly, she wrote "The Passage of the Mountain of St. Gothard," a travel poem dedicated, in part, to them. After her return to England in 1792, Lady Georgiana had a joyous reunion with her three children by the duke (Little G, Harry-O, and Hart, who would become the sixth Duke of Devonshire).

Back at Chatsworth, Georgiana was now a middle-aged woman who suffered from debilitating headaches. In 1796, a series of operations on her right eye, intended to relieve these symptoms, only made matters worse. The condition spread to her left eye as well. She was subjected to a tourniquet tied around her neck, a cruel device concocted for the dubious purpose of flushing out the eye, which almost choked her to death. When she did not recover by September of that year, she agreed to undergo electric shocks recommended by the inventor Erasmus Darwin. Recovering from this treatment, she lost the use of her right eye completely and thereafter kept from public view. She spent her time on a fossil collection at Devonshire House and catalogued the books in the library. She earned the respect of noted chemist and family member Henry Cavendish, and her fossil collection at Chatsworth is still of considerable importance.

Nonetheless, in the early 1800s, Lady Georgiana remained active in politics. Her political diary, which she kept in 1801, shows that she enjoyed the confidence of Charles James Fox and the Whigs, as well as the entourage surrounding the Prince of Wales. She shaped events through her private parties.[74] After Pitt's death on January 23, 1806, Lady Georgiana arranged a rapprochement between the powerful Grenville faction and the Foxite Whigs, which became known as the Ministry of All the Talents. The Grenvilles were more politically conservative than Fox but proved instrumental in wresting power from the Tories. Lady Georgiana also kept the Whigs from allowing vanity to splinter their alliance. She kept Richard Sheridan from exerting undue influence on the Prince of Wales, thus hurting Fox's supremacy with the Whigs. The road to the prince's heart was vanity; she therefore praised him for having "assembled around you the Old Opposition, Lord Moira, the Grenvilles, Lord Fitzwilliam and Windham . . . I fear

Sheridan tormenting you with his jealousies and idle dreams."[75] The Duke of Bedford thought enough of her poetic talent and political acumen to ask her to write an inscription for his bust of Charles James Fox, which she did.

In addition to her political activity, Lady Georgiana also continued to write, describing her personal troubles, as one gallstone after another kept her confined to Devonshire House. Her poem captures her whimsy, creativity, and self-deprecating irony:

ENQUIRIES AT DEVONSHIRE HOUSE

Is she sick; or at Chiswick; in or gone out
Is she shamming a headache; or giving a rout
She's been ill—
Twas a stone—but she's now in good trim
A stone! You amaze me—more likely a whim,
But what is its substance? A feather or lead!
Is it soft as her heart, or as light as her head,
Is it gall cries a foe—is it gold cries a Dun
—alas the poor Duchess of either has none
But smile on the errors she tries to disown
And perhaps it will prove the philosopher's stone.[76]

It was likely her debts and the anxiety that attended them that led to a breakdown in Georgiana's health. She died on March 30, 1806, but not before seeing Charles James Fox in office and throwing an enormous party that recalled her earlier victory celebration for him in 1784. But Fox did not survive Lady Georgiana for long. Troubled by gout and succumbing to the effects of a life of dissipation, he died at Georgiana's ancestral home at Chiswick on September 13, 1806. Georgiana was forty-nine when she died; Fox was fifty-seven. A few years later, in October 1809, Lady Elizabeth Foster married the Duke of Devonshire. The duke did not tell his children until a few days later.

Lady Georgiana's Works

This account of Georgiana's life does not mention many of her literary works. Georgiana's youthful effusions include lyrics ("The Butterfly" and "The Table"),[77] a play about her mother (*Zyllia*), a poem on her father's birthday (May 1787), as well as *Emma; or, The Unfortunate Attachment: A Sentimental Novel.* Her mature work includes *The Sylph;* "A Negro Song," a poem in *Travels in the Interior Districts of Africa;* and two plays, *The Hungarian* and *The Hebrew Mother,* the former of which had some small influence on Lord Byron's *Werner.*[78] No less important are works described by her biographers: the diary she kept during the Regency crisis; her poem to Eliza Courtney, her illegitimate daughter by Charles Grey; and the self-admonitions she wrote on blue notebook paper and stuffed into books in the Chatsworth archives. *The Sylph* and "The Passage of the Mountain of St. Gothard" have long been ascribed to the Duchess of Devonshire but not, perhaps, taken truly seriously as works of art. The first, published in 1779, was dismissed as a roman à clef, and the latter, begun while she was in exile but published in 1799, was gently satirized by Coleridge in the *Morning Post* on December 24, 1799. As late as April 1802, the *Morning Herald* reported that Georgiana had an opera in the works. That same year, she discussed the possibility of publishing a sacred drama, possibly *The Hebrew Mother,* and a children's story. She made arrangements to publish these works anonymously with Joseph Johnson but withdrew.[79]

Our understanding of Georgiana's literary significance has a long way to go. Many of her inmost thoughts were excised from her letters by Elizabeth Foster (who edited them at Lady Georgiana's request), but these poems and stories tell the anguish she felt and the suffering she endured. The raw emotion she committed to the page in her novels, combined with the broad range of her literary allusions, makes them compelling more than two hundred years later.

There are several reasons for their relevance today. To begin, *The Sylph* gives insight into the social mores of the English nobility, a class not often represented by one of its own. To be sure, Lady Georgiana's frivolous behavior was satirized by T. S. Surr in *A Winter in London* (1802),[80] but *The Sylph* shows the duchess's own perspective on her early years as a married woman, charting Lady Julia Stanley's transformation from Welsh country girl to London society hostess. At the same time, this bildungsroman illustrates what the genre owed to court cases and newspapers, such as the *Morning Chronicle* series "Tête à Tête." Georgiana is as interested in wife-swapping, Rosicrucianism, forgery, and army corruption as she is in polishing her prose. *The Sylph* is thus an exposé, a work of muckraking journalism done up as a novel and thrown in the face of the very social class Lady Georgiana led. It functions as both apologia and self-indictment.

These functions were lost on her contemporary readers, however, because Thomas Lowndes, *The Sylph*'s publisher, allowed book buyers to believe that the novel was written by the author of *Evelina*. Most literary historians view Fanny Burney's novel of manners as a precursor to Jane Austen. The daughter of the well-respected musicologist Charles Burney, Fanny was twenty-six, unmarried, and innocent when she earned praise and admiration for her success as a young, and at first anonymous, novelist. In January 1778, by popular demand she revealed her authorship of *Evelina*. Thomas Lowndes capitalized on Burney's success that November by also attributing *The Sylph* to her, a technique that infuriated Charles Burney, since *The Sylph* included scandalous episodes that would endanger his daughter's reputation. Ever since that time, Lady Georgiana's novel has suffered by comparison. "*The Sylph* was less a novel than an exposé of the corrupting mores of the ton," her most recent biographer notes.[81] This is undoubtedly true to a point. Yet Georgiana's novel gives new insight into the manners of aristocratic Georgian women of the late eighteenth century. A history of the novel would be incomplete without it. This epistolary work, while inspired by Rousseau, borrows from Richardson's *Clarissa* in its depiction of the attempted rape of Julia and from *Pamela* when the colonel places the novel "in the hands of" Nancy in order to "prevail over the ignorant mind of a young rustic!"[82] Lady Georgiana also borrows from sentimentalism, at its height during the decades in which she published her novels. In *Emma,* she makes use of the erratic punctuation employed by Henry Mackenzie's *The Man of Feeling* (1770) and Laurence Sterne's *A Sentimental Journey Through France and Italy* (1768). And in *The Sylph*, Lord Stanley actually calls himself a "sentimental traveller" (the phrase Yorick uses to describe himself in *A Sentimental Journey*). His marriage to Julia begins as an erotic travel adventure, not unlike that of Sterne's hero. Finally, Georgiana's *Emma* is imbued with a wide range of verse penned by Edmund Waller, Thomas Gray, William Shenstone, Fanny Greville, and James Thomson, as well as passages from Proverbs and Revelations. *The Sylph* quotes Alexander Pope, Matthew Prior, James

Beattie, Isaac Bickerstaffe, John Milton, and William Shakespeare, as well as Samuel, Jeremiah, and other sources. The novel anticipates William Hazlitt's artful use of quotation in his essays, which weld poetry and prose by alluding to verse, sometimes in mid-sentence, without identifying sources. A common enough technique, few novelists exhibit Lady Georgiana's grace, erudition, and literary tact in employing it.

The Sylph begins with a masterful letter by Lord Stanley, exposing his libertine creed while describing the results of a hunting expedition to Lord Biddulph.[83] Stanley breaks his leg while ogling a "brace" of females. He then becomes so enamored of the woman who saves him after his fall that he marries her, unable to have her in any other way (as Julia herself ruefully admits). "Don't everybody marry?" Stanley asks. "Those who have estates to have heirs of their own and those who have *nothing* to get *something.*" The newlyweds travel to London, but no sooner does Julia leave her beloved sister than she begins to regret her union with this London rake on holiday. Stanley, it turns out, is the quintessential roué. He provides his wife with two advisers, Lady Besford and Lady Anne Parker, the latter of whom continues as his mistress. Lord Biddulph, Stanley's erstwhile friend, longs to revenge himself on Stanley because Stanley has stolen his former mistress, Lucy Gardiner.[84] Meanwhile, Julia writes to her sister, providing an ingénue's portrait of London society: the French hairdresser, the mantua maker, and the milliner. "I always looked on taste as genuine and inherent to ourselves; but here, taste is to be acquired; and what is infinitely more astonishing still, it is variable," Julia writes about her dancing master, shortly after she arrives from Wales.

With some prompting from Julia, who longs for guidance in her new life, her father, Edward Grenville, writes her a letter, recounting how he came to withdraw from London society after a series of emotional setbacks that left him disgusted with the world. He had married a wealthy woman whose family never accepted him. Upon her death, she had not yet come into her inheritance, and the father of the heir, a cousin, denied him any part of it. Maria Maynard, the heiress, sympathized with him and followed the unhappy widower to the army. Cross-dressing so she would not be detected, she met him in camp. She delivered an impassioned speech about female bravery, declaring her intention to join the battle alongside

Grenville, which she did, and so was with Grenville when he was wounded in battle. The army captain who professed friendship with Grenville attempted to seduce Maria, we later learn, but was no longer interested in her after she fell prey to smallpox. Later, after becoming father to Julia and her sister and recovering his fortune, Grenville is widowed again when Maria dies after giving birth to a third child. As a result of her father's heartbreak, Julia grew up with him and her sister in relative seclusion in Wales. She now tries to use this account of her father's romantic history to make sense of her own unhappiness in marriage.

In a mere year and a half, Julia is profoundly altered by her marriage to Stanley. Against this backdrop of corruption appears a German baron, Ton-hausen, who is everything that effeminate London rakes are not. Considerate and manly, Ton-hausen rescues Julia Stanley on three occasions. He prevents her hair from catching fire, single-handedly removes her from a crowded theater, and inquires solicitously after her health when she suffers a miscarriage brought on by her debacle at the theater. Unable to communicate much with her directly, however, for fear of compromising his reputation, the baron disguises himself as a benevolent sylph, who corresponds with her in private, guiding her every move. Despite his precaution of disguising himself as an aerial spirit, Ton-hausen must leave England when Lady Anne Parker insinuates that Lady Stanley is about to have an affair with him. By the end of the novel, Julia discovers that Ton-hausen and the Sylph are the same person and that both are really Henry Woodley, her childhood friend from Wales, who refused to even propose to Lady Julia when they were younger because of his impoverished state. Having come into a fortune after the death of his friend, Frederick, he is now in a position to disclose his love and ask for her hand in marriage. It is the old story of impoverished virtue hiding its face in shame, while rich villains declare themselves too boldly.

Transformations play a key role in the novel. When Stanley spies Julia from a distance, he tumbles down a mountain and breaks his leg. He is Actaeon to Julia's Artemis: like Actaeon, Stanley is figuratively torn to pieces for spying, through a telescope, on a woman he had no right to see. Lady Stanley also recalls Actaeon when, beset by a French hairstylist, she runs from her image like Actaeon trying to escape his own hounds. Finally, Biddulph compares his attempt to rape Lady Stanley to Zeus raping Calista, one of Diana's nymphs, by disguising himself as Artemis. Biddulph confesses, "Like Calista of old, she soon discovered the God under the semblance of Diana. Heavens!"

In this novel, falling—breaking a leg, as Stanley does (or twisting an ankle[85] as Edward Grenville's wife does)—suggests vulnerability to eros, which twists the body into unrecognizable shapes. Sometimes these Ovidian transformations cross gender lines, as when Julia is compared to Actaeon. Other transformations, such as those caused by smallpox or the disfigurement of death, have legal implications. Maria Maynard's father pours quicklime on the grave of the corpse he claims is his daughter to make it unrecognizable by the authorities, ensuring that his son by a second marriage will inherit his estate, not his daughter. Though Maria's father fabricates a change in his supposed daughter's appearance, smallpox does, in fact, alter his real daughter forever, which causes the captain to lose interest in her. The same transformation from smallpox occurs to Baron Ton-hausen, who somehow seems more attractive precisely because of his alteration, as Maria Finch and Julia Stanley note. The ultimate transformation of the novel, when the Sylph reveals himself to be Henry Woodley, who had loved Julia since childhood, completes the metamorphoses.

The Sylph appears to Julia many times throughout the novel, but she does not recognize him as Baron Ton-hausen and Henry Woodley until the end. Recognition is painful; ultimately Baron Ton-hausen must leave London to avoid rumors of an affair between him and Julia. At the end of the novel, Woodley explains why it was necessary that Julia not recognize him. He did not have enough income to propose to Julia and did not wish to put her and her father in the difficult position of turning him down if he did. By disguising his identity, he watches and admires her from afar, proving his moral worth and transforming himself into a successful suitor in the process: "Spencer opposed my resolution of returning to Germany . . . *He* it was that urged me to take the name of Ton-hausen." The masquerade scene furthers the theme of misrecognition. "When the face is masked, the mind is uncovered," the Sylph writes. "From the conduct and language of those who frequent masquerades, we may judge of the principles of their souls." Masquerades expose the hypocrisy of London social life, where few are who they pretend to be. This is true for Julia as well. She conceals, through her insistence that she loves her husband, the fact that she is physically repulsed by him. This repulsion is evidenced in her account of Biddulph, when he dresses as her husband.

> Well then, pleased as I was with Sir William's ready compliance with my request of returning, suppose me seated in my chair and giving way to some hopes that he would yet see his errors and some method be pitched on to relieve all. He was ready to hand me out of the chair and led me upstairs into my dressing room. I had taken off my mask, as it was very warm; he still kept his on and talked in the same kind of voice he practised at the masquerade. He paid me most profuse compliments on the beauty of my dress and, throwing his arms round my waist, congratulated himself on possessing such an angel, at the same time kissing my face and bosom with such a strange kind of eagerness as made me suppose he was intoxicated; and, under that idea, being very desirous of disengaging myself from his arms, I struggled to get away from him. He pressed me to go to bed; and, in short, his behaviour was unaccountable: at last, on my persisting to entreat him to let me go, he blew out one of the candles. I then used all my force and burst from him, and at that instant his mask gave way; and in the dress of my husband (Oh, Louisa! Judge, if you can, of my terror), I beheld that villain Lord Biddulph.

The phrase "strange kind of eagerness," combined with the further assertion that "his behaviour was unaccountable," is rather humorous. After all, Lady Julia believes Biddulph to be her husband. Why would a husband's sexual eagerness be "unaccountable"? For all his villainy, Biddulph does capture a truth which Lady Julia will not own: "I might indeed have supposed my caresses were disagreeable, when offered under the character of a husband," Biddulph states. "I had been more blest, at least better received, had I worn the dress of the baron." The masquerade, a common enough event in the late eighteenth century, clearly shows that for Julia an imaginary lover is more appealing than her spouse.

But Julia steers clear of this ugly truth and insists on romance, a spiritualized love, rather than lust, as her primary motivation in seeking the baron's company. What is an attractive illusion for her as a woman is not possible for her lover. In a world where social position and gold are necessary, Woodley must quickly transform himself from penniless supplicant into deserving bridegroom. That wealth and moral virtue do not always coincide is not lost on the earnest novelist, who continually contrasts the corrupt wealthy (Lord Biddulph and Lord Stanley) with the virtuous poor (Nancy, Woodley, and Julia's father in his youth). Woodley, of course, breaks this mold. Lady Georgiana uses Rosicrucianism and its concern with hidden appearances to show how Woodley's virtue reveals itself. When he, disguised as Ton-hausen, takes Julia to the chemist to provide her with reviving drops—that, incidentally, coincide with her miscarriage—a physical and psychological rebirth takes place. He worships Julia on his knees, as she worships the Sylph. Julia's regard for the Sylph—commemorated in the pendant she gives him that depicts her kneeling in gratitude—contrasts with Biddulph's and Lord L.'s false acts of self-prostration: they worship only themselves. The pendant is important, for it crystallizes the spiritual message of self-denial. It is described as consisting of "an altar on which is inscribed these words: *To Gratitude,* an elegant figure of a woman making an offering on her knees, and a winged cherub bearing the incense to heaven." One cannot imagine Jane Austen or Mary Wollstonecraft recommending such an act of self-prostration. For Lady Georgiana, however, the Rosicrucian machinery and the jewelry that alludes to it enable her to be realistic and fantastic at the same time, pointing out discrepancies between moral and immoral characters. Left without a guide, Julia uses her own imagination to induct herself into a chemical bond with the Sylph. Rosicrucianism was a sect of Freemasonry that accepted women. The sect, founded by Christian Rosenkreutz, was particularly popular in Germany, where Ton-hausen spends his formative years. The Rosicrucians believed that human beings were united by mystical bonds that could be strengthened through moral self-restraint. The ceremony Julia creates, while not actually Rosicrucian, emulates the theatrical rites of Freemasonry that became so popular at the end of the eighteenth century.

The discipline of the seekers of the rosy cross was legendary, and Lady Georgiana makes use of it in her novel. Rosicrucianism involves allusions to blood telegraphy, a perpetual lamp, telepathy, optics, healing by transplantation, homeopathic healing, magnetic healing, magnetized water, digitations, returning to life, astral projection, and mesmerism. Strange as these topics may sound, Lady Georgiana was not alone in her interests—they can be found, even today, treated in the occult section of most bookstores. Thomas Jefferson attended a meeting of mesmerism while ambassador to

France; Goethe became interested in astral projections and Rosicrucian optics (he met Mesmer in Constance in 1788), and Mary Shelley would take up the subject in *Frankenstein,* including an account of Paracelsus, considered to be the origin of modern Rosicrucianism. Robert Fludd (1574–1637) was only the most famous seventeenth-century Rosicrucian; his adherents in Britain included William Maxwell (1619–69). Fludd defined magnetism in a way that sheds light on the treatment of good and evil in Lady Georgiana's book: "When two human beings approach one another, their magnetism is either active or passive. In sympathy and attraction the bodily radiation travels from the center to the periphery. Should the magnetic radiations of the two individuals interpenetrate and mingle, there is an affinity between them; if, on the other hand, the radiations are broken and thrown back, there is a negative magnetism and aversion, because where there is antipathy the radiations retreat from the periphery to the center."[86] The breaking of Stanley's leg—he is literally thrown back when he sees Julia—suggests their "negative magnetism." Lady Georgiana overlays the Artemis story with these references to magnetism to achieve her effects. Schopenhauer acknowledged the growing prestige of such work a generation later: "Nowadays, anyone who denies the effectiveness of magnetism should be regarded not as a sceptic but as an ignoramus."[87] Lady Georgiana's interest in fossils—spurred, perhaps, by her cousin Henry Cavendish, a chemist—may have sprung from her interest in magnetism. "Back of everything magnetism," Joyce writes in *Ulysses.*[88]

Lady Georgiana includes a series of interpolated stories that reinforce the contrast between virtue and vice—opposite poles of magnetism—which Rosicrucians believed to be crucial to moral development. Julia's story is juxtaposed with her sister's, her mother's, Nancy's, and Maria Finch's, all of which it resembles in many ways. Julia writes to Louisa about her disastrous marriage, and she solicits her father to write about his first marriage, which ended in his wife's death and his withdrawal from the world. No sooner do we learn about Maria's seduction by an army officer than the story of Nancy, stalked by a designing British officer, provides a third story that reinforces the theme of worldly evil. "I shall still have the delightful privilege of a husband, and Will Parker shall bear the name," the colonel says. "What say you?" Lord Biddulph poses the identical question to Lady Stanley as did Lord L. and Edward Grenville's superior officer. In this world of illicit proposals, Lady D——'s actual rape by Lord L. foreshadows Julia's averted catastrophe with Biddulph; she recognizes him just in time. Grenville's return to Wales, after being disappointed by the world, precedes Julia's and Woodley's returns. Julia's faithful servant, Winifred, finds her counterpart in her mother's servant, Hannah, who actually outdoes Winifred by dying in the service of her mistress. Both Lord Stanley and Lord Biddulph whistle Italian airs—emblematic of their continental indifference to English chivalry—shortly after insulting Lady Stanley. Lady Besford warns Julia that men crave variety; Lady Melford repeats the advice, in almost identical language, and the phrase regarding the mysterious human heart, taken from Jeremiah 17:5–10, appears no less than three times: "the heart of man is deceitful above all things." Lady Besford rejects the sexual double standard which Lady Melford endorses, but both address it, another instance of repetition. Julia's letters begin to resemble Lady Besford's—the woman who initially horrified Julia—especially when she quotes Lady Besford's view that "one can form no opinion of what a woman is while she is single." And the final series of marriages—Maria Finch's to Sir George Brudenel, Louisa's to James Spencer, and Julia's to the transformed and enriched Woodley—reinforce the parallel experiences they have undergone, as well as the three-in-one theme that has both religious and symbolic significance. (The Sylph is Woodley, Ton-hausen, and a Rosicrucian spirit—father, son, and holy ghost.)

These are not the only thematic echoes and reverberations in this carefully constructed novel. There is a certain symmetry to the work which underscores its feminist theme. The novel begins with Lord Stanley's false letter and ends with Maria Finch Brudenel's true one. Female friendship trumps male treachery. Women prove more faithful than men: Maria Maynard, Julia's mother, has the romantic courage to follow Edward Grenville into battle, while Grenville is hapless, passive, and despairing. Maria Finch and Julia Stanley overcome rumors that they are rivals for the attentions of Baron Ton-hausen by appearing in public together. Their solidarity is shown when Lady Georgiana has Julia write, "I own, I like her for having refused Colonel Montague." Women behave straightforwardly, but men rely on ruses and duplicity. The artful Henry Woodley retreats from the field of love entirely, only to adopt various disguises and deceptions to win his lover, Julia. Women return men to their best selves. Love triumphs when mere lust is refined, usually under the ministrations of a woman. Woodley's artful seduction of Julia, complete with masquerade ball, suggests that she has more than met her match. Maria advises her friend to tie down her lover of ever-changing forms so he cannot escape. If Stanley is Actaeon, in other words, Woodley is Proteus (an early sea god described in Homer's *Odyssey* [4.432] who can foretell the future but avoids doing so by changing shapes).

In this novel, niceties of behavior—foppishness, social manners, sentimental affection for parents—give way to forms of barbarism perhaps unknown in less "civilized" societies. Lord L.'s speech proposing an act of bribery and rape underscores the absurd attention to appearances encouraged by London society:

> Without further preface, Lord L. threw himself on his knees before her— and said if her heart could not suggest the restitution, which the most ardent of lovers might expect and hope for—he must take the liberty of informing her that bestowing on him the delightful privilege of a husband was the only means of securing her from the resentment of one.

Lord L.'s polite circumlocutions belie his grotesque intent. One of many kneeling actions in the novel, this dramatic act of self-prostration recalls (by reversing) Julia's pendant depicting her offering incense to the Sylph.

Without an omniscient narrator, such as Jane Austen's, the reader of Lady Georgiana's novel sifts through Julia's professions of innocence. While Julia suggests that greed resides elsewhere (among Jewish moneylenders, for example), her acquiescence in the aristocratic fascination with bragg, loo, picquet, and faro and her obsession with keeping up appearances show her to be unreliable. She makes excuses for herself, stating to Louisa that she sees nothing in her heart to condemn while at the same time acknowledging that the heart is deceitful. No sooner does she say she will never take an "amour" than she describes one in Baron Ton-hausen. Lady Stanley is innocent enough to need the Sylph to guide her through London high society, but there is bad faith here, for she takes no moral responsibility: "No one seemed to interest themselves about me," she complains. Her female guides, Lady Besford and Lady Anne Parker, are even more perilous than Lord Biddulph. "It is, I believe, a received opinion that more women are seduced from the path of virtue by their own sex than by ours," Maria Finch recounts the wronged Nancy's father as saying. Patriarchal society paid lip service to male authority while expecting women to think for themselves and save their husbands from ruin (even if this meant suffering passively). Lady Stanley ultimately chooses the mysteries of a desexualized Rosicrucianism to liberate her from the almost unbelievably corrupt society that surrounds her. Rosicrucianism's link to Protestantism and moral self-improvement gives the novel its characteristic and pleasant spiritualism which elevates Julia above the depraved Londoners who try to pull her down to their level.

In addition to her interest in Rosicrucianism, Lady Georgiana was an avid reader of Rousseau. She breast-fed her children as he suggested one should do in *Emile* and underlined passages of her copy of *Julie, où La Nouvelle Héloïse* at Chatsworth. Lady Georgiana's own Julie recognizes that social institutions, as Rousseau saw in *The Social Contract,* clap on the chains that bind us; marriage is a true mind-forged manacle for the Stanleys, encouraging them to spend time apart at social gatherings, to gamble and spend more than they can afford. Fashion is a hydra-headed beast that must be placated in the form of jewels, gambling debts, and expensive fashions for the hair, carriage, and home. The late eighteenth century, though perhaps not for the first time, saw the birth of consumer society.[89] The need to consume conspicuously was apparent in the behavior of Lady Georgiana's close friend Lady Melbourne, whose breakfasts and dinners found their way into newspapers, along with a description of her china. She also traded her home at Piccadilly with the Duke of York's Whitehall when he commented, in an offhand way, on its superior decorations. Lady Melbourne benefited from the proximity of Whitehall to Parliament, for she knew that throwing extravagant parties led to social promotion for her family. Though Lady Georgiana could feel superior to the social-climbing Lady Melbourne—of whom she was "a *little afraid,*" as she confessed to her friend—she could afford to do so because she already had the greatest prize, the Duke of Devonshire.[90] That she obtained him and then repented her choice makes *The Sylph* an especially interesting novel to read, for social as well as literary reasons. Lady Georgiana led the very society she mocks in this novel, showing her conflicted feelings about her own social success. Given Lady Georgiana's gambling debts and treatment of tradesmen, there is a curious dissonance between Julia's idealistic remarks and Lady Georgiana's neglect of tradesmen's bills, adding a further level of disingenuousness to the polite poses of the novel: "Do you not think I was cut to the soul when I had this painful reflexion to make, that many honest and industrious tradesmen are every day dunning for their lawful demands, while we are thus throwing away hundreds after hundreds, without affording the least heartfelt satisfaction?" Julia asks. Later she worries about "the laudably industrious tradesman defrauded of his due." As a necessary complement to her gambling addiction, Lady Georgiana inherited the tendency to moral hypocrisy that allowed her to worry about tradesmen on the one hand and to ignore their bills on the other. Julia makes a number of speeches in this novel that redound to her credit, but her cold treatment of her husband and her defense of her conduct show that she wants it both ways. (Louisa exposes this trait, but she is soon worn down by Julia's exculpatory evidence showing her husband's neglect.) One poignant aspect of the novel is that its epistolary form allows us to see only partial truths, told from different people's perspectives, as Mary Poovey has pointed out about Austen's *Lady Susan*.[91] This heightens the pathos of *The Sylph*, which shows the wide gulf between male and female ways of seeing the world. Despite these gender differences, however, conspicuous consumption trumps all human values, and no self-respecting woman condescends to marry a man who cannot improve, or at least allow her to maintain, her social position.

In its concern with fashion's effects on morality, Lady Georgiana's novel treats themes congenial to Pope's *Rape of the Lock*. Although taking its epigraph from this poem, *The Sylph* does not follow Pope's mock-heroic model entirely. Lady Georgiana's novel presents us with a real attempt at rape. In both her title and her allusions to a Rosicrucian hero, Lady Georgiana followed Pope's example, though there is nothing epic or mock-epic in her epistolary novel. In his dedication to the second edition of *The Rape of the Lock*, Alexander Pope wrote:

> The Rosicrucians are a people I must bring you acquainted with. The best account I know of them is in a French book call'd *Le Comte de Gabalis*, which both in its title and size is so like a Novel, that many of the Fair Sex have read it for one by mistake. According to these Gentlemen, the four Elements are inhabited by Spirits, which they call Sylphs, Gnomes, Nymphs, and Salamanders. The Gnomes or Demons of Earth delight

in mischief; but the Sylphs, whose habitation is in the Air, are the best-condition'd Creatures imaginable. For they say any mortals may enjoy the most intimate familiarities with these gentle Spirits, upon a condition very easy to all true Adepts, an inviolate preservation of Chastity.[92]

Alexander Pope developed the epic machinery of the sylphs in a subsequent draft of the poem but was interested in Freemasonry throughout his life (and was a mason himself). Pope's sylphs in *The Rape of the Lock* inspired Georgiana's novel in a number of respects. First, they are closely associated with fashion. They prepare Belinda (the warrior) for conquest in Canto I:

> The busy sylphs surround their darling Care;
> These set the Head, and those divide the Hair,
> Some fold the Sleeve, whilst others plait the Gown;
> And Betty's prais'd for Labours not her own.

(Pope, *The Rape of the Lock*, 1.145–48)

Where Julia resists the attentions of her French hairdresser, Belinda accepts the "darling Care" of her "busy sylphs." Julia is a victim; Belinda, a woman warrior.

But there are other differences. Though Georgiana's novel contains disparaging references to Jews, Gabalis's book (Pope's source) is based, in part, on the Kabbalah and includes an occult interpretation of the scriptures with specific references to the art of communing with spirits.[93] Pope follows rabbinical ideas about how women longed to mate with sylphs, for example, because his sylphs have a preexistence as human beings. The conceit that "angels and devils are nought but souls of men departed," viewed as foolish by Robert Burton, was accepted by Dryden, Virgil, and Ovid.[94] Sylphs in Gabalis's volume can change their shape and sex at will. Like Milton's angels, Pope's sylphs are indestructible. If their bodies are divided they can, as Burton explains, with "admirable celerity . . . come together again."[95] For Pope, as for Lady Georgiana, transmigrated souls protect their friends on earth and battle enemies.

Like the gods that guide epic heroes, sylphs are guardians of maidens. De Villars rejects the rabbis' view that angels consorted with women, thereby bringing about their own fall: "They were not angels," De Villars states, "but sylphs—sylphs who needed such contact to make them immortal."[96]

Pope rejects De Villars and allows the sylphs supervision of the toilette. For Gabalis, all sprites are "good," but Pope follows the traditional categories of spirits, making the gnomes "bad," guilty of contriving impediments for mortals. In the same way that the Spanish game of ombre plays an important role in Pope's poems, faro and piquet dominate the lives and even the destinies of Lady Georgiana's central characters.

Another departure from Gabalis lies in the poet's presentation of Ariel, drawn from Shakespeare's *Tempest*. In Pope's poem, Ariel is the chief spirit who warns Belinda of her impending fate:

> Of these am I, who thy Protection claim,
> A watchful Sprite, and Ariel is my Name,
> In the clear Mirror of thy ruling Star
> I saw, alas! some dread Event impend,
> But Heav'n revels not what, nor how or where:
> Warn'd by thy Sylph, oh Pious Maid beware!
> This to disclose is all thy Guardian can.
> Beware of all, but most beware of Man!
>
> (Pope, *The Rape of the Lock*, 1.105–14)

Though they can see the future, sylphs are powerless to prevent it. Belinda's sylphs fail to protect her from the man who cuts a lock of her hair, for example: one of them, placing himself between the offending blades, finds himself cut in two. This mock-heroic treatment of spirituality is not unlike Lady Georgiana's tongue-in-cheek references to the supernatural appearances of Julia's Sylph.

Alexander Pope and Lady Georgiana use sylphs for similar thematic purposes. Sylphs defend a woman's chastity in both *The Rape of the Lock* and *The Sylph*, and they are only drawn to chaste women:

> What guards the Purity of melting Maids,
> In Courtly Balls, and Midnight Masquerades,
> . . . .
> 'Tis but their Sylph, the wise Celestials know,
> Tho' Honour is the Word with Men below.
>
> (Pope, *The Rape of the Lock*, 1.71–78)

In Pope's poem, the sylphs protect the heroine from titled men like Lord Stanley who would "early taint the Female Soul":

> Some Nymphs there are, too conscious of their Face,
> For Life predestin'd to the Gnomes' Embrace.
> These swell their Prospects and exalt their Pride,
> When Offers are disdain'd, and Love deny'd.
> Then gay Ideas crowd the vacant Brain
> While Peers and Dukes, and all their sweeping Train,
> And Garters, Stars and Coronets appear,
> And in soft Sounds, *Your Grace* salutes their Ear.
> 'Tis these that early taint the Female Soul.

(Pope, *The Rape of the Lock*, 1.79–87)

To be loved by a gnome is to fall prey to the "gay Ideas [that] crowd the vacant Brain"—to lack a certain spiritual refinement. A sylph offers pleasures that mere "Peers and Dukes, and all their sweeping Train" cannot begin to satisfy. Titled positions, the narrator of Pope's poem suggests, are those which "early taint the Female Soul." Biddulph and Stanley in *The Sylph* and the lover in *The Rape of the Lock* all exhibit this quality of preferring the corporeal to the incorporeal. "My person still invites his caresses," Lady Julia complains of her husband, "but for the softer sentiments of the soul, that ineffable tenderness which depends not on the tincture of the skin, of that—alas!—he has no idea. A voluptuary in love, he professes not that delicacy which refines all its joys. His is all passion; sentiment is left out of the catalogue." In Pope's *Rape of the Lock*, chastity is not unrelated to the desire for immortality. Humans long to mate with sylphs, according to the Comte de Gabalis, because they want to live forever, for spiritual as well as physical reasons. Each group has an escape clause, however: "Just as sylphs may choose not to mate with humans for fear that immortality may lead to eternal damnation, so men who mate with sylphs have the option of rejecting their immortality in case they should be damned."[97] Alexander Pope and Lady Georgiana were well informed about Rosicrucianism, though each writer treats the subject with levity, as have other authors who used the movement as a literary device. Anatole France's *The Revolt of the Angels* is only one example.

Though Lady Georgiana's epigraph encourages readers to attribute *The Sylph*'s title solely to Pope's poem, the late-eighteenth-century novelist may well have had something more contemporary at hand—a one-act play titled *The Sylph* (1771; for full text, see the appendix) by Germain François Poullain de Saint-Foix, who borrowed the story from Crébillon Fils' 1730 story of that title.[98] Translated into English and published in 1771, this brief but fascinating adaptation depicts a marquis' effort to seduce his lover by posing as her chambermaid (among other identities he assumes) in order to gain his lover's interest. The play anticipates Lady Georgiana's novel in three respects: a man's disguise takes three forms, he uses his spiritual identity to dupe a woman into falling in love with him, and he seduces her in such a way as to cast doubt, however temporarily, on his moral character. In addition, there are minor plot devices, such as the gift of a painting (in Lady Georgiana's novel, a jeweled inscription) and the important use of a maid, Finetta (Winifred in *The Sylph*), as a go-between.

The plot of the 1771 play is complex but quickly resolved. After the death of her aunt, a young woman—named Julia like Georgiana's heroine—who has inherited the estate of the setting (thus making her eminently marriageable to the impatient marquis) pores over "a cursed pack of Kabbalistic . . . books." Arriving from Paris for the express purpose of marrying her, the marquis is annoyed by this spiritual development in his intended. Finetta expresses amazement that the marquis, Julia's suitor, has passed himself off as Buggaboe; her adopted niece, Florina; and also as Ziblis, "one of those aerial beings which she is so very desirous of getting acquainted with." Exhibiting an admirable self-restraint, according to the young lady's nurse, the marquis plays the role of *cavalier servente*, attending to the young lady and appearing before her in a form that she finds flattering. He quickly disabuses the gullible maid of her belief in "ghosties," as she calls them, informing her that he was Ziblis—and two other characters—all along. Surprised by Julia's sudden arrival, he dons Florina's dress and expresses his doubts regarding the reality of "these hobgoblins, these sylphs, gnomes, and salamanders . . . such a new race of beings that [he] shan't be easily brought to credit them." But Julia responds by linking Sylphs to Neroides: to Aeolus, who rules the waves, and his children. "The forests too have their inhabitants," Julia explains, the fauns and satyrs.—According to the systems of our forefathers, there was neither grove nor fountain unprovided with its nymph or its naiad—they thought each element peopled with a race of intelligent beings, who, having the power of making themselves visible when they chose it, participated with mankind in their passions and were frequently engaged in intrigues with simple mortals.—These were their sylphs.—Ah, girl, were but your eyes enlightened by the knowledge of the Kabbalah!

Once a young woman attains knowledge of what love is, Julia continues,

During the night, in dreams, which he contrives to excite, he takes care to be the principal object of her ideas—in the morn, he renews the pleasing illusion—in the gayest hours of the spring, 'tis her sylph who perpetually causes those pleasing reveries, in which the mind is employed in meditating on that reciprocal tenderness which gives new graces to all the works of nature.—'Tis amazing, Florina, how many artful methods the sylph has recourse to, that, by little and little, he may search to the bottom the heart which he wishes to find worthy of a sincere attachment.

In Lady Georgiana's novel, Julia's lover plays a similarly relentless role as spiritual seducer, probing her inmost thoughts in order to become her future husband. Both sylphs penetrate to the secret cores of the women who fall in love with them.

Like Pope's sylphs, who attend Arabella in her boudoir, the marquis appropriates the person of Florina and attends Julia as she prepares her toilette. The intimacy is not just spiritual but erotic—with enough of both the worldly and the ethereal to satisfy both genders. But Julia objects that the sylph, in taking Florina's form, will become a rival to himself. So drawn is she to the spiritual that Poullain de Saint-Foix's Julia seems to object to the sylph taking any form at all. "Yet some form I must have," he notes. "You, my Julia, have eyes, have lips, have hands—I must provide myself with the like, else we shall be at a sad loss." Julia, it turns out, wants to ascend to the ethereal, to become, in short, a sylphid. The marquis, truly disturbed at this development, cleverly appeals to Julia's vanity. He informs her that sylphids are not nearly as pretty as mortal women. If she transforms herself into a sylphid, moreover, there is no turning back. The competing impulses of man and woman as depicted in this work, for the earthly and the spiritual, respectively, are thus played out in a comic vein until Julia accepts the more material version of the marquis. She discovers, as Finetta announces, that "*the sylph, Florina, and the marquis* are one and the same person." The marquis, meanwhile, by showing his delicacy and playing at sylphs, has transformed himself into a lover more suitable to Julia, who has material desires of her own.

In Georgiana's novel, Woodley's poverty forestalls their union; in Saint-Foix's one-act play, the heroine's fickleness is to blame for the misadventures that occur. It was only "the notions in which you had been educated respecting the Kabbalah and your prejudice against mankind which reduced a lover, who adored you, to these disguises," the marquis states.

In crafting her novel, Lady Georgiana makes use of the Rosicrucian idea of the chemical wedding, a magical union between two like-minded souls. She also anticipates the moralistic tone of a prose tract titled *The Sylph* (1784), presumed to be by P. P. London (though published anonymously), in which a man sets himself up as a spiritual adviser to a woman, guiding her every move. In the world of late eighteenth-century Protestant England, such a guide was obviously needed, since the price a woman paid for any deviation from propriety was enormous. "And the woman once fallen forever must fall," Byron wrote of Lady Frances Webster twenty years later.[99] In most tales of sylphs—whether dramatic, expository, or fictional—the writer insists upon "that sublime purity which alone can fit us for the commerce with such aerial beings," as Julia states in Saint-Foix's play.

In addition to Pope's *Rape of the Lock* and Saint-Foix's *Sylph*, Lady Georgiana's novel owes something to the dramatic literature that precedes it. Her close friendship with David Garrick—he wrote her a birthday ode and served as godfather to her first child—would have brought Edward Moore's play *The Gamester* to her notice. Sarah Siddons, whom Lady Georgiana patronized, had played one of the leading roles. *The Gamester* appeared more often than any other English drama between the time it was first staged by David Garrick in 1753 and the late nineteenth century. The play, redone on occasion as *Beverley*, told the story of a man who poisons himself when overcome by gambling debts. Dedicated to the prime minister, Lord Pelham, the play plucked at the heartstrings of middle-class Londoners, who enjoyed seeing the vices of the upper classes exposed. Actors were so moved by Moore's drama that advance notice appeared in the press, thereby stimulating interest in the play. In fact, Garrick found the role so emotionally and physically draining—he shed tears during performances—that he ended the successful run early. Garrick's prologue to *The Gamester* highlighted the theme of gambling, showing how a love of display, licentious sexuality, and financial risk were leading England to ruin.

> Ye slaves of passion, and ye dupes of France,
> Wake all your pow'rs from this destructive trance!
> Shake off the chains of this tyrant vice:
> Hear other calls than those of cards and dice!

> (Garrick, Prologue to *The Gamester*, lines 23–26)[100]

The dangers of gambling affected Lady Georgiana's generation as surely as they did the one that came before.

When Baron Grimm in his *Correspondance Littéraire* reviewed Bernard-Joseph Saurin's Parisian adaptation, *Béverlei*, psychological themes emerged more prominently. The director of the play, he felt, had mistakenly relied on coincidences and plot devices, forgoing the mental drama that was its real subject: "The loss of every honest and virtuous sentiment, would be the poison that would make the spectator tremble; this is the true catastrophe with which the gamester is threatened."[101] Grimm's perceptive point highlights the melodramatic aspects of Edward Moore's drama: its reliance on the sentimentality of the sleeping boy, innocent of his father's imminent self-murder, as the father holds the poison cup from which he will drink. Eschewing gothic elements, Lady Georgiana attains a more realistic focus on Lord Stanley's suicide, showing how Biddulph's betrayal of their friendship is at least as horrific as Stanley's betrayal of his wife.

After writing the prologue to *The Gamester*, Garrick penned his own drama, *Bon Ton*, about high life, one that, first produced in 1775, was republished no fewer than five times in two decades. The play is forgettable in many respects, but it offers in its prologue, by George Colman, a nice summary of the weaknesses that attended participants in the fashionable world, four years before Lady Georgiana published *The Sylph*. The ton concerned itself only with the weekend, the space "twixt Saturday and Monday."[102] Being a member of the bon ton involved drinking tea with "china and gilt spoons," dancing "Cow-tillions" in satins, and attending fashionable clubs, balls, and masquerades.[103] Ultimately, it meant gambling and a willingness to lose vast amounts at gaming tables: "'tis losing thousands ev'ry night at lu!" Colman's prologue highlights the extent to which fashion represents a departure from nature, a juxtaposition Georgiana also develops in *The Sylph*. "Nature it thwarts, and contradicts all reason," Colman writes:

> 'Tis stiff French stays, and fruit when out of season!
> A rose, when half a guinea is the price;
> A set of bays, scarce bigger than six mice;
> To visit friends, you never wish to see;
> Marriage 'twixt those, who never can agree;
> Old dowagers, drest, painted, patch'd, and curl'd;
> This is Bon Ton, and this we call the world!
>
> (Colman, Prologue to *Bon Ton*, lines 32–38)

Like Lady Georgiana and David Garrick, Colman traces the corruption of the bon ton to the importation of French customs.

> French, French, my boy's the thing! Jafez! Prate, chatter!
> Trim be the mode, whipt-syllabub the matter!
> Walk like a Frenchman! For on English pegs
> Moves native awkwardness with two left legs—
>
> . . . .
>
> Hearts may be black, but all should wear clean faces;
> The graces boy! the graces, graces, graces!
>
> (Colman, Prologue to *Bon Ton*, lines 43–46, 56–57)

That eminently English writer Lord Chesterfield enjoined his son, as Colman's imaginary speaker does here, to observe *les bienseances*. Lady Georgiana's novel alludes directly to Chesterfield, criticizing his notions of the English gentleman (as she had in *Emma*) even as she blames grand tours to Paris and Italy for effecting their ruin. Samuel Johnson, a close friend of the Spencer family, stated that Chesterfield's famous book taught the "morals of a whore, and the manners of a dancing master."[104]

In *Bon Ton*, both women and men marry for vanity, without loving one another, but become jealous when the other partner finds a more suitable mate. Garrick exposes how pride trumps vanity, as husband and wife, though busy with affairs of their own, exert their energies to find out who the other's lover is without any wish to replace them. The laughter the play elicits is hollow—something like attending a sermon done up as a two-act play. This is true not because the play is moralistic but because it sermonizes to no purpose. Garrick's satire is light but perhaps too light to keep the play entertaining. Unlike Sheridan's *School for Scandal,* which makes vice appealing by showing its verbal ingenuity ("The malice of a good thing is the barb that makes it stick," Sheridan's Lady Sneerwell states),[105] Garrick's *Bon Ton* strives to laugh gently at aristocratic excess without insisting on firm moral distinctions. He points out the absurdities of his contemporaries without shooing them away from the theater, where they pay to see such behavior displayed, and thus he earns his bread and butter.

Like Garrick's *Bon Ton,* Pope's poem also exposed upper-class vanity and vice through sexual metaphors and double entendres. Unlike Garrick, however, Pope was aware of another world that governs mortal actions. Replace the sylphs with saints, and one sees the Catholic dimensions of Pope's poem quite clearly. Though it is absurd to think of a sylph being cut in two by scissors in its effort to defend Arabella's lock, the very image is piquant and charming. Clearly Lady Georgiana was attracted to the idea of Rosicrucianism, also explored by Pope. In her endless letters and religious fanaticism, Georgiana's mother had made religion seem like a series of chores performed for a punishing God. The idea that the world was watched by four categories of daimon spirits must have made the path of virtue seem more appealing to her daughter, if only because it was less lonely. If sylphs existed, London life could be altered one person at a time. Left to the paltry consciences of hardened rakes like Stanley and Biddulph, nothing would change.

During the time that Lady Georgiana wrote her novel, forgery had become "the emblematic crime of the period."[106] Perhaps the court case that most clearly galvanized opinion on this last subject was that of the Perreaus and Rudd. Mrs. Rudd stood accused of having forged a bond; she turned state's evidence to escape the death penalty, and Robert and Daniel Perreau, twins, were hung at the scaffold. The trial garnered interest because Mrs. Rudd accused Daniel, her partner, of forcing her to sign the forged bond at knifepoint. Her eloquent defense of her actions, published as various pamphlets, transfixed a generation and resulted in her acquittal.

Robert, by contrast, appeared stupefied by the charge of criminality; his brother had played the stock market and lived a somewhat disreputable life, while Robert was a family man who left two children behind and a disconsolate wife. Coming on the heels of victories in North America (the war was going well for the British in 1779) and catastrophic losses incurred by speculating about the war in the Falkland Islands, the Perreau and Rudd case captured the imagination of Georgiana's generation from March 1775 to January 1776, for it suggested that something was wrong with the soul of this burgeoning empire. "In the period between the end of the Perreaus' trial and the trial of Mrs. Rudd, at least one hundred letters and seventeen correspondences were published that dealt with the case," *The Perreaus and Mrs. Rudd,* an excellent book on the subject, explains. "Not only does this represent a substantial number of letters for the period, but they tended to be much longer than usual, longer even than those dealing with the war in America."[107]

Forgery is central to *The Sylph,* the issue around which all else unravels. The Sylph passes himself off as someone he is not; masquerade parties exploit the tension between appearance and reality. Commercial transactions, by contrast, depend upon a person being who he says he is. At a time of intense class consciousness, when appearing wealthy was almost as good as possessing wealth, England was likely to produce such characters as the Perreaus and Rudd and novels such as *The Sylph.* Lady Georgiana committed many financial indiscretions, but it is not clear that she ever committed forgery. The crime had a certain frisson that attends even Lady Georgiana's novelistic depiction. In a letter to Lord Stanley, George Brudenel explains that he has received a "forged deed of conveyance" for the Pemberton estate. The Pemberton estate had not been Lord Stanley's to dispose of, and he has forged the signature of his uncle, dismissively called "old Squaretoes." Lady Julia offers to sell her jewels to make up the funds, not realizing that Lord Stanley has already pawned them. Biddulph explains why forgery is worse than bankruptcy:

> "Believe me," said he, "the execution is the least part of the evil. That event happens daily among the great people: but there is an affair of another nature, the stain of which can never be wiped off. Sir William, by his necessities, has been plunged into the utmost difficulties and to

extricate himself has used some unlawful means; in a word, he has committed a forgery."

"Impossible!" cried I, clasping my hands together in agony.

"It is too true; Sir George Brudenel has the forged deed now in his hands, and nothing can save him from an ignominious death but the raising a large sum of money, which is quite out of his power. Indeed, I might with some difficulty assist him."

"And will you not step forth to save him?" I asked with precipitation.

"What would *you* do to save him?" he asked in his turn, attempting to take my hand.

"Can you ask me such a question? To save his life, what would I not do?"

"You have the means in your power."

"Oh! Name them quickly, and ease my heart this load of distraction! It is more—much more than I can bear."

"Oh! My lovely angel!" cried the horrid wretch. "Would you show some tenderness to me? Would you but listen to the most faithful, most enamoured of men, much might be done. You would, by your sweet condescension, bind me forever to your interest, might I but flatter myself I should share your affection. Would you but give me the slightest mark of it, oh!—how blest I should be! Say, my adorable Julia, can I ever hope to touch your heart?"

So fearful is he of hanging for forgery that Lord Stanley is coerced into selling his wife to Biddulph. After that last indignity, he takes his life. Financial forgery and sexual forgery are thus linked. A woman's commodification as wife—she is literally chattel that can be transferred from one man to another by means of a piece of paper—was never so materially represented.

Lady Georgiana's novel touches upon a number of contemporary events and does so with great compression. The intricate structure of the novel, its deft use of the epistolary form (particularly through repetition of key phrases by different correspondents), and its consistent and intelligent use of allusion all make it something more than a hastily written novel. In *The Sylph*, readers found themselves introduced to the world of aristocratic England: London decadence, outrageous debts incurred by gambling, the importation of French hairstyles into London before the French Revolution, the spread of Rosicrucianism and evangelical Christianity, the fear of paper money and the heavy price exacted against forgers, the indelicate practice of wife-swapping, the cruel discipline imposed by army officers against their subordinates, and the rank barbarism of the upper classes barely concealed beneath a patina of Chesterfieldian decorum. These topics are treated with a freshness that transports the reader back to that time period much better than any history could. Such attention to changing customs and decorum increase a novel's value. *The Sylph* takes its place as a work written between Fanny Burney's *Evelina* and Jane Austen's *Sense and Sensibility*, by a writer who patronized novelist Charlotte Smith, poet Mary Robinson, and the leading actresses of her day, such as Sarah Siddons. It fulfills the promise of being both a work of art and a secret history of late-eighteenth-century British aristocratic life.

Notes

1. Brian Masters, *Georgiana* (London: Hamish Hamilton, 1981), 143.

2. Masters, 61.

3. James Raven and Antonia Forster, with the assistance of Stephen Bending, *The English Novel, 1770–1829: A Bibliographical Survey of Prose Fiction Published in the British Isles*, vol. 1 (Oxford: Oxford University Press, 2000), 1.228.

4. Amanda Foreman, *Georgiana* (New York: HarperCollins, 1998), 60. Foreman's book updates but does not replace Brian Masters's work, *Georgiana*, which includes much important information on Lady Georgiana's travels abroad and has a rich chapter on Sheridan's *School for Scandal*.

5. Masters, 79.

6. Foreman, 390.

7. Masters, 1.

8. Masters, 4.

9. Foreman, 8.

10. Foreman, 12.

11. Masters, 11.

12. Brian Dolan, *Ladies of the Grand Tour: British Women in Pursuit of Enlightenment and Adventure in Eighteenth-Century Europe* (London: HarperCollins, 2001).

13. Masters, 11.

14. Foreman, 13.

15. Masters, 16.

16. Foreman, 15; Masters, 17.

17. Masters, 17.

18. Foreman, 17.

19. Masters, 17.

20. Masters, 23.

21. Foreman, 17.

22. Foreman, 17.

23. Foreman, 17.

24. Masters, 18, 19.

25. Masters, 3.

26. Masters, 27.

27. Masters, 25.

28. Masters, 35.

29. Masters, 35.

30. Masters, 37.

31. Masters, 36.

32. Masters, 39.

33. Foreman, 41.

34. Masters, 64. By the time of the French Revolution, which Fox supported, Georgiana had outgrown her political mentor. She saw the dangers the revolution posed to aristocrats and did not oppose, as Fox did, the war with France.

35. Foreman, 56.

36. Foreman, 56.

37. Masters, 55.

38. Georgiana Cavendish, Duchess of Devonshire, "The Duchess's Diary," in *Sheridan: A Life. Sheridan: From New and Original Material; Including a Manuscript Diary by Georgiana Duchess of Devonshire,* ed. Walter Sichel (London: Constable, 1909), 2:400.

39. Foreman, 409.

40. Lady Sneerwell, Mrs. Candour, and the archetypical macaroni Sir Benjamin Backbite of Sheridan's *School for Scandal* were all drawn from the people Sheridan met in Georgiana's circle (Masters, 64–66).

41. Masters, 46.

42. Richard Sheridan, "The School for Scandal," in *The School for Scandal and Other Plays* (New York: Penguin, 1988), 1:i, p. 196. Quoted in Masters, 65.

43. Masters, 64.

44. Masters, 66.

45. Masters, 67.

46. Horace Walpole wrote this to Horace Mann in 1770. Horace Mann (1706–86), diplomatist, is not to be confused with Horace Mann (1796–1859), the American educational reformer. David Cecil attributes the comment to Lady Melbourne;

see *Lord M., or The Later Life of Lord Melbourne* (New York: Bobbs-Merrill, 1939), 30.

47. She also wrote "Sweet Is the Vale." Both were published with different arrangements in Great Britain and the United States. Like most of Lady Georgiana's creative works, this musical composition was very popular.

48. Masters, 68. Thanks to Pasquale-Anne Brault of the Department of Modern Languages at DePaul University for her help with this translation. Any awkwardness in the final version is mine.

49. Masters, 69.

50. Foreman, 54.

51. Foreman, 59.

52. Foreman, 54.

53. Foreman, 61.

54. Foreman, 65.

55. Masters, 90.

56. Masters, 95.

57. Foreman, 415n36.

58. Foreman, 124.

59. Masters, 102.

60. Masters, 106.

61. Masters, 124.

62. Masters, 124.

63. Based on circumstantial evidence in archives at Chatsworth, Foreman assumes, with justification, that Lady Georgiana may well have had affairs with Charles James Fox and the Duke of Dorset (Foreman, 129, 183).

64. Masters, 125.

65. Foreman, 129.

66. Masters, 132.

67. Masters, 136.

68. Masters, 138.

69. Masters, 155.

70. Foreman, 87.

71. Foreman, 130.

72. Foreman, 192.

73. Masters, 156.

74. Foreman, 331.

75. Foreman, 382.

76. Foreman, 382.

77. "The Butterfly" and "The Table" were printed for the first time from a manuscript in the Beinecke Library, Yale University, in Duchess of Devonshire, *Emma*.

78. Foreman, 431n8; for an update of Foreman's informative note, see Duchess of Devonshire, *Emma*, 32n17).

79. Mary Poovey, *The Proper Lady and the Woman Writer: Ideology as Style in the Works of Mary Wollstonecraft, Mary Shelley, and Jane Austen* (Chicago: University of Chicago Press, 1984).

80. Foreman, 355.

81. Foreman, 392n45.

82. Samuel Richardson, *Pamela; or, Virtue Rewarded*, ed. Peter Sabor, with an introduction by Margaret Doody, 1740 (New York: Penguin, 1980).

83. The very name Biddulph calls to mind Frances Sheridan, *Memoirs of Miss Sidney Biddulph*, ed. Sue Townsend (New York: Pandora, 1987). It is a text that Lady Georgiana, an intimate of Richard Sheridan, must have known, since the work was by his mother.

84. This conventional device appears in a number of works of the period, especially in plays such as Garrick's *Bon Ton* and Moore's *Gamester*.

85. Jane Austen uses an identical plot device to bring Willoughby and Marianne together in *Sense and Sensibility*. Marianne twists her ankle, and Willoughby rescues her.

86. Willy Schrodter, *A Rosicrucian Notebook: The Secret Sciences Used by Members of the Order* (New York: Weiser Books, 1992), 73.

87. Schrodter, 81.

88. Joyce, quoted in Schrodter, 91.

89. Colin Campbell, *The Romantic Ethic and the Spirit of Modern Consumerism* (Oxford: Oxford University Press, 1987).

90. Masters, 47.

91. Poovey, 186.

92. Alexander Pope, *Pope: Poetical Works*, ed. Herbert Davis with a new introduction by Pat Rogers. 1st ed. reprint (London: Oxford University Press, 1990), 1.87. Pope's comments are drawn from Gabalis's introduction. Pope's brief explanation for his choice of the sylphs appears in his dedicatory letter to Arabella Fermor, the model for Belinda: "The Machinery, Madam, is a Term invented by the Criticiks, to signify that Part which the Deities, Angels, or Daemons, are made to act in a Poem: For the ancient poets are in one respect like any modern Ladies; Let an Action be never so trivial in itself, they always make it appear of the utmost importance. These Machines I determin'd to raise on a very new and odd Foundation, the *Rosicrucian* Doctrine of Spirits" (1.86).

93. Comte de Gabalis, *Discourses on the Secret Sciences and Mysteries, in Accordance with the Principles of the Ancient Magi and the Wisdom of the Kabalistic Philosophers* (London: William Rider, 1922), 4.

94. Alexander Pope, *The Rape of the Lock and Other Poems*, ed. Geoffrey Tillotson (New Haven: Yale University Press, 1940), 380.

95. Pope, *The Rape of the Lock and Other Poems*, 380.

96. Pope, *The Rape of the Lock and Other Poems*, 380.

97. Diana J. Prola, "The Sylph in Pope's *Rape of the Lock*" (master's thesis, California State University, Hayward, 1974), 12.

98. Claude Prosper Jolyot de Crébillon (Crébillon Fils), *Le sylphe ou songe de Madame de R***. Écrit par elle-même à Madame de S****, in *Œuvres complètes*, 4 vols., ed. Jean Sgard (Paris: Gallimard, Classiques Garnier, 1999–2003).

99. *Byron's Letters and Journals*, ed. Leslie Marchand (Cambridge: Belknap Press, 1982–92), 2:200.

100. David Garrick, prologue to *The Gamester*, by Edward Moore, in *Poetical Works of David Garrick*, ed. Benjamin Blom (New York: Ayer, 1968), 114–15. For the text of *The Gamester*, I have consulted Edward Moore, *The Foundling: A Comedy* and *The Gamester: A Tragedy*, ed. Anthony Amberg (Newark: University of Delaware Press, 1996).

101. Moore, *The Gamester*, 331.

102. George Colman, prologue to *Bon Ton*, by David Garrick, in David Garrick, *Bon Ton; or, High Life Above Stairs. A Comedy, in Two Acts as It Is Performed at the Theatre Royal, in Drury-lane* (London: T. Becket, 1775), line 5.

103. Colman, lines 22, 24.

104. James Boswell, *Life of Johnson*, ed. Pat Rogers (Oxford: Oxford University Press, 1998), 188.

105. Sheridan, 1.1.196.

106. Donna T. Andrew and Randall MacGowen, *The Perreaus and Mrs. Rudd: Forgery and Betrayal in Eighteenth-Century London* (Berkeley: University of California Press, 2001), 180.

107. Andrew and MacGowen, 180.

CHRONOLOGY OF EVENTS FROM THE LIFE OF GEORGIANA, DUCHESS OF DEVONSHIRE

1772   Lady Spencer and her family tour Europe to recover from the deaths of two infant daughters; visit court of Marie Antoinette. Lady Georgiana writes *Emma; or, The Unfortunate Attachment.*

1773   *Emma; or, The Unfortunate Attachment* is published.

1774   Lady Georgiana marries on June 7.

1778   Lady Georgiana lives with her husband at Coxheath while military drills take place to forestall French invasion; incurs large gambling debts; blackmailed by a man named Wilkinson; confesses debts to her husband who pays them.

1779   Lady Georgiana publishes *The Sylph.*

1782   Lady Georgiana meets Elizabeth Foster.

1783   Birth of Georgiana's first daughter, Lady Georgiana Cavendish.

1784   Lady Georgiana campaigns for the election of Charles James Fox; receives widespread publicity in caricatures and newspapers; witnesses the Prince of Wales's suicide attempt and marriage proposal to the Catholic widow Lady Maria Fitzherbert.

1785   Birth of Georgiana's second daughter, Lady Harriet Cavendish.

1787   Thomas Coutts loans Lady Georgiana large sums; she promises to introduce his daughters to members of the French court; Comte Perregaux helps her manage forty thousand to fifty thousand pounds worth of debts in France.

1790   Birth of Georgiana's son, William (Harrington, known as Hart) Spencer, 1790, sixth Duke of Devonshire.

1792   Lady Georgiana bears a child, Eliza Courtney, by Charles Grey and is banished by Duke of Devonshire; travels with mother, sister, and Bess, as well as servants, through Nice, Lausanne, and Rome, visiting Mt. Vesuvius and other sights.

1793   France declares war on Britain.

1794   Georgiana returns to England after her husband welcomes her home; reunited with their children.

1796   Lady Georgiana undergoes painful operations on her right eye and infection spreads to her left eye; retires from public life; collects and studies fossils at Chatsworth.

1802   Duke of Richmond and Elizabeth Foster consider marriage.

1806   Lady Georgiana helps bring together the "Ministry of All the Talents" (1804–6) with Charles James Fox as Prime Minister; dies at Chiswick.

1809   Elizabeth Foster marries the Duke of Devonshire.

THE SYLPH

"Ye Sylphs and Sylphids, to your chief give ear!
Fays, Fairies, Genii, Elves, and Dæmons, hear!
Ye know the spheres, and various tasks assigned
By laws eternal to the aërial kind.
Some in the fields of purest ether play,
And bask and whiten in the blaze of day.
Some guide the course of wandering orbs on high,
Or roll the planets through the boundless sky . . ."

"Our humbler province is to tend the Fair,
Not a less pleasing, though less glorious care . . ."

Pope's *Rape of the Lock*
(Canto 2, lines 73–80; 91–92)

LETTER 1

To Lord Biddulph

It is a certain sign of a man's cause being bad, when he is obliged to quote precedents in the follies of others to excuse his own. You see, I give up my cause at once. I am convinced I have done a silly thing, and yet I can produce thousands who daily do the same with, perhaps, not so good a motive as myself. In short, not to puzzle you too much, which I know is extremely irksome to a man who loves to have everything as clear as a proposition in Euclid; your friend (now don't laugh) is married. Married! Aye, why not? Don't everybody marry? Those who have estates to have heirs of their own and those who have *nothing* to get *something;* so, according to my system, everybody marries. Then why that stare of astonishment? That look of unbelief? Yes, thou infidel, I am married, and to such a woman! Though, notwithstanding her beauty and other accomplishments, I shall be half afraid to present her in the world, she's such a rustic! One of your sylvan deities. But I was mad for her. "So you have been for half the women in town." Very true, my lord, so I have, till I either gained them or saw others whose image obliterated theirs. You well know, love with me has ever been a laughing god, "Rosy lips and cherub smiles"—none of its black despairing looks have I experienced.

What will the world say? How will some exult that I am at last taken in! What, the gay seductive Stanley shackled!

But, I apprehend, your lordship will wish to be informed how the "smiling mischief" seized me. Well, you shall have the full and true particulars of the matter how, the time when, and place where. I must, however, look back. Perhaps I have been too precipitate—I might possibly have gained the charming maid at a less expense than "adamantine everlasting chains."—But the bare idea of losing her made every former resolution of never being enslaved appear as nothing.—Her looks "would warm the cool bosom of age," and tempt an Anchorite to sin.

I could have informed you in a much better method, and have led you on through a flowery path; but as all my elaborate sketches must have ended in this disastrous truth, *I am married,* I thought it quite as well to let you into that important secret at once. As I have divided my discourse under three heads, I will, according to some able preachers, begin with the first.

I left you as you may remember (though perhaps the burgundy might have washed away your powers of recollection) pretty early one morning at the Thatched House, to proceed as far as Wales to visit Lord G.—I did not find so much sport as I expected in his lordship's grounds; and within doors, two old-fashioned maiden sisters did not promise such as is suited to my taste, and therefore pretended letters from town, which required my attendance, and in consequence made my *congé* and departed. On my journey—as I had no immediate business anywhere, save that which has ever been my sole employ, amusement—I resolved to make little deviations from the right road and like a sentimental traveller pick up what I could find in my way conducive to the chief end in my life. I stopped at a pleasant village some distance from Abergavenny, where I rested some time, making little excursive progressions round the country. Rambling over the cloud-capt mountains one morning, a morning big with the fate of moor game and your friend—from the ridge of a precipice I beheld, to me, the most delicious game in the hospitable globe, a brace of females, unattended, and, by the style of their dress, though far removed from the vulgar, yet such as did not bespeak them of *our* world.—I drew out my glass to take a nearer ken, when such beauties shot from one in particular that fired my soul and ran thrilling through every vein. That instant they turned from me and seemed to be bending their footsteps far away. Mad with the wish of a nearer view, and fearful of losing sight of them, I hastily strove to descend. My eyes still fixed on my lovely object, I paid no regard to my situation, and, while my thoughts and every faculty were absorbed in this pleasing idea, scrambled over rocks and precipices fearless of consequences—which however might have concluded unfortunately and spoiled me for adventure—for, without the least warning, which is often the case, a piece of earth gave way, and down my worship rolled to the bottom. The height from whence I had fallen, and the rough encounters I had met with, stunned me for some time, but when I came to my recollection, I was charmed to see my beautiful girls running towards me. They had all seen my fall, and, from my lying still, concluded I was killed; they expressed great joy on hearing me speak and most obligingly endeavoured to assist me in rising, but their united efforts were in vain; my leg was broken. This was a great shock to us all. In the sweetest accents they condoled me on my misfortune and offered every assistance and consolation in their power. To a genius so enterprising as myself, any accident which furthered my wishes of making an acquaintance with the object I had been pursuing appeared trivial when the advantages presented themselves to my view. I sat therefore *like Patience on a monument* and bore my misfortune with a stoical philosophy. I wanted much to discover who they were, as their appearance was rather equivocal and might have pronounced them belonging to any station in life. Their dress was exactly the same: white jackets and petticoats, with light green ribbons, &c. I asked some questions, which I hoped would lead to the point I wished to be informed in: their answers were polite, but not satisfactory, though I cannot say they were wholly evasive, as they seemed artlessly innocent, or, if at all reserved, it was the reserve which native modesty teaches. One of them said I was in great need of instant assistance, and she had interest enough to procure some from a house not very distant from us to which they were both going. I entreated the younger one to stay, as I should be the most wretched of all mortals if left to myself. "We go," said she, "in order to relieve that wretchedness."

I fixed my eyes on her with the most tender languor I could assume and, sighing, told her it was in her power alone to give me ease, since she was the cause of my pain: her charms had dazzled my eyes and occasioned that false step which had brought me sooner than expected at her feet.

She smiled and answered then it was doubly incumbent on her to be as quick as possible in procuring me every accommodation necessary. At that instant they spied a herdsman, not far off. They called aloud, and talking with him some little time, without saying a word further to me, tripped away like two fairies. I asked the peasant who those lovely girls were. He not answering, I repeated my question louder, thinking him deaf; but, staring at me with a stupid astonishment, he jabbered out some barbarous sounds, which I immediately discovered to be a Welsh language I knew no more than the Hottentot. I had flattered myself with being, by this fellow's assistance, able to discover the real situation of these sweet girls: indeed I hoped to have found them within my reach; for, though I was at that moment as much in love as a man with a broken leg and bruised body could be supposed, yet I had then not the least thoughts of matrimony, I give you my honour. Thus disappointed in my views, I rested as contented as I could—hoping better fortune by and by.

In a little time a person, who had the appearance of a gentleman, approached, with three other servants, who carried a gate, on which was laid a feather bed. He addressed me with the utmost politeness and assisted to place me on this litter and begged to have the honour of attending me to his house. I returned his civilities with the same politeness and was carried to a very good-looking house on the side of a wood and placed on a bed in a room handsomely furnished. A surgeon came a few hours after. The fracture was reduced; and as I was ordered to be kept extremely quiet, everyone left the room, except my kind host, who sat silently by the bedside. This was certainly genuine hospitality, for I was wholly unknown, as you may suppose: however, my figure, being that of a gentleman, and my distressed situation were sufficient recommendations.

After lying some time in a silent state, I ventured to breathe out my grateful acknowledgements; but Mr. Grenville stopped me short, nor would suffer me to say one word that might tend to agitate my spirits. I told him I thought it absolutely necessary to inform him who I was, as the event of my accident was uncertain. I therefore gave a concise account of myself. He desired to know if I had any friend to whom I would wish to communicate my situation. I begged him to send to the village I had left that morning for my servant, as I should be glad of his attendance. Being an adroit fellow, I judged he might be of service to me in gaining some intelligence about the damsels in question: but I was very near never wanting him again; for, a fever coming on, I was for some days hovering over the grave. A good constitution at last got the better, and I had nothing to combat but my broken limb, which was in a fair way. I had a most excellent nurse, a housekeeper in the family. My own servant likewise waited on me. Mr. Grenville spent a part of every day with me; and his agreeable conversation, though rather too grave for a fellow of my fire, afforded me great comfort during my confinement: yet still something was wanting, till I could hear news of my charming wood nymphs.

One morning I strove to make my old nurse talk and endeavoured to draw her out; she seemed a little shy. I asked her a number of questions about my generous entertainer; she rung a peal in his praise. I then asked if there were any pretty girls in the neighbourhood, as I was a great admirer of beauty. She laughed and told me not to let my thoughts wander that way yet a while; I was yet too weak.

"Not to talk of beauty, my old girl," said I.

"Aye, aye," she answered, "but you look as if talking would not content you." I then told her I had seen the loveliest girl in the world among the Welsh mountains, not far from hence, who I found was acquainted with this family, and I would reward her handsomely if she could procure for me an interview with her, when she should judge I was able to talk of love in a proper style. I then described the girls I had seen and freely confessed the impression one of them made on me.

"As sure as you are alive," said the old cat, "it was my daughter you saw."

"Your daughter!" I exclaimed. "Is it possible for your daughter to be such an angel?"

"Good lack! Why not? What, because I am poor, and a servant, my daughter is not to be flesh and blood?"

"By heaven! But she is," said I, "and such flesh and blood that I would give a thousand pounds to take her to town with me. What say you, mother; will you let me see her?"

"I cannot tell," said she, shaking her head. "To be sure my girl is handsome, and might make her fortune in town; for she's as virtuous as she's poor."

"I promise you," said I, "if she is not foolish enough to be too scrupulous about one, I will take care to remove the other. But, when shall I see her?"

"Lord! You must not be in such a hurry: all in good time." With this assurance, and these hopes, I was constrained to remain satisfied for some time: though the old wench every now and then would flatter my passions by extolling the charms of her daughter, and above all, commending her sweet compliant disposition, a circumstance I thought in my favour, as it would render my conquest less arduous. I occasionally asked her of the family whom she served. She seemed rather reserved on this subject, though copious enough on any other. She informed me, however, that Mr. Grenville had two daughters, but no more to be compared with hers than she was, and that, as soon as I was able to quit my bedchamber, they would be introduced to me.

As my strength increased, my talkative nurse grew more eloquent in the praises of her child, and by those praises inflamed my passion to the highest pitch. I thought every day an age till I again beheld her; resolving to begin my attack as soon as possible and indulging the idea that my task would, through the intervention of the mother, be carried on with great facility. Thus I whiled away the time when I was left to myself. Yet, notwithstanding I recovered most amazingly fast considering my accident, I thought the confinement plaguey tedious and was heartily glad when my surgeon gave me permission to be conveyed into a dressing room. On the second day of my emigration from my bedchamber, Mr. Grenville informed me he would bring me acquainted with the rest of his family. I assured him I should receive such an indulgence as a mark of his unexampled politeness and humanity and should endeavour to be grateful for such favour. I now attained the height of my wishes, and at the same time sustained a sensible and mortifying disappointment, for, in the afternoon, Mr. Grenville entered the room, and in either hand one of the lovely girls I had seen, and who were the primary cause of my accident. I attained the summit of my wishes in again beholding my charmer; but when she was introduced under the character of daughter to my host, my fond hopes were instantly crushed. How could I be such a villain as to attempt the seduction of the daughter of a man to whom I was bound by so many ties? This reflexion damped the joy which flushed in my face when I first saw her. I paid my compliments to the fair sisters with an embarrassment in my air not usual to a man of the world, but which, however, was not perceptible to my innocent companions. They talked over my adventure and congratulated my recovery with so much good nature as endeared them both to me at the same time that I inwardly cursed the charms that enslaved me. Upon the whole, I do not know whether pain or pleasure was predominant through the course of the day; but I found I loved her more and more every moment. Uncertain what my resolves or intentions were, I took my leave of them and returned to my room with matter for reflexion sufficient to keep me waking the best part of the night. My old tabby did not administer a sleeping potion to me, by the conversation I had with her afterwards on the subject in debate.

"Well, sir," she asked, "how do you like my master's daughters?"

"Not so well as I should your daughter, I can tell you. What the devil did you mean by your cursed long harangues about her beauty, when you knew all the while she was not attainable?"

"Why not? She is disengaged; is of a family and rank in life to do any man credit; and you are enamoured of her."

"True; but I have no inclination to marry."

"And you cannot hope to succeed on any other terms, even if you could form the plan of dishonouring the daughter of a man of some consequence in the world, and one who has shown you such kindness!"

"Your sagacity happens to be right in your conjecture."

"But you would have no scruples of conscience in your design on *my* daughter."

"Not much, I confess; money well applied would have silenced the world, and I should have left it to her and your prudence to have done the rest."

"And do you suppose, sir," said she, "that the honour of my daughter is not as valuable to me, because I am placed so much below you, as that of the daughter of the first man in the world? Had this been my child and, by the various artifices you might have put in practice, you had triumphed over her virtue, do you suppose, I say, a little paltry dross would have been a recompense? No, sir, know me better than to believe any worldly advantages would have silenced my wrongs. My child, thank heaven, is virtuous, and far removed from the danger of meeting with such as I am sorry to find you are: one who would basely rob the poor of the only privilege they possess, that of being innocent, while you cowardly shrink at the idea of attacking a woman who, in the eye of a venal world, has a sufficient fortune to varnish over the loss of reputation. I confess I knew not the depravity of your heart, till the other day, I by accident heard part of a conversation between you and your servant; before that, I freely own, though I thought you not so strict in morals as I hoped, yet I flattered myself your principles were not corrupted, but imputed the warmth of your expressions to youth and a life unclouded by misfortune. I further own, I was delighted with the impression which my young lady had made on you. I fancied your passion disinterested, because you knew not her situation in life; but now I know you too well to suffer her to entertain a partiality for one whose sentiments are unworthy a man of honour, and who can never esteem virtue though in her loveliest form."

"Upon my soul! Mother," cried I (affecting an air of gaiety in my manner, which was foreign to my heart, for I was cursedly chagrined), "you have really a fine talent for preaching; why what a delectable sermon have you delivered against *simple fornication*. But come, come, we must not be enemies. I assure you, with the utmost sincerity, I am not the sad dog you think me. I honour and revere virtue even in you, who, you must be sensible, are rather too advanced in life for a Venus, though I doubt not in your youth you made many a Welsh heart dance without a harp. Come, I see you are not so angry as you were. Have a little compassion on a poor young fellow who cannot, if he wishes it, run away from your frowns. I am tied by the leg, you know, my old girl. But to tell you the serious truth, the cause of the air of dissatisfaction which I wore was my apprehension of not having merit to gain the only woman that ever made any impression on my heart; and likewise my fears of your not being my friend, from the ludicrous manner in which I had before treated this affair."—I added some more prevailing arguments and solemnly attested heaven to witness my innocence of actual seduction, though I had, I confessed with blushes, indulged in a few fashionable pleasures, which, though they might be styled crimes among the Welsh mountains, were nothing in our world. In short, I omitted nothing (as you will suppose by the lies I already told of my *innocence of actual seduction,* and such stuff—) that I thought conducive to conciliating her good opinion, or at least a better than she seemed to have at present.

When I argued the matter over in my own mind, I knew not on what to determine. Reflexion never agreed with me: I hate it confoundedly—it brings with it a consumed long string of past transactions that *bore* me to death and is worse than a fit of the hypochondriac. I endeavoured to lose my disagreeable companion in the arms of sleep; but the devil a bit: the idea of the raptures I should taste in those of my lovely Julia drove the drowsy God from my eyelids—yet my pleasurable sensations were damped by the enormous purchase I must in all probability pay for such a delightful privilege. After examining the business every way, I concluded it as I do most things which require mature deliberation—left it to work its way in the manner it could, making chance, the first link in the chain of causes, ruler of my fate.

I now saw my Julia daily, and the increase of passion was the consequence of every interview. You have often told me I was a fellow of no speculation or thought: I presume to say that in the point in question, though you may conceive me running hand over head to destruction, I have shown a great deal of forethought and that the step I have taken is an infallible proof of it. Charming as both you and I think the Lady Bettys and Lady Bridgets, and faith have found them too, I believe neither you nor I ever intended to take any one of them *for better, for worse;* yet we have never made any resolution against entering into the pale of matrimony. Now though I like a little *badinage,* and sometimes something more, with a married woman—I would much rather that my wife, like Caesar's, should not be suspected: where then is it so likely to meet with a woman of real virtue as in the lap of innocence? The women of our world marry that they may have the greater privilege for leading dissipated lives. Knowing them so well as I do, I could have no chance of happiness with one of their class—and yet one must one time or other "settle soberly and raise a brood."—And why not now, while every artery beats rapidly, and nature is alive?

However, it does not signify bringing this argument, or that, to justify my procedure; I could not act otherwise than I have done. I was mad, absolutely dying for her. By heaven! I never saw so many beauties under one form. There is not a limb nor feature which I have not adored in as many different women; here, they are all assembled with the greatest harmony: and yet she wants the polish of the world: a *je ne sais quoi,* a *tout ensemble,* which nothing but mixing with people of fashion can give: but, as she is extremely docile, I have hopes that she will not disgrace the name of Stanley.

Shall I whisper you a secret—but publish it not in the streets of Askalon—I could almost wish my whole life had passed in the same innocent tranquil manner it has now for several weeks. No tumultuous thought, which, as they are too often excited by licentious excess, must be lost and drowned in wine. No cursed qualms of conscience, which will appal the most hardy of us, when nature sickens after the fatigue of a debauch. Here all is peaceful, because all is innocent: and yet what voluptuary can figure a higher joy than I at present experience in the possession of the most lovely of her sex, who thinks it her duty to contribute to my pleasure, and whose every thought I can read in her expressive countenance? Oh! That I may ever see her with the same eyes I do at this moment! Why cannot I renounce the world, the ways which I have seen and despise from my soul?

What attachments have I to it, guilty ones excepted? Ought I to continue them, when I have sworn—Oh! Christ! What is come to me now? Can a virtuous connexion with the sex work miracles? But you cannot inform me—having never made such: and who the devil can, till they marry—and then it is too late: the die is cast.

I hope you will thank me for making you my confidant—and, what is more, writing you so enormous a long letter. Most likely I shall enhance your obligation by continuing my correspondence, as I do not know when I shall quit what appears to me my earthly paradise. Whether you will congratulate me from your heart I know not, because you may possibly imagine, from some virtuous emanations which have burst forth in the course of this epistle, that you shall lose your old companion. No, no, not quite so bad neither—though I am plaguey squeamish at present, a little town air will set all to right again, and I shall no doubt fall into my old track with redoubled alacrity from this recess. So don't despair, my old friend: you will always find me,

Your lordship's devoted,

W. Stanley

❦ ❦ ❦ ❦ ❦ ❦ ❦ ❦ ❦
LETTER 2
❦ ❦ ❦ ❦ ❦ ❦ ❦ ❦ ❦

To the Same

What a restless discontented animal is man! Even in Paradise unblest. Do you know I am, though surrounded with felicity, languishing for sin and sea-coal in your regions. I shall be vapoured to death if I stay here much longer. Here is nothing to exercise the bright genius with which I am endued: all one calm sunshine:

> And days of peace do still succeed
> To nights of calm repose.

How unfit to charm a soul like mine! I, who love everything that the moderns call pleasure. I must be amongst you, and that presently. My Julia, I am certain, will make no resistance to my will. Faith! She is the wife for me. Mild, passive, duteous, and innocent: I may lead my life just as I please; and she, dear creature! will have no idea but that I am a very good husband:

And when I am weary of wandering all day,
To thee my delight in the evening I come.

I did intend, when first I began my correspondence with your lordship, to have informed you of the whole process of this affair; but, upon my soul, you must excuse me. From being idle, I have become perfectly indolent;—besides, it is unfashionable to talk so much of one's wife. I shall only say, I endeavoured, by all those little attentions which are so easily assumed by us, to gain her affections,—and at the same time, to make sure work, declared myself in form to her father.

One day, when I could hobble about, I took occasion to say to Mr. Grenville that I was meditating a return for his civilities, which was no other than running away with his daughter Julia: that, in the whole course of my life, I had never seen a woman whom I thought so capable of making me happy; and that, were my proposals acceptable to him and her, it would be my highest felicity to render her situation such. I saw the old man was inwardly pleased.—In very polite terms he assured me he should have no objection to such an alliance if Julia's heart made none; that although, for very particular reasons, he had quarrelled with the world, he did not wish to seclude his children from partaking of its pleasures. He owned he thought Julia seemed to have an inclination to see more of it than he had had an opportunity of showing her; and that, as he had forever renounced it, there was no protector, after a father, so proper as a husband. He then paid me some compliments, which perhaps had his acquaintance been of as long standing as yours and mine he might have thought rather above my desert: but he knows no more of me than he has heard from me,—and the devil is in it if a man won't speak well of himself when he has an opportunity.

It was some time before I could bring myself to the pious resolution of marrying.—I was extremely desirous of practising a few manoeuvres first, just to try the strength of the citadel;—but madame housekeeper would have blown me up. "You are in love with my master's daughter," said she one day to me;

"If you make honourable proposals, I have not a doubt but they will be accepted;—if I find you endeavouring to gain her heart in a clandestine manner,—remember you are in my power. My faithful services in this family have given me some influence, and I will certainly use it for their advantage. The best and loveliest of her sex shall not be left a prey to the artful insinuating practices of a man too well versed in the science of deceit. Marry her; she will do you honour in this world, and by her virtues ensure your happiness in the next."

I took the old matron's advice, as it so perfectly accorded with my own wishes. The gentle Julia made no objection.—Vanity apart, I certainly have some attractions; especially in the eyes of an innocent young creature, who yet never saw a reasonable being besides her father; and who had likewise a secret inclination to know a little how things go in the world. I shall very soon gratify her wish, by taking her to London.—I am sick to death of the constant *routine* of circumstances here—*the same today, tomorrow, and forever.* Your mere good kind of people are really very insipid sort of folks and as such totally unsuited to my taste. I shall therefore leave them to their pious meditations in a short time and whirl my little Julia into the giddy circle, where alone true joy is to be met with.

I shall not invite her sister to accompany her; as I have an invincible dislike to the idea of marrying a whole family. Besides, sisters sometimes are more quick sighted than wives: and I begin to think (though from whence she has gained her knowledge I know not, I hope honestly!) that Louisa is mistress of more penetration than my *rib*.—She is more serious, consequently more observing and attentive.

The day of our departure is fixed.—Our *suite* will be a Welsh *fille de chambre*, yclep'd Winifred, and an old male domestic, who at present acts in capacity of groom to me, and who I foresee will soon be the butt of my whole house;—as he is chiefly composed of Welsh materials, I conclude we shall have fine work with him among our *beaux d'esprits* of the motley tribe.—I shall leave Taffy to work his way as he can. Let everyone fight their own battles I say.—I hate to interfere in any kind of business. I burn with impatience to greet you and the rest of your confederates. Assure them of my best wishes.—I was going to say services,—but alas! I am not my own master! I am married. After that, may I venture to conclude myself yours?

W. Stanley

LETTER 3

To Miss Grenville

How strange does it seem, my dearest Louisa, to address you at this distance! What is it that has supported me through this long journey and given me strength to combat with all the softer feelings, to quit a respectable parent and a beloved sister, to leave such dear and tender relations, and accompany a man to whom four months since I was wholly a stranger! I am a wretched reasoner at best.—I am therefore at a loss to unravel this mystery. It is true, it became my duty to follow my husband; but that a duty so newly entered into should supersede all others is certainly strange. You will say, you wonder these thoughts did not arise sooner;—they did, my dear; but the continual agitation of my spirits since I am married prevented my paying any attention to them. Perhaps those who have been accustomed to the bustles of the world would laugh at my talking of the agitation of spirits in the course of an affair which was carried on with most methodical exactness; but then it is their being accustomed to bustles which could insure their composure on such an important occasion. I am young and inexperienced—and what is worst of all, a perfect stranger to the disposition of Sir William. He may be a very good sort of man; yet he may have some faults, which are at present unknown to me.—I am resolved, however, to be as indulgent to them as possible, should I discover any.—And as for my own, I will strive to conceal them, under an implicit obedience to his will and pleasure.

As to giving you an account of this hurrying place, it is totally out of my power. I made Sir William laugh very heartily several times at my ignorance. We came into town at a place called Piccadilly, where there was such a crowd of carriages of all sorts that I was perfectly astonished and absolutely frightened. I begged Sir William would order the drivers to stop till they were gone by.—This entreaty threw him almost into a convulsion of laughter at my simplicity;—but I was still more amazed when he told me they would continue driving with the same vehemence all night. For my part, I could not hear my own voice for the continual rattle of coaches, &c.—I still could not help thinking it must be some particular rejoicing day, from the immense concourse of people I saw rushing from all quarters;—and yet Sir William assured me the town was very empty. "Mercy defend us!" cried Winifred, when I informed her what her master had said, "What a place must it be when it is full, for the people have not room to walk as it is!" I cautioned Win to discover her ignorance as little as possible;—but I doubt both mistress and maid will be subjects of mirth some time to come.

I have not yet seen anything, as there is a ceremony to be observed among people of rank in this place. No married lady can appear in public till she has been properly introduced to their majesties. Alas! What will become of me upon an occasion so singular!—Sir William has been so obliging as to bespeak the protection of a lady, who is perfect mistress of the *etiquettes* of courts. She will pay me a visit previous to my introduction; and under her tuition, I am told, I have nothing to fear. All my hopes are that I may acquit myself so as to gain the approbation of my husband. Husband! What a sound has that, when pronounced by a girl barely seventeen,—and one whose knowledge of the world is merely speculative;—one who, born and bred in obscurity, is equally unacquainted with men and manners.—I have often revolved in my mind what could be the inducement of my father's total seclusion from the world; for what little hints I (and you, whose penetration is deeper than mine) could gather, have only served to convince us, he must have been extremely ill treated by it, to have been constrained to make a vow never again to enter into it,—and in my mind the very forming of a vow looks as if he had loved it to excess and therefore made his retreat from it more solemn than a bare resolution, lest he might, from a change of circumstances or sentiments, again be seduced by its attractions, and by which he had suffered so much.

Do you know I have formed the wish of knowing some of those incidents in his history which have governed his actions? Will you, my dear Louisa, hint this to him? He may, by such a communication, be very serviceable to me, who am such a novice.

I foresee I shall stand in need of instructors; otherwise I shall make but an indifferent figure in the drama. Everything, and everybody, makes an appearance so widely opposite to my former notions that I find myself every moment at a loss, and know not to whom to apply for information. I am apprehensive I shall tire Sir William to death with my interrogatories; besides, he gave me much such a hint as I gave Win, not to betray my ignorance to every person I met with; and yet, without asking questions, I shall never attain the knowledge of some things which to me appear extremely singular. The ideas I possessed while among the mountains seem entirely useless to me here. Nay, I begin to think, I might as well have learnt nothing; and that the time and expense which were bestowed on my education were all lost, since I even do not know how to walk a minuet properly. Would you believe it? Sir William has engaged a dancing master to put me into a genteel and polite method of acquitting myself with propriety on the important circumstance of moving about a room gracefully. Shall I own I felt myself mortified when he made the proposition? I could even have shed tears at the humiliating figure I made in my own eyes; however, I had resolution to overcome such an appearance of weakness and turned it off with a smile, saying I thought I had not stood in need of any accomplishments, since I had had sufficient to gain his affections. I believe he saw I was hurt, and therefore took some pains to reassure me. He told me that though my person was faultless, yet, from my seclusion from it, I wanted an air of the world. He himself saw nothing but perfection in me; but he wished those who were not blinded by passion should think me not only the most beautiful but likewise the most polished woman at court. Is there not a little vanity in this, Louisa? But Sir William is, I find, a man of the world; and it is my duty to comply with everything he judges proper to make me what he chooses.

Monsieur Fierville pays me great compliments. "Who is he?" you will ask. Why, my dancing master, my dear. I am likewise to take some lessons on the harpsichord, as Sir William finds great fault with my fingering and thinks I want taste in singing. I always looked on taste as genuine and inherent to ourselves; but here, taste is to be acquired; and what is infinitely more astonishing still, it is variable. So, though I may dance and sing in taste now, a few months hence I may have another method to learn, which will be the taste then. It is a fine time for teachers, when scholars are never taught. We used to think to be made perfect mistress of anything was sufficient; but in this world it is very different; you have a fresh lesson to learn every winter. As a proof, they had last winter one of the first singers in the world at the opera house; this winter they had one who surpassed her. This assertion you and I think nonsense, since, according to our ideas, nothing can exceed perfection: the next who comes over will be superior to all others that ever arrived. The reason is, everyone has a different mode of singing, a taste of their own, which by arbitrary custom is for that cause to be the taste of the whole town. These things appear incomprehensible to me; but I suppose use will reconcile me to them, as it does others by whom they must once have been thought strange.

I think I can discover Sir William Stanley has great pride, that is, he is a slave to fashion. He is ambitious of being a leading man. His house, his equipage, and wife—in short, everything which belongs to him—must be admired; and I can see, he is not a little flattered when they meet with approbation, although from persons of whose taste and knowledge of life he has not the most exalted idea.

It would look very ungrateful of me, if I was to make any complaints against my situation; and yet would it not be more so to my father and you, if I was not to say, I was happier whilst with you? I certainly was. I will do Sir William the justice to say he contributed to make my last two months' residence very pleasant. He was the first lover I ever had, at least the first that ever told me he loved. The distinction he paid me certainly made some impression on my heart. Every female has a little vanity; but I must enlarge my stock before I can have a proper confidence in myself in this place.

My singing master has just been announced. He is a very great man in his way, so I must not make him wait; besides, my letter is already a pretty reasonable length. Adieu, my dearest sister! Say everything duteous and affectionate for me to my father; and tell yourself that I am ever yours,

Julia Stanley

LETTER 4

To Colonel Montague

Dear Jack,

I was yesterday introduced to the loveliest woman in the universe, Stanley's wife. Yes, that happy dog is still the favourite of Fortune. How does he triumph over me on every occasion! If he had a soul of worth, what a treasure would he possess in such an angel! But he will soon grow tired even of her. What immense pains did he take to supplant me in the affections of Lucy Gardiner, though he has since sworn to you and many others he proposed no other advantage to himself than rivalling me and conquering her prejudices in my favour. He thinks I have forgot all this, because I did not call him to an account for his ungenerous conduct, and because I still style him my friend; but let him have a care; my revenge only slept till a proper opportunity called it forth. As to retaliating, endeavouring to obtain any of his mistresses was too trivial a satisfaction for me, as he is too phlegmatic to be hurt by such an attempt. I flatter myself I shall find an opening by and by to convince him I have neither forgotten the injury nor am of a temper to let slip an occasion of piercing his heart by a method effectual and secure. Men who delight to disturb the felicity of others are most tenacious of their own. And Stanley, who has allowed himself such latitude of intrigue in other men's families, will very sensibly feel any stain on his. But of this in future; let me return to Lady Stanley. She is not a perfect beauty: which, if you are of my taste, you will think rather an advantage than not; as there is generally a formality in great regularity of features, and most times an insipidity. In her there are neither. She is in one word *animated nature.* Her height is proper, and excellently well proportioned, I might say, exquisitely formed. Her figure is such as at once creates esteem and gives birth to the tenderest desires. Stanley seemed to take pleasure in my commendations. "I wanted you to see her, my lord," said he. "You are a man of taste. May I introduce Julia, without blushing through apprehension of her disgracing me? You know my sentiments. I must be applauded by the world; lovely as I yet think her, she would be the object of my hate, and I should despise myself, if she is not admired by the whole court; it is the only apology I can make to myself for marrying at all." What a brute of a fellow it is! I suppose he must be cuckolded by half the town to be convinced his wife has charms.

Lady Stanley is extremely observant of her husband at present, because he is the only man who has paid her attention; but when she finds she is the only woman who is distinguished by his indifference, which will soon be the case, she will likewise see, and be grateful for, the assiduities paid her by other men. One of the first of those I intend to be. I shall not let you into the plan of operations at present; besides, it is impossible, till I know more of my ground, to mark out any scheme. Chance often performs that for us, which the most judicious reflexion cannot bring about; and I have the whole campaign before me.

I think myself pretty well acquainted with the failings and weak parts in Stanley; and you may assure yourself I shall avail myself of them. I do not want penetration; and doubt not, from the free access which I have gained in the family, but I shall soon be master of the ruling passion of her ladyship. She is, as yet, a total stranger to the world; her character is not yet established; she cannot know herself. She only knows she is handsome; that secret, I presume, Nature has informed her of. Her husband has confirmed it, and she liked him because she found in him a coincidence of opinion. But all that rapturous nonsense will, and must soon, have an end. As to the beauties of mind, he has no more idea of them than we have of a sixth sense; what he knows not he cannot admire. She will soon find herself neglected; but at the same time she will find the loss of a husband's praises amply supplied by the *devoirs* of a hundred, all equal, and many superior to him. At first, she may be uneasy; but repeated flattery will soon console her; and the man who can touch her heart needs fear nothing. Everything else, as Lord Chesterfield justly observes, will then follow of course. By which assertion, whatever the world may think, he certainly pays a great compliment to the fair sex. Men may be rendered vicious by a thousand methods; but there is only one way to subdue women.

Whom do you think he has introduced as *chaperons* to his wife? Lady Besford and Lady Anne Parker. Do not you admire his choice? Oh! They will be charming associates for her! But I have nothing to say against it, as I think their counsels will further my schemes. Lady Besford might not be so much amiss; but Lady Anne! Think of her, with whom he is belied if he has not had an affair. What madness! It is like him, however. Let him then take the consequences of his folly; and such clever fellows as you and I the advantages of them. Adieu, dear Jack! I shall see you, I hope, as soon as you come to town. I shall want you in a scheme I have in my head, but which I do not think proper to trust to paper.

Yours,

Biddulph

LETTER 5

To Lady Stanley

I have lost you, my Julia; and who shall supply your loss? How much am I alone! And yet, if you are happy, I must and will be satisfied. I should, however, be infinitely more so if you had any companion to guide your footsteps through the devious path of life: I wish you some experienced director. Have you not yet made an acquaintance which may be useful to you? Though you are prevented appearing in public, yet I think it should have been Sir William's first care to provide you with some agreeable sensible female friend, one who may love you as well as your Louisa, and may, by having lived in the world, have it more in her power to be of service to you.

My father misses you as much as I do; I will not repeat all he says, lest you should think he repents of his complying with Sir William's importunity. Write to us very often, and tell us you are happy; that will be the only consolation we can receive in your absence. Oh, this vow! It binds my father to this spot. Not that I wish to enter into the world. I doubt faithlessness and insincerity are very prevalent there, since they could find their way among our mountains. But let me not overcloud your sunshine. I was, you know, always of a serious turn. May no accident make you so, since your natural disposition is cheerfulness itself!

I read your letter to my father; he seemed pleased at your wish of being acquainted with the incidents of his life: he will enter on the task very soon. There is nothing, he says, which can, from the nature of things, be a guide to you in your passage through the world, any farther than not placing too much confidence in the prospect of felicity with which you see yourself surrounded; but always to keep in mind, we are but in a state of probation here, and consequently but for a short time: that, as our happiness is liable to change, we ought not to prize the possession so much as to render ourselves miserable when that change comes; neither, when we are oppressed with the rod of affliction, should we sink into despair, as we are certain our woe, like ourselves, is mortal. Receive the blessing of our only parent, joined with the affectionate love of a tender sister.

Adieu!

Louisa Grenville

፝ ፝ ፝ ፝ ፝ ፝ ፝ ፝ ፝ ፝

LETTER 6

፝ ፝ ፝ ፝ ፝ ፝ ፝ ፝ ፝ ፝

To James Spencer, Esq.

It is high time, my dear Spencer, to account to you for the whimsical journey, as you called it, which your friend undertook so suddenly. I meant not to keep that, or even my motives for it, a secret from you. The esteem you have ever shown me merited my most unlimited confidence.

You said you thought I must have some other view than merely to visit the ruins of a paternal estate lost to me by the extravagant folly of my poor father. You said true, I had indeed some other view. But alas! How blasted is that view! Long had my heart cherished the fondest attachment for the loveliest and best of human beings, who inhabited the mountains, which once my father owned. My fortune was too circumscribed to disclose my flame; but I secretly indulged it, from the remote hope of having it one day in my power to receive her hand without blushing at my inferiority in point of wealth. These thoughts, these wishes, have supported me through an absence of two years from my native land, and all that made my native land dear to me.

Her loved idea heightened every joy I received and softened every care. I knew I possessed her esteem; but I never, from the first of my acquaintance, gave the least hint of what I felt for, or hoped from, her. I should have thought myself base in the highest degree to have made an interest in her bosom, which I had nothing to support on my side but the sanguine wishes of youth, that some turn of Fortune's wheel might be in my favour. You know how amply, as well as unexpectedly, I am now provided for by

24

our dear Frederick's death. How severely have I felt and mourned his loss! But he is happier than in any situation which our friendship for him could have found.

I could run any lengths in praising one so dear to me; but he was equally so to you, and you are fully acquainted with my sentiments on this head; besides, I have something more to the purpose at present to communicate to you.

All the satisfaction I ever expected from the acquisition of fortune was to share it with my love. Nothing but that hope and prospect could have enabled me to sustain the death of my friend. In the bosom of my Julia I fondly hoped to experience those calm delights which his loss deprived me of for some time. Alas! That long-indulged hope is sunk in despair! Oh! My Spencer! She's lost, lost to me forever! Yet what right had I to think she would not be seen, and, being seen, admired, loved, and courted? But from the singularity of her father's disposition who had vowed never to mix in the world; a disappointment of the tenderest kind which her elder sister had met with; and the almost monastic seclusion from society in which she lived; joined to her extreme youth, being but seventeen the day I left you in London: all these circumstances, I say, concurred once to authorize my fond hopes,—and these hopes have nursed my despair. Oh! I knew not how much I loved her till I saw her snatched from me forever. A few months sooner and I might have pleaded some merit with the lovely maid from my long and unremitted attachment. My passion was interwoven with my existence,—with that it grew, and with that only will it expire.

> My dear-lov'd Julia! from my youth began
> The tender flame, and ripen'd in the man;
> My dear-lov'd Julia! to my latest age,
> No other vows shall e'er my heart engage.

Full of the fond ideas which seemed a part of myself, I flew down to Woodley Vale, to reap the long-expected harvest of my hopes.—Good God! What was the fatal news I learnt on my arrival! Alas! She knew not of my love and constancy;—she had a few weeks before given her hand, and no doubt her heart, to Sir William Stanley, with whom an accident had brought her acquainted. I will not enlarge upon what were my feelings on this occasion.—Words would be too faint a vehicle to express the anguish of my soul. You, who know the tenderness of my disposition, must judge for me.

Yesterday I saw the dear angel, from the inn from whence I am writing; she and her happy husband stopped here for fresh horses. I had a full view of her beauteous face. Ah! How much has two years improved each charm in her lovely person! Lovely and charming, but not for me. I kept myself concealed from her—I could hardly support the sight of her at a distance; my emotions were more violent than you can conceive. Her dress became her best in the world; a riding habit of stone-coloured cloth, lined with rose colour, and frogs on the same—the collar of her shirt was open at the neck and discovered her lovely ivory throat. Her hair was in a little disorder, which, with her hat, served to contribute to, and heighten, the almost irresistible charms of her features. There was a pensiveness in her manner, which rendered her figure more interesting and touching than usual. I thought I discovered the traces of a tear on her cheek. She had just parted with her father and sister; and, had she shown less concern, I should not have been so satisfied with her. I gazed till my eyeballs ached; but, when the chaise drove from the door—oh! What then became of me! "She's gone! She's gone!" I exclaimed aloud, wringing my hands, "and never knew how much I loved her!" I was almost in a state of madness for some hours—at last, my storm of grief and despair a little subsided, and I, by degrees, became calm and more resigned to my ill fate. I took the resolution, which I shall put in execution as soon as possible, to leave England. I will retire to the remaining part of my Frederick's family—and, in their friendship, seek to forget the pangs which a habitual tenderness has brought upon me.

You who are at ease may have it in your power to convey some small satisfaction to my wounded breast. But why do I say *small satisfaction*? To me it will be the highest to hear that my Julia is happy. Do you then, my dear Spencer, enquire, among your acquaintance, the character of this Sir William Stanley? His figure is genteel, nay, rather handsome; yet he does not look the man I could wish for her. I did not discover that look of tenderness, that soft impassioned glance, which virtuous love excites; but you will not expect a favourable picture from a rival's pen.

I mentioned a disappointment which the sister of my Julia had sustained: it was just before I left England. While on a visit to Abergavenny, she became acquainted with a young gentleman of fortune, who, after taking some pains to render himself agreeable, had the satisfaction of gaining the affections of one of the most amiable girls in the world. She is all that a woman can be, except being my Julia. Louisa was at that time extremely attached to a lady in the same house with her, who was by no means a favourite with her lover. They used frequently to have little arguments concerning her. He would not allow her any merit. Louisa fancied she saw her own image reflected in the bosom of her friend. She is warm in her attachments. Her zeal for her friend at last awakened a curiosity in her lover, to view her with more scrutiny. He had been accustomed to pay an implicit obedience to Louisa's opinion; he fancied he was still acquiescing only in that opinion when he began to discover she was handsome, and to find some farther beauties which Louisa had not painted in so favourable a light as he now saw them. In short, what at first was only a compliment to his mistress now seemed the due of the other. He thought Louisa had hardly done her justice; and in seeking to repair the fault, he injured the woman who doted on him. Love, which in some cases is blind, is in others extremely quick sighted. Louisa saw a change in his behaviour—a studied civility—an apprehension of not appearing sufficiently assiduous—frequent expressions of fearing to offend—and all those mean arts and subterfuges which a man uses who wants to put it in a woman's power to break with him that he may basely shelter himself behind, what he styles, her cruelty. Wounded to the soul with the duplicity of his conduct, she one day insisted on knowing the motives which induced him to act in so disingenuous a manner by her. At first his answers were evasive; but she peremptorily urged an explicit satisfaction. She told him the most unfavourable certainty would be happiness to what she now felt, and that *certainty* she now called on him in justice to grant her. He then began by palliating the fatal inconstancy of his affections by the encomiums which she had bestowed on her friend; that his love for her had induced him to love those dear to her; and some unhappy circumstances had arisen, which had bound him to her friend beyond his power of inclination to break through. This disappointment, in so early a part of Louisa's life, has given a tenderness to her whole frame, which is of advantage to most women, and her in particular. She has, I question not, long since beheld this unworthy wretch in the light he truly deserved; yet, no doubt, it was not till she had suffered many pangs. The heart will not recover its usual tone in a short time, that has long been racked with the agonies of love; and even when we fancy ourselves quite recovered, there is an aching void which still reminds us of former anguish.

I shall not be in town these ten days at least, as I find I can be service-able to a poor man in this neighbourhood whom I believe to be an object worthy of attention. Write me, therefore, what intelligence you can obtain; and scruple not to communicate the result of your inquiry to me speedily. Her happiness is the wish next my heart. Oh! May it be as exalted and per-manent as I wish it! I will not say anything to you; you well know how dear you are to the bosom of your

Henry Woodley

ŦŦŦŦŦŦŦŦŦŦ
LETTER 7
ŦŦŦŦŦŦŦŦŦŦ

To Henry Woodley, Esq.

No, my dear Harry, I can never consent to your burying yourself abroad; but I will not say all I could on that subject till we meet. I think I shall then be able to offer you some very powerful reasons that you will esteem suf-ficient to induce you to remain in your native land.—I have a scheme in my head, but which I shall not communicate at present.

Sir William Stanley is quite a man of fashion.—Do you know enough of the world to understand all that title comprehends? If you do, you will sincerely regret your Julia is married to *a man of fashion*. His passions are the rule and guide of his actions. To what mischiefs is a young creature exposed in this town, circumstanced as Lady Stanley is—without a friend or relation with her to point out the artful and designing wretch who means to make a prey of her innocence and inexperience of life!

The most unsafe and critical situation for a woman is to be young, hand-some, and married to a man of fashion; these are thought to be lawful prey to the specious of our sex. As a man of fashion, Sir William Stanley would blush to be found too attentive to his wife;—he will leave her to seek what companions chance may throw in her way, while he is associating with rakes of quality, and glorying in those scenes in which to be discovered he should really blush. I am told he is fond of deep play—attaches himself to women of bad character and seeks to establish an opinion that he is quite the *ton* in everything. I tremble for your Julia.—Her beauty, if she had no other merit making her fashionable, will induce some of those wretches, who are ever upon the watch to ensnare the innocent, to practise their diabolical artifices to poison her mind. She will soon see herself neglected by her husband;—and that will be the signal for them to begin their attack.—She is totally unhackneyed in the ways of men, and consequently can form no idea of the extreme depravity of their hearts. May the innate virtue of her mind be her guide and support!—But to escape with honour and reputation will be a difficult task. I must see you, Harry. I have something in my mind. I have seen more of the world than you have.—For a whole year I was witness of the disorder of this great town and, with blushes I write, have too frequently joined in some of its extravagances and follies. But, thank heaven! My eyes were opened before my morals became corrupt, or my fortune and constitution impaired.—Your virtue and my Frederick's confirmed me in the road I was then desirous of pursuing,—and I am now convinced I shall never deviate from the path of rectitude.

I expect you in town with all the impatience of a friend zealous for your happiness and advantage: but I wish not to interfere with any charitable or virtuous employment.—When you have finished your affairs, remember your faithful

J. Spencer

LETTER 8

To Miss Grenville

Surrounded with mantua makers, milliners, and hairdressers, I blush to say I have hardly time to bestow on my dear Louisa. What a continual bustle do I live in, without having literally anything to do! All these wonderful preparations are making for my appearance at court, and, in consequence of that, my visiting all the places of public amusement. I foresee my head will be turned with this whirl of folly, as I am inclined to call it in contradiction to the opinion of mankind.—If the people I am among are of any character at all, I think I may comprise it in few words: to me they seem to be running about all the morning and throwing away time in concerting measures to throw away more in the evening. Then, as to dress, to give an idea of that, I must reverse the line of an old song.

What was our *shame*, is now our *pride*.

I have had a thousand patterns of silks brought me to make choice, and such colours as yet never appeared in a rainbow. A very elegant man, one of Sir William's friends I thought, was introduced to me the other morning.—I was preparing to receive him as a visitor, when, taking out his pocketbook, he begged I would do him the honour to inspect some of the most fashionable patterns, and of the newest taste. He gave me a list of their names as he laid them on the cuff of his coat. This you perhaps will think unnecessary, and that, as colours affect the visual orb the same in different people, I might have been capable of distinguishing blue from red, and so on, but the case is quite otherwise; there are no such colours now. "This your ladyship will find extremely becoming,—it is *la cheveaux de la Regne;*—but the colour *de puce* is esteemed before it, and mixed with *d'Artois* forms the most elegant assemblage in the world; the *Pont sang* is immensely rich; but to suit your ladyship's complexion, I would rather recommend the *feuille morte,* or *la noisette.*" Fifty others, equally unintelligible, he ran off with the utmost facility. I thought, however, so important a point should be determined by wiser heads than mine;—therefore requested him to leave them with me, as I expected some ladies on whose taste I had great reliance. As I cannot be supposed from the nature of things to judge for myself with any propriety, I shall leave the choice of my clothes to Lady Besford and Lady Anne Parker, two ladies who have visited me and are to be my protectors in public.

I was extremely shocked when I sent for a mantua maker to find a man was to perform that office. I even refused a long time to admit him near me—and, thinking myself perfectly safe that I should have him on my side, appealed to Sir William. He laughed at my ridiculous scruples, as he called them, and further told me custom justified everything; nothing was indecent or otherwise, but as it was the *ton*.—I was silent, but neither satisfied nor pleased,—and submitted, I believe, with but an ill grace.

Lady Besford was so extremely polite to interest herself in everything concerning my making a fashionable appearance and procured for me a French friseur of the last importation, who dressed hair to a miracle, *au dernier goût*. I believe, Louisa, I must send you a dictionary of polite phrases, or you will be much at a loss, notwithstanding you have a pretty competent knowledge of the French tongue. I blush twenty times a day at my own stupidity,—and then Sir William tells me, "It is so immensely *bore* to blush," which makes me blush ten times more, because I don't understand what he means by that expression, and I am afraid to discover my ignorance; and he has not the patience to explain every ambiguous word he uses, but cries, shrugging up his shoulders, *ah! quel savage!* and then composes his ruffled spirits by humming an Italian air.

Well, but I must tell you what my dress was in which I was presented. My gown was a silver tissue, trimmed with silver net, and tied up with roses, as large as life, I was going to say. Indeed it was very beautiful, and so it ought, for it came to a most enormous sum. My jewels are *magnifique*, and in immense quantities. Do you know I could not find out half their purposes, or what I should do with them; for such things I never saw. What should poor Win and I have done by ourselves?—Lady Besford talked of sending her woman to assist me in dressing.—I told her I had a servant to whom I had been accustomed for a long time.—"Ah! For heaven's sake, my dear creature!" exclaimed my husband. "Don't mention the *tramontane*. She might do tolerably well for the Welsh mountains, but she will cut a most *outré* figure in the *beau monde*. I beg you will accept of Lady Besford's polite offer till you can provide yourself with a *fille de chambre* that knows on which side her right hand hangs." Alas! Poor Winifred Jones! Her mistress has but few advantages over her. Lady Besford was lavish in the encomiums of her woman, who had the honour of being dresser to one of the actresses many years.

Yesterday morning the grand talk of my decoration was to commence. Ah! Good Lord! I can hardly recollect particulars. I am morally convinced my father would have been looking for his Julia, had he seen me, and would have spent much time before he discovered me in the midst of feathers, flowers, and a thousand gew-gaws beside, too many to enumerate. I will, if I can, dissect my head for your edification, as it appeared to me when monsieur permitted me to view myself in the glass. I was absolutely ready to run from it with fright, like poor Actaeon when he had suffered the displeasure of Diana, and, like him, was in danger of running my new-acquired ornaments against everything in my way.

Monsieur alighted from his chariot about eleven o'clock and was immediately announced by Griffith, who—poor soul!—stared as if he thought him one of the finest men in the world. He was attended by a servant, who brought in two very large caravan boxes and a number of other things. Monsieur then prepared to begin his operations.—Sir William was at that time in my dressing room. He begged—for God's sake!—that Monsieur would be so kind as to exert his abilities, as everything depended on the just impression my figure made.—Monsieur bowed and shrugged, just like an overgrown monkey. In a moment I was overwhelmed with a cloud of powder.

"What are you doing? I do not mean to be powdered," I said.

"Not powdered!" repeated Sir William. "Why, you would not be so barbarous as to appear without,—it positively is not decent."

"I thought," answered I, "you used to admire the colour of my hair—how often have you praised its glossy hue!—and called me your nut-brown maid!"

"Pho! Pho!" said he, blushing, perhaps lest he should be suspected of tenderness, as that is very vulgar. "I can bear to see a woman without powder in summer; but now the case is otherwise. Monsieur knows what he is about. Don't interrupt or dictate to him. I am going to dress. Adieu, *ma charmante*!"

With a determination of being passive, I sat down under his hands—often, I confess, wondering what kind of being I should be in my metamorphosis,—and rather impatient of the length of time, to say nothing of the pain I felt under the pulling and frizzing and rubbing in the exquisitely scented *pommade de Venus*. At length the words *vous êtes fini, madame, au dernier goût* were pronounced; and I rose with precaution, lest I should discompose my new-built fabric, to give a glance at myself in the glass;—but where, or in what language, shall I ever find the words to express my astonishment at the figure which presented itself to my eyes! What, with curls, flowers, ribbons, feathers, lace, jewels, fruit, and ten thousand other things, my head was at least from one side to the other full half an ell wide and from the lowest curl that lay on my shoulder up to the top, I am sure

I am within compass if I say three-quarters of a yard high; besides six enormous large feathers—black, white, and pink—that reminded me of the plumes which nodded on the immense casque in the castle of Otranto. "Good God!" I exclaimed, "I can never bear this." The man assured me I was dressed quite in taste. "Let me be dressed as I will," I answered. "I must and will be altered. I would not thus expose myself for the universe." Saying which, I began pulling down some of the prodigious and monstrous fabric.—The *dresser of the actresses* exclaimed loudly, and the friseur remonstrated. However, I was inflexible: but to stop the volubility of the Frenchman's tongue, I inquired how much I was indebted to him for making me a monster. A mere trifle! Half a guinea the dressing, and for the feathers, pins, wool, false curls, *chignon, toque, pomades,* flowers, wax fruit, ribbon, &c. &c. &c. he believes about four guineas would be the difference. I was almost petrified with astonishment. When I recovered the power of utterance, I told him I thought at least he should have informed me what he was about before he ran me to so much expense; three-fourths of the things were useless, as I would not by any means appear in them.

It was the same to him, he said, they were now my property. He had run the risk of disobliging the Duchess of D—— by giving me the preference of the finest bundles of radishes that had yet come over; but this it was to degrade himself by dressing commoners. Lady Besford had entreated this favour from him; but he must say, he had never been this ill-treated since his arrival in the kingdom. In short, he flew out of the room in a great rage, leaving me in the utmost disorder. I begged Mrs. Freeman (so her ladyship's woman is called) to assist me a little in undoing what the impertinent Frenchman had taken such immense pains to effect. I had sacrificed half a bushel of trumpery when Lady Besford was ushered into my dressing room. "Lord bless me! My dear Lady Stanley, what, still *déshabillé?* I thought you had been ready and waiting for me." I began, by way of apology, to inform her ladyship of monsieur's insolence. She looked serious and said, "I am sorry you offended him; I fear he will represent you at her grace's *ruelle,* and you will be the jest of the whole court. Indeed, this is a sad affair. He is the first man in his walk of life."

"And if he was the last," I rejoined, "it would be the better; however, I beg your ladyship's pardon for not being ready. I shall not detain you many minutes."

My dear Louisa, you will laugh when I tell you that poor Winifred, who was reduced to be my gentlewoman's gentlewoman, broke two laces in endeavouring to draw my new French stays close. You know I am naturally small at bottom. But now you might literally span me. You never saw such a doll. Then, they are so intolerably wide across the breast that my arms are absolutely sore with them; and my sides so pinched!—But it is the *ton;* and pride feels no pain. It is with these sentiments the ladies of the present age heal their wounds; to be admired is a sufficient balsam.

Sir William had met with the affronted Frenchman and, like Lady Besford, was full of apprehensions lest he should expose me; for my part, I was glad to be from under his hands at any rate and feared nothing when he was gone, only still vexed at the strange figure I made. My husband freely condemned my behaviour as extremely absurd; and on my saying I would have something to cover, or at least shade, my neck, for I thought it hardly decent to have that entirely bare while one's head was loaded with super-fluities, he exclaimed to Lady Besford, clapping his hands together, "Oh! God! This ridiculous girl will be an eternal disgrace to me!" I thought this speech very cutting. I could not restrain a tear from starting.

"I hope not, Sir William," said I. "But, lest I should, I will stay at home till I have properly learnt to submit to insult and absurdity without emotion."

My manner made him ashamed; he took my hand and, kissing it, begged my pardon, and added, "My dear creature, I want you to be admired by the whole world; and, in compliance with the taste of the world, we must sub-mit to some things which, from their novelty, we may think absurd; but use will reconcile them to you." Lady Besford encouraged me; and I was pre-vailed on to go, though very much out of spirits. I must break off here, for the present. This letter has been the work of some days already. Adieu!

[*In continuation.*]

My apprehensions increased each moment that brought us near St. James's, but there was nothing for it, so I endeavoured all in my power to argue my-self into a serenity of mind and succeeded beyond my hopes. The amiable condescension of Their Majesties, however, contributed more than any-thing to compose my spirits, or, what I believe to be nearer the true state of the case, I was absorbed in respect for them and totally forgot myself. They were so obliging as to pay Sir William some compliments; and the king said if all my countrywomen were like me, he should be afraid to trust his son thither. I observed Sir William with the utmost attention; I saw his eyes were on me the whole time; but, my Louisa, I cannot flatter myself so far as to say they were the looks of love; they seemed to me rather the eyes of scrutiny which were on the watch, yet afraid they should see something unpleasing. I longed to be at home, to know from him how I had acquitted myself. To my question, he answered, by pressing me to his bosom, crying, "Like an angel, by heaven! Upon my soul, Julia, I never was so charmed with you in my life."

"And upon my honour," I returned, "I could not discover the least symptom of tenderness in your regards. I dreaded all the while that you was thinking I should disgrace you."

"You was never more mistaken. I never had more reason to be proud of my family. The circle rang with your praises. But you must not expect tenderness in public; my love, if you meet with it in private, you will have no cause of complaint."

This will give you a strange idea of the world I am in, Louisa. I do not above half like it and think a ramble, arm in arm with you upon our native mountains, worth it all. However, my lot is drawn; and, perhaps, as times and husbands go, *I have no cause of complaint.*

Yours most sincerely,

Julia Stanley

ʭ ʭ ʭ ʭ ʭ ʭ ʭ ʭ ʭ ʭ
LETTER 9
ʭ ʭ ʭ ʭ ʭ ʭ ʭ ʭ ʭ ʭ

To Lady Stanley

My dearest child,

The task you set your father is a heavy one; but I cheerfully comply with any request of my Julia's. However, before I enter upon it, let me say a little to you: Are you happy, my child? Do you find the world such as you thought it while it was unknown to you? Do the pleasures you enjoy present you with an equivalent for your renunciation of a fond father, and a tender sister? Is their affection amply repaid by the love of your husband? All these, and a thousand other equally important questions, I long to put to my beloved. I wish to know the true state of your heart. I then should be able to judge whether I ought to mourn or rejoice in this separation from you. Believe me, Julia, I am not so selfish to wish you here merely to augment my narrow circle of felicity if you can convince me you are happier where you are. But can all the bustle, the confusion you describe, be productive of happiness to a young girl born and educated in the lap of peaceful retirement? The novelty may strike your mind; and, for a while, you may think yourself happy, because you are amused and have not time to define what your reflexions are: but in the sober hour, when stillness reigns and the soul unbends itself from the fatigues of the day, what judgement then does cool reason form? Are you satisfied? Are your slumbers peaceful and calm? Do you never sigh after the shades of Woodley and your rural friends? Answer these questions fairly and candidly, my Julia—prove to me you are happy and your heart as good and innocent as ever, and I shall descend to the silent tomb with peaceful smiles.

Perhaps the resolution I formed of retiring from a world in which I had met with disgust was too hastily concluded on. Be that as it may—it was sacred, and as such I have, and will, keep it. I lost my confidence in mankind; and I could find no one whose virtues could redeem it. Many years have elapsed since; and the manners and customs change so frequently that I should be a total stranger among the inhabitants of this present age.

You have heard me say I was married before I had the happiness of being united to *your* amiable mother. I shall begin my narrative from the commencement of that union, only premising that I was the son of the younger branch of a noble family whose name I bear. I inherited the blood but very little more of my ancestors. However, a taste for pleasure, and an indulgence of some of the then fashionable follies which in all ages and all times are too prevalent, conspired to make my little fortune still more contracted. Thus situated, I became acquainted with a young lady of a large fortune. My figure and address won her heart; her person was agreeable; and although I might not be what the world calls in love, I certainly was attached to her. Knowing the inferiority of my fortune, I could not presume to offer her my hand, even after I was convinced she wished I should; but some circumstances arising, which brought us more intimately acquainted, at length conquered my scruples; and, without consulting any other guide than our passions, we married. My finances were now extremely straitened; for although my wife was heiress of upwards of thirty thousand pounds, yet, till she came of age, I could read no advantage of it; and to that period she wanted near four years. We were both fond of pleasure and foolishly lived as if we were in actual possession of double that income. I found myself deeply involved; but the time drew near that was to set all to rights; and I had prevailed on my wife to consent to retrenchment. We had formed a plan of retiring for some time in the country, to look after her estate; and, by way of taking a polite leave of our friends (or rather acquaintances, for when they were put to the test, I found them undeserving of that appellation); by way, I say, of quitting town with *éclat,* my wife proposed giving an elegant entertainment on her birthday, which was on the twenty-fourth of December. Christmas Day fell that year upon a Monday: unwilling to protract this day of joy till the Tuesday, my wife desired to anticipate her natal festival, and accordingly Saturday was appointed. She had set her heart on dancing in the evening and was extremely mortified on finding pain in her ankle, which she attributed to a strain. It was so violent during dinnertime that she was constrained to leave the table. A lady who retired with her told her the surest remedy for a strain was to plunge the leg in cold water, which would procure instant relief. Impatient of the disappointment and anguish, she too fatally consented. I knew nothing of what was doing in my wife's dressing room till my attention was roused by repeated cries. Terribly alarmed—I flew thither and found her in the agonies of death. Good God! What was my distraction at that moment! I then recollected what she had often told me, of all her family being subject to the gout at a very early age. Every medical assistance was procured with all speed. The physician, however, gave but small hopes, unless the disorder could be removed from her head and stomach, which it had attacked with the greatest violence. How was all our mirth in one sad moment overthrown! The day, which had risen with smiles, now promised to set in tears. In the few lucid intervals which my unhappy wife could be said to have, she incessantly prayed to live till she could secure her fortune to my use, which could be done no other way than making her will, since, having had no children, the estate, should she die before she came of age—or even then, without a bequest—would devolve upon a cousin with whose family we had preserved no intimacy, owing to the illiberal reflexions part of them had cast on my wife for marrying a man without an answerable fortune. My being allied to a noble family was no recommendation to those who had acquired their wealth by trade and were possessed of the most sordid principles. I would not listen to the persuasion of my friends, who urged me to get the writings executed, to which my wife might set her hand: such measures appeared both selfish and cruel; or, rather, my mind was too much absorbed in my present affliction to pay any attention to my future security.

In her greatest agonies and most severe paroxysms, she knew and acknowledged her obligations to me for the unremitted kindness I had shown her during our union. "Oh! My God!" she would exclaim, "Oh! My God! Let me but live to reward him! I ask not length of years—though in the bloom of life, I submit with cheerful resignation to thy will. My God! I ask not length of days; I only petition for a few short hours of sense and recollection, that I may, by the disposition of my affairs, remove all other distress from the bosom of my beloved husband, save what he will feel on this separation."

Dear soul! She prayed in vain. Nay, I doubt her apprehension and terrors, lest she should die, increased the agonies of her body and mind.

Unknown to me, a gentleman, by the request of my dying wife, drew up a deed; the paper lay on the bed: she meant to sign it as soon as the clock struck twelve. Till within a few minutes of that time, she continued tolerably calm, and her head perfectly clear; she flattered herself and endeavoured to convince us she should recover—but, alas! This was only a little gleam of hope, to sink us deeper in despair. Her pain returned with redoubled violence from this short recess; and her senses never again resumed their seat. She suffered the most excruciating agonies till two in the morning—then winged her flight to heaven—leaving me the most forlorn and disconsolate of men.

I continued in a state of stupefaction for several days, till my friends roused me by asking what course I meant to pursue. I had the whole world before me and saw myself, as it were, totally detached from any part of it. My own relations I had disobliged by marrying the daughter of a tradesman. They were no doubt glad of an excuse to rid themselves of an indigent person who might reflect dishonour on their nobility—of them I had no hopes. I had as little probability of success in my application to the friends of my late wife; yet I thought, in justice, they should not refuse to make me some allowances for the expenses our manner of living had brought on me—as they well knew they were occasioned by my compliance with her taste—at least so far as to discharge some of my debts.

I waited on Mr. Maynard, the father of the lady who now possessed the estate, to lay before him the situation of my affairs. He would hardly hear me out with patience. He upbraided me with stealing an heiress, and with meanly taking every method of obliging a dying woman to injure her relations. In short, his behaviour was rude, unmanly, and indecent. I scorned to hold converse with so sordid a wretch and was leaving his house with the utmost displeasure when his daughter slipped out of the room. She begged me, with many tears, not to impute her father's incivility to her—wished the time was come when she should be her own mistress, but hoped she should be able to bring her father to some terms of accommodation, and assured me, she would use all her influence with him to induce him to do me justice.

Her influence over the mind of such a man as her father had like to have little weight—as it proved. She used all her eloquence in my favour, which only served to instigate him against me. He sent a very rude abrupt message to me, to deliver up several articles of household furniture, and other things, which had belonged to my wife; which, however, I refused to do, unless I was honoured with the order of Miss Maynard. Her father could not prevail on her to make the requisition; and, enraged at my insolence, and her obstinacy, as he politely styled our behaviour, he swore he would be revenged. In order to make his words good, he went severally to each of the tradespeople to whom I was indebted and, collecting the sums, prevailed on them to make over the debts to him, thereby becoming the sole creditor; and how merciful I should find him, I leave you to judge, from the motive by which he acted.

In a few days there was an execution in my house, and I was conveyed to the King's Bench. At first I took the resolution of continuing there contentedly, till either my cruel creditor should relent or that an act of grace should take place. A prison, however, is dreadful to a free mind; and I solicited those who had, in the days of my prosperity, professed a friendship for me: some few afforded me a temporary relief but dealt with a scanty hand; others disclaimed me—none would bail me or undertake my cause: many who had contributed to my extravagance now condemned me for launching into expenses beyond my income; and those who refused their assistance thought they had a right to censure my conduct. Thus did I find myself deserted and neglected by the whole world and was taught how little dependence we ought to place on the goods of it.

When I had been an inmate of the house of bondage some few weeks, I received a note from Miss Maynard. She deplored, in the most pathetic terms, the steps her father had taken, which she had never discovered till that morning, and entreated my acceptance of a trifle to render my confinement less intolerable: and if I could devise any methods wherein she could be serviceable, she should think herself most happy. There was such a delicacy and nobleness of soul ran through the whole of this little *billet*, as, at the same time that it showed the writer in the most amiable light, gave birth to the liveliest gratitude in my bosom. I had, till this moment, considered her only as the daughter of Mr. Maynard—as one whose mind was informed by the same principles as his own. I now beheld her in another view; I looked on her only in her relation to my late wife, whose virtues she inherited with her fortune. I felt a veneration for the generosity of a young girl who, from the narrow sentiments of her father, could not be mistress of any large sum; and yet she had, in the politest manner (making it a favour done to herself), obliged me to accept of a twenty-pound note. I had a thousand conflicts with myself, whether I should keep or return it; nothing but my fear of giving her pain could have decided it. I recollected the tears she shed the last time I saw her: on reading over her note again, I discovered the paper blistered in several places; to all this, let me add, her image seemed to stand confessed before me. Her person, which I had hardly ever thought about, now was present to my imagination. It lost nothing by never having been the subject of my attention before. I sat ruminating on the picture I had been drawing in my mind, till, becoming perfectly enthusiastic in my ideas, I started up and, clasping my hands together,—"Why," exclaimed I aloud, "why have I not twenty thousand pounds to bestow on this adorable creature!" The sound of my voice brought me to myself, and I instantly recollected I ought to make some acknowledgement to my fair benefactress. I found the task a difficult one. After writing and rejecting several, I at last was resolved to send the first I had attempted, knowing that, though less studied, it certainly was the genuine effusions of my heart. After saying all my gratitude dictated, I told her that, next to her society, I should prize her correspondence above everything in this world but that I begged she would not let compassion for an unfortunate man lead her into any inconveniences, but be guided entirely by her own discretion. I would, in the meantime, entreat her to send me a few books—the subject I left to her, they being her taste would be their strongest recommendation. Perhaps I said more than I ought to have done, although at that time I thought I fell infinitely short of what I might have said; and yet, I take God to witness, I did not mean to engage her affection; and nothing was less from my intention than basely to practise on her passions.

In one of her letters, she asked me if my debts were discharged what would be my dependence or scheme of life: I freely answered, my dependence would be either to get a small place, or else serve my king in the war now nearly breaking out, which rather suited the activity of my disposition. She has since told me she shed floods of tears over that expression—*the activity of my disposition;* she drew in her imagination the most affecting picture of a man, in the bloom and vigour of life, excluded from the common benefits of his fellow creatures by the merciless rapacity of an inhuman creditor. The effect this melancholy representation had on her mind, while pity endeared the object of it to her, made her take the resolution of again addressing her father in my behalf. He accused her of ingratitude, in thus repaying his care for her welfare. Hurt by the many harsh things he said, she told him the possession of ten times the estate could convey no pleasure to her bosom, while it was tortured with the idea that he who had the best right to it was secluded from every comfort of life; and that, whenever it should be in her power, she would not fail to make every reparation she could for the violence offered to an innocent, injured man.

This brought down her father's heaviest displeasure. He reviled her in the grossest terms—asserted she had been fascinated by me, as her ridiculous cousin had been before, but that he would take care his family should not run the risk of being again beggared by such a spendthrift, and that he should use such precautions as to frustrate any scheme I might form of seducing her from her duty. She fought to exculpate me from the charges her father had brought against me; but he paid no regard to her asseverations and remained deaf and inexorable to all her entreaties. When I learnt this, I wrote to Miss Maynard, entreating her, for her own sake, to resign an unhappy man to his evil destiny. I begged her to believe I had sufficient resolution to support confinement, or any other ill, but that it was an aggravation to my sufferings (which to sustain was very difficult) to find her zeal for me had drawn on her the ill-usage of her father. I further requested she would never mention me to him, and if possible, never think of me, if those thoughts were productive of the least disquiet to her. I likewise mentioned my hearing of an act of grace that would soon release me from my bonds; and then I was determined to offer myself a volunteer in the service, where, perhaps, I might find a cannonball my best friend.

A life so different to what I had been used brought on a disorder, which the agitation of my spirits increased so much as to reduce me almost to the gates of death. An old female servant of Miss Maynard's paid me a visit, bringing me some nutritive delicacies, which her kind mistress thought would be serviceable to me. Shocked at the deplorable spectacle I made, for I began to neglect my appearance—which a man is too apt to do when not at peace with himself—shocked, I say, she represented me in such a light to her lady as filled her gentle soul with the utmost terror for my safety. Guided alone by the partiality she honoured me with, she formed the resolution of coming to see me. She gave me half an hour's notice of her intention. I employed the intermediate time in putting myself into a condition of receiving her with decency. The little exertion I made had nearly exhausted my remaining strength, and I was more dead than alive when the trembling, pale, and tottering guest made her approach in the house of woe. We could neither of us speak for some time. The benevolence of her heart had supported her during her journey thither; but now the native modesty of her sex seemed to point the impropriety of visiting a man, unsolicited, in prison. Weak as I was, I saw the necessity of encouraging the drooping spirits of my fair visitor. I paid her my grateful acknowledgements for her inestimable goodness. She begged me to be silent on that head, as it brought reflexions she could ill support. In obedience to her, I gave the conversation another turn; but still I could not help reverting to the old subject. She then stopped me by asking what was there so extraordinary in her conduct? And whether, in her situation would I not have done as much for her?

"Oh! Yes!" I cried with eagerness. "That I would, and ten times more."
I instantly felt the impropriety of my speech.

"Then I have been strangely deficient," said she, looking at me with a gentle smile.

"I ask a thousand pardons," said I, "for the abruptness of my expression. I meant to evince my value for you, and my sense of what I thought you deserved. You must excuse my method, I have been long unused to the association of human beings, at least such as resemble you. You have already conferred more favours than I could merit at your hands."

Miss Maynard seemed disconcerted—she looked grave. "It is a sign you think so," said she, in a tone of voice that showed she was piqued, "as you have taken such pains to explain away an involuntary compliment.—But I have already exceeded the bounds I prescribed to myself in this visit—it is time to leave you."

I felt abashed and found myself incapable of saying anything to clear myself from the imputation of insensibility or ingratitude without betraying the tenderness which I really possessed for her, yet which I thought, circumstanced as I was, would be ungenerous to the last degree to discover, as it would be tacitly laying claim to hers. The common rules of politeness, however, called on me to say something.—I respectfully took her hand, which trembled as much as mine. "Dear Miss Maynard," said I, "how shall I thank you for the pleasure your company has conveyed to my bosom?" Even then thinking I had said too much, especially as I by an involuntary impulse found my fingers compress hers, I added, "I plainly see the impropriety of asking you to renew your goodness—I must not be selfish or urge you to take any step for which you may hereafter condemn yourself."

"I find, sir," she replied, "your prudence is greater than mine. I need never apprehend danger from such a monitor."

"Don't mistake me," said I, with a sigh I could not repress.

"I doubt I have," returned she, "but I will endeavour to develop your character. Perhaps, if I do not find myself quite perfect, I may run the risk of taking another lesson, unless you should tell me it is imprudent." So saying, she left me. There was rather an affectation of gaiety in her last speech, which would have offended me had I not seen it was only put on to conceal her real feelings from a man who seemed coldly insensible of her invaluable perfections both of mind and body.—Yet how was I to act?

I loved her with the utmost purity, and yet fervour. My heart chid me for throwing cold water on the tenderness of this amiable girl;—but my reason told me I should be a villain to strive to gain her affections in such a situation as I was. Had I been lord of the universe, I would have shared it with my Maria. You will ask how I could easily forget the lowness of my fortune in my connexion with her cousin? I answer, the case was widely different.—I then made a figure in life equal to my birth, though circumstances were contracted.—Now, I was poor and in prison:—then, I listened only to my passions—now, reason and prudence had some sway with me. My love for my late wife was the love of a boy;—my attachment to Maria the sentiments of a man, and a man visited by, and a prey to, misfortune. On reflexion, I found I loved her to the greatest height. After passing a sleepless night of anguish, I came to the resolution of exculpating myself from the charge of insensibility, though at the expense of losing sight of her I loved forever. I wrote her a letter, wherein I freely confessed the danger I apprehended from the renewal of her visit.—I opened my whole soul before her, but at the same time told her I laid no claim to anymore from her than compassion; showed her the rack of constraint I put on myself, to conceal the emotions of my heart, lest the generosity of hers might involve her in a too strong partiality for so abject a wretch. I hoped she would do me the justice to believe that as no man ever loved more, so no one on earth could have her interest more at heart than myself, since to those sentiments I sacrificed everything dear to me. Good God! What tears did this letter cost me! I sometimes condemned myself and thought it false generosity.— Why should I, said I to myself, why should I thus cast happiness away from two, who seem formed to constitute all the world to each other?—How vigorous are thy mandates, O Virtue! How severe thy decree! And oh! How much do I feel in obeying thee! No sooner was the letter gone than I repented the step I had pursued.—I called myself ungrateful to the bounty of heaven, who thus, as it were, had inspired the most lovely of women with an inclination to relieve my distress and had likewise put the means in her hands.—These cogitations contributed neither to establish my health nor compose my spirits. I had no return to my letter; indeed I had not urged one. Several days I passed in a state of mind which can be only known to those who have experienced the same. At last a packet was brought me. It contained an ensign's commission in a regiment going to Germany and a paper sealed up, on which was written, "It is the request of M.M. that Mr. Grenville does not open *this* till he has crossed the seas."

There was another paper folded in the form of a letter but not sealed; *that* I hastily opened and found it contained only a few words and a bank bill of a hundred pounds. The contents were as follow:

True love knows not the nice distinctions you have made,—at least, if I may be allowed to judge from my own feelings, I think it does not. I may, however, be mistaken; but the error is too pleasing to be relinquished; and I would much rather indulge it than listen at present to the cold prudential arguments which a too refined and ill-placed generosity points out. When you arrive at the place of your destination, you may gain a further knowledge of a heart capable at the same time of the tenderest partiality and a firm resolution of conquering it.

Every word of this billet was a dagger to my soul. I then ceased not to accuse myself of ingratitude to the loveliest of women, as guilty of false pride instead of generosity. If she placed her happiness in my society, why should I deprive her of it? As she said my sentiments were too refined, I asked myself if it would not have been my supreme delight to have raised her from the dregs of the people to share the most exalted situation with me. Why should I then think less highly of her attachment of which I had received such proofs than I was convinced mine was capable of? For the future, I was determined to sacrifice these nice punctilios, which were ever opposing my felicity, and that of an amiable woman, who clearly and repeatedly told me, by her looks, actions, and a thousand little nameless attentions I could not mistake, that her whole happiness depended on me.

I thought nothing could convince her more thoroughly of my wish of being obliged to her than the acceptance of her bounty; I made no longer any hesitation about it. That very day I was released from my long confinement by the grace act, to the utter mortification of my old prosecutor. I drove immediately to some lodgings I had provided in the Strand, from whence I instantly dispatched a billet-doux to Maria, in which I said these words:

The first moment of liberty I devote to the lovely Maria, who has my heart a slave. I am a convert to your assertion that love makes not distinctions. Otherwise, could I support the reflexion that all I am worth in the world I owe to you? But to you the world owes all the charms it has in my eyes. We will not, however, talk of debtor and creditor, but permit me to make up in adoration what I want in wealth. Fortune attends the brave.—I will therefore flatter myself with returning loaded with the spoils of the enemy, and in such a situation, that you may openly indulge the partiality which makes the happiness of my life, without being put to the blush by sordid relations.

I shall obey your mandates the more cheerfully, as I think I am perfectly acquainted with every perfection of your heart; judge then how I must value it. Before I quit England, I shall petition for the honour of kissing your hand;—but how shall I bid you adieu!

The time now drew nigh when I was to take leave of my native land—and, what was dearer to me, my Maria.—I was too affected to utter a word;—her soul had more heroic greatness.—"Go," said she, "pursue the paths of glory; have confidence in Providence, and never distrust me. I have already experienced some hazards on your account; but perhaps my father may be easier in his mind when he is assured you have left England."

I pressed her to explain herself. She did so by informing me her father suspected her attachment and, to prevent any ill consequence arising, had proposed a gentleman to her for a husband, whom she had rejected with firmness. "No artifice, or ill-usage," continued she, "shall make any change in my resolution;—but I shall say no more; the packet will more thoroughly convince you of what I am capable."

"Good God!" said I in an agony. "Why should your tenderness be incompatible with your duty?"

"I do not think it," she answered;—"it is my duty to do justice; and I do no more by seeking to restore you to your own."

We settled the mode of our future correspondence; and I tore myself from the only one I loved on earth. When I joined the regiment, I availed myself of the privilege given me to inspect the papers. Oh! How was my love, esteem, and admiration increased! The contents were written at a time when she thought me insensible, or at least too scrupulous. She made a solemn vow never to marry; but as soon as she came of age, to divide the estate with me, making over the remainder to any children I might have; but the whole was couched in terms of such delicate tenderness as drew floods of tears from my eyes and riveted my soul more firmly to her. I instantly wrote her and concealed not a thought or sentiment of my heart,—*that* alone dictated every line. In the letter she returned, she sent me her picture in a locket and on the reverse a device with her hair; this was an inestimable present to me.—It was my sole employ, while off duty, to gaze on the lovely resemblance of the fairest of women.

For some months our correspondence was uninterrupted.—However, six weeks had now passed since I expected a letter. Love is industrious in tormenting itself. I formed ten thousand dreadful images in my own mind and sunk into despair from each. I wrote letter after letter, but had still no return. I had no other correspondent in England.—Distraction seized me. "She's dead!" cried I to myself. "She's dead! I have nothing to do but follow her." At last I wrote to a gentleman who lived in the neighbourhood of Mr. Maynard, conjuring him, in the most affecting terms, to inform me of what I yet dreaded to be told.—I waited with dying impatience till the mails arrived.—A letter was brought to me from this gentleman.—He said, Mr. Maynard's family had left L. sometime;—they proposed going abroad; but he believed they had retired to some part of Essex;—there had a report prevailed of Miss Maynard's being married; but if true, it was since they had left L. This news was not very likely to clear or calm my doubts. What could I think?—My reflexions only served to awaken my grief. I continued two years making every inquiry, but never received the least satisfactory account.

A prey to the most heartfelt affliction, life became insupportable to me.—Was she married? I resolved in my mind all the hardships she must have endured before she would be prevailed on to falsify her vows to me, which were registered in heaven.—Had death ended her distress, I was convinced it had been hastened by the severity of an unnatural father.— Whichsoever way I turned my thoughts, the most excruciating reflexions presented themselves, and in each I saw her sufferings alone.

In this frame of mind, I rejoiced to hear we were soon to have a battle, which would in all probability be decisive. I was now raised to the rank of captain-lieutenant. A battalion of our regiment was appointed to a most dangerous post. It was to gain a pass through a narrow defile, and to convey some of our heavy artillery to cover a party of soldiers, who were the flower of the troops, to endeavour to flank the enemy. I was mortified to find I was not named for this service. I spoke of it to the captain, who honoured me with his friendship.—"It was my care for you, Grenville," said he, "which prevented your name being enrolled. I wish, for the sakes of so many brave fellows, this manoeuvre could have been avoided. It will be next to a miracle if we succeed; but success must be won with the lives of many; the first squadron must look on themselves as a sacrifice."

"Permit me then," said I, "to head that squadron; I will do my duty to support my charge; but if I fall, I shall bless the blow which rids me of an existence intolerable to me."

"You are a young man, Grenville," replied the captain. "You may experience a change in life which will repay you for the adversities you at present complain of. I would have you courageous and defy dangers, but not madly rush on them; that is to be despairing, not brave; and consequently displeasing to the Deity, who appoints us our task and rewards us according to our acquittal of our duty. The severest winter is followed oftentimes by the most blooming spring."

"It is true," said I. "But when will spring visit the mouldering urn? Ah! When will it dawn on the gloom of the grave? Will you, however, allow me to offer an exchange with the commanding officer?"

My captain consented; and the lieutenant was very glad to exchange his post for one of equal honour but greater security.

I was sitting in my tent the evening of the important day, ruminating on the past events of my life, and then naturally fell into reflexions of what, in all probability, would be the consequence of the morrow's attack. We looked on ourselves as devoted men; and though, I dare say, not one in the whole corps was tired of his life, yet they all expressed the utmost eagerness to be employed. Death was the ultimate wish of my soul. "I shall, before tomorrow's sun goes down," said I, addressing myself to the resemblance of my Maria; "I shall, most lovely of women, be reunited to thee; or, if yet thy sufferings have not ended thy precious life, I shall yet know where thou art, and be permitted, perhaps, to hover over thee, to guide thy footsteps, and conduct thee to those realms of light, whose joys will be incomplete without thee." With these rhapsodies I was amusing my mind when a serjeant entered and acquainted me that there was, without, a young man enquiring for me who said he must be admitted, having letters of the greatest importance from England. My heart beat high against my breast, my respiration grew thick and difficult, and I could hardly articulate these words,—"For God's sake, let me see him! Support me, Oh, God! What is it I am going to hear?"

A cold sweat bedewed my face, and a universal tremor possessed my whole frame.

A young gentleman, wrapped up in a Hussar cloak, made his appearance. "Is this Lieutenant Grenville?"

I bowed. "I am told, sir," said I, in a tremulous voice, "you have letters from England; relieve my doubts I beseech you."

"Here sir, is one," said the youth, extending his hand, which trembled exceedingly.—I hastily snatched it, ready to devour the contents;—what was my agitation, when I read these words!

> If, after a silence of two long years, your Maria is still dear to you, you will rejoice to hear that she still lives for you alone. If her presence is wished for by you, you will find her at no great distance from you. But, if you love with the tenderness she does, how great, how ecstatic, will be your felicity, to raise your eyes and fix them on hers!

The paper dropped from my enervate hand while I raised my eyes and beheld, Oh! My God! Under the disguise of a young officer, my beloved, my faithful, long-lost Maria!

"Great God!" cried I, in a transport of joy, clasping my hands together. "Have then my prayers been heard! Do I again behold her?" But my situation recurring to my imagination—the dangers which I had unnecessarily engaged myself in for the morrow; her disguise; the unprotected state in which I should leave her, in camp, where too much licentiousness reigned—all these ideas took instant possession of my mind and damped the rising joy her loved presence had at first excited. The agonizing pangs which seized me are past description. "Oh! My God!" I exclaimed in the bitterness of soul. "Why did we thus meet! Better,—Oh! How much better would it have been that my eyes had closed in death than to see all they adored thus exposed to the horrid misery and carnage of destructive war." The conflict became too powerful; and in all the energy of woe I threw myself on the ground. Poor Maria flung herself on a seat and covered her face in her great coat.—Audible sobs burst from her bosom—I saw the convulsive heavings, and the sight was as daggers to me.—I crawled on my knees to her and, bending over her,—"Oh! My Maria!" said I. "These pangs I feel for you; speak to me, my only love; if possible, ease my sufferings by thy heavenly welcome voice."

She uttered not a word; I sought to find her hand; she pushed me gently from her, then rising,—"Come, thou companion of my tedious and painful travel; come, my faithful Hannah," said she to one I had not taken notice of, who stood in the entrance of the tent. "Let us be gone; here we are unwelcome visitors. Is it thus," continued she, lifting up her hands to heaven, "is it thus I am received? Adieu! Grenville! My love has still pursued you with unremitting constancy: but it shall be your torment no longer. I will no longer tax your compassion for a fond wretch, who perhaps deserves the scorn she meets."

She was leaving the tent. I was immovably rooted to the ground while she spoke.—I caught her by the coat. "Oh! Leave me not, dearest of women, leave me not! You know not the love and distress which tear this wretched bosom by turns. Injure me not, by doubting the first,—and if you knew the latter, you would find me an object entitled to your utmost pity. Oh! That my heart was laid open to your view! Then would you see it had wasted with anguish on the supposition of your death. Yes, Maria, I thought you dead. I had a too exalted idea of your worth to assign any other cause; I never called you cruel or doubted your faith. Your memory lived in my fond breast, such as my tenderness painted you. But you can think meanly of me and put the most ungenerous construction on the severest affliction that ever tore the heart of man."

"Oh! My Grenville," said she, raising me. "How have I been ungenerous? Is the renunciation of my country, relations, and even sex a proof of want of generosity? Will you never know, or, knowing, understand me? I believe you have suffered, greatly suffered; your pallid countenance too plainly evinces it; but we shall now, with the blessing of heaven, soon see an end to them.—A few months will make me mistress of my fortune. In the meantime, I will live with my faithful Hannah retired; only now and then let me have the consolation of seeing you and hearing from your lips a confirmation that I have not forfeited your affection."

I said all that my heart dictated to reassure my lovely heroic Maria and calm her griefs. I made her take some refreshment; and, as the night was now far spent, and we yet had much to say, we agreed to it in the tent. My dear Maria began to make me a little detail of all that had passed. She painted out the persecutions of her father in the liveliest colours, the many artifices he used to weaken her attachment to me, the feigning me inconstant; and, when he found her opinion of my faith too firmly rooted, he procured a certificate of my death. As she was then released from her engagement, he more strongly urged her to marry; but she as resolutely refused. On his being one day more than commonly urgent, she knelt down and said, in the most solemn manner, "Thou knowest, O God! Had it pleased thee to have continued him I doted on in this life, that I was bound, by the most powerful asseverations, to be his, and only his:—hear me now, O God! While I swear still to be wedded in his memory. In thy eye, I was his wife; I attest thee to witness that I will never be any other. In his grave shall all my tenderness be buried, and with him shall it rise to heaven." Her father became outrageous and swore if she would not give him a son he would give her a mother and, in consequence, married the housekeeper—a woman sordid as himself, and whose principles and sentiments were as low as her birth.

The faithful Hannah had been discharged sometime before, on finding out she aided our correspondence. My letters had been for a long time intercepted. Maria, one day, without the least notice, was taken out of her chamber and conveyed to a small house in the hundreds of Essex, to some relations of her new mother's, in hopes, as she found, that grief and the unhealthiness of the place might make an end of her before she came of age. After a series of ill-usage and misfortunes, she at length was so fortunate as to make her escape. She wrote to Hannah, who came instantly to her; from her she learnt I was still living. She then formed the resolution of coming over to Germany, dreading again falling into the hands of her cruel parent. The plan was soon fixed on and put in execution. To avoid the dangers of travelling, they agreed to put on men's clothes; and Maria, to ensure her safety, dressed herself like an English officer charged with the dispatches to the British army.

While she was proceeding in her narrative, I heard the drum beat to arms. I started and turned pale. Maria hastily demanded the cause of this alteration! I informed her we were going to prepare for battle. "And what, oh! What is to become of you? Oh! Maria! The service I am going on is hazardous to the last degree. I shall fall a sacrifice; but what will become of you?"

"Die with you," said she firmly, rising and drawing her sword. "When I raise my arm," continued she, "who will know it is a woman's? Nature has stamped me with that sex, but my soul shrinks not at danger. In what am I different from the Romans, or even from some of the ancient Britons? They could lose their lives for less cause than what I see before me. As I am firmly resolved not to outlive you—so I am equally determined to share your fate. You are certainly desirous my sex should remain concealed. I wish the same—and, believe me, no womanish weakness on my part shall betray it. Tell your commander I am a volunteer under your direction. And, assure yourself, you will find me possessed of sufficient courage to bear any and everything, for your sake."

I forbore not to point out the horrors of war in the most dreadful colours. "I shudder at them," said she, "but am not intimidated." In short, all my arguments were in vain. She vowed she would follow me: "Either you love me, Grenville, or you love me not—if the first, you cannot refuse me the privilege of dying with you; if the last, sad fate should be mine, the sooner I lose my life the better."

While I was yet using dissuasives, the captain entered my tent. "Come, Grenville," said he, "make preparations, my good lad. There will be hot work today for us all. I would have chosen a less dangerous situation for you: but this was your own desire. However, I hope heaven will spare you."

"I could have almost wished I had not been so precipitate, as here is a young volunteer who will accompany me."

"So young, and so courageous!" said the captain, advancing towards my Maria. "I am sure, by your looks, you have never seen service."

"But I have gone through great dangers, sir," she answered, blushing, "and, with so brave an officer as Lieutenant Grenville, I shall not be fearful of meeting even death."

"Well said, my little hero," rejoined he. "Only that as a volunteer you have a right to choose your commander, I should be happy to have the bringing you into the field myself. Let us, however, as this may be the last time we meet on earth, drink one glass to our success. Grenville, you can furnish us." We soon then bid each other a solemn adieu!

I prevailed on Maria and poor Hannah (who was almost dead with her fears) to lie down on my pallet-bed, if possible, to procure a little rest. I retired to the outside of the tent and, kneeling down, put up the most fervent prayers to heaven that the heart of man could frame. I then threw myself on some baggage and slept with some composure till the second drum beat.

Hannah hung round her mistress; but such was her respect and deference that she opened not her lips. We began our march, my brave heroine close at my side, with all the stillness possible. We gained a narrow part of the wood, where we wanted to make good our pass; but here, either by the treachery of our own people or the vigilance of the enemy, our scheme was entirely defeated. We marched on without opposition, and, flushed with the appearance of success, we went boldly on, till, too far advanced to make a retreat, we found ourselves surrounded by a party of the enemy's troops. We did all in our power to recover our advantage and lost several men in our defence. Numbers, however, at last prevailed; and those who were not left dead on the field were made prisoners, among whom were my Maria and myself. I was wounded in the side and in the right arm. She providentially escaped unhurt. We were conveyed to the camp of the enemy, where I was received with the respect that one brave man shows another. I was put into the hospital, where my faithful Maria attended me with the utmost diligence and tenderness.

When the event of this day's disaster was carried to the British camp, it struck a damp on all. But poor Hannah, in a frenzy of distress, ran about, wringing her hands, proclaiming her sex and that of the supposed volunteer, and entreating the captain to use his interest to procure our release. She gave him a brief detail of our adventures and concluded by extolling the character of her beloved mistress. The captain, who had at that time a great regard for me, was touched at the distressful story and made a report to the commander in chief, who, after getting the better of the enemy in an engagement, proposed an exchange of prisoners, which being agreed to, and I being able to bear the removal, we were once more at liberty.

I was conveyed to a small town near our encampment, where my dear Maria and old Hannah laid aside their great Hussar cloaks, which they would never be prevailed upon to put off, and resumed their petticoats. This adventure caused much conversation in the camp; and all the officers were desirous of beholding so martial a female. But, notwithstanding the extraordinary step she had been induced to take, Miss Maynard possessed all the valued delicacy of her sex in a very eminent degree and therefore kept very recluse, devoting herself entirely to her attendance on me.

Fearful that her reputation might suffer, now her sex was known, I urged her to complete my happiness by consenting to our marriage. She at first made some difficulties, which I presently obviated; and the chaplain of the regiment performed the ceremony, my captain acting as father and, as he said, bestowing on me the greatest blessing man could deserve.

I was now the happiest of all earthly creatures; nor did I feel the least allay, but in sometimes, on returning from duty in the field, finding my Maria uncommonly grave. On enquiry she used to attribute it to my absence; and indeed her melancholy would wear off, and she would resume all her wonted cheerfulness.

About three months after our marriage, my dear wife was seized with the smallpox, which then raged in the town. I was almost distracted with my apprehensions. Her life was in imminent danger. I was delivered myself up to the most gloomy presages. "How am I marked out for misfortune!" said I. "Am I destined to lose both my wives on the eve of their coming of age?" Her disorder was attended with some of the most alarming symptoms. At length, it pleased heaven to hear my prayers, and a favourable crisis presented itself. With joy I made a sacrifice of her beauty, happy in still possessing the mental perfections of this most excellent of women. The fear of losing her had endeared her so much the more to me that every mark of her distemper, reminding me of my danger, served to render her more valuable in my eyes. My caresses and tenderness were redoubled; and the loss of charms, which could not make her more engaging to her husband, gave my Maria no concern.

Our fears, however, were again alarmed on Hannah's account. That good and faithful domestic caught the infection. Her fears, and the attention on her beloved mistress, had injured her constitution before this baleful distemper seized her. She fell sacrifice to it. Maria wept over the remains of one who had rendered herself worthy of the utmost consideration. It was a long time before she could recover her spirits. When the remembrance of her loss had a little worn off, we passed our time very agreeably; and I, one day, remarking the smiles I always found on my Maria's face, pressed to know the melancholy which had formerly given to me so much uneasiness. "I may now," said she, "resolve your question without any hazard; the cause is now entirely removed. You know there was a time when I was thought handsome; I never wished to appear so in any other eyes than yours; unfortunately, another thought so and took such measures to make me sensible of the impression my beauty had made, as rendered me truly miserable. Since I am as dear to you as ever, I am happy in having lost charms that were fated to inspire an impious passion in one who, but for me, might have still continued your friend."

I asked no more. I was convinced she meant the captain, who had sought to do me some ill offices, but which I did not resent, as I purposed quitting the army at the end of the campaign. By her desire, I took no notice of his perfidy, only by avoiding every opportunity of being in his company.

One day, about a fortnight after Maria came of age, I was looking over some English newspapers, which a brother officer had lent me to read, in which I saw this extraordinary paragraph:

> Last week was interred the body of Miss Maria Maynard, daughter of James Maynard, Esq.; of L. in Bedfordshire, aged twenty years, ten months, and a fortnight. Had she lived till she attained the full age of twenty-one, she would have been possessed of an estate worth upwards of forty thousand pounds, which now comes to her father, the above-mentioned James Maynard, Esq.
>
> *By a whimsical and remarkable desire of the deceased, a large quantity of quicklime was put into the coffin.*

This piece of intelligence filled us with astonishment, as we could not conceive what end it was likely to answer: but, on my looking up to Maria, by way of gathering some light from her opinion, and seeing not only the whole form of her face but the entire cast of her countenance changed, it immediately struck into my mind that it would be a difficult matter to prove her identity—especially as by the death of Hannah we had lost our only witness. This may appear a very trivial circumstance to most people; but, when we consider what kind of man we had to deal with, it will wear a more serious aspect. It was plain he would go to very great lengths to secure the estate, since he had taken such extraordinary measures to obtain it: he had likewise another motive, for by this second marriage he had a son. It is well known that the property of quicklime is to destroy the features in a very short space, by which means, should we insist on the body's being taken up, no doubt he had used the precaution of getting a suppositious one, and, in all probability, the corrosive quality of the lime would have left it very difficult to ascertain the likeness after such methods being used to destroy it. We had certainly some reason for our apprehensions that the father would disown his child, when it was so much his interest to support his own assertion of her death, and when he had gone so far as actually to make a sham funeral, and, above all, when no one who had been formerly acquainted with her could possibly know her again, so totally was she altered both in voice and features. However, the only step we could take was to set off for England with all expedition—which accordingly we did.

I wrote Mr. Maynard a letter in which I enclosed one from his daughter. He did not deign to return any answer. I then consulted some able lawyers; they made not the least doubt of my recovering my wife's fortune as soon as I proved her identity. That I could have told them; but the difficulty arose how I should do it. None of the officers were in England who had seen her both before and after the smallpox and whose evidence might have been useful.

Talking over the affair to an old gentleman who had been acquainted with my first wife's father—and who likewise knew Maria: "I have not a doubt," said he, "but this lady is the daughter of old Maynard, because you both tell me so—otherwise I could never have believed it. But I do not well know what all this dispute is about: I always understood you was to inherit your estate from your first wife. She lived till she came of age; did she not?"

"According to law," said I, "she certainly did; she died that very day; but she could not make a will."

"I am strangely misinformed," replied he, "if you had not a right to it from that moment. But what say the writings?"

"Those I never saw," returned I. "As I married without the consent of my wife's relations, I had no claim to demand the sight of them; and, as she died before she could call them hers, I had no opportunity."

"Then you have been wronged, take my word for it. I assert that her fortune was hers on the day of marriage, unconditionally. I advise you to go to law with the old rogue (beg your pardon, madame, for calling your father so); go to law with him for the recovery of your first wife's estate; and let him thank heaven his daughter is so well provided for."

This was happy news for us. I changed my plan and brought an action against him for detaining my property. In short, after many hearings and appeals, I had the satisfaction of casting him. But I became father to your sister and yourself before the cause was determined. We were driven to the utmost straits while it was in agitation. At last, however, right prevailed; and I was put in possession of an estate I had unjustly been kept out of many years.

Now I thought myself perfectly happy. "Fortune," said I, "is at length tired of persecuting me; and I have before me the most felicitous prospect." Alas! How short-sighted is man! In the midst of my promised scene of permanent delight, the most dreadful of misfortunes overtook me. My loved Maria fell into the most violent disorder, after having been delivered of a dead child.—Good God! What was my situation, to be reduced to pray for the death of her who made up my whole scheme of happiness! Dear, dear, Maria! Thy image still lives in my remembrance; that,

—Seeks thee still in many a former scene;
Seeks thy fair form, thy lovely beaming eyes,
Thy pleasing converse, by gay lively sense
Inspir'd: whose moral wisdom mildly shone,
Without the toil of art; and virtue glow'd
In all her smiles, without forbidding pride.

Oh! My Julia, such was thy mother! My heart has never tasted happiness since her lamented death. Yet I cease not to thank heaven for the blessings it has given me in thee and my Louisa. May I see you both happy in a world that to me has lost its charms!

The death of my Maria seemed to detach me from all society. I had met with too many bad people in it to have any regard for it; and now the only chain that held me was broken. I retired hither and, in my first paroxysms of grief, vowed never to quit this recluse spot, where, for the first years of your infancy, I brooded my misfortunes, till I became habituated and inured to melancholy. I was always happy when either you or your sister had an opportunity of seeing a little of the world. Perhaps my vow was a rash one, but it is sacred.

As your inclination was not of a retired turn, I consented to a marriage, which, I hope, will be conducive to your felicity. Heaven grant it may! Oh! Most gracious Providence, let me not be so curst as to see my children unhappy! I feel I could not support such an afflicting stroke. But I will not anticipate an evil I continually pray to heaven to avert.

Adieu, my child! May you meet with no accident or misfortune to make you out of love with the world!

Thy tender and affectionate father,

E. Grenville

༖ ༖ ༖ ༖ ༖ ༖ ༖ ༖ ༖
LETTER 10
༖ ༖ ༖ ༖ ༖ ༖ ༖ ༖ ༖

To Miss Grenville

I have just perused my father's long packet: I shall not, however, comment upon it till I have opened my whole mind to you in a more particular manner than I yet have done.

The first part of my father's letter has given me much concern, by awakening some doubts, which I knew not subsisted in my bosom. He asks such questions relative to my real state of happiness as distresses me to answer. I have examined my most inward thoughts. Shall I tell you, my Louisa, the examination does not satisfy me? I believe in this life, and particularly in this town, we must not search too deeply—to be happy, we must take both persons and things as we in general find them, without scrutinizing too closely. The researches are not attended with that pleasure we would wish to find.

The mind may be amused, or, more properly speaking, employed, so as not to give it leisure to think; and, I fancy, the people in this part of the world esteem reflexion an evil, and therefore keep continually hurrying from place to place to leave no room or time for it. For my own part, I sometimes feel some little compunction of mind from the dissipated life I lead and wish I had been cast in a less tumultuous scene. I even sometimes venture to propose to Sir William a scheme of spending a little more time at home—telling him it would be more for our advantage with respect to our health, as the repeated hurries in which we are engaged must, in future, be hurtful to us. He laughs at my sober plan. "Nothing," he says, "is so serviceable to the body, as unbending to the mind"—as to the rest, my notions are owing to the prejudices of education; but in time he hopes my rusticity will yield to the *ton*. "For God's sake," he continues, "make yourself ready—you know you are to be at the opera—" or somewhere or other.

So away goes reflexion; and we are whirled away in the stream of dissipation with the rest of the world. This seems a very sufficient reason for everything we do—*The rest of the world does so:* that's quite enough.

But does it convey to the heart that inward secret pleasure which increases on reflexion? Too sure it does not. However, it has been my invariable plan, from which I have not nor do intend to recede, to be governed in these matters by the will of my husband: he is some years older than me and has had great experience in life. It shall be my care to preserve my health and morals;—in the rest, *he* must be my guide.

My mind is not at the same time quite at ease. I foresee I shall have some things to communicate to you which I shall be unwilling should meet my father's eye. Perhaps the world is altered since he resided in it; and from the novelty to him, the present modes may not meet his approbation. I would wish carefully to conceal everything from him which might give him pain, and which it is not in his power to remedy. To you, my Louisa, I shall ever use the most unbounded confidence. I may sometimes tell you I am dissatisfied; but when I do so, it will not be so much out of a desire of complaint as to induce you to give me your advice. Ah! You would be ten times fitter to live in the world than I. Your solidity and excellent judgement would point out the proper path, and how far you might stray in it unhurt, while my vivacity impels me to follow the gay multitude; and when I look back, I am astonished to behold the progress I have made. But I will accustom myself to relate every circumstance to you: though they may in themselves be trivial, yet I know your affection to me will find them interesting. Your good sense will point out to you what part of our correspondence will be fit for my father's ear.

I mentioned to you two ladies to whose protection and countenance I had been introduced by Sir William. I do not like either of them and wish it had suited him to have procured me inmates more adapted to my sentiments. And now we are upon the subject, I must say, I should have been better pleased with my husband if he had proposed your coming to town with me. He may have a high opinion of my integrity and discretion; but he ought in my mind to have reflected how very young I was; and, he scruples not frequently to say how totally unlearned in polite life.—Should I not then have had a real protector and friend? I do not mention my early years by way of begging an excuse for any impropriety of conduct; far from it: there is no age in which we do not know right from wrong; nor is extreme youth an extenuation of guilt: but there is a time of life which wants attention and should not be left too much to its own guidance.

With the best propensities in the world, we may be led, either by the force of example or real want of judgement, too far in the flowery path of pleasure. Every scene I engage in has the charm of novelty to recommend it. I see all to whom I am introduced do the same; besides, I am following the taste of Sir William; but I am (if I may be allowed to say so) too artless. Perhaps what I think is his inclination may be only to make trial of my natural disposition. Though he may choose to live in the highest *ton*, he may secretly wish his wife a more retired turn. How then shall I act? I do everything with a cheerful countenance; but that proceeds from my desire of pleasing him. I accommodate myself to what I think is his taste; but, owing to my ignorance of mankind, I may be defeating my own purpose. I once slightly hinted as much to Lady Besford. She burst out into a fit of laughter at my duteous principles. I supposed I was wrong by exciting her mirth: this is not the method of reforming me from my errors; but thus I am in general treated. It reminds me of a character in the *Spectator*, who, being very beautiful, was kept in perfect ignorance of everything and who, when she made any enquiry in order to gain knowledge, was always put by with "You are too handsome to trouble yourself about such things." This, according to the present fashion, may be polite; but I am sure it is neither friendly nor satisfactory.

Her ladyship, the other day, showed me a very beautiful young woman, Lady T. "She is going to be separated from her husband," said she. On my expressing surprise,—"Pshaw! There is nothing surprising in those things." She added, "It is customary in this world to break through stone walls to get together this year and break a commandment the next to get asunder. But with regard to her ladyship, I do not know that she has been imprudent; the cause of their disagreement proceeds from a propensity she has for gaming; and my lord is resolved not to be any longer answerable for her debts, having more of that sort on his own hands than he can well discharge." Thus she favours me with sketches of the people of fashion.

Alas! Louisa, are these people to make companions of?—They may, for want of better, be acquaintances but never can be friends.

By her account, there is not a happy couple that frequents St. James's.—Happiness in her estimate is not an article in the married state. "Are you not happy?" I asked one day.

"Happy? Why yes, probably I am; but you do not suppose my happiness proceeds from my being married, any further than that state allowing greater latitude and freedom than the single. I enjoy title, rank, and liberty by bearing Lord Besford's name. We do not disagree, because we very seldom meet. He pursues his pleasures one way, I seek mine another; and our dispositions being very opposite, they are sure never to interfere with each other. I am, I give you my word, a very unexceptionable wife and can say, what few women of quality would be able to do that spoke truth, that I never indulged myself in the least liberty with other men till I had secured my lord a lawful heir." I felt all horror and astonishment.—She saw the emotion she excited. "Come, don't be prudish," said she. "My conduct in the eye of the world is irreproachable. My lord kept a mistress from the first moment of his marriage. What law allows those privileges to a man and excludes a woman from enjoying the same? Marriage now is a necessary kind of barter, and an alliance of families;—the heart is not consulted;—or, if that should sometimes bring a pair together;—judgement being left far behind, love seldom lasts long. In former times, a poor foolish woman might languish out her life in sighs and tears for the infidelity of her husband. Thank heaven! They are now wiser; but then they should be prudent. I extremely condemn those who are enslaved by their passions and bring a public disgrace on their families by suffering themselves to be detected; such are justly our scorn and ridicule; and you may observe they are not taken notice of by anybody. There is a decency to be observed in our amours; and I shall be very ready to offer you my advice, as you are young and inexperienced. One thing let me tell you; never admit your *cicisbeo* to an unlimited familiarity; they are first suspected. Never take notice of your favourite before other people; there are a thousand ways to make yourself amends in secret for that little, but necessary, sacrifice in public."

"Nothing," said I, "but the conviction that you are only bantering me, should have induced me to listen to you so long; but be assured, madame, such discourses are extremely disagreeable to me."

"You are a child," said she, "in these matters; I am not therefore angry or surprised; but, when you find all the world like myself, you will cease your astonishment."

"Would to heaven," cried I, "I had never come into such a depraved world! How much better had it been to have continued in ignorance and innocence in the peaceful retirement in which I was bred! However, I hope, with the seeds of virtue which I imbibed in my infancy, I shall be able to go through life with honour to my family, and integrity to myself. I mean never to engage in any kind of amour, so shall never stand in need of your ladyship's advice, which, I must say, I cannot think Sir William would thank you for, or can have the least idea you would offer."

She assured me Sir William knew too much of the world to expect, or even wish, his wife to be different from most women who composed it but that she had nothing further to say.—I might sometime hence want a *confidante,* and I should not be unfortunate if I met with no worse than her, who had ever conducted herself with prudence and discretion.

I then said I had married Sir William because I preferred him,—and that my sentiments would not alter.

"If you can answer for your future sentiments," replied Lady Besford, "you have a greater knowledge, or at least a greater confidence, in yourself than most people have.—As to your preference of Sir William, I own I am inclined to laugh at your so prettily deceiving yourself.—Pray how many men had you seen, and been addressed by, before your acquaintance with Sir William? Very few, I fancy, that were likely to make an impression on your heart, or that could be put in a competition with him, without an affront from the comparison. So, because you thought Sir William Stanley a handsome man, and genteeler in his dress than the boors you had been accustomed to see—add to which his being passionately enamoured of you—you directly conclude you have given him the preference to all other men and that your heart is devoted to him alone: you may think so; nay, I dare say, you do think so; but, believe me, a time may come when you will think otherwise. You may possibly likewise imagine, as Sir William was so much in love, that you will be forever possessed of his heart:—it is almost a pity to overturn so pretty a system; but, take my word for it, Lady Stanley, Sir William will soon teach you another lesson; he will soon convince you the matrimonial shackles are not binding enough to abridge him of the fashionable enjoyments of life and that, when he married, he did not mean to seclude himself from those pleasures, which, as a man of the world, he is entitled to partake of, because love was the principal ingredient and main spring of your engagement. That love may not last forever. He is of a gay disposition, and his taste must be fed with variety."

"I cannot imagine," I rejoined, interrupting her ladyship, "I cannot imagine what end it is to answer, that you seem desirous of planting discord between my husband and me.—I do not suppose you have any views on him, as, according to your principles, his being married would be no obstacle to that view.—Whatever may be the failings of Sir William, as his wife, it is my duty not to resent them and my interest not to see them. I shall not thank your ladyship for opening my eyes or seeking to develop my sentiments respecting the preference I have showed him anymore than he is obliged to you for seeking to corrupt the morals of a woman whom he has made the guardian of his honour. I hope to preserve that and my own untainted, even in this nursery of vice and folly. I fancy Sir William little thought what instructions you would give when he begged your protection. I am, however, indebted to you for putting me on my guard: and, be assured, I shall be careful to act with all the discretion and prudence you yourself would wish me." Some company coming in put an end to our conversation. I need not tell you that I shall be very shy of her ladyship in future. Good God! Are all the world, as she calls the circle of her acquaintance, like herself? If so, how dreadful to be cast in such a lot! But I will still hope detraction is among the catalogue of her failings and that she views the world with jaundiced eyes.

As to the male acquaintances of Sir William, I cannot say they are higher in my estimation than the other sex. Is it because I am young and ignorant, that they, one and all, take the liberty of almost making love to me? Lord Biddulph, in particular, I dislike; and yet he is Sir William's most approved friend. Colonel Montague is another who is eternally here. The only unexceptional one is the foreign gentleman, Baron Ton-hausen. There is a modest diffidence in his address which interests one much in his favour. I declare, the only blush I have seen since I left Wales was on his cheek when he was introduced. I fancy he is as little acquainted with the vicious manners of the court as myself, as he seemed under some confusion on his first conversation. He is but newly known to Sir William; but, being a man of rank, and politely received in the *beau monde,* he is a welcome visitor at our house. But though he comes often, he is not obtrusive like the rest. They will never let me be at quiet—forever proposing this or the other scheme—which, as I observed before, I comply with, more out of the conformity to the will of Sir William than to my own taste. Not that I would have you suppose that I do not like any of the public places I frequent. I am charmed at the opera and receive a very high, and, I think, rational delight at a good play. I am far from being an enemy to pleasure—but then I would wish to have it under some degree of subordination. Let it be the amusement, not the business of life.

Lord Biddulph is what Lady Besford stiles my *cicisbeo*—that is, he takes upon him the task of attending me to public places, calling my chair, handing me refreshments, and such like; but I assure you, I do not approve of him in the least: and Lady Besford may be assured, I shall, at least, follow her kind advice in this particular, not to admit him to familiarities; though his lordship seems ready enough to avail himself of all opportunities of being infinitely more assiduous than I wish him.

Was this letter to meet the eye of my father, I doubt he would repent his ready acquiescence to my marriage. He would not think the scenes in which I am involved an equivalent for the calm joys I left in the mountains. And was he to know that Sir William and I have not met these three days but at meals, and then surrounded with company; he would not think the tenderness of a husband a recompense for the loss of a father's and sister's affection. I do not, however, do well to complain. I have no just reasons, and it is a weakness to be uneasy without a cause. Adieu then, my Louisa; be assured, my heart shall never know a change, either in its virtuous principles or in its tender love to you. I might have been happy, superlatively so, with Sir William in a desert, but in this vale of vice, it is impossible, unless one can adapt one's sentiments to the style of those one is among. I will be everything I can without forgetting to be what I ought in order to merit the affection you have ever showed to your faithful

Julia Stanley

LETTER 11

To Lady Stanley

Three days, my Julia, and never met but at meals! Good God! To what can this strange behaviour be owing? You say you tell me every circumstance. Have you had any disagreement; and is this the method your husband takes to show his resentment? Ah! Julia, be not afraid of my showing your letters to my father; do you think I would precipitate him with sorrow to the grave, or at least wound his reserved bosom with such anguish? No, Julia, I will burst my heart in silence, but never tell my grief. Alas! My sister, friend of my soul, why are we separated? The loss of your loved society I would sacrifice could I but hear you were happy. But can you be so among such wretches? Yet be comforted, my Julia; have confidence in the rectitude of your own actions and thoughts; but, above all, petition heaven to support you in all trials. Be assured, while you have the protection of the Almighty, these impious vile wretches will not, cannot, prevail against you. Your virtue will shine out more conspicuously while surrounded with their vices.

That horrid Lady Besford! I am sure you feel all the detestation you ought for such a character. As you become acquainted with other people (and they cannot be all so bad)—you may take an opportunity of shaking her off. Dear creature! How art thou beset! Surely, Sir William is very thoughtless; with his experience, he ought to have known how improper such a woman was for the protector of his wife. And why must this Lord—what's his odious name?—why is he to be your *escorte*? Is it not the husband's province to guard and defend his wife? What a world are you cast in!

I find poor Win has written to her aunt Bailey and complains heavily of her situation. She says Griffith is still more discontented than herself, since he is the jest of all the other servants. They both wish themselves at home again. She likewise tells Mrs. Bailey that she is not fit to dress you according to the fashion and gives a whimsical account of the many different things you put on and pull off when you are, what she calls, high-dressed. If she is of no use to you, I wish you would send her back before her morals are corrupted. Consider, she has not had the advantage of education, as you have had, and, being without those resources within, may the more easily fall a prey to some insidious betrayer; for, no doubt, in such a place,

> Clowns as well can act the rake,
> As those in a higher sphere.

Let her return, then, if she is willing, as innocent and artless as she left us. Oh! That I could enlarge that wish! I should have been glad you had had Mrs. Bailey with you; she might have been of some service to you. Her long residence in *our* family would have given her some weight in *yours,* which I doubt is sadly managed by Win's account. The servants are disorderly and negligent. Don't you think of going into the country? Spring comes forward very fast; and next month is the fairest of the year.

Would to heaven you were here!—I long ardently for your company and, rather than forgo it, would almost consent to share it with the dissipated tribe you are obliged to associate with;—but that privilege is not allowed me. I could not leave my father. Nay, I must further say, I should have too much pride to come unasked; and you know Sir William never gave me an invitation.

I shed tears over the latter part of your letter, where you say, *I could be happy, superlatively so, with Sir William in a desert, but here it is impossible.* Whatever he may think, he would be happy too; at least he appeared so while with us. Oh! That he could have been satisfied with our calm joys which mend the heart and left those false delusive ones which corrupt and vitiate it!

Dearest Julia, adieu!

Believe me your faithful

Louisa Grenville

To Miss Grenville

Louisa! My dearest girl! Who do you think I have met with?—No other than Lady Melford! I saw her this day in the drawing room. I instantly recognized her ladyship and, catching her eye, made my obeisance to her. She returned my salute in a manner which seemed to say, "I don't know you; but I wish to recollect you."—As often as I looked up, I found I engaged her attention. When their majesties were withdrawn, I was sitting in one of the windows with Lady Anne Parker and some other folks about me.—I then saw Lady Melford moving towards me. I rose and pressed her to take my place. "You are very obliging," said she. "I will, if you please, accept part of it, as I wish to be informed who it is that is so polite as to pay such civility to an old woman." Lady Anne, finding we were entering on conversation, wished me a good day and went off.

"I am perfectly well acquainted with your features," said her ladyship, "but I cannot call to my memory what is your name."

"Have you then quite forgotten Julia Grenville, to whom you were so kind while she was on a visit with your grandfather at L.?"

"Julia Grenville! Aye, so it is; but, my dear, how came I to meet you in the drawing room at St. James's, whom I thought still an inmate of the mountains? Has your father rescinded his resolution of spending his life there? And where is your sister?"

"My father," I replied, "is still in his favourite retreat; my sister resides with him.—I have been in town sometime and am at present an inhabitant of it."

"To whose protection could your father confide you, my dear?"

"To the best protector in the world, madame," I answered, smiling— "To a husband."

"A husband!" she repeated, quite astonished. "What, child, are you married? And who, my dear, is this husband that your father could part with you to?"

"That gentleman in the blue and silver velvet, across the room,—Sir William Stanley. Does your ladyship know him?"

"By name and character only," she answered. "You are very young, my dear, to be thus initiated in the world. Has Sir William any relations, female ones I mean, who are fit companions for you?—This is a dangerous place for young inexperienced girls to be left to their own guidance."

I mentioned the ladies to whom I had been introduced. "I don't know them," said Lady Melford. "No doubt they are women of character, as they are the friends of your husband. I am, however, glad to see you and hope you are happily married. My meeting you here is owing to having attended a lady who was introduced; I came to town from D. for that purpose."

I asked her ladyship if she would permit me to wait on her while she remained in town.

She obligingly said she took it very kind in a young person showing such attention to her and should always be glad of my company.

The counsel of Lady Melford may be of service to me. I am extremely happy to have seen her. I remember with pleasure the month I passed at L. I reproach myself for not writing to Jenny Melford. I doubt she thinks me ungrateful, or that the busy scenes in which I am immersed have obliterated all former fond remembrances. I will soon convince her that the gay insignificant crowd cannot wear away the impression which her kindness stamped on my heart in early childhood.

Your letter is just brought to my hands. Yes, my dear Louisa, I have not a doubt but that while I deserve it I shall be in the immediate care of heaven. Join your prayers to mine; and they will, when offered with heartfelt sincerity, be heard.

I have nothing to apprehend from Lady Besford.—Such kind of women can never seduce me. She shows herself too openly; and the discovery of her character gives me no other concern than as it too evidently manifests in my eyes the extreme carelessness of Sir William: I own *there* I am in some degree piqued. But if *he* is indifferent about my morals and well-doing in life, it will more absolutely become my business to take care of myself,—an arduous task for a young girl surrounded with so many incitements to quit the strait paths, and so many examples of those that do.

As to the economy of my family, I fear it is but badly managed.—However, I do not know how to interfere, as we have a housekeeper who is empowered to give all orders, &c. If Win is desirous of returning, I shall not exert my voice to oppose her inclinations, though I own I shall be very sorry to lose the only domestic in my family in whom I can place the least confidence, or who is attached to me from any other motive than interest. I will never, notwithstanding my repugnance to her leaving me, offer any objections which may influence her conduct; but I do not think, with you, her morals will be in any danger, as she in general keeps either in my apartments or in the housekeeper's.

I do not know how Griffith manages; I should be concerned that he should be ill-used by the rest of the servants; his dialect, and to them singular manners, may excite their boisterous mirth; and I know, though he is a worthy creature, yet he has all the irascibility of his countrymen; and therefore they may take a pleasure in thwarting and teasing the poor Cambro-Briton; but of this I am not likely to be informed, as being so wholly out of my sphere.

I could hardly help smiling at that part of your letter wherein you say you think the husband the proper person to attend his wife to public places. How different are your ideas than those of the people of this town, or at least to their practice!—A woman who would not blush at being convicted of a little affair of gallantry would be ready to sink with confusion should she receive those *tendres* from a husband in public, which when offered by any other man is accepted with pleasure and complacency. Sir William never goes with me to any of these fashionable movements. It is true, we often meet, but very seldom join, as we are in general in separate parties. *Whom God hath joined, let no man put asunder* is a part of the ceremony; but here it is the business of everyone to endeavour to put a man and wife asunder;—fashion not making it decent to appear together.

These *etiquettes*, though so absolutely necessary in polite life, are by no means reconcilable to reason, or to my wishes. But my voice would be too weak to be heard against the general cry; or, being heard, I should be thought too insignificant to be attended to.

"Conscience makes cowards of us all," some poet says; and your Julia says, "Fashion makes fools of us all"; but she only whispers this to the dear bosom of her friend. Oh! My Louisa, that you were here with me!—It is

69

with this wish I end all my letters; mentally so, if I do not openly express myself.—Absence seems to increase my affection.—One reason is, because I cannot find anyone to supply to me the loss I sustain in you; out of the hundreds I visit, not one with whom I can form a friendly attachment. My attachment to Sir William, which was strong enough to tear me from your arms, is not sufficient to suppress the gushing tear, or hush the rising sigh, when I sit and reflect on what I once possessed and what I so much want at this moment. Adieu, my dear Louisa! Continue your tender attention to the best of fathers,—and love me always.

Julia Stanley

ᵼ ᵼ ᵼ ᵼ ᵼ ᵼ ᵼ ᵼ ᵼ ᵼ ᵼ ᵼ

LETTER 13

ᵼ ᵼ ᵼ ᵼ ᵼ ᵼ ᵼ ᵼ ᵼ ᵼ ᵼ ᵼ

To the Same

I spent a whole morning with Lady Melford, more to my satisfaction than anyone I have passed since I left you. But this treat cannot be repeated; her ladyship leaves town this day. She was so good as to say she was sorry her stay was so short and wished to have had more time with me. I can truly join with her. Her conversation was friendly and parental. She cautioned me against falling into the levities of the sex—which unhappily, she observed, were now become so prevalent—and further told me how cautious I ought to be of my female acquaintance, since the reputation of a young woman rises and falls in proportion to the merit of her associates. I judged she had Lady Besford in her mind. I answered I thought myself unhappy in not having you with me, and likewise possessing so little penetration, that I could not discover who were, or who were not, proper companions; that, relying on the experience of Sir William, I had left the choice of them to him, trusting he would not introduce those whose characters and morals were reprehensible; but whether it proceeded from my ignorance or from the mode of the times I could not admire the sentiments of either of the ladies with whom I was more intimately connected but wished to have the opinion of one whose judgement was more matured than mine.

Lady Melford replied the circle of her acquaintance was rather confined;—and that her short residences at a time in town left her an incompetent judge: "But, my dear," she added, "the virtuous principles instilled into you by your excellent father, joined to the innate goodness of your heart, must guide you through the warfare of life. Never for one moment listen to the seductive voice of folly, whether its advocate be man or woman.—If a man is profuse in flattery, believe him an invidious betrayer who only watches a favourable moment to ruin your peace of mind forever. Suffer no one to lessen your husband in your esteem: no one will attempt it but from sinister views: disappoint all such, either by grave remonstrances or lively sallies. Perhaps some will officiously bring you information of the supposed infidelity of your husband, in hopes that they may induce you to take a fashionable revenge.—Labour to convince such how you detest all informers; speak of your confidence in him,—and that nothing shall persuade you but that he acts as he ought. But, since the heart of man naturally loves variety and, from the depravity of the age, indulgences, which I call criminal, are allowed to them, Sir William may not pay that strict obedience to his part of the marriage contract as he ought; remember, my dear, his conduct can never exculpate any breach in yours. Gentleness and complacency on your part are the only weapons you should prove to any little irregularity on his. By such behaviour, I doubt not, you will be happy, as you will deserve to be so."

Ah! My dear Louisa, what a loss shall I have in this venerable monitress! I will treasure up her excellent advice and hope to reap the benefit of it.

If I dislike Lady Besford, I think I have more reason to be displeased with Lady Anne Parker.—She has more artifice and is consequently a more dangerous companion. She has more than once given hint of the freedoms which Sir William allows in himself.—The other night at the opera she pointed out one of the dancers and assured me, "Sir William was much envied for having subdued the virtue of that girl. That," continued she, "was her *vis-à-vis* that you admired this morning; she lives in great taste; I suppose her allowance is superb." It is quite the *ton* to keep opera girls, though, perhaps, the men who support them never pay them a visit.—I therefore concluded this affair was one of that sort. Such creatures can never deprive me of my husband's heart, and I should be very weak to be uneasy about such connexions.

Last night, however, a circumstance happened, which, I own, touched my heart more sensibly. Lady Anne insisted on my accompanying her to the opera. Sir William dined out and, as our party was sudden, knew not of my intention of being there. Towards the end of the opera, I observed my husband in one of the upper boxes with a very elegant-looking woman, dressed in the genteelest taste, to whom he appeared very assiduous.— "There is Sir William," said I.—"Yes," said Lady Anne, "but I dare say, he did not expect to see you here."

"Possibly not," I answered. A little female curiosity urged me to ask if she knew who that lady was. She smiled and answered she believed she did. A very favourite air being then sung, I dropped the conversation, though I could not help now and then stealing a look at my husband. I was convinced he must see and know me, as my situation in the house was very conspicuous; but I thought he seemed industriously to avoid meeting my eyes.—The opera being ended, we adjourned to the coffee room, and having missed Sir William a little time before, naturally expected to see him there, as it is customary for all the company to assemble there previous to going to their carriages.

A great number of people soon joined us. Baron Ton-hausen had just handed me a glass of orgeat and was chatting in an agreeable manner when Lord Biddulph came up. "Lady Stanley," said he with an air of surprise, "I thought I saw you this moment in Sir William's chariot. I little expected the happiness of meeting you here."

"You saw Sir William, my lord, I believe," said Lady Anne, "but as to the lady you are mistaken—though I should have supposed you might have recognized your old friend Lucy Gardiner; they were together in one of the boxes.—Sly wretch! He thought we did not see him."

"Oh! You ladies have such penetrating eyes," replied his lordship, "that we poor men—and especially the married ones, ought to be careful how we conduct ourselves. But, my dear Lady Stanley, how have you been entertained? Was not Rauzzini exquisite?"

"Can you ask how her ladyship has been amused when you have just informed her her *caro sposo* was seen with a favourite Sultana?"

"Pshaw!" said his lordship. "There is nothing in that—*tout la mode de François.* The conduct of a husband cannot discompose a lady of sense. What says the lovely Lady Stanley?"

"I answer," I replied very seriously, "Sir William has an undoubted right to act as he pleases. I never have or ever intended to prescribe rules to him; sufficient, I think, to conduct myself."

"Bravo!" cried Lord Biddulph. "Spoke like a heroine: and I hope my dear Lady Stanley will act as she pleases too."

"I do when I can," I answered.—Then, turning to Lady Anne, "Not to break in on your amusement," I continued, "will you give me leave to wait on you to Brook Street? You know you have promised to sup with me."

"Most cheerfully," said she;—"but will you not ask the beaux to attend us?"

Lord Biddulph said he was most unfortunately engaged to Lady D——'s route. The baron refused, as if he wished to be entreated. Lady Anne would take no denial; and, when I assured him his company would give me pleasure, he consented.

I was handed to the coach by his lordship, who took that opportunity of condemning Sir William's want of taste and lavishing the utmost encomiums on your Julia—with whom they passed as nothing. If Sir William is unfaithful, Lord Biddulph is not the man to reconcile me to the sex. I see his motives in too glaring colours. No, the soft timidity of Ton-hausen, which, while it indicates the profoundest respect, still betrays the utmost tenderness—he it is alone who could restore the character of mankind and raise it again in my estimation. But what have I said? Dear Louisa, I blush at having discovered to you that I am, past all doubt, the object of the baron's tender sentiments. Ah! Can I mistake those glances, which modest reserve and deference urge him to correct? Yet fear me not. I am married. My vows are registered in the book of heaven; and as, by their irreversible decree, I am bound to *honour* and *obey* my husband, so will I strive to *love* him, and him alone; though I have long since ceased to be the object of his? Of what consequence, however, is that? I am indissolubly united to him; he was the man of my choice—to say he was almost the first man I almost ever saw—and to plead my youth and inexperience—oh! What does that avail? Nor does his neglect justify the least on my part.

"For man the lawless libertine may rove."

But this is a strange digression. The baron accompanied us to supper. During our repast, Lady Anne made a thousand sallies to divert us. My mind, however, seemed that night infected by the demon of despair. I could not be cheerful—and yet, I am sure, I was not jealous of this Lucy Gardiner. Melancholy was contagious: Ton-hausen caught it—I observed him sometimes heave a suppressed sigh. Lady Anne was determined to dissipate the gloom which enveloped us and began drawing, with her satirical pen, the characters of her acquaintance.

"Baron," said she, "did you not observe Lord P. with his round unthinking face, how assiduous he was to Miss W., complimenting her on the brilliancy of her complexion, though he knows she wore more *rouge* than almost any woman of quality—extolling her *forest of hair,* when most likely he saw it this morning brought in a bandbox—and celebrating the pearly whiteness of her teeth, when he was present at their transplanting. But he is not a slave to propriety, or even common sense. No, dear creature, he has a soul above it. But did you take notice of Lady L., how she ogled Captain F. when her booby lord turned his head aside? What a ridiculous sop is that! The most glaring proofs will not convince him of his wife's infidelity. 'Captain F.,' said he to me yesterday at court; 'Captain F., I assure you, Lady Anne, is a great favourite with me.'

"'It is a family partiality,' said I. 'Lady L. seems to have no aversion to him.'

"'Ah, there you mistake, fair lady. I want my lady to have the same affection for him I have. He has done all he can to please her, and yet she does not seem satisfied with him.'

"'Unconscionable!' cried I. 'Why then, she is never to be satisfied.'

"'Why, so I say, but it proceeds from the violence of her attachment to me. Oh! Lady Anne, she is the most virtuous and discreetest lady. I should be the happiest man in the world, if she would but show a little more consideration to my friend.'

"I think it a pity he does not know his happiness, as I have not the least doubt of F. and her ladyship having a pretty good understanding together."

Thus was the thoughtless creature running on unheeded by either of us when her harangue was interrupted by an alarming accident happening to me. I had sat some time, leaning on my hand, though—God knows!—paying very little attention to Lady Anne's sketches, when some of the superfluous ornaments of my headdress, coming rather too near the candle, caught fire, and the whole farrago of ribbons, lace, and gew-gaws was instantly in flames. I shrieked out in the utmost terror and should have been a very great sufferer—perhaps been burnt to death—had not the baron had the presence of mind to roll my head, flames and all, up in my shawl, which fortunately hung on the back of my chair, and, by such precaution, preserved the *capital*. How ridiculous are the fashions, which render us liable to such accidents! My fright, however, proved more than the damage sustained. When the flames were extinguished, I thought Lady Anne would have expired with mirth, owing to the disastrous figure I made with my singed feathers, &c. The whimsical distress of the heroine of the Election Ball presented itself to her imagination; and the pale face of the affrighted baron during the conflagration heightened the picture. "Even such a man," she cried, "so dead in look, so woebegone! Excuse me, dear Ton-hausen—the danger is over now. I must indulge my risible faculties."

"I will most readily join with your ladyship," answered the baron, "as my joy is in proportion to what were my apprehensions. But I must condemn a fashion which is so injurious to the safety of the ladies."

The accident, however, disconcerted me not a little and made me quite unfit for company. They saw the chagrin painted on my features and soon took leave of me.

I retired to my dressing room and sent for Win to inspect the almost ruined fabric; but such is the construction nowadays that a head might burn for an hour without damaging the genuine part of it. A lucky circumstance! I suffered but little damage—in short, nothing which Monsieur Corross could not remedy in a few hours.

My company staying late, and this event besides, retarded my retiring to rest till near three in the morning. I had not left my dressing room when Sir William entered.

"Good God! Not gone to bed yet, Julia? I hope you did not sit up for me. You know that is a piece of ceremony I would choose to dispense with; as it always carries a tacit reproach under an appearance of tender solicitude."

I fancied I saw in his countenance a consciousness that he deserved reproach and a determination to begin first to find fault. I was vexed and answered, "You might have waited for the reproach at least, before you prejudged my conduct. Nor can you have any apprehensions that I should make such, having never taken that liberty. Neither do you do me justice in supposing me capable of the meanness you insinuate on finding me up at this late hour. That circumstance is owing to an accident, by which I might have been a great sufferer, and which, though you so unkindly accuse me of being improperly prying and curious, I will, if you permit me, relate to you in order to justify myself." He certainly expected I should ask some questions which would be disagreeable to him; and therefore, finding me totally silent on that head, his features became more relaxed; he enquired, with some tenderness, what alarming accident I hinted at. I informed him of every circumstance.—My account put him into good humour; and we laughed over the droll scene very heartily. Observing, however, that I was very *en déshabillé*, "My dear girl," cried he, throwing his arms around me, "I doubt you will catch cold, notwithstanding you so lately represented a burning mountain. Come," continued he, "will you go to bed?" While he spoke, he pressed me to his bosom and expressed in his voice and manner more warmth of affection than he had discovered since I forsook the mountains. He kissed me several times with rapture; and his eyes dwelt on me with an ardour I have long been unused to behold. The adventure at the opera returned to my imagination. These caresses, thought I, have been bestowed on one whose prostituted charms are more admired than mine. I sighed—"Why do you sigh, Julia?" asked my husband.

"I know not," I answered. "I ought not to sigh at the very moment I am receiving proofs of your affection. But I have not lately received such proofs, and therefore perhaps I sighed."

"You are a foolish girl, Julia, yet a good one too," cried he, kissing me again. "Foolish to fancy I do not love you; and a good girl not to ask impertinent questions. That is, your tongue is silent, but you have wicked eyes, Julia, that seek to look into my inmost thoughts."

"Then I will shut them," said I, affecting to laugh—but added, in a more serious tone—"I will see no further than you would wish me; to please you, I will *be blind, insensible and blind.*"

"But, as you are not deaf, I will tell you what well I know—that I was at the opera—and with a lady too.—Do not, however, be jealous, my dear: the woman I was with was perfectly indifferent to me. I met her by accident—but I had a mind to see what effect such a piece of flirtation would have on you. I am not displeased with your behaviour; nor would I have you so with mine."

"I will in all my best obey you," said I.

"Then go to bed," said he—"*To bed my love, and I will follow thee.*"

You will not scruple to pronounce this a reasonable long letter, my dear Louisa, for a modern fine lady.—Ah! Shield me from that character! Would to heaven Sir William was no more of the modern fine gentleman in his heart! I could be happy with him.—Yes, Louisa—was I indeed the object of his affections, not merely so of his passions, which, I fear, I am, I could indeed be happy with him. My person still invites his caresses, but for the softer sentiments of the soul, that ineffable tenderness which depends not on the tincture of the skin, of that—alas!—he has no idea. A voluptuary in love, he professes not that delicacy which refines all its joys. His is all passion; sentiment is left out of the catalogue. Adieu!

Julia Stanley

[*In continuation.*]

I hope my dearest Louisa will not be too much alarmed at a whole fortnight's silence. Ah! Louisa, the event which occasioned it may be productive of very fatal consequences to me—yet I will not despair. No, I will trust in a good God and the virtuous education I have had. They will arm me to subdue inclinations irreversible fate has rendered improper. But to the point.

Two or three nights after I wrote my last, I went to the play.—Lady Anne, Colonel Montague, and a Miss Finch were the party. Unhappily, the afterpiece represented was one obtruded on the public by an author obnoxious to some of them; and there were two parties formed: one to condemn, the other to support. Wholly unacquainted with a thing of this kind, I soon began to be alarmed at the clamour which rang from every part of the house. The glass chandeliers first fell a victim to a hotheaded wretch in the pit; and part of the shattered fragments was thrown into my lap. My fears increased to the highest degree—no one seemed to interest themselves about me. Colonel Montague being an admirer of Miss Finch, his attention was paid to her. The ladies were ordered out of the house. I was ready enough to obey the summons and was rushing out when my passage was stopped by a concourse of people in the lobby. The women screaming, men swearing—altogether—I thought I should die with terror. "Oh! Let me come out, let me come out!" I cried with uplifted hands.—No one regarded me. And I might have stood screaming in concert with the rest till this time had not the baron most seasonably come to my assistance. He broke through the crowd with incredible force and flew to me.

"Dearest Lady Stanley," cried he, "recover your spirits—you are in no danger. I will guard you to your carriage."

Others were equally anxious about their company, and everyone striving to get out first increased the difficulty. Many ladies fainted in the passages, which, being close, became almost suffocating. Every moment our difficulties and my fears increased. I became almost insensible. The baron most kindly supported me with one arm—and with the other strove to make way. The men even pushed with rudeness by me. Ton-hausen expostulated and raved by turns: at length he drew his sword, which terrified me to such a degree that I was sinking to the earth—and really gave myself up totally to despair. The efforts he made at last gained us a passage to the great door—and, without waiting to ask any questions, he put me into a coach that happened to be near: as to my carriage, it was not to be found—or probably some others had used the same freedom that we had with one unknown to us.

As soon as we were seated, Ton-hausen expressed his joy in the strongest terms that we had so happily escaped any danger. I was so weak that he thought it necessary to support me in his arms; and though I had no cause to complain of any freedom in his manner, yet the warmth of his expression, joined to my foregoing fright, had such an effect on me that, though I did not wholly lose my senses, I thought I was dying—I never fainted in my life before; to my ignorance, then, must be imputed my fears and foolish behaviour in consequence. "Oh! Carry me somewhere," cried I, gasping. "Do not let me die here! For God's sake, do not let me die in the coach!"

"My angel," said the baron, "do not give way to such imaginary terrors. I will not let down the glasses—you will be better presently." But finding my head, which I could no longer support, drop on his shoulder and a cold damp bedew my face, he gave a loose to his tenderness, which showed itself in his attention to my welfare. He pressed me almost frantic to his bosom, called on me in the most endearing terms. He thought me insensible. He knew not I could hear the effusions of his heart. Oh! Louisa, he could have no idea how they sunk in mine. Among the rest, these broken sentences were distinct: "Oh! My God! What will become of me! Dearest, most loved of women, how is my heart distracted! And shall I lose thee thus? Oh! How shall I support thy loss! Too late found—ever beloved of my soul! Thy Henry will die with thee!" Picture to yourself, my Louisa, what were my sensations at this time. I have no words to express them—or, if I could, they would be unfit for me to express. The sensations themselves ought not to have found a passage in my bosom. I will drive them away, Louisa. I will not give them harbour. I no longer knew what was become of me: I became dead to all appearance. The baron, in a state of distraction, called to the coachman to stop anywhere where I could receive assistance. Fortunately we were near a chemist's. Ton-hausen carried me in his arms to a back room—and, by the application of drops, etc. I was restored to life. I found the baron kneeling at my feet and supporting me. It was a long time before he could make me sensible where I was. My situation in a strange place, and singularity of our appearance, affected me extremely—I burst into tears and entreated the baron to get me a chair to convey me home. "A chair! Lady Stanley; will not you then permit me to attend you home? Would you place yourself under the protection of two strangers rather than allow me that honour?"

"Ah! Excuse me, Baron," I answered, "I hardly know what I said. Do as you please, only let me go home." And yet, Louisa, I felt a dread on going into the same carriage with him. I thought myself extremely absurd and foolish; yet I could not get the better of my apprehensions. How vain they were! Never could any man behave with more delicate attention, or more void of that kind of behaviour which might have justified my fears. His despair had prompted the discovery of his sentiments. He thought me incapable of hearing the secret of his soul; and it was absurd to a degree for me, by an unnecessary circumspection, to let him see I had unhappily been a participator of his secret. There was, however, an awkward consciousness in my conduct towards him I could not divest myself of. I wished to be at home. I even expressed my impatience to be alone. He sighed but made it obvious he saw and felt it. Thank God! At last we got home.

"It would be rude," said he, "after your ladyship has so frequently expressed your wish to be alone, to obtrude my company a moment longer than absolutely necessary; but, if you will allow me to remain in your drawing room till I hear you are a little recovered, I shall esteem it a favour."

"I have not a doubt of being much better," I returned, "when I have had a little rest. I am extremely indebted to you for the care you have taken. I must repay it, by desiring you to have some consideration for yourself: rest will be salutary for both; and I hope to return you a message in the morning that I am not at all the worse for this disagreeable adventure. Adieu, Baron, take my advice." He bowed and cast on me such a look—he seemed to correct himself.—Oh! That look! What was not expressed in it! Away, away, all such remembrances.

The consequences, however, were not to end here. I soon found other circumstances which I had not thought on. In short, my dear Louisa, I must now discover to you a secret, which I had determined to keep sometime longer at least. Not even Sir William knew of it. I intended to have surprised you all; but this vile playhouse affair put an end to my hopes, and very near to my life. For two days, my situation was very critical. As soon as the danger was over, I recovered apace. The baron was at my door several times in the day to enquire after me. And Win said, who once saw him, that he betrayed more anxiety than anyone beside.

Yesterday was the first of my seeing any company. The baron's name was the first announced. The sound threw me into a perturbation I laboured to conceal. Sir William presented him to me. I received his compliment with an awkward confusion. My embarrassment was imputed, by my husband, to the simple bashfulness of a country rustic—a bashfulness he generally renders more insupportable by the ridiculous light he chooses to make me appear in, rather than encouraging in me a better opinion of myself, which, sometimes, he does me the honour of saying I ought to entertain. The baron had taken my hand in the most respectful manner. I suffered him to lift it to his lips. "Is it thus," said Sir William, "you thank your deliverer? Had I been in your place, Julia, I should have received my champion with open arms—at least have allowed him a salute. But the baron is a modest young man. Come, I will set you the example."—Saying which, he caught me in his arms and kissed me. I was extremely chagrined and felt my cheeks glow, not only with shame, but anger.

"You are too violent, Sir William," said I very gravely. "You have excessively disconcerted me."

"I will allow," said he, "I might have been too eager: now you shall experience the difference between the ecstatic ardour of an adoring husband and the cool complacency of a friend. Nay, nay," continued he, feeling a dissenting look, "you must reward the baron, or I shall think you either very prudish or angry with me." Was there ever such inconsiderate behaviour? Ton-hausen seemed fearful of offending—yet not willing to lose so fair an opportunity. Oh! Louisa, as Sir William said, I *did* experience a difference. But Sir William is no adoring husband. The baron's lips trembled as they touched mine; and I felt an emotion to which I was hitherto a stranger.

I was doomed, however, to receive still more shocks. On the baron's saying he was happy to see me so well recovered after my fright and hoped I had found no disagreeable consequence—"No disagreeable consequence!" repeated Sir William with the most unfeeling air. "Is the loss of a son and heir then nothing? It may be repaired," he continued, laughing, "to be sure; but I am extremely disappointed." Are you not enraged with your brother-in-law, Louisa? How indelicate! I really could no longer support these mortifications, though I knew I should mortally offend him; I could not help leaving the room in tears; nor would I return to it till summoned by the arrival of other company. I did not recover my spirits the whole evening.

Good God! How different do men appear sometimes from themselves! I often am induced to ask myself whether I really gave my hand to the man I now see in my husband. Ah! How is he changed! I reflect for hours together on the unaccountableness of his conduct. How he is carried away by the giddy multitude. He is swayed by every passion, and the last is the ruling one—

Is everything by starts, and nothing long.

A time may come when he may see his folly; I hope before it be too late to repair it. Why should such a man marry? Or why did fate lead him to our innocent retreat? Oh! Why did I foolishly mistake a rambling disposition, and a transient liking, for a permanent attachment? But why do I run on thus? Dear Louisa, you will think me far gone in a frenzy. But, believe me, I will ever deserve your tender affection.

Julia Stanley

LETTER 14

To Lady Stanley

Good heavens! What a variety of emotions has your last letter excited in my breast! Surely, my Julia did not give it a second perusal! I can make allowance for the expressions of gratitude which you (in a manner lavish, not) bestow on the baron. But oh! Beware, my beloved sister, that your gratitude becomes not too warm; that sentiment, so laudable when properly placed, should it be an introduction to what my fears and tenderness apprehend, would change to the most impious.—You already perceive a visible difference between him and your husband.—I assert, no woman ought to make a comparison,—'tis dangerous, 'tis fatal. Sir William was the man of your choice;—it is true you were young; but still you ought to respect your choice as sacred.—You are still young; and although you may have seen more of the world, I doubt your sentiments are little mended by your experience. The knowledge of the world—at least so it appears to me—is of no further use than to bring one acquainted with vice and to be less shocked at the idea of it. Is this then a knowledge which we should wish to attain?—Ah! Believe me, it had been better for you to have blushed unseen and lost your sweetness in the desert air than to have, in *the busy haunts of men,* hazarded the privation of *that peace which goodness bosoms ever.* Think what I suffer; and, constrained to treasure up my anxious fears in my own bosom, I have no one to whom I can vent my griefs: and indeed to whom could I impart the terrors which fill my soul, when I reflect on the dangers by which my sister, the darling of my affections, is surrounded? Oh, Julia! You know how fatally I have experienced the interest a beloved object has in the breast of a tender woman; how ought we then to guard against the admission of a passion destructive to our repose, even in its most innocent and harmless state, while we are single?—But how much more should *you* keep a strict watch over every outlet of the heart, lest it should fall prey to the insidious enemy;—you respect his silence;—you pity his sufferings.—Reprobate respect!—Abjure pity!—They are both in your circumstances dangerous; and a well-experienced writer has observed more women have been ruined by pity than have fallen a sacrifice to appetite and passion. Pity is a kindred virtue, and from the innocence and complacency of her appearance, we suspect no ill; but dangers inexplicable lurk beneath the tear that trembles in her eye; and, without even knowing that we do so, we make a fatal transfer to our utter and inevitable disadvantage. From having the power of bestowing compassion, we become objects of it from others; though too frequently, instead of receiving it, we find ourselves loaded with the censure of the world. We look into our own bosoms for consolation: Alas! It is flown with our innocence; and in its room we feel the sharpest stings of self-reproof. Me, Julia, my tears obliterate each mournful passage of my pen.

⚜⚜⚜⚜⚜⚜⚜⚜⚜⚜

LETTER 15

⚜⚜⚜⚜⚜⚜⚜⚜⚜⚜

To Miss Grenville

Enough, my dearest sister, enough have you suffered through your unremitting tenderness to your Julia;—yet believe her, while she vows to the dear bosom of friendship, no action of hers shall call a blush on your cheek. Good God! What a wretch should I be if I could abuse such sisterly love! If, after such friendly admonitions, enforced with so much moving eloquence, your Julia should degenerate from her birth, and forget those lessons of virtue early inculcated by the best of fathers! Oh! Rest assured, my dearest dear Louisa, be satisfied, your father cannot be so vile,—remember the same blood flows through our veins; one parent stock we sprang from, nurtured by one hand, listening at the same time to the same voice of reason, learning the same pious lesson—why then these apprehensions of my degeneracy? Trust me, Louisa, I will not deceive you; and God grant I may never deceive myself! The wisest of men has said, "The heart of man is deceitful above all things." I, however, will strictly examine mine; I will search into it narrowly; at present the search is not painful, I have nothing to reproach myself with; I have, I hope, discharged my filial and fraternal duties; my matrimonial ones are inviolate: I have studied the temper of Sir William, in hopes I should discover a rule of my actions; but how can I form a system from one so variable as he is? Would to heaven he was more uniform! Or that he would suffer himself to be guided by his own under-standing, and not by the whim or caprice of others so much inferior to him-self! All this I have repeated frequently to you, together with my wish to leave London, and the objects with which I am daily surrounded.—Does such a wish look as if I was improperly attached to the world, or any par-ticular person in it? You are too severe, my love; but when I reflect that your rigidity proceeds from your unrivalled attachment, I kiss the rod of my chastisement;—I long to fold my dear lecturer in my arms and convince her that one whose heart is filled with the affection that glows in mine can find no room for any sentiment incompatible with virtue, of which she is the express image. Adieu!

LETTER 16

To Miss Grenville

If thy Julia falls, my beloved sister, how great will be her condemnation! With such supports, and I hope I may add with an inward rectitude of mind, I think she can never deviate from the right path. You see, my Louisa, that not you alone are interested in my well-doing. I have a secret, nay I may say, celestial friend and monitor,—a friend it certainly is, though unknown;—all who give good counsel must be my true and sincere friends. From whom I have received it, I know not; but it shall be my study to merit the favour of this earthly or heavenly conductor through the intricate mazes of life. I will no longer keep you in ignorance of my meaning, but without delay will copy for you a letter I received this morning; the original I have too much veneration to part with, even to you, who are dearer to me than almost all the world beside.—

I cannot help anticipating the surprise your ladyship will be under from receiving a letter from an unknown hand; nor will the signature contribute to develop the cloud behind which I choose to conceal myself.

My motives, I hope, will extenuate the boldness of my task; and I rely likewise on the amiable qualities you so eminently possess to pardon the temerity of anyone who shall presume to criticize the conduct of one of the most lovely of God's works.

I feel for you as a man, a friend, or, to sum up all, a guardian angel. I see you on the brink of a steep precipice. I shudder at the danger which you are not sensible of. You will wonder at my motive and the interest I take in your concerns.—It is from my knowledge of the goodness of your heart: were you less amiable than you are, you would be below my solicitude; I might be charmed with you as a woman, but I should not venerate you;—nay, should possibly—enchanted as everyone must be with your personal attractions, join with those who seek to seduce you to their own purposes. The sentiments I profess for you are such as a tender father would feel—such as your own excellent father cherishes; but they are accompanied by a warmth which can only be equalled by their purity; such sentiments shall I ever experience while you continue to deserve them, and every service in my power shall be exerted in your favour. I have long wished for an opportunity of expressing to you the tender care I take in your conduct through life. I now so sensibly feel the necessity of apprizing you of the dangers which surround you, that I waive all forms, and thus abruptly introduce myself to your acquaintance—unknown, indeed, to you, but knowing you well, reading your thoughts, and seeing the secret motives of all your actions. Yes, Julia, I have watched you through life. Nay, start not, I have never seen any action of yours but what had virtue for its guide.—But to remain pure and uncontaminated in this vortex of vice requires the utmost strength and exertion of virtue. To avoid vice, it is necessary to know its colour and complexion; and in this age, how many various shapes it assumes! My task shall be to point them out to you, to show you the traps, the snares, and pitfalls which the unwary too frequently sink into;—to lead you by the hand through those intricate paths beset with quicksands and numberless dangers;—to direct your eyes to such objects as you may with safety contemplate and induce you to shut them forever against such as may by their dire fascination entice you to evil;—to conduct you to those endless joys hereafter, which are to be the reward of the virtuous; and to have myself the ineffable delight of partaking them with you, where no rival shall interrupt my felicity.

I am a Rosicrucian by principle; I need hardly tell you, they are a sect of philosophers who by a life of virtue and self-denial have obtained a heavenly intercourse with aerial beings;—as my internal knowledge of you (to use the expression) is in consequence of my connexion with the Sylphiad tribe, I have assumed the title of my familiar counsellor. This, however, is but a preface to what I mean to say to you;—I have hinted I knew you well;—when I thus expressed myself, it should be understood, I spoke in the person of the Sylph, which I shall occasionally do, as it will be writing with more perspicuity in the first instance; and, as he is employed by me, I may, without the appearance of robbery, safely appropriate to myself the knowledge he gains.

Every human being has a guardian angel; my skill has discovered yours; my power has made him obedient to my will; I have a right to avail myself of the intelligences he gains; and by him I have learnt everything that has passed since your birth;—what your future fortune is to be, even he cannot tell; his view is circumscribed to a small point of time; he only can tell what will be the consequence of taking this or that step, but your free agency prevents his impelling you to act otherwise than as you see fit. I move upon a more enlarged sphere; he tells me what will happen; and as I see the remote, as well as immediate consequence, I shall, from time to time, give you my advice.—Advice, however, when asked, is seldom adhered to; but when given voluntarily, the receiver has no obligation to follow it.—I shall in a moment discover how this is received by you; and your deviation from the rules I shall prescribe will be a hint for me to withdraw my counsel where it is not acceptable. All that then will remain for me will be to deplore your too-early initiation in a vicious world, where to escape unhurt or uncontaminated is next to a miracle.

I said I should soon discover whether my advice would be taken in the friendly part it is offered: I shall perceive it the next time I have the happiness of beholding you, and I see you every day; I am never one moment absent from you in idea, and in my *mind's eye* I see you each moment; only while I conceal myself from you can I be of service to you;—press not then to discover who I am; but be convinced—nay, I shall take every opportunity to convince you—that I am the most sincere and disinterested of your friends; I am a friend to your soul, Julia, and I flatter myself mine is congenial with yours.

I told you you were surrounded with dangers; the greatest perhaps comes from the quarter least suspected; and for that very reason, because, where no harm is expected, no guard is kept. Against such a man as Lord Biddulph, a watchful sentinel is planted at every avenue. I caution you not against him; there you are secure; no temptation lies in that path; no precipice lurks beneath those footsteps. You never can fall unless your heart takes part with the tempter; and I am morally certain a man of Lord Biddulph's craft can never touch yours; and yet it is of him you seem most apprehensive. Ask yourself, is it not because he has the character of a man of intrigue? Do you not feel within your own breast a repugnance to the assiduities he at all times takes pains to show you? Without doubt, Lord Biddulph has designs upon you;—and few men approach you without. Oh! Julia, it is difficult for the most virtuous to behold you daily and suppress those feelings your charms excite. In a breast inured to too-frequent indulgence in vicious courses, your beauty will be a consuming fire; but in a soul whose delight is moral rectitude, it will be a cherishing flame that animates, not destroys. But how few the latter! And how are you to distinguish the insidious betrayer from the open violator? To you they are equally culpable; but only one can be fatal. Ask your own heart—the criterion by which I would have you judge—ask your own heart, which is entitled to your detestation most: the man who boldly attacks you, and by his threats plainly tells you he is a robber, or the one who, under the semblance of imploring your charity, deprives you of your most valued property? Will it admit of a doubt? Make the application: examine your-self, and I conjure you examine your acquaintance; but be cautious whom you trust. Never make any of your male visitors the *confidant* of anything which passes between yourself and husband. This can never be done without a manifest breach of modest decorum. Have I not said enough for the present? Yet let me add thus much, to secure to myself your confi-dence. I wish you to place an unlimited one in me; continue to do so, while I continue to merit it; and by this rule you shall judge of my merit. The moment you discover that I urge you to anything improper or take advantage of my self-assumed office and insolently prescribe when I should only point out or that I should seem to degrade others in your eyes, and particularly your husband, believe me to be an impostor, and treat me as such; disregard my sinister counsel, and consign me to that scorn and derision I shall so much deserve. But, while virtue inspires my pen, afford me your attention; and may that God whom I attest to prove my truth ever be indulgent to you, and forever and ever protect you!

So prays

Your Sylph

Who can it be, my Louisa, who takes this friendly interest in my welfare? It cannot be Lady Melford; the address bespeaks it to be a man; but what man is the question; one too who sees me every day: it cannot be the baron, for he seems to say Ton-hausen is a more dangerous person than Lord Biddulph. But why do I perplex myself with guessing? Of what consequence is it who is my friend, since I am convinced he is sincere? Yes! Thou friendly monitor, I will be directed by thee! I shall now act with more confidence, as my Sylph tells me he will watch over and apprise me of every danger. I hope his task will not be a difficult one; for, though ignorant, I am not obstinate—on the contrary, even Sir William, whom I do not suspect of flattery, allows me to be extremely docile. I am, my beloved Louisa, most affectionately, yours,

Julia Stanley

LETTER 17

To Lady Stanley

Blessed, forever blessed, be the friendly monitor! Oh! My Julia, how fortunate are you, thus to become the care of heaven, which has raised you up a guide with all the dispositions but with more enlarged abilities than thy poor Louisa! And much did you stand in need of a guide, my sister: be not displeased that I write thus. But why do I deprecate your anger? You who were ever so good, so tender, and indulgent to the apprehensions of your friends. Yet, indeed, my dear, you are reprehensible in many passages of your letters, particularly the last. You say you cannot suspect Sir William of flattery; would you wish him to be a flatterer? Did you think him such when he swore your charms had kindled the brightest flames in his bosom? No, Julia, you gave him credit then for all he said: but, allowing him to be changed, are you quite the same? No; with all the tenderness of my affection, I cannot but think you are altered since your departure from the vale of innocent simplicity. It is the knowledge of the world which has deprived you of those native charms above all others. Why are you not resolute with Sir William to leave London? Our acquiescence in matters which are hurtful both to our principles and constitution is a weakness. Obedience to the will of those who seek to seduce us from the right road is no longer a virtue but a reprehensible participation of our leader's faults. Be assured, your husband will listen to your persuasive arguments. Exert all your eloquence; and, Heaven, I beseech thee, grant success to the undertaking of the dearest of all creatures to,

Louisa Grenville

ψ ψ ψ ψ ψ ψ ψ ψ ψ ψ
LETTER 18
ψ ψ ψ ψ ψ ψ ψ ψ ψ ψ

To Miss Grenville

Ah! My dear Louisa, you are single, and know not the trifling influence a woman has over her husband in this part of the world. Had I the eloquence of Demosthenes or Cicero, it would fail. Sir William is wedded—I was going to say, to the pleasures of this bewitching place. I corrected myself in the instant; for, was he wedded, most probably he would be as tired of it as he is of his wife. If I was to be resolute in my determination to leave London, I must go by myself; and, notwithstanding such a circumstance might accord with his wishes, I do not choose to begin the separation. All the determination I can make is to strive to act so as to deserve a better fate than has fallen to my lot. And, beset as I am on all sides, I shall have some little merit in so doing. But you, my love, ought not to blame me so severely as you do. Indeed, Louisa, if you knew the slights I hourly receive from my husband, and the conviction which I have of his infidelity, you would not criticise my expressions so harshly. I could add many more things which would justify me in the eye of the world were I less cautious than I am; but his failings would not extenuate any on my side.

Would you believe that any man who wished to preserve the virtue of his wife would introduce her to the acquaintance and protection of a woman with whom he had had an intrigue? What an opinion one must have in future of such a man! I am indebted for this piece of intelligence to Lord Biddulph. I am grateful for the information, though I despise the motive which induced him. Yes, Louisa! Lady Anne Parker is even more infamous than Lady Besford—nay, Lord Biddulph offered to convince me they still had their private assignations. My pride, I own it, was more wounded than my love from this discovery, as it served to confirm me in my idea that Sir William never had a proper regard for me, but that he married me merely because he could obtain me on no other terms. Yet, although I was sensibly pained with this news, I endeavoured to conceal my emotions from the disagreeable prying eyes of my informer. I affected to disbelieve his assertions and ridiculed his ill-policy in striving to found his merit on such base and detestable grounds. He had too much *effronterie* to be chagrined with my raillery. I therefore assumed a more serious air and plainly told him no man would dare to endeavour to convince a woman of the infidelity of her husband, but from the basest and most injurious motives; and, as such, was entitled to my utmost contempt; that, from my soul, I despised both the information and the informer and should give him proofs of it if ever he should again have the confidence to repeat his private histories to the destruction of the peace and harmony of families. To extenuate his fault, he poured forth a most elaborate speech, abounding with flattery, and was proceeding to convince me of his adoration; but I broke off the discourse by assuring him I saw through his scheme from the first; but the man who sought to steal my heart from my husband must pursue a very different course from that he had followed, as it was very unlikely I should withdraw my affections from one unworthy object to place them on another infinitely worse. He attempted a justification, which I would not allow him opportunity of going on with, as I left the room abruptly. However, his lordship opened my eyes, respecting the conduct of Lady Anne. I have mentioned, in a former letter, that she used to give hints about my husband. I am convinced it was her jealousy which prompted her to give me, from time to time, little anecdotes of Sir William's *amours*. But ought I to pardon him for introducing me to such a woman? Oh! Louisa! Am I to blame if I no longer respect such a man?

Yesterday I had a most convincing proof that there are a sort of people who have all the influence over the heart of a man which a virtuous wife ought to have—but seldom has: by some accident, a hook of Sir William's waistcoat caught hold of the trimming of my sleeve. He had just received a message and, being in a hurry to disengage himself, lifted up the flap of the waistcoat eagerly and snatched it away, by which means, two or three papers dropped out of the pocket; he seemed not to know it, but flew out of the room, leaving them on the ground. I picked them up, but, I take heaven to witness, without the least intention or thought of seeing the contents—when one being open, and seeing my name written in a female hand, and the signature of *Lucy Gardiner,* my curiosity was excited to the greatest degree—yet I had a severe conflict first with myself; but *femaleism* prevailed, and I examined the contents, which were as follows, for I wrote them down:

Is it thus, Sir William, you repay my tenderness in your favour? Go, thou basest of all wretches! Am I to be made continually a sacrifice to every new face that strikes thy inconstant heart? If I was contented to share you with a wife, and calmly acquiesced, do not imagine I shall rest in peace till you have given up Lady Anne. How have you sworn you would see her no more! How have you falsified your oath! You spent several hours *tête-à-tête* with her yesterday. Deny it not. I could tear myself to pieces when I reflect that I left Biddulph, who adored me, whose whole soul was devoted to me,—to be slighted thus by you.—Oh! That Lady Stanley knew of your baseness! Yet she is only your wife. Her virtue may

console her for the infidelity of her husband; but I have sacrificed everything, and how am I repaid! Either be mine alone or never again approach

    Lucy Gardiner

The other papers were of little consequence. I deliberated sometime
what I should do with this precious *morceau;* at last I resolved to burn it
and give the remainder, with as much composure as possible, to Sir William's *valet* to restore to his master. I fancied he would hardly challenge
me about the *billet,* as he is the most careless man in the universe. You will
perceive there is another cause for Lord Biddulph seeking to depreciate my
husband. He has private revenge to gratify, for the loss of his mistress. Oh!
What wretches are these men! Is the whole world composed of such?—No!
Even in this valley of vice I see some exceptions, some who do honour to
the species to which they belong. But I must not whisper to myself their
perfections; and it is less dangerous for me to dwell upon the vices of the
one than the virtues of the other.

    Adieu!

ቑ ቑ ቑ ቑ ቑ ቑ ቑ ቑ ቑ

LETTER 19

ቑ ቑ ቑ ቑ ቑ ቑ ቑ ቑ ቑ

To Miss Grenville

To keep my mind constantly employed upon different objects, and prevent
my thoughts attaching themselves to improper ones, I have lately attended
the card tables. From being an indifferent spectator of the various fashionable games, I became an actor in them; and at length play proved very
agreeable. As I was an utter novice at games of skill, those of chance presented themselves as the best. At first I risked only trifles; but, by little and
little, my party encroached upon the rules I had laid down, and I could no
longer avoid playing their stake. But I have done with play forever. It is no
longer the innocent amusement I thought it; and I must find out some other
method of spending my time—since this might in the end be destructive.

The other night, at a party, we made up a set at bragg, which was my favourite game. After various vicissitudes, I lost every shilling I had in my pocket and, being a broken-merchant, sat silently by the table. Everybody was profuse in the offers of accommodating me with cash; but I refused to accept their contribution. Lord Biddulph, whom you know to be justly my aversion, was very earnest; but I was equally peremptory. However, some-time after, I could not resist the entreaty of Baron Ton-hausen, who, in the genteelest manner, entreated me to make use of his purse for the evening; with great difficulty he prevailed on me to borrow ten guineas—and was once more set up. Fortune now took a favourable turn, and when the party broke up, I had repaid the baron, replaced my original stock, and brought off ninety-five guineas. Flushed with success, and more attached than ever to the game, I invited the set to meet the day after the next at my house. I even counted the hours till the time arrived. Rest departed from my eye-lids, and I felt all the eagerness of expectation.

About twelve o'clock of the day my company were to meet, I received a packet, which I instantly knew to be from my ever-watchful Sylph. I will give you the transcript.

TO LADY STANLEY

I should be unworthy of the character I have assumed if my pen was to lie dormant while I am sensible to the unhappy predilection which your ladyship has discovered for gaming. Play under proper restrictions—which however in this licentious town can never take place—may not be altogether prejudicial to the morals of those who engage in it for trifling sums. Your ladyship finds it not practicable always to follow your own inclinations, even in that particular. The triumphant joy which sparkled in your eyes when success crowned your endeavours plainly indicated you took no common satisfaction in the game. You, being a party so deeply interested, could not discover the same appearances of joy and tri-umph in the countenances of some of those you played with; nor, had you made the observation, could you have guessed the cause. It has been said by those who will say anything to carry on an argument which can-not be supported by reason that cards prevent company falling upon topics of scandal; it is a scandal to human nature that it should want such a resource from so hateful and detested a vice. But be it so. It can only be so while the sum played for is too trifling a concern to excite the anxiety which avaricious minds experience; and everyone is more or less avaricious who gives up his time to cards.

If your ladyship could search into the causes of the unhappiness which prevails in too many families in this metropolis, you would find the source to be gaming either on the one side or the other. Whatever appears licentious or vicious in men, in your sex becomes so in a tenfold degree. The passionate exclamation, the half-uttered imprecation, and the gloomy pallidness of the losing gamester ill accords with the female delicacy. But the evil rests not here. When a woman has been drawn in to lose larger sums than her allowance can defray—even if she can submit to let her tradespeople suffer from her extravagant folly;—it most commonly happens that they part with their honour to discharge the account; at least, they are always suspected. Would not the consideration of being obnoxious to such suspicion be sufficient to deter any woman of virtue from running the hazard? You made a firm resolution of not borrowing from the purses of any of the gentlemen who wished to serve you; you for some time kept that resolution; but remember, it lasted no longer than when one particular person made the offer. Was it your wish to oblige him? Or did the desire of gaming operate in that instant more powerful than in any other? Whatever was your motive, the party immediately began to form hopes of you; hopes which, being founded in your weakness, you may be certain were not to your advantage.

To make a more forcible impression on your mind, your ladyship must allow me to lay before you a piece of private history, in which a noble family of this town was deeply involved. The circumstances are indubitable facts—their names I shall conceal under fictitious ones. A few years since, Lord and Lady D—— were the happiest of pairs in each other. Love had been the sole motive of their union; and love presided over every hour of their lives. Their pleasures were mutual, and neither knew an enjoyment in which the other did not partake. By an unhappy mischance, Lady D—— had an attachment to cards—which yet, however, she only looked on as the amusement of an idle hour. Her person was beautiful, and as such made her an object of desire in the eyes of Lord L. Her virtue and affection for her husband would have been sufficient to have damped the hopes of a man less acquainted with the weakness of human

94

nature than Lord L. Had he paid her a more than ordinary attention, he would have awakened her suspicions and put her on her guard; he therefore pursued another method. He availed himself of her love of play—and would now and then, seemingly by accident, engage her in a party at picquet, which was her favourite game. He contrived to lose trifling sums to increase her inclination for play. Too fatally he succeeded. Her predilection gathered strength every day. After having been very unsuccessful for some hours at picquet, Lord L. proposed a change of the game, a proposal which Lady D—— could not object to, as having won so much of his money. He produced a pair of dice. Luck still ran against him. A generous motive induced Lady D—— to offer him his revenge the next evening at her own house. In the morning preceding the destined evening, her lord signified his dislike of gaming with dice and instanced some families to whom it had proved destructive. Elate, however, with good fortune—and looking on herself engaged in honour to give Lord L. a chance of recovering his losses, she listened not to the hints of her husband, nor did they recur to her thoughts till too late to be of any service to her.

The time so ardently expected by Lord L. now arrived, the devoted time which was to put the long-destined victim into the power of her insidious betrayer. Fortune, which had hitherto favoured Lady D——, now deserted her—in a short time, her adversary reimbursed himself, and won considerably besides. Adversity only rendered her more desperate. She hazarded still larger stakes; every throw, however, was against her; and no otherwise could it be, since his dice were loaded, and which he had the dexterity to change unobserved by her. He lent her money, only to win it back from her; in short, in a few hours, she found herself stripped of all the cash she had in possession, and two thousand five hundred pounds in debt. The disapprobation which her husband had expressed towards dice playing, and her total inability to discharge this vast demand without his knowledge, contributed to make her distress very great. She freely informed Lord L. she must be his debtor for some time—as she could not think of acquainting Lord D—— with her imprudence. He offered to accept of part of her jewels, till it should be convenient to her to pay the whole—or, if she like it better, to play it off. To the first, she said, she could not consent, as her husband would miss them—and to the last she would by no means agree, since she suffered too much already in her own mind from the imprudent part she had acted by risking so much more than she ought to have done. He then, approaching her, took her hand in his and, assuming the utmost tenderness in his air, proceeded to inform her it was in her power amply to repay the debt, without the knowledge of her husband—and confer the highest obligations upon himself. She earnestly begged an explanation—since there was nothing she would not submit to, rather than incur the censure of so excellent a husband. Without further preface, Lord L. threw himself on his knees before her—and said if her heart could not suggest the restitution, which the most ardent of lovers might expect and hope for—he must take the liberty of informing her that bestowing on him the delightful privilege of a husband was the only means of securing her from the resentment of one. At first, she seemed thunderstruck and unable to articulate a sentence. When she recovered the use of speech, she asked him what he had seen in her conduct to induce him to believe she would not submit to any ill consequences which might arise from the just resentment of her husband, rather than not show her detestation of such an infamous proposal. "Leave me," added she. "Leave me," in perfect astonishment at such insolence of behaviour. He immediately rose, with a very different aspect—and holding a paper in his hand, to which she had signed her name in acknowledgement of the debt—"Then, madame," said he, with the utmost *sang-froid*—"I shall, tomorrow morning, take the liberty of waiting on Lord D—— with this."

"Stay, my lord, is it possible you can be so cruel and hard a creditor?— I consent to make over to you my annual allowance, till the whole is discharged."

"No, madame," cried he, shaking his head. "I cannot consent to any such subterfuges, when you have it in your power to pay this moment."

"Would to heaven I had!" answered she.

"Oh, that you have, most abundantly!" said he.—"Consider the hours we have been *tête-à-tête* together; few people will believe we have spent all the time at play. Your reputation then will suffer; and, believe me while I attest heaven to witness, either you must discharge the debt by blessing me with the possession of your charms, or Lord D—— shall be made acquainted with every circumstance. Reflect," continued he, "two thousand five hundred pounds is no small sum, either for your husband to pay or me to receive.—Come, madame, it grows late.—In a little time, you will not have it in your power to avail yourself of the alternative. Your husband will soon return—and then you may wish in vain that you had yielded to my love, rather than have subjected yourself to my resentment."

She condescended to beg of him, on her knees, for a longer time for consideration; but he was inexorable, and at last she fatally consented to her own undoing. The next moment, the horror of her situation, and the sacrifice she had made, rushed on her tortured imagination. "Give me the fatal paper," cried she, wringing her hands in the utmost agony, "give me that paper, for which I have parted with my peace forever, and leave me. Oh! Never let me in future behold you.—What do I say? Ah! Rather let my eyes close in everlasting darkness;—they are now unworthy to behold the face of heaven!"

"And do you really imagine, madame (all-beautiful as you are), the life-less half-distracted body you gave to my arms a recompense for five and twenty hundred pounds?—Have you agreed to your bargain? Is it with tears, sighs, and reluctant struggles you meet your husband's caresses? Be mine as you are his, and the bond is void—otherwise, I am not such a spendthrift as to throw away thousands for little less than a rape."

"Oh! Thou most hateful and perfidious of all monsters! Too dearly have I earned my release—do not then, do not withhold my right."

"Hush, madame, hush," cried he with the most provoking coolness. "Your raving will but expose you to the ridicule of your domestics. You are at present under too great an agitation of spirits to attend to the calm dictates of reason. I will wait till your ladyship is in a more even temper. When I receive your commands, I will attend them, and hope the time will soon arrive when you will be better disposed to listen to a tender lover who adores you, rather than to seek to irritate a man who has you in his power." Saying which, he broke from her leaving her in a state of mind of which you, madame, I sincerely hope, will never be able to form the slightest idea. With what a weight of woe she stole up into her bedchamber, unable to bear the eye of her domestic! How fallen in her own esteem, and still bending under the penalty of her bond, as neither prayers nor tears (and nothing else was she able to offer) could obtain the release from the inexorable and cruel Lord L.

How was her anguish increased when she heard the sound of her lord's footstep! How did she pray for instant death! To prevent any conversation, she feigned sleep—sleep, which now was banished from her eyelids. Guilt had driven the idea of rest from her bosom. The morning brought no comfort on its wings—to her the light was painful. She still continued in bed. She framed the resolution of writing to the destroyer of her repose. She rose for that purpose; her letter was couched in terms that would have pierced the bosom of the most obdurate savage. All the favour she entreated was to spare the best of husbands, and the most amiable and beloved of men, the anguish of knowing how horrid a return she had made, in one fatal moment, for the years of felicity she had tasted with him: again offered her alimony, or even her jewels, to obtain the return of her bond. She did not wish for life. Death was now her only hope;—but she could not support the idea of her infamy. What advantage could he (Lord L.) propose to himself from the possession of her person, since tears, sighs, and the same reluctance would still accompany every repetition of her crime—as her heart, guilty as it now was, and unworthy as she had rendered herself of his love, was, and ever must be, her husband's only. In short, she urged everything likely to soften him in her favour. But this fatal and circumstantial disclosure of her guilt and misfortunes was destined to be conveyed by another messenger than she designed. Lord D——, having that evening expected someone to call on him, on his return enquired if any one had been there.

He was answered, "Only Lord L."

"Did he stay?"

"Yes, till after eleven."—Without thinking of any peculiarity in this, he went up to bed. He discovered his wife was not asleep—to pretend to be so alarmed him. He heard her frequently sigh; and, when she thought him sunk in the peaceful slumber she had forfeited, her distress increased. His anxiety, however, at length gave way to fatigue; but with the morning his doubts and fears returned; yet, how far from guessing the true cause! He saw a letter delivered to a servant with some caution, whom he followed, and insisted on knowing for whom it was intended. The servant, ignorant of the contents, and not at all suspicious he was doing an improper thing, gave it up to his lordship. Revenge lent him wings, and he flew to the base destroyer of his conjugal happiness.—You may suppose what followed.—In an hour Lord D—— was brought home a lifeless corpse. Distraction seized the unhappy wife; and the infamous cause of this dreadful calamity fled his country. He was too hardened, however, in guilt to feel much remorse from this catastrophe and made no scruple of relating the circumstances of it.

To you, madame, I surely need make no comment. Nor do I need say anymore to deter you from so pernicious a practice as gaming. Suspect a Lord L. in everyone who would induce you to play; and remember they are the worst seducers, and the most destructive enemies, who seek to gain your heart by ruining your principles.

Adieu, madame! Your ever watchful angel will still hover over you. And may that God, who formed both you and me, enable me to give you good counsel, and dispose your heart to follow it!

Your faithful Sylph

Alas, my Louisa! What would become of your Julia without this respectable monitor? Would to heaven I knew who he was! Or how I might consult him upon some particular circumstances! I examine the features of my guests in hopes to discover my secret friend; but my senses are perplexed and bewildered in the fruitless search. It is certainly a weakness; but, absolutely, my anxiety to obtain this knowledge has an effect on my health and spirits; my thoughts and whole attention rest solely on this subject. I call it a weakness, because I ought to remain satisfied with the advantages which accrue to me from this correspondence without being inquisitively curious who it may be; yet I wish to ask some questions. I am uneasy, and perhaps in some instances my Sylph would solve my doubts; not that I think him endued with a preternatural knowledge; yet I hardly know what to think neither. However, I bless and praise the goodness of God that has raised me up a friend in a place where I may turn my eyes around and see myself deprived of every other.

Even my protector—he who has sworn before God and man;—but you, Louisa, will reprehend my indiscreet expressions. In my own bosom, then, shall the sad repository be.

Adieu!

LETTER 20

To Miss Grenville

As you have entertained an idea that Sir William could not be proof against any occasional exertion of my eloquence, I will give you a sketch of a matrimonial *tête-à-tête*, though it may tend to subvert your opinion of both parties.

Yesterday morning I was sitting in my dressing room when Sir William, who had not been at home all night, entered it: he looked as if he had not been in bed, his hair disordered, and, upon the whole, as forlorn a figure as you ever beheld, I was going to say; but you form very little idea of these rakes of fashion after a night spent as they usually spend it. To my inquiry after his health, he made a very slight or rather peevish answer and flung himself into a chair, with both hands in his waistcoat pockets and his eyes fixed on the fire, before which he had placed himself. As he seemed in an ill humour, and I was unconscious of having given him cause, I was regardless of the consequences and pursued my employment, which was looking over and settling some accounts relative to my own expenses. He continued his posture in the strictest silence for near a quarter of an hour, a silence I did not feel within myself the least inclination to break through: at last he burst forth into this pretty soliloquy.

"Damn it! Sure there never was a more unfortunate dog than I am! Everything goes against me. And then to be so situated too!"

Unpromising as the opening sounded, I thought it would be better to bear a part in the conversation.—"If it is not impertinent, Sir William," said I, "may I beg to know what occasions the distress you seem to express? Or at least inform me if it is in my power to be of service to you."

"No, no, you can be of no use to me—though," continued he, "you are in part the cause."

"I the cause!—for God's sake, how?" cried I, all astonishment.

"Why, if your father had not taken advantage of my cursed infatuation for you, I should not have been distressed in pecuniary matters by making so large a settlement."

"A cursed infatuation! Do you call it? Sure, that is a harsh expression! Oh! How wretched would my poor father feel could he imagine the affection which he fancied his unhappy daughter had inspired you with would be styled by yourself, and to *her* face, a *cursed infatuation!*" Think you, Louisa, I was not pained to the soul? Too sure I was—I could not prevent tears from gushing forth. Sir William saw the effect his cruel speech had on me; he started from his seat, and took my hand in his. A little resentment, and a thousand other reasons, urged me to withdraw it from his touch.—"Give me your hand, Julia," cried he, drawing his chair close to mine and looking at my averted face,—"give me your hand, my dear, and pardon the rashness of my expressions; I did not mean to use such words;—I recall them, my love: it was ungenerous and false in me to arraign your father's conduct. I would have doubled and trebled the settlement to have gained you; I would, by heavens! My Julia.—Do not run from me in disgust; come, come, you shall forgive me a thoughtless expression, uttered in haste, but seriously repented of."

"You cannot deny your sentiments, Sir William; nor can I easily forget them. What my settlement is, as I never wished to outlive you, so I never wished to know how ample it was. Large I might suppose it to be, from the conviction that you never pay any regard to consequences to obtain your desires, let them be what they will. I was the whim of the day; and if you have paid too dearly for the trifling gratification, I am sorry for it; heartily sorry for it, indeed, Sir William. You found me in the lap of innocence and in the arms of an indulgent parent, happy, peaceful, and serene; would to heaven you had left me there!" I could not proceed; my tears prevented my utterance.

"Pshaw!" cried Sir William, clapping his fingers together and throwing his elbow over the chair which turned his face nearer me. "How ridiculous this is! Why, Julia, I am deceived in you; I did not think you had so much resentment in your composition. You ought to make some allowance for the *derangement* of my affairs. My hands are tied by making a larger settlement than my present fortune would admit; and I cannot raise money on my estate because I have no child, and it is entailed on my uncle, who is the greatest curmudgeon alive. Reflect on all these obstacles to my release from some present exigencies; and do not be so hard-hearted and inexorable to the prayers and entreaties of your husband."—During the latter part of this speech, he put his arm around my waist and drew me almost on his knees, striving by a thousand little caresses to make me pardon and smile on him; but, Louisa, caresses, which I now know came not from the heart, lose the usual effect on me; yet I would not be, as he said, inexorable. I therefore told him I would no longer think of anything he would wish me to forget.—With the utmost appearance of tenderness he took my hand-kerchief and dried my eyes, laying his cheek close to mine and pressing my hands with warmth,—in short, acting over the same farce as (once) in-duced me to believe I had created the most permanent flame in his bosom. I could not bear the reflexion that he should suffer from his former attach-ment to me; and I had hopes that my generosity might rouse him from his lethargy and save him from the ruin which was likely to involve him.

I told him I would with the greatest cheerfulness relinquish any part of my settlement, if by that means he could be extricated from his present and future difficulties.

"Why, to be sure, a part of it would set me to rights as to the present; but as for the future, I cannot look into futurity, Julia."

"I wish you could, Sir William, and reflect in time."

"Reflect! Oh, that is so *outré*! I hate reflexion. Reflexion cost poor D——r his life the other day: he, like me, could not bear reflexion."

"I tremble to hear you thus lightly speak of that horrid event. The more so, as I too much fear the same fatal predilection has occasioned your distress: but may the cheerfulness with which I resign my future depen-dence awaken in you a sense of your present situation and secure you from fresh difficulties!"

"Well said, my little *monitress*! Why you are quite an *orator* too. But you shall find I can follow your lead and be *just* at least, if not so generous as yourself. I would not for the world accept the whole of your jointure. I do not want it; and if I had as much as I could raise on it, perhaps I might not be much richer for it. *Riches make to themselves wings, and fly away*, Julia. There is a sentence for you. Did you think your rattle-pated husband had ever read the book of books from whence that sentence is drawn?"

I really had little patience to hear him run on in this ludicrous and trifling manner. What an argument of his insensibility!

To stop him, I told him I thought we had better not lose time, but have the writings prepared which would enable me to do my duty as an obedient wife and enable him to pay his debts like a man of honour and integrity; and then he need not fear his treasure flying away, since it would be laid up where neither thieves could break through nor rust destroy.

The writings are preparing to dispose of an estate which was settled on me; it brings in at present five hundred a year, which I find is but a quarter of my jointure. Ah! Would to heaven he could take all, provided it would make change in his sentiments! But that I despair of, without the interposition of a miracle. You never saw such an alteration as an hour made in him. So alert and brisk! And apishly fond! I mean affectedly so; for, Louisa, a man of Sir William's cast never could love sincerely,—never could experience that genuine sentimental passion,

> Which, selfish joy disdaining, seeks alone
> to bless the dearer object of its soul.

No, his passions are turbulent—the madness of the moment—eager to please himself—regardless of the satisfaction of the object.—And yet I thought he loved—I likewise thought I loved. Oh! Louisa! How was I deceived! But I check my pen. Pardon me, and, if possible, excuse your sister.

Julia Stanley

☙ ☙ ☙ ☙ ☙ ☙ ☙ ☙ ☙ ☙

LETTER 21

☙ ☙ ☙ ☙ ☙ ☙ ☙ ☙ ☙ ☙

To Colonel Montague

What are we to make of this divine and destructive beauty? This Lady Stanley? Did you not observe with what eager avidity she became a votary to the gaming table and bragged away with the best of us? You must: you was witness to the glow of animation that reigned despotic over every lovely feature when she had got a pair-royal of braggers in her snowy fingers. But I am confoundedly bit! She condescended to borrow of that pattern of Germanic virtue, Baron Ton-hausen. Perhaps you will say, Why did not you endeavour to be the Little Premium? No, I thought I played a better game: it was better to be the second lender; besides, I only wanted to excite in her a passion for play; and, or I am much deceived, never a woman entered into it with more zeal. But what a turn to our affairs! I am absolutely cast off the scent, totally ignorant of the doubles she has made. I could hardly close my eyes from the pleasing expectations I had formed of gratifying the wishes of my heart in both those interesting passions of love and revenge. Palpitating with hopes and fears, I descended from my chariot at the appointed hour. The party were assembled, and my devoted victim looked as beautiful as an angel of light; her countenance wore a solemnity, which added to her charms by giving an irresistible and persuasive softness to her features. I scrutinized the lineaments of her lovely face; and, I assure you, she lost nothing by the strict examination. Gods! What a transporting creature she is! And what an insensible brute is Stanley! But I recall my words, as to the last;—he was distractedly in love with her before he had her; and perhaps, if she was *my* wife, I should be as indifferent about her as *he* is, or as *I* am about the numberless women of all ranks and conditions with which I have "trifled away the dull hours."—While I was in contemplation anticipating future joys, I was struck all of a heap, as the country girls say, by hearing Lady Stanley say,—"It is in vain—I have made a firm resolution never to play again; my resolution is the result of my own reflexions on the uneasiness which those bits of painted paper have already given me. It is altogether fruitless to urge me; for from the determination I have made, I shall never recede. My former winnings are in the sweepstake pool at the commerce table, which you will extremely oblige me to sit down to; but for me, I play no more.—I shall have a pleasure in seeing you play; but I own I feel myself too much discomposed with ill fortune; and I am not unreasonable enough to be pleased with the misfortunes of others. I have armed my mind against the shafts of ridicule that I see pointed at me; but, while I leave others the full liberty of following their own schemes of diversion, I dare say, none will refuse me the same privilege."—We all stared with astonishment; but the devil a one offered to say a word, except against sitting down to divide her property;—there we entered into a general protest; so we set down, at least I can answer for myself, to an insipid game.—Lady Stanley was marked down as a fine *pigeon* by some of our ladies, and as a delicious *morceau* by the men. The gentle baron seemed all aghast. I fancy he is a little disappointed in his expectations too.—Perhaps he has formed hopes that his soft sighs and respectful behaviour may have touched the lovely Julia's heart. He felt himself flattered no doubt at her giving him the preference in borrowing from his purse. Well then, his hopes are *dérangé,* as well as mine.—But, *courage, mi lord,* I shall play another game now; and peradventure as safe a one, if not more so, than what I planned before.—I will not, however, anticipate a pleasure (which needs no addition should I succeed) or add to my mortification should I fail by expatiating on it at present.

Adieu! Dear Montague! Excuse my *boring* you with these trifles;—for to a man in love, everything is trifling except the *trifle* that possesses his heart; and to one who is not under the guidance of the *soft deity, that* is the *greatest* trifle (to use a Hibernicism) of all.

I am yours most cordially,

Biddulph

ᚼ ᚼ ᚼ ᚼ ᚼ ᚼ ᚼ ᚼ ᚼ ᚼ
LETTER 22
ᚼ ᚼ ᚼ ᚼ ᚼ ᚼ ᚼ ᚼ ᚼ ᚼ

To Miss Grenville

Well, my dear Louisa, the important point I related the particulars of in my last is quite settled, and Sir William has been able to satisfy some rapacious creditors. Would to heaven I could tell you, the butcher, baker, &c., were in the list! No, my sister; the creditors are a vile set of gamblers, or, in the language of the *polite* world—*blacklegs.* Thus is the purpose of my heart entirely frustrated and the laudably industrious tradesman defrauded of his due. But how long will they remain satisfied with being repeatedly put by with empty promises, which are never kept? Good God! How is this to end? I give myself up to the most gloomy reflexions and see no point of time when we shall be extricated from the cruel dilemmas in which Sir William's imprudence has involved us. I vainly fancied I should gain some advantages, at least raise myself in his opinion, from my generosity; but I find, on the contrary, he only laughs at me for being such a simpleton to suppose the sale of five hundred a year would set him to rights. It is plain I have got no credit by my condescension, for he has not spent one day at home since; and his temper, when I do see him, seems more uncertain than ever.—Oh! Louisa! And do all young women give up their families, their hand, and virgin affections to be thus recompensed? But why do I let fall these expressions? Alas! They fall with my tears; and I can no more suppress the one than the other; I ought, however, and indeed do endeavour against both. I seek to arm my soul to support the evils with which I see myself surrounded. I beseech heaven to afford me strength, for I too plainly see I am deprived of all other resources. I forget to caution you, my dear sister, against acquainting my father that I have given up my part of my jointure; and lest, when I am unburdening the weight of my over-charged bosom to you, I should in future omit this cautionary reserve, do you, my Louisa, keep those little passages a secret within your own kind, sympathizing breast and add not to my affliction by planting such daggers in the heart of my dear—more dear than ever—parent? You know I have pledged my honour to you; I will never, by my own conduct, accumulate the distresses this fatal union has brought on me. Though every vow on his part is broken through, yet I will remember I am *his* wife,—and, what is more, *your* sister. Would you believe it? He—Sir William I mean—is quite displeased that I have given up cards and very politely told me I should be looked on as a fool by all his acquaintances,—and himself not much better, for marrying such an ignorant uninstructed rustic. To this tender and husband-like speech, I returned no other answer than that my conscience should be the rule and guide of my actions; and *that,* I was certain, would never lead me to disgrace him. I left the room, as I found some difficulty in stifling the resentment which rose at his indignant treatment. But I shall grow callous in time; I have so far conquered my weakness, as never to let a tear drop in his presence. Those indications of self-sorrow have no effect on him, unless, indeed, he had any point to gain by it; and then he would feign a tenderness foreign to his nature, but which might induce the ignorant uninstructed fool to yield up everything to him.

Perhaps he knows it not; but I might have instructors enough;—but he has taught me sufficient of evil, thank God!—to make me despise them all. From my unhappy connexions with one, I learn to hate and detest the whole race of rakes; I might add, of both sexes. I tremble to think what I might have been had I not been blessed with a virtuous education and had the best of patterns in my beloved sister. Thus I was early initiated in virtue; and let me be grateful to my kind Sylph, whose knowledge of human nature has enabled him to be so serviceable to me: he is a sort of second conscience to me:—What would the Sylph say? I whisper to myself. Would he approve? I flatter myself that, insignificant as I am, I am yet in the care of heaven; and while I depend on that merciful Providence and its vicegerents, I shall not fall into those dreadful pits that are open on every side: but, to strengthen my reliances, let me have the prayers of my dear Louisa, for every support is necessary for her faithful Julia.

LETTER 23

To the Same

I have repeatedly mentioned to my Louisa how earnestly I wished to have more frequent communications with my Sylph. A thought struck me the other day of the practicability of effecting such a scheme. I knew I was safe from detection, as no one on earth, yourself excepted, knew of his agency in my affairs. I therefore addressed an advertisement to my invisible friend, which I sent to the *St. James's Chronicle,* couched in this concise manner.

TO THE SYLPH

Grateful for the friendly admonition, the receiver of the Sylph's favour is desirous of having the power of expressing it more largely than is possible through this channel. If still entitled to protection, begs to be informed how a private letter may reach his hand.

I have not leisure nor inclination to make a long digression, or would tell you the *St. James's* is a newspaper which is the fashionable vehicle of intelligence; and from the circumstance alone of its admission into all families, and meeting all eyes, I chose it to convey my wishes to the Sylph. The next evening I had the satisfaction of finding those wishes answered, and the further pleasure (as you will see by the enclosed copy) of being assured of his approbation of the step I have taken.

And now for a little of family affairs. You know I have a certain allowance of what is called pin money;—my quarter having been due for some time, I thought I might as well have it in my own possession,—not that I am poor, for I assure you on the contrary, I have generally a quarter in hand, though I am not in debt. I sent Win to Harris, the steward, for my stipend. She returned with his duty to me, acquainting me it was not in his power at present to honour my note, not having any cash in hand. Surprised at his inability of furnishing a hundred and fifty pounds, I desired to speak with him, when he gave me so melancholy a detail of his master's circumstances as makes me dread the consequences. He is surrounded with Jew brokers, for, in this Christian land, Jews are the money negotiators; and such wretches as you would tremble to behold are admitted into the private recesses of the Great and caressed as their better angels. These infernal agents procure them money, for which they pay fifty, a hundred, and sometimes two hundred percent. Am I wrong in styling them *infernal*? Do they not make the silly people who trust in them pay very dear for the means of accomplishing their own destruction? Like those miserable beings they used to call *witches*, who were said to sell their souls to the Devil for everlasting to have the power of doing temporary mischief upon earth.

These now form the bosom associates of my husband. Ah! Wonder not the image of thy sister is banished thence! Rather rejoice with me that he pays that reverence to virtue and decency as to distinguish me from that dreadful herd of which his chief companions are composed.

I go very little from home.—In truth, I have no creature to go with.—I avoid Lord Biddulph, because I hate him; and (dare I whisper it to my Louisa?) I estrange myself from the baron lest I should be too partial to the numerous good qualities I cannot but see, and yet which it would be dangerous to contemplate too often. Oh, Louisa! Why are there not many such men? His merit should not so forcibly strike me if I could find anyone in the circle of my acquaintances who could come in competition with him, for, be assured, it is not the tincture of the skin which I admire, not because *fairest*, but *best*. But where shall a married woman find excuse to seek for, and admire, merit in any other than her husband? I will banish this too, too amiable man from my thoughts. As my Sylph says, such men (under the circumstances I am in) are infinitely more dangerous than a Biddulph. Yet, can one fall by the hand of virtue?—Alas! This is deceitful sophistry. If I give myself up to temptation, how dare I flatter myself I shall *be delivered from evil?*

Could two men be more opposite than what Sir William appeared at Woodley Vale and what he now is?—For too surely *that* was appearance—*this* reality. Think of him then sitting in your library, reading by turns with my dear father some instructive and amusing author, while *we* listened to their joint comments; what lively sallies we discovered in him; and how we all united in approving the natural flow of good spirits, chastened as we thought with the principles of virtue! See him now—but my pen refuses to draw the pain-inspiring portrait. Alas! It would but be a copy of what I have so repeatedly traced in my frequent letters, a copy from which we should turn with disgust, bordering on contempt. This we should do were the character unknown or indifferent to us. But how must that woman feel—who sees in the picture the well-known features of a man whom she is bound by her vows to love, honour, and obey? Your tenderness, my sister, will teach you to pity so unhappy a wretch. I will not, however, tax that tenderness too much. I will not dwell on the melancholy theme.

But I lose sight of my purpose, in thus contrasting Sir William *to himself;* I meant to infer, from the total change which seems to have taken place in him, that other men may be the same, could the same opportunity of developing their characters present itself. Thus, though the baron wears this semblance of an angel—yet it may be assumed. What will not men do to carry a favourite point? He saw the open and avowed principles of libertinism in Lord Biddulph disgusted me from the first. He, therefore, may conceal the same invidious intention under the seducing form of every virtue. The simile of the robber and the beggar, in the Sylph's first letter, occurs to my recollection. Yet, perhaps, I am injuring the baron by my suspicion. He may have had virtue enough to suppress those feelings in my favour, which my situation should certainly destroy in a virtuous breast.—Nay, I believe, I may make myself wholly easy on that head. He has, for some time, paid great attention to Miss Finch, who, I find, has totally broke with Colonel Montague. Certainly, if we should pay any deference to appearance, she will make a much better election by choosing Baron Tonhausen than the colonel. She has lately—Miss Finch, I should say—has lately spent more time with me than any other lady—for my two first companions I have taken an opportunity of civilly dropping. I took care to be from home whenever they called by *accident*—and always to have some *prior* engagement when they proposed meeting by *design.*

Miss Finch is by much the least reprehensible character I have met with.—But, as Lady Besford once said, one can form no opinion of what a woman is while she is single. *She* must keep within the rules of decorum. The single state is not a state of freedom. Only the married ladies have that privilege. But, as far as one can judge, there is no danger in the acquaintance of Miss Finch. I own, I like her for having refused Colonel Montague, and yet (Oh! Human nature!), on looking over what I have written, I have expressed myself disrespectfully on the supposition that she saw Ton-hausen with the same eyes as a certain foolish creature that shall be nameless.

ᵜ ᵜ ᵜ ᵜ ᵜ ᵜ ᵜ ᵜ ᵜ ᵜ

LETTER 24

ᵜ ᵜ ᵜ ᵜ ᵜ ᵜ ᵜ ᵜ ᵜ ᵜ

To Lady Stanley

[*Enclosed in the foregoing.*]

The satisfaction of a benevolent heart will ever be its own recompense, but not its *only* reward, as you have sweetly assured me, by the advertisement that blessed my eyes last night. I beheld, with pleasure, that my admonitions have not lost their intended effect. I should have been most cruelly disappointed, and have given up my knowledge of the human heart as imperfect, had I found you incorrigible to my advice. But I have heretofore told you I was thoroughly acquainted with the excellencies of your mind. Your renunciation of your favourite game, and cards in general, give every reason to justify my sentiments of you. I have formed the most exalted idea of you.—And you alone can destroy the altar I have raised to your divinity. All the incense I dare hope to receive from you is a just and implicit observance of my dictates, while they are influenced by virtue, of which none but you can properly judge, since to none but yourself *they* are addressed. Doubts, I am convinced, may arise in your mind concerning this invisible agency. As far as is necessary, I will satisfy those doubts. But to be forever concealed from your knowledge as to identity, your own good sense will see too clearly the necessity of, to need any illustration from my pen. If I admired you before—how much has that admiration increased from the cheerful acquiescence you have paid to my injunctions! Go on, then, my beloved charge! Pursue the road of *virtue;* and be assured, however rugged the path and tedious the way, you will, one day, arrive at the goal and find *her* "in her own form—how lovely!" I had almost said as lovely as yourself.

Perhaps, you will think this last expression too warm and savouring more of the man—than the Rosicrucian philosopher.—But be not alarmed. By the most rigid observance of virtue it is we attain this superiority over the rest of mankind; and only by this course can we maintain it—we are not, however, divested of our sensibilities; nay, I believe, as they have not been vitiated by contamination, they are more *tremblingly alive* than other mortals usually are. In the human character, I could be of no use to you; in the Sylphiad, of the utmost. Look on me, then, only in the light of a preternatural being—and, if my sentiments should sometimes flow in a more earthly style—yet, take my word as a Sylph, they shall never be such as shall corrupt your heart. To guard it from the corruptions of mortals is my sole view in the lecture I have given, or shall from time to time give you.

I saw and admired the laudable motive which induced you to give up part of your settlement. Would to heaven, for your sake, it had been attended with the happy consequences you flattered yourself with seeing. Alas! All the produce of that is squandered after the rest. Beware how you are prevailed on to resign anymore; for, I question not, you will have application made you very soon for the remainder, or at least part of it: but take this advice of your true and disinterested friend. The time may come, and from the unhappy propensities of Sir William I much fear it will not be long ere it does come, when both he and you may have no other resource than what your jointure affords you. By this ill-placed benevolence you will deprive yourself of the means of supporting him, when all other means will have totally failed. Let this be your plea to resist his importunities.

When you shall be disposed to make me the repository of your confidential thoughts, you may direct to A.B. at Anderton's Coffee House. I rely on your prudence to take no measures to discover me. May you be as happy as you deserve, or, in one word, as I wish you!

Your careful

Sylph

ᵭᵭᵭᵭᵭᵭᵭᵭᵭ
LETTER 25
ᵭᵭᵭᵭᵭᵭᵭᵭᵭ

To the Sylph

It is happy for me if my actions have stood so much in my favour as to make any return for the obligations which I feel I want words to express. Alas! What would have become of me without the friendly, the paternal admonitions of my kind Sylph! Spare me not, tell me all my faults—for, notwithstanding your partiality, I find them numerous. I feel the necessity of having those admonitions often enforced, and am apprehensive I shall grow troublesome to you.

Will, then, my friend allow me to have recourse to him on any important occasion—or what may appear so to me? Surely an implicit observance of his precepts will be the least return I can make for his disinterested interposition in my favour—and thus, as it were, stepping in between me and ruin. Believe me, my heart overflows with a grateful sense of these unmerited benefits—and feels the strongest resolution to persevere in the paths of rectitude so kindly pointed out to me by the hand of heaven.

I experience a sincere affliction that the renunciation of part of my future subsistence should not have had the desired effect, but *none* that I have parted with it. My husband is young, and blest with a most excellent

112

constitution, which even *his* irregularities have not injured. I am young likewise, but of a more delicate frame, which the repeated hurries I have for many months past lived in (joined to a variety of other causes, from anxieties and inquietude of mind) have not a little impaired so that I have not a remote idea of living to want what I have already bestowed, or may hereafter resign, for the benefit of my husband's creditors. Yet in this, as well as everything else, I will submit to your more enlightened judgment—and abide most cheerfully by your decision.

Would to heaven Sir William would listen to such an adviser! He yet might retrieve his affairs. We yet might be happy. But, alas! He will not suffer his reason to have any sway over his actions. He hurries on to ruin with hasty strides—nor ever casts one look behind.

The perturbation these sad reflexions create in my bosom will apologize to my worthy guide for the abruptness of this conclusion, as well as the incorrectness of the whole. May heaven reward you!—prays your ever grateful,

Julia Stanley

LETTER 26

To Miss Grenville

I feel easier in my mind, my dearest Louisa, since I have established a sort of correspondence with the Sylph. I can now, when any intricate circumstance arises which your distance may disable you from being serviceable in, have an almost immediate assistance in, or at least the concurrence of— my Sylph, my guardian angel!

In a letter I received from him the other day, he told me a time might come when he should lose his influence over me; however remote the period, as there was a possibility of his living to see it, the *idea* filled his mind with sorrow. The only method his skill could divine, of still possessing the privilege of superintending my concerns, would be to have some pledge from me. He flattered himself I should not scruple to indulge this only weakness of *humanity* he discovered, since I might rest assured he had it neither in his will nor inclination to make an ill use of my condescension. The rest of the letter contained advice as usual. I only made this extract to tell you my determination on this head. I think to send a little locket with my hair in it. The *design* I have formed in my own mind and, when it is completed, will describe it to you.

I have seriously reflected on what I had written to you in my last concerning Miss Finch and (let me not practise disingenuity to my beloved sister) the Baron Ton-hausen. Miss Finch called on me yesterday morning—she brought her work. "I am come," said she, "to spend some hours with you."

"I wish," returned I, "you would enlarge your plan and make it the whole day."

"With all my heart," she replied, "if you are to be alone, for I wish to have a good deal of chat with you, and hope we shall have no male impertinents break in upon our little female *tête-à-tête*."

I knew Sir William was out for the day, and gave orders I should not be at home to anyone.

As soon as we were quite by ourselves, "Lord!" said she, "I was monstrously flurried coming hither, for I met Montague in the park and could hardly get clear of him—I was fearful he would follow me here." As she first mentioned him, I thought it gave me a kind of right to ask her some questions concerning that gentleman and the occasion of her rupture with him. She answered me very candidly—"To tell you the truth, my dear Lady Stanley, it is but lately I had much idea that it was necessary to love one's husband in order to be happy in marriage."

"You astonish me," I cried.

"Nay, but hear me. Reflect how we young women who are born in the air of the court are bred. Our heads are filled with nothing but pleasure—let the means of procuring it be, almost, what you will. We marry—but without any notion of its being a union for life—only a few years; and then we make a second choice. But I have lately thought otherwise; and in consequence of these my more serious reflexions am convinced Colonel Montague and I might make a fashionable couple, but never a happy one. I used to laugh at his gaieties and foolishly thought myself flattered by the attentions of a man whom half my sex had found dangerous; but I never loved him; that I am now more convinced of than ever; and as to reforming his morals—oh! It would not be worth the pains, if the thing was possible.

"Let the women be ever so exemplary, their conduct will have no influence over these professed rakes, these rakes upon principle, as that iniquitous Lord Chesterfield has taught our youth to be. Only look at yourself, I do not mean to flatter you; what effect has your mildness, your thousand and ten thousand good qualities, for I will not pretend to enumerate them, had over the mind of your husband? None. On my conscience, I believe it has only made him worse, because he knew he never should be censured by such a pattern of meekness. And what chance should such a one as I have with one of these *modern* husbands? I fear me, I should become a *modern* wife. I think I am not vain-glorious when I say I have not a bad heart and am ambitious of emulating a good example. On these considerations alone, I resolved to give the colonel his dismission. He pretended to be much hurt by my determination; but I really believe the loss of my fortune his greatest disappointment, as, I find, he has two, if not more, mistresses to console him."

"It would hardly be fair," said I, "after your candid declaration, to call any part in question, or else I should be tempted to ask you if you had really no other motive for your rejection of the colonel's suit?"

"You scrutinize pretty closely," returned Miss Finch, blushing. "But I will make no concealments; I have a man in my eye, with whom, I think, the longer the union lasted, the happier I, at least, should be."

"Do I know the happy man?"

"Indeed you do; and one of some consequence too."

"It cannot be Lord Biddulph?"

"Lord Biddulph!—No, indeed!—Not Lord Biddulph, I assure your ladyship; tho' *he* has a title, but not an English one."

To you, my dear Louisa, I use no reserve. I felt a sickishness and chill all over me; but recovering instantly, or rather, I fear, desirous of appearing unaffected by what she said, I immediately rejoined—"So then, I may wish the *baron* joy of his conquest." A faint smile, which barely concealed my anguish, accompanied my speech.

"Why should I be ashamed of saying I think the baron the most amiable man in the world? Tho' it is but lately I have allowed his superior merit the preference; indeed, I did not know so much of him as within these few weeks I have had opportunity."

"He is certainly very amiable," said I. "But don't you think it very close?" (I felt ill.) "I believe I must open the window for a little air. Pursue your panegyric, my dear Miss Finch. I was rather overcome by the warmth of the day; I am better now—pray proceed."

"Well then, it is not because he is handsome that I give him this preference, for I do not know whether Montague has not a finer person. Observe, I make this a doubt, for I think those marks of the smallpox give an additional expression to his features. What say you?"

"I am no competent judge," I answered, "but, in my opinion, those who do most justice to Baron Ton-hausen will forget, or overlook, the graces of his person in the contemplation of the more estimable, because more permanent, beauties of his mind."

"What an elegant panegyrist you are! In three words you have comprised his eulogium, which I should have spent hours about, and not so completed at last. But the opportunity I hinted at having had of late, of discovering more of the baron's character, is this: I was one day walking in the park with some ladies; the baron joined us; a well-looking old man, but meanly dressed, met us; he fixed his eyes on Ton-hausen; he started, then, clasping his hands together, exclaimed with eagerness, 'It is, it must be he! O, sir! O, thou best of men!' 'My good friend,' said the baron, while his face was crimsoned over, 'my good friend, I am glad to see you in health, but be more moderate.' I never before thought him handsome; but such a look of benevolence accompanied his soft accents that I fancied him something more than mortal. 'Pardon my too lively expressions,' the old man answered, 'but gratitude—oh for such benefits! You, sir, may, and have a right to command my lips; but my eyes—my eyes will bear testimony.' His voice was now almost choked with sobs, and the tears flowed plentifully. I was extremely moved at this scene, and had likewise a little female curiosity excited to develop this mystery. I saw the baron wished to conceal his own and the old man's emotions, so walked a little aside with him. I took that opportunity of whispering my servant to find out, if possible, where this man came from and discover the state of this adventure. The ladies and myself naturally were chatting on this subject when the baron rejoined our party. 'Poor fellow,' said he, 'he is so full of gratitude for my having rendered a slight piece of service to his family and fancies he owes every blessing in life to me, for having placed two or three of his children out in the world.' We were unanimous in praising the generosity of the baron and were making some reflexions on the infrequency of such examples among the affluent when Montague came up; he begged to know on whom we were so severe; I told him in three words—and pointed to the object of the baron's bounty. He looked a little chagrined, which I attributed to my commendations of this late instance of worth, as, I believe, I expressed myself with that generous warmth which a benevolent action excites in a breast capable of feeling, and wishing to emulate, such patterns. After my return home, my servant told me he had followed the old man to his lodgings, which were in an obscure part of the town, where he saw him received by a woman nearly his own age, a beautiful girl of eighteen, and two little boys. James, who is rather an *adroit* fellow, further said that, by way of introduction, he told them to whom he was servant, that his lady was attached to their interest from something the baron had mentioned concerning them, and had, in earnest of her future intentions, sent them a half guinea. At the name of the baron, the old folks lifted up their hands and blessed him; the girl blushed and cast down her eyes; and, said James, 'I thought, my lady, she seemed to pray for him with greater fervour than the rest.' 'He is the noblest of men!' echoed the old pair. 'He is indeed!' sighed the young girl. 'My heart, my lady, ran over at my eyes to see the thankfulness of these poor people. They begged me to make their grateful acknowledgments to your ladyship for your bounty and hoped the worthy baron would convince you it was not thrown away on base or forgetful folks.' James was not farther inquisitive about their affairs, judging, very properly, that I should choose to make some inquiries myself.

"The next day I happened to meet the baron at your house. I hinted to him how much my curiosity had been excited by the adventure in the park. He made very light of it, saying his services were only common ones; but that the object having had a tolerable education, his expressions were rather adapted to his own feelings than to the merit of the benefit. 'Ah! Baron,' I cried, 'there is more in this affair than you think proper to communicate. I shall not cease persecuting you till you let me a little more into it. I feel myself interested, and you must oblige me with a recital of the circumstances, for which purpose I will set you down in my *vis-à-vis.*'

"'Are you not aware, my dear Miss Finch, of the pain you will put me to in resounding my own praise?—What can be more perplexing to a modest man?'

"'A truce with your modesty in this instance,' I replied; 'be *just* to yourself, and *generously indulgent* to me.'

"He bowed, and promised to gratify my desire.

"When we were seated, 'I will now obey you, madame,' said the baron. 'A young fellow, who was the lover of the daughter to the old man you saw yesterday, was inveigled by some soldiers to enlist in Colonel Montague's regiment. The present times are so critical that the idea of a soldier's life is full of terror in the breast of a tender female. Nancy Johnson was in a state of distraction, which the consciousness of her being rather too severe in a late dispute with her lover served to heighten, as she fancied herself the cause of his resolution. Being a fine young man of six feet, he was too eligible an object for the colonel to wish to part from. Great intercession, however, was made, but to no effect, for he was ordered to join the regiment. You must conceive the distress of the whole family; the poor girl brokenhearted, her parents hanging over her in anguish, and, ardent to restore the peace of mind of their darling, forming the determination of coming up to town to solicit his discharge from the colonel. By accident I became acquainted with their distressed situation and, from my intimacy with Montague, procured them the blessing they sought for. I have provided him with a small place and made a trifling addition to her portion. They are shortly to be married, and of course, I hope happy. And now, madame,' he continued, 'I have acquitted myself of my engagement to you.'

"I thanked him for his recital and said I doubted not his pleasure was near as great as theirs, for to a mind like his, a benevolent action must carry a great reward with it.

"'Happiness and pleasure,' he answered, 'are both comparative in some degree; and to feel them in their most exquisite sense, must be after having been deprived of them for a long time—we see ourselves possessed of them when hope had forsaken us. When the happiness of man depends on relative objects, he will be frequently liable to disappointment. I have found it so. I have seen every prop on which I had built my schemes of felicity sink one after the other; no other resource was then left but to endeavour to form that happiness in others, which fate had forever prevented my enjoying; and when I succeed, I feel a pleasure which for a moment prevents obtruding thoughts from rankling in my bosom. But I ask your pardon—I am too serious—tho' my *tête-à-têtes* with the ladies are usually so.'

"I told him such reflexions as his conversation gave rise to excited more heartfelt pleasure than the broadest mirth could e'er bestow; that *I* too was serious, and I hoped should be a better woman as long as I lived from the resolution I had formed of attending, for the future, to the happiness of others more than I had done. Here our conversation ended, for we arrived at his house. I went home full of the idea of the baron and his recital, which, tho' I gave him credit for, I did not implicitly believe, at least as to circumstance, tho' I might to substance. I was kept waking the whole night in comparing the several parts of the baron's and James's accounts. In short, the more I ruminated, the more I was convinced there was more in it than the baron had revealed; and Montague being an actor in the play did not a little contribute to my desire of *peeping behind the curtain* and having the whole *drama* before me. Accordingly, as soon as I had breakfasted, I ordered my carriage and took James for my guide. When we came to the end of the street, I got out, and away I tramped to Johnson's lodgings. I made James go up first and apprise them of my coming; and, out of the goodness of his heart, in order to relieve their minds from the perplexity which inferiority always excites, James told them I was the best lady in the world and might, for charity, pass for the baron's sister. I heard this as I ascended the staircase. But, when I entered, I was really struck with the figure of the young girl. Divested of all ornament—without the aid of dress, or any external advantage, I think I never beheld a more beautiful object. I apologized for the abruptness of my appearance amongst them, but added I doubted not, as a friend of the baron's and an encourager of merit, I should not be unwelcome; I begged them to go on with their several employments. They received me with that kind of embarrassment which is usual with people circumstanced as they are, who fancy themselves under obligations to the affluent for treating them with common civility. That they might recover their spirits, I addressed myself to the two little boys and emptied my pockets to amuse them. I told the good old pair what the baron had related to me, but fairly added, I did not believe he had told me all the truth, which I attributed to his delicacy. 'Oh!' said the young girl, 'with the best and most noble of minds, the baron possesses the greatest delicacy; but I need not tell you so; you, madame, I doubt not, are acquainted with his excellencies; and may he, in you, receive his earthly reward for the good he has done to us! Oh, madame! He has saved me, both soul and body; but for him, I had been the most undone of all creatures. Sure he was our better angel, sent down to stand between us and destruction.'

"'Wonder not, madame,' said the father, 'at the lively expressions of my child; gratitude is the best master of cloquence; she feels, madame—we all feel the force of the advantages we derive from that worthy man. Good God! What had been our situation at this moment had we not owed our deliverance to the baron!'

"'I am not,' said I, 'entirely acquainted with the whole of your story; the baron, I am certain, concealed great part; but I should be happy to hear the particulars.'

"The old man assured me he had a pleasure in reciting a tale which reflected so much honour on the baron; 'and let me,' said he, 'in the pride of my heart, let me add, no disgrace on me or mine; for, madame, poverty, in the eye of the right-judging, is no disgrace. Heaven is my witness, I never repined at my lowly station till by that I was deprived of the means of rescuing my beloved family from their distress. But what would riches have availed me had the evil befallen me from which that godlike man extricated us? Oh! Madame, the wealth of worlds could not have conveyed one ray of comfort to my heart if I could not have looked all round my family, and said, "Tho' we are poor, we are virtuous, my children."'

"'It would be impertinent to trouble you, madame, with a prolix account of my parentage and family. I was once master of a little charity school, but by unavoidable misfortunes I lost it. My eldest daughter, who sits there, was tenderly beloved by a young man in our village, whose virtues would have reflected honour on the most elevated character. He did ample justice to his merit. We looked forward to the *happy* hour that was to render our child so and had formed a thousand little schemes of rational delight to enliven our evening of life; in one short moment the sun of our joy was overcast and promised to set in lasting night. On a fatal day, my Nancy was seen by a gentleman in the army, who was down on a visit to the neighbouring squire, my landlord; her figure attracted his notice, and he followed her to our peaceful dwelling. Her mother and I were absent with a sick relation, and her protector was out at work with a farmer at some distance. He obtruded himself into our house and begged a draught of ale; my daughter, whose innocence suspected no ill, freely gave him a mug, of which he just sipped; then, putting it down, swore he would next taste the nectar of her lips. She repelled his boldness with all her strength, which, however, would have availed her but little had not our next-door neighbour, seeing a fine-looking man follow her in, harboured a suspicion that all was not right and taken an opportunity of coming in to borrow something. Nancy was happy to see her and begged her to stay till our return, pretending she could not procure her what she wanted till then. Finding himself disappointed, Colonel Montague (I suppose, madame, you know him) went away, when Nancy informed our neighbour of his proceedings. She had hardly recovered herself from her perturbation when we came home. I felt myself exceedingly alarmed at her account, more particularly as I learnt the colonel was a man of intrigue and proposed staying some time in the country. I resolved never to leave my daughter at home by herself, or suffer her to go out without her intended husband. But the vigilance of a fond father was too easily eluded by the subtleties of an enterprising man who spared neither time nor money to compass his illaudable schemes. By presents he corrupted that neighbour, whose timely interposition had preserved my child inviolate. From the friendship she had expressed for us, we placed the utmost confidence in her and, next to ourselves, entrusted her with the future welfare of our daughter. When the outposts are corrupted, what *fort* can remain unendangered? It is, I believe, a received opinion that more women are seduced from the path of virtue by their own sex than by ours. Whether it is that the unlimited faith they are apt to put in their own sex weakens the barriers of virtue and renders them less powerful against the attacks of the men or that, suspecting no sinister view, they throw off their guard, it is certain that an artful and vicious woman is infinitely a more to be dreaded companion than the most abandoned libertine. This false friend used from time to time to administer the poison of flattery to the tender unsuspicious daughter of innocence. What female is free from the seeds of vanity? And unfortunately, this bad woman was but too well versed in this destructive art. She continually was introducing instances of handsome girls who had made their fortunes merely from that circumstance. That, to be sure, the young man, her sweetheart, had merit; but what a pity a person like hers should be lost to the world! That she believed the colonel to be too much a man of honour to seduce a young woman, though he might like to divert himself with them. What a fine opportunity it would be to raise her family, like *Pamela Andrews,* and accordingly placed in the hands of my child those pernicious volumes. Ah! Madame, what wonder such artifices should prevail over the ignorant mind of a young rustic! Alas! They sunk too deep. Nancy first learnt to disrelish the honest, artless effusions of her first lover's heart. His language was insipid after the luscious speeches and ardent but dishonourable warmth of Mr. B. in the books before mentioned. Taught to despise simplicity, she was easily led to suffer the colonel to plead for pardon for his late boldness. My poor girl's head was now completely turned, to see such an accomplished man kneeling at her feet suing for forgiveness, and using the most refined expressions, and elevating her to Goddess, that he might debase her to the lowest dregs of humankind. Oh! Madame, what have most such wretches to answer for! The colonel's professions, however, at present, were all within the bounds of honour. A man never scruples to make engagements which he never purposes to fulfil, and which he takes care no one shall ever be able to claim. He was very profuse of promises, judging it the most likely method of triumphing over her virtue by appearing to respect it. Things were proceeding thus, when, finding the colonel's continued stay in our neighbourhood, I became anxious to conclude my daughter's union, hoping that, when he should see her married, he would entirely lay his schemes aside, for, by his hovering about our village, I could not remain satisfied or prevent disagreeable apprehensions arising. My daughter was too artless to frame any excuse to protract her wedding, and equally *so,* not to discover, by her confusion, that her sentiments were changed. My intended son-in-law saw too clearly that *change;* perhaps he had heard more than I had. He made rather a too sharp observation on the alteration in his mistress's features. Duty and respect kept her silent to me, but to him she made an acrimonious reply. He had been that day at market and had taken a too free draught of ale. His spirits had been elevated by my information that I would that evening fix his wedding day. The damp on my daughter's brow had therefore a greater effect on him. He could not brook her reply, and his answer to it was a sarcastic reflexion on those women who were undone by the redcoats. This touched too nearly; and, after darting a look of the most ineffable contempt on him, Nancy declared, whatever might be the consequence, she would never give her hand to a man who had dared to treat her on the eve of her marriage with such unexampled insolence; so saying, she left the room. I was sorry matters had gone so far and wished to reconcile the pair, but both were too haughty to yield to the intercessions I made; and he left us with a fixed resolution of making her repent, as he said. As is too common in such cases, the public house seemed the properest asylum for the disappointed lover. He there met with a recruiting serjeant of the colonel's, who, we since find, was sent on purpose to our village to get Nancy's future husband out of the way. The bait unhappily took, and before morning he was enlisted in the king's service. His father and mother, half distracted, ran to our house to learn the cause of this rash action in their son. Nancy, whose virtuous attachment to her former lover had only been lulled to sleep, now felt it rouse with redoubled violence. She pictured to herself the dangers he was now going to encounter and accused herself with being the cause. Judging of the influence she had over the colonel, she flew into his presence; she begged, she conjured him, to give the precipitate young soldier his discharge. He told her he could freely grant anything to her petition, but that it was too much his interest to remove the only obstacle to his happiness out of the way for him to be able to comply with her request. "However," continued he, taking her hand, "my Nancy has it in her power to preserve the young man." "Oh!" cried she, "how freely would I exert that power!" "Be mine this moment," said he, "and I will promise on my honour to discharge him." "By that sacred word," said Nancy, "I beg you, sir, to reflect on the cruelty of your conduct to me! What generous professions you have made voluntarily to me! How sincerely have you promised me your friendship! And does all this end in a design to render me the most criminal of beings?" "My angel," cried the colonel, throwing his arms round her waist and pressing her hand to his lips, "give not so harsh a name to my intentions. No disgrace shall befall you. You are a sensible girl; and I need not, I am sure, tell you that, circumstanced as *I* am in life, it would be utterly impossible to marry you I adore you; you know it, do not then play the sex upon me and treat me with rigour because I have candidly confessed I cannot live without you. Consent to bestow on me the possession of your charming person, and I will hide your lovely blushes in my fond bosom, while you shall whisper to my enraptured ear that I shall still have the delightful privilege of a husband, and Will Parker shall bear the name. This little delicious private treaty shall be known only to ourselves. Speak, my angel, or rather let me read your willingness in your lovely eyes." "If I have been silent, sir," said my poor girl, "believe me, it is the horror which I feel at your proposal which struck me dumb. But, thus called upon, let me say, I bless heaven for having allowed me to see your cloven foot while yet I can be out of its reach. You may wound me to the soul, and"—no longer able to conceal her tears—"you have most sorely wounded me through the side of William; but I will never consent to enlarge him at the price of my honour. We are poor people. He has not had the advantages of education as you have had; but, lowly as his mind is, I am convinced he would first die before I should suffer for his sake. Permit me, sir, to leave you, deeply affected with the disappointments I have sustained, and more so, that in part I have brought them on myself." Luckily, at this moment a servant came in with a letter. "You are now engaged, sir," she added, striving to hide her distress from the man. "Stay, young woman," said the colonel, "I have something more to say to you on this head." "I thank you, sir," said she, curtseying, "but I will take the liberty of sending my father to hear what further you may have to say on this subject."

"'He endeavoured to detain her, but she took this opportunity of escaping. On her return, she threw her arms 'round her mother's neck, unable to speak for sobs. Good God! What were our feelings on seeing her distress! Dying to hear, yet dreading to enquire. My wife folded her speechless child to her bosom, and in all the agony of despair besought her to explain this mournful silence. Nancy slid from her mother's encircling arms and sunk upon her knees, hiding her face in her lap: at last sobbed out she was undone forever; her William would be hurried away, and the colonel was the basest of men. These broken sentences served but to add to our distraction. We urged a full account; but it was a long time before we could learn the whole particulars. The poor girl now made a full recital of all her folly, in having listened so long to the artful addresses of Colonel Montague, and the no less artful persuasions of our perfidious neighbour, and concluded by imploring our forgiveness. It would have been the height of cruelty to have added to the already deeply wounded Nancy. We assured her of our pardon and spoke all the comfortable things we could devise. She grew tolerably calm, and we talked composedly of applying to some persons whom we hoped might assist us. Just at this juncture, a confused noise made us run to the door, when we beheld some soldiers marching, and dragging with them the unfortunate William, loaded with irons and handcuffed. On my hastily demanding why he was thus treated like a felon, the serjeant answered he had been detected in an attempt to desert but that he would be tried tomorrow and might escape with five hundred lashes; but, if he did not mend his manners for the future, he would be shot, as all such cowardly dogs ought to be; and added, they were on the march to the regiment. Figure to yourself, madame, what was now the situation of poor Nancy. Imagination can hardly picture so distressed an object. A heavy stupor seemed to take entire possession of all her faculties. Unless strongly urged, she never opened her lips, and then only to breathe out the most heart-piercing complaints. Towards the morning, she appeared inclinable to doze; and her mother left her bedside and went to her own. When we rose, my wife's first business was to go and see how her child fared; but what was her grief and astonishment to find the bed cold and her darling fled! A small scrap of paper, containing these few distracted words, was all the information we could gain:

> My dearest father and mother, make no inquiry after the most forlorn of all wretches. I am undeserving of your least *regard*. I fear I have forfeited *that* of heaven. Yet pray for me: I am myself unable, as I shall prove myself unworthy. I am in despair; what that despair may lead to, I dare not tell: I dare hardly think. Farewell. May my brothers and sisters repay you the tenderness which has been thrown away on N. Johnson!

"'My wife's shrieks reached my affrighted ears; I flew to her and felt a thousand conflicting passions while I read the dreadful scroll. We ran about the yard and little field, every moment terrified with the idea of seeing our beloved child's corpse, for what other interpretation could we put on the alarming notice we had received, but that to destroy herself was her intention? All our inquiry failed. I then formed the resolution of going up to London, as I heard the regiment was ordered to quarters near town, and *hoped* there. After a fruitless search of some days, our strength, and what little money we had collected, nearly exhausted, it pleased the mercy of heaven to raise us up a friend, one, who, like an angel, bestowed every comfort upon us; in short, all comforts in one—our dear wanderer: restored her to us pure and undefiled, and obtained us the felicity of looking forward to better days. But I will pursue my long detail with some method and follow my poor distressed daughter thro' all the sad variety of woe she was doomed to encounter. She told us that as soon as her mother had left her room, she rose and dressed herself, wrote the little melancholy note, then stole softly out of the house, resolving to follow the regiment and to preserve her lover by resigning herself to the base wishes of the colonel, that she had taken the gloomy resolution of destroying herself as soon as his discharge was signed, as she could not support the idea of living in infamy. Without money, she followed them, at a painful distance, on foot, and sustained herself from the springs and a few berries; she arrived at the market town where they were to take up their quarters; and the first news that struck her ear was that a fine young fellow was just then receiving part of five hundred lashes for desertion; her trembling limbs just bore her to the dreadful scene; she saw the back of her William streaming with blood; she heard his agonizing groans! She saw—she heard no more! She sunk insensible on the ground. The compassion of the crowd around her soon, too soon, restored her to a sense of her distress. The object of it was, at this moment, taken from the halberts and was conveying away to have such applications to his lacerated back as should preserve his life to a renewal of his torture. He was led by the spot where my child was supported; he instantly knew her. "Oh! Nancy," he cried, "what do I see?" "A wretch," she exclaimed, "but one who will do you justice. Could my death have prevented this, freely would I have submitted to the most painful. Yes, my William, I would have died to have released you from those bonds and the exquisite torture I have been witness to; but the cruel colonel is deaf to entreaty; nothing but my everlasting ruin can preserve you. Yet you shall be preserved; and heaven will, I hope, have that mercy on my poor soul which this basest of men will not show." The wretches who had the care of poor William hurried him away, nor would suffer him to speak. Nancy strove to run after them but fell a second time, through weakness and distress of mind. Heaven sent amongst the spectators that best of men, the noble-minded baron. Averse to such scenes of cruel discipline, he came that way by accident; struck with the appearance of my frantic daughter, he stopped to make some inquiry. He stayed till the crowd had dispersed and then addressed

himself to this forlorn victim of woe. Despair had rendered her wholly un-
reserved; and she related, in few words, the unhappy resolution she was
obliged to take to secure her lover from a repetition of his sufferings. "If
I will devote myself to infamy to Colonel Montague," said she, "my dear
William will be released. Hard as the terms are, I cannot refuse. See, see!"
she screamed out, "how the blood runs! Oh! Stop thy barbarous hand!" She
raved and then fell into a fit again. The good baron entreated some people
who were near to take care of her. They removed the distracted creature to
a house in the town, where some comfortable things were given her by an
apothecary, which the care of the baron provided.

"'By his indefatigable industry, the baron discovered the basest collu-
sion between the colonel and serjeant: that, by the instigation of the former,
the latter had been tampering with the young recruit about procuring his discharge for a sum of money, which he, being at that time unable to advance,
the serjeant was to connive at his escape and receive the stipulated reward
by instalments. This infamous league was contrived to have a plea for tormenting poor William, hoping, by that means, to effect the ruin of Nancy. The
whole of this black transaction being unravelled, the baron went to Colonel
Montague, to whom he talked in pretty severe terms. The colonel, at first,
was very warm and wanted much to decide the affair, as he said, in an honourable way. The baron replied it was too *dishonourable* a piece of business to
be thus decided; that he went on sure grounds; that he would prosecute the
serjeant for wilful and corrupt perjury; and how honourably it would sound,
that the colonel of the regiment had conspired with such a fellow to procure
an innocent man so ignominious a punishment. As this was not an affair of
common gallantry, the colonel was fearful of the exposure of it; therefore,
to hush it up signed the discharge, remitted the remaining infliction of discipline, and gave a note of two hundred pounds for the young people to begin
the world with. The baron generously added the same sum. I had heard my
daughter was near town; the circumstances of her distress were aggravated
in the accounts I had received. Providence, in pity to my age and infirmities,
at last brought us together. I advertised her in the papers; and our guardian
angel used such means to discover my lodgings, as had the desired effect.
My children are now happy; they were married last week. Our generous protector gave Nancy to her faithful William. We propose leaving this place soon,
and shall finish our days in praying for the happiness of our benefactor.'

"You will suppose," continued Miss Finch, "my dear Lady Stanley, how much I was affected with this little narrative. I left the good folks with my heart filled with resentment against Montague and complacency towards Ton-hausen. You will believe I did not hesitate long about the dismission of the former; and my frequent conversations on this head with the latter has made him a very favourable interest in my bosom. Not that I have the vanity to think he possesses any predilection in my favour; but, till I see a man I like as well as him, I will not receive the addresses of anyone."

We joined in our commendation of the generous baron. The manner in which he disclaimed all praise, Miss Finch said, served only to render him still more praiseworthy. He begged her to keep this little affair a secret, and particularly from me. I asked Miss Finch, why he should make that request.

"I know not indeed," she answered, "except that, knowing I was more intimate with you than anyone beside, he might mention your name by way of enforcing the restriction." Soon after this, Miss Finch took leave.

Oh, Louisa! Dare I, even to your indulgent bosom, confide my secret thoughts? How did I lament not being in the park the day of this adventure. *I* might then have been the envied *confidante* of the amiable Ton-hausen. They have had frequent conversations in consequence. The softness which the melancholy detail gave to Miss Finch's looks and expressions have deeply impressed the mind of the baron. Should I have shown less sensibility? I have, indeed, rather sought to conceal the tenderness of my soul. I have been constrained to do so. Miss Finch has given hers full scope, and has riveted the chain which her beauty and accomplishments first forged. But what am I doing? Oh! My sister, chide me for thus giving loose to such expressions. How much am I to blame! How infinitely more prudent is the baron! He begged that *I*, of all persons, should not know his generosity. Heavens! What an idea does that give birth to! He has seen—Oh! Louisa, what will become of me, if he should have discovered the struggles of my soul? If he should have searched into the recesses of my heart, and developed the thin veil I spread over the feelings I have laboured incessantly to overcome! He then, perhaps, wished to conceal his excellencies from me, lest I should be too partial to them. I ought then to copy his discretion. I will do so; yes, Louisa, I will drive his image from my bosom! I ought—I know it would be my interest to see him married to Miss Finch, or anyone who would make him happy. I am culpable in harbouring the remotest desire of his preserving his attachment to me. He has had virtue enough to conquer so *improper* an attachment; and, if improper in him, how infinitely more so in me! But I will dwell no longer on this forbidden subject; let me set bounds to my pen, as an earnest that I most truly mean to do so to my thoughts.

Think what an enormous packet I shall send you. Preserve your affection for me, my dearest sister; and, truth to my asseverations, you shall have no cause to blush for

Julia Stanley

To Miss Grenville

This morning I dispatched to Anderton's Coffee House the most elegant locket with hair that you ever saw. May I be permitted to say thus much when the design was all my own? Yet, why not give myself praise when I can? The locket is in the form and size of that bracelet I sent you; the device, an altar on which is inscribed these words: *To Gratitude,* an elegant figure of a woman making an offering on her knees, and a winged cherub bearing the incense to heaven. A narrow plait of hair, about the breadth of penny ribbon, is fastened on each side of the locket near the top by three diamonds and united with a bow of diamonds, by which it may hang to a ribbon. I assure you, it is exceedingly pretty. I hope the Sylph will approve of it. I forget to tell you, as the hair was taken from my head by your dear hand before I married, I took the fancy of putting the initials J.G. instead of J.S. It was a whim that seized me, because the hair did never belong to J.S.

Adieu!

LETTER 28

From the Sylph to Lady Stanley

Will my amiable charge be ever thus increasing my veneration, my almost adoration of her perfections? Yes, Julia; still pursue these methods, and my whole life will be too confined a period to render you my acknowledgements. Its best services have, and ever shall be, devoted to your advantage. I have no other business and, I am sure, no other pleasure in this world than to watch over your interest; and, if I should at anytime be so fortunate as to have procured you the smallest share of felicity, or saved you from the minutest inquietude, I shall feel myself amply repaid; repaid! Where have I learnt so cold an expression? From the earthborn sons of clay? I shall feel a bliss beyond the sensation of a mortal!

None but a mind delicate as your own can form an idea of the sentimental joy I experienced on seeing the letters J.G. on the most elegant of devices, an emblem of the lovely giver! There was a purity, a chasteness of thought, in the design which can only be conceived; all expression would be faint; even my Julia can hardly define it. Wonder not at my boundless partiality to you. You know not, you see not, yourself as I *know* and *see* you. I pierce through the recesses of your soul; each fold expands itself to my eye; the struggles of your mind are open to my view; I see how nobly your virtue towers over the involuntary tribute you pay to concealed merit. But be not uneasy. Feel not humiliated that the secret of your mind is discovered to me. Heaven sees our thoughts and reads our hearts; we know it, but feel no restraint therefrom. Consider me as heaven's agent, and be not dismayed at the idea of having a window in your breast, when only the sincerest, the most disinterested of your friends is allowed the privilege of looking through it. Adieu! May the blest above (thy only superiors), guard you from ill!

So prays your

Sylph

LETTER 29

To the Sylph

Though encouraged by the commendations of my Sylph, I tremble when you tell me the most retired secrets of my soul are open to your view. You say you have seen its struggles. Oh! That you alone have seen them! Could I be assured that one *other* is yet a stranger to those struggles, I should feel no more humiliated (though that word is not sufficiently strong to express my meaning) than I do in my confessions to heaven, because I am taught to believe that our thoughts are involuntary, and that we are not answerable for them unless they tend to excite us to evil actions. Mine—thank God!— have done me no other mischief than robbing me of that *repose,* which, perhaps, had I been blest with insensibility might have been my portion. But a very large share of insensibility must have been dealt out to me to have guarded me from my sense of merit in one person and my feeling no affliction at the want of it in another, that *other* too, with whose fate mine is unavoidably connected. I must do myself that justice to say my heart would have remained fixed with my hand had my husband remained the same. Had *he* known no change, my affections would have centred in him; that is, I should have passed through life a duteous and observant partner of his cares and pleasures. When I married, I had never loved any but my own relations; indeed I had seen no *one* to love. The language, and its emotions, were equally strangers to my ears or heart. Sir William Stanley was the first man who used the one, and consequently, in a bosom so young and inexperienced as mine, created the other. He told me he loved. I blushed, and felt confused; unhappily, I construed these indications of self-love into an attachment for him. Although this bore but a small relation to love, yet, in a breast where virtue and a natural tenderness resided, it would have been sufficient to have guarded my heart from receiving any other impression. He did so till repeated flights and irregularities on one hand, and on the other all the virtues and graces that can adorn and beautify the mind, raised a conflict in my bosom that has destroyed my peace and hurt my constitution. I have a beloved sister, who deserves all the affection I bear her; from her I have concealed nothing. She has read every secret of my heart, for, when I wrote to her, reserve was banished from my pen. This unfortunate predilection, which, believe me, I have from the first combated with all my force, has given my Louisa, who has the tenderest soul, the utmost uneasiness. I have very lately assured her my resolves to conquer this fatal attachment are fixed and permanent. I doubt (and she thinks perhaps) I have too often indulged myself in dwelling upon the dangerous subject in my frequent letters. I have given my word I will mention him no more. Oh! My Sylph! How has he risen in my esteem from a recent story I have heard of him! How hard is my fate (you read my thoughts, so that to endeavour to soften the expression would be needless) that I am constrained to obey the man I can neither love nor honour!—and, alas!—love the man who is not, nor can be, anything to me.

I have vowed to my sister, myself, and now to you that, however hardly treated, yet virtue and rectitude shall be my guide. I arrogate no great merit to myself in still preserving myself untainted in this vortex of folly and vice. No one falls all at once; and I have no temptation to do so. The man I esteem above all others is superior to all others. His manners refined, generous, virtuous, humane; oh!—when shall I fill the catalogue of his excellent qualities? He pays a deference to me, at least used to do, because I was tinctured with the licentious fashion of the times; he would lose that esteem for me were I to act without decency and discretion; and I hope I know enough of my heart to say I should no longer feel an attachment for him, did he countenance vice. Alas! What is to be inferred from this but that I shall carry this fatal preference with me to the grave! Let me, however, descend to *it* without bringing disgrace on myself, sorrow on my beloved relations, and repentance on my Sylph for having thrown away his counsels on an ingrate, and I will peacefully retire from a world for whose pleasures I have very little taste.

Adieu.

LETTER 30

To Lady Stanley

My dearest sister,

It is with infinite pleasure I receive your promise of no longer indulging your pen with a subject which has too much engaged your thoughts of late; a pleasure heightened by the assurance that your silence in future shall be an earnest of banishing an image from your idea which I cannot but own, from the picture you have drawn, is very amiable, and, for that reason, very dangerous. I will, my Julia, emulate your example; this shall be the last letter that treats on this to-be-forbidden theme. Permit me, therefore, to make some comment on your long letter. Sure never two people were more strongly contrasted than the baron and the colonel. The one seems the kindly sun, cherishing the tender herbage of the field; the other, the blasting mildew, breathing its pestiferous venom over every beautiful plant and flower. However, do you, my love, only regard them as virtue and vice personified; look on them as patterns and examples; view them in no other light; for in *no other* can they be of any advantage to you. You are extremely reprehensible (I hope, and believe, I shall never have occasion to use such harsh language again) in your strictures on the supposed change in the baron's sentiments. You absolutely seem to regret, if not express anger, that *he* has had virtue sufficient to resist the violence of an improper attachment. The efforts he has made, and my partiality for you supposes them not to have been easily made, ought to convince you the conquest over ourselves is possible, though oftentimes difficult. It is, I believe (and I may say I am certain from my own experience), a very mistaken notion that we nourish our afflictions by keeping them to ourselves. I said I know so experimentally. While I indulged myself, and your tenderness induced you to do the same, in lamenting in the most pathetic language the perfidy of Mr. Montgomery and Emily Wingrove, I increased the wounds which that *perfidy* occasioned; but, when I took the resolution of never mentioning their names, or ever suffering myself to dwell on former scenes, burning every letter I had received from either; though these efforts cost me floods of tears, and many sleepless nights, yet, in time, my reflexions lost much of their poignancy; and I chiefly attribute it to my steady adherence to my laudable resolution. He deserved not my tenderness, even if only because he was married to another. This is the first time I have suffered my pen to write his name since that determination; nor does he now ever mix with my thoughts unless by chance, and then quite as an indifferent person. I have recalled his idea for no other reason than to convince you that, although painful, yet self-conquest is attainable. You will not think I am endued with less sensibility than you are; and I had long been authorized to indulge my attachment to this ingrate, and had long been cruelly deceived into a belief that his regard was equal to mine; while, from the first, *you* could have no *hope* to lead you on by flowery footsteps to the confines of *disappointment* and *despair,* for to those goals does that fallacious phantom too frequently lead. You envy Miss Finch the distinction which accident induced the baron to pay her, by making her his *confidante.* Had you been on the spot, it is possible you might have shared his confidence; but, believe me, I am thankful to heaven that chance threw you not in his way; with your natural tenderness, and your unhappy predilection, I tremble for what might have been the consequence of frequent conversations in which pity and compassion bore so large a share as perhaps might have superseded every other consideration. I wish from my soul, and hope my Julia will soon join my wish, that the baron may be in earnest in his attention to Miss Finch. I wish to have him married, that his engagements may increase, and prevent your seeing him so often as you now do, for undoubtedly your difficulty will be greater; but consider, my dear Julia, your triumph will be *greater* likewise. It is sometimes harder to turn one's eyes from a pleasing object than one's thoughts; yet there is nothing which may not be achieved by resolution and perseverance; both of which, I question not, my beloved will exert, if it be but to lighten the oppressed mind of her faithful

Louisa Grenville

ᣔᣔᣔᣔᣔᣔᣔᣔᣔᣔ
LETTER 31
ᣔᣔᣔᣔᣔᣔᣔᣔᣔᣔ

To the Sylph

Will my kind guardian candidly inform me if he thinks I may comply with
the desire of Sir William in going next Thursday to the masquerade at the
Pantheon? Without your previous advice, I would not willingly consent. Is
it a diversion of which I may participate without danger? Though I doubt
there is hardly decency enough left in this part of the world that *vice* need
wear a mask; yet do not people give a greater scope to their licentious inclinations while under that veil? However, if you think I may venture with
safety, I will indulge my husband, who seems to have set his mind on my
accompanying his party thither. Miss Finch has promised to go if I go and,
as she has been often to those motley meetings, assures me she will take
care of me. Sir William does not know of my application to that lady; but
I did so merely to gain time to inform you, that I might have your sanction
(or be justified by your advising the contrary) either to accept or reject the
invitation.

I am ever your obliged,

J.S.

ᣔᣔᣔᣔᣔᣔᣔᣔᣔᣔ
LETTER 32
ᣔᣔᣔᣔᣔᣔᣔᣔᣔᣔ

From the Sylph

When the face is masked, the mind is uncovered. From the conduct and
language of those who frequent masquerades, we may judge of the principles of their souls. A modest woman will blush in the dark; and a man

of honour would scorn to use expressions while behind a visor which he would not openly avow in the face of day. A masquerade is then the criterion by which you should form your opinion of people; and, as I believe I have before observed to my Julia that female companions are either the safest or most dangerous of any, you may make this trial whether Miss F. is or is not one in whom you may confide. When I say *confide,* I would not be understood that you should place an unlimited confidence in her; there is no occasion to lay our hearts bare to the inspection of all our intimates; we should lessen the compliment we mean to pay to our particular friends by destroying that distinguishing mark. But you want a female companion. Indeed, for your sake, I should wish you one older than Miss F. and a married woman; yet, unless she was very prudent, *you* had better be the *leader* than the *led;* therefore, upon the whole, perhaps it is as well as it is.

I shall never enough admire your amiable condescension in asking (in a manner) my permission to go to the Pantheon. And at the same time I feel the delicacy of your situation, and the effect it must have on a woman of your exquisite sensibility, to be constrained to appeal to another in an article wherein her husband ought to be the properest guide. Unhappily for you, Sir William will find so many engagements that the protection of his wife must be left either to her own discretion or to strangers. But your Sylph, my Julia, will never desert you. You request my leave to go thither. I freely grant that, and even more than you desire. I will meet my charge among the motley group. I do not demand a description of your dress; for—oh!—what disguise can conceal you from him whose heart only vibrates in union with yours? I will not inform you how I shall be habited that night, as I have not a doubt that I shall soon be discovered by you, though I shall be invisible to all beside. Only you will see me; and I, of course, shall only see *you;* you, who are all and everything in this world to your faithful attendant.

Sylph

〽〽〽〽〽〽〽〽〽〽
LETTER 33
〽〽〽〽〽〽〽〽〽〽

To the Sylph

Will you ever thus be adding to my weight of obligation! Yes! My Sylph!
Be still thus kind, thus indulgent; and be assured your benevolence shall be
repaid by my steady adherence to your virtuous counsel. Adieu! Thursday
is eagerly wished for by yours,

J.S.

〽〽〽〽〽〽〽〽〽〽
LETTER 34
〽〽〽〽〽〽〽〽〽〽

To Miss Grenville

Enclosed my Louisa will find some letters which have passed between the
Sylph and your Julia. I have sent them to inform you of my being present
at a masquerade, in compliance with the taste of Sir William, who was very
desirous of my exhibiting myself there. As he has of late never intimated
an inclination to have me in any of his parties till this whim seized him, I
thought it would not become me to refuse my consent. You will find, however, I was not so dutiful a wife as to pay an implicit obedience to his mandate without taking the concurrence of my guardian angel on the subject.
My dear, you must be first circumstanced as I am (which heaven forbid!)
before you can form an idea of the satisfaction I felt on the assurances of
my Sylph's being present. No words can convey it to you. It seemed as if
I was going to enjoy the ultimate wish of my heart. As to my dress, I told
Sir William I would leave the choice of it to him, not doubting in matters
of elegant taste he would be far superior to me. I made him this compli-

ment, as I have been long convinced he has no other pleasure in possessing me than what is excited by the admiration which other people bestow me. Nay, he has said, unless he heard everybody say his wife was one of the handsomest women at court, he would never suffer her to appear there, or anywhere else.

That I might do credit to his taste, I was to be most superbly brilliant; and Sir William desired to see my jewels. He objected to their manner of being set, though they were quite new-done when we married. But now these were detestable, horridly *outré,* and so barbarously antique that I could only appear as Rembrandt's wife, or some such relic of ancient history. As I had promised to be guided by him, I acquiesced in what I thought a very unnecessary expense, but was much laughed at when I expressed my amazement at the jeweller's saying the setting would come to about two hundred pounds. This is well worthwhile for an evening's amusement, for they are now in such whimsical forms that they will be scarce fit for any other purpose. And oh! My Louisa! Do you not think I was cut to the soul when I had this painful reflexion to make, that many honest and industrious tradesmen are every day dunning for their lawful demands, while we are thus throwing away hundreds after hundreds, without affording the least heartfelt satisfaction?

Well, at last my dress was completed; but what character I assumed I know not, unless I was the epitome of the folly of this world. I thought myself only an agent to support all the frippery and finery of *Tavistock Street;* but, however, I received many compliments on the figure I made; and some people of the first fashion pronounced me to be quite the thing. They say one may believe the women when they praise one of their own sex; and Miss Finch said I had contrived to heighten and improve every charm with which Nature had endowed me. Sir William seemed to tread on air, to see and hear the commendations which were lavished on me from all sides. To a man of his taste, I am no more than any fashionable piece of furniture or new equipage, or, what will come nearer our idea of things, a beautiful prospect, which a man fancies he shall never be tired of beholding, and therefore builds himself a house within view of it; by the time he is fixed, he hardly remembers what his motive, nor ever feels any pleasure but in pointing out its various perfections to his guests; his vanity is awhile gratified, but even that soon loses its *goût;* and he wonders how others can be pleased with objects now grown familiar, and, consequently, indifferent to him. But I am running quite out of the course. Suppose me now dressed and mingling with a fantastic group of all kind of forms and figures, striving to disengage my eyes from the throng, to single out my Sylph. Our usual party was there: Miss Finch, Lady Barton, a distant relation of hers, the baron, Lord Biddulph, and some others; but it was impossible to keep long together. Sometimes I found myself with one; then they were gone, and I was *tête-à-tête* with somebody else; for a good while I observed a mask, who looked like a fortune-teller, followed me about, particularly when the baron and Miss Finch were with me. I thought I must say something, so I asked him if he would tell me my fortune. "Go into the next room," said he, in a whisper, "and you shall see one more learned in the occult science than you think; but I shall say no more while you are surrounded with so many observers." Nothing is so easy as to get away from your company in a crowd: I slipped from them and went into a room which was nearly empty, and still followed by the conjuror. I seated myself on a sofa and just turned my head round when I perceived the most elegant creature that imagination can form placed by me. I started, half-breathless with surprise. "Be not alarmed, my Julia," said the phantom (for such I at first thought it). "Be not alarmed at the appearance of your Sylph." He took my hand in his, and, pressing it gently, speaking all the while in a soft kind of whisper, "Does my amiable charge repent her condescension in teaching me to believe she would be pleased to see her faithful adherent?" I begged him to attribute my tremor to the hurry of spirits so new a scene excited and, in part, to the pleasure his presence afforded me. But, before I proceed, I will describe his dress: his figure in itself seems the most perfect I ever saw; the finest harmony of shape: a waistcoat and breeches of silver tissue, exactly fitted to his body; buskins of the same, fringed, &c.; a blue silk mantle depending from one shoulder, to which it was secured by a diamond epaulette, falling in beautiful folds upon the ground; this robe was starred all over with plated silver, which had a most brilliant effect; on each shoulder was placed a transparent wing of painted gauze, which looked like peacock's feathers; a cap, suitable to the whole dress, which was certainly the most elegant and best contrived that can be imagined. I gazed on him with the most perfect admiration. Ah! How I longed to see his face, which the envious mask concealed. His hair hung in sportive ringlets, and just carelessly restrained from wandering too far by a white ribbon. In short, the most luxuriant fancy could hardly create a more captivating object. When my astonishment a little subsided, I found utterance. "How is it possible I should be so great a favourite of fortune as to interest you in my welfare?"

"We have each our task allotted us," he answered, "from the beginning of the world, and it was my happy privilege to watch over your destiny."

"I speak to you as a man," said I, "but you answer only as a Sylph."

"Believe me," he replied, "it is the safest character I can assume. I must divest myself of my feelings as a *man,* or I should be too much enamoured to be serviceable to you: I shut my eyes to the beauties of your person, which excites tumultuous raptures in the chastest bosom, and only allow myself the free contemplation of your interior perfections. There your virtue secures me and renders my attachment as pure as your own pure breast. I could not, however, resist this opportunity of paying my personal *devoir* to you, and yet I feel too sensibly I shall be a sufferer from my indulgence; but I will never forget that I am placed over you as your guardian angel and protector, and that my sole business on earth is to secure you from the wiles and snares which are daily practised against youth and beauty. What does my excellent pupil say? Does she still cheerfully submit herself to my guidance?" While he spoke this, he had again taken my hand and pressed it with rapture to his bosom, which, beating with violence, I own caused no small emotion in mine.

I gently withdrew my hand and said, with as composed a voice as I could command, "Yes, my Sylph, I do most readily resign myself to your protection, and shall never feel a wish to put any restriction on it while I am enabled to judge of you from your own criterion; while virtue presides over your lessons, while your instructions are calculated to make me a good and respectable character, I can form no wish to depart from them."

He felt the delicacy of the reproof and, sighing, said, "Let me never depart from that sacred character! Let me still remember I am your Sylph! But I believe I have before said a time may come when you will no longer stand in need of my interposition. Shall I own to you, I sicken at the idea of my being useless to you?"

"The time can never arrive in which you will not be serviceable to me, or, at least, when I shall not be inclined to ask and follow your advice."

"Amiable Julia! May I venture to ask you this question? If fate should ever put it in your power to make a second choice, would you consult your Sylph?"

"Hear me," cried I, "while I give you my hand on it, and attest heaven to witness my vow that if I should have the fate (which may that heaven avert!) to outlive Sir William, I will abide by your decision; neither my hand nor affections shall be disposed of without your concurrence. My obligations to you are unbound; my confidence in you shall likewise be the same; I can make no other return than to resign myself solely to your guidance in that and every other concern of moment to me."

"Are you aware of what you have said, Lady Stanley?"

"It is past recall," I answered, "and if the vow could return again into my bosom, it should only be to issue thence more strongly ratified."

"Oh!" cried he, clasping his hands together, "Oh! Thou merciful Father, make me but worthy of this amiable and most excellent of all thy creatures confidence! None but the most accurst of villains could abuse such goodness. The blameless purity and innocent simplicity of your heart would make a convert of a libertine."

"Alas!" said I. "That, I fear, is impossible; but how infinitely happy should I be if my utmost efforts could work the least reformation in my husband! Could I but prevail on him to quit this destructive place and retire into the peaceful country, I should esteem myself a fortunate woman."

"And could you really quit these gay scenes, nor *cast one longing lingering look behind?*"

"Yes," I replied with vivacity, "nor even cast a thought on what I had left behind!"

"Would no one be remembered with a tender regret? Would your Sylph be entirely forgotten?"

"My Sylph," I answered, "is possessed of the power of omnipresence; he would still be with me, wherever I went."

"And would no other ever be thought of? You blush, Lady Stanley; the face is the needle which points to the polar star, the heart; from that information, may I not conclude someone whom you would leave behind would mix with your ideas in your retirement, and that, even in solitude, you would not be alone?"

I felt my cheeks glow while he spoke; but, as I was a mask, I did not suppose the Sylph could discover the emotion his discourse caused. "Since," said I in a faltering voice, "you are capable of reading my heart, it is unnecessary to declare its sentiments to you; but it would be my purpose, in retirement, to obliterate every idea which might conduce to rob my mind of peace; I should endeavour to reform as well as my husband; and if he would oblige me by such a compliance to my will, I should think I could do no less than seek to amuse him, and should, indeed, devote my whole time and study to that purpose."

"You may think I probe too deep: but is not your desire of retirement stronger since you have conceived the idea of the baron's entertaining a *penchant* for Miss Finch than it has been heretofore?"

I sighed—"Indeed you do probe very deep; and the pain you cause is exquisite: but I know it is your friendly concern for me; and it proves how needful it is to apply some remedy for the wound, the examination of which is so acute. Instruct me, ought I to wish him married? Should I be happier if he was so? And if he married Miss Finch, should I not be as much exposed to danger as at present, for his amiable qualities are more of the domestic kind?"

"I hardly know how to answer to these interrogatories; nor am I judge of the heart and inclinations of the baron; only thus much: if you have ever had any cause to believe him impressed with your idea, I cannot suppose it possible for Miss Finch, or any other woman, to obliterate that idea. But, *the heart of man is deceitful above all things.* For the sake of your interest, I wish Sir William would adopt your plan, tho' I have my doubts that his affairs are not in the power of any economy to arrange; and this consideration urges me to enforce what I have before advised, that you do not surrender up any farther part of your jointure, as *that* may, too soon, be your sole support; and I have seen a recent proof of what mean subterfuges some men are necessitated to fly to in order to extricate themselves for a little time. But the room fills; our conversation may be noticed; and, in this age of dissipation and licentiousness, to escape censure we must not stray within the limits of impropriety. Your having been so long *tête-à-tête* with any character will be observed. Adieu, therefore, for the present—see, Miss Finch is approaching."

I turned my eye towards the door—the Sylph rose—I did the same— he pressed my hand on his quitting it; I cast my eye round, but I saw him no more; how he escaped my view I know not. Miss Finch by this time bustled through the crowd and asked me where I had been and whether I had seen the baron, whom she had dispatched to seek after me?

The baron then coming up rallied me for hiding myself from the party and losing a share of merriment which had been occasioned by two whimsical masks making themselves very ridiculous to entertain the company. I assured them I had not quitted that place after I missed them in the great room; but, however, adding that I had determined to wait there till some of the party joined me, as I had not courage to venture a *tour* of the rooms by myself. To be sure all this account was not strictly true; but I was obliged to make some excuse for my behaviour, which otherwise might have caused some suspicion. They willingly accompanied me through every room, but my eyes could nowhere fix on the object they were in search of, and therefore returned from their survey dissatisfied. I complained of fatigue, which was really true, for I had no pleasure in the hurry and confusion of the multitude, and it grew late. I shall frighten you, Louisa, by telling you the hour; but we did not go till twelve at night. I soon met with Sir William, and on my expressing an inclination to retire, to my great astonishment, instead of censuring, he commended my resolution and hasted to the door to procure my carriage. When you proceed, my dear Louisa, you will wonder at my being able to pursue, in so methodical a manner, this little narrative; but I have taken some time to let my thoughts subside, that I might not anticipate any circumstance of an event that may be productive of very serious consequences. Well then, pleased as I was with Sir William's ready compliance with my request of returning, suppose me seated in my chair and giving way to some hopes that he would yet see his errors and some method be pitched on to relieve all. He was ready to hand me out of the chair and led me upstairs into my dressing room. I had taken off my mask, as it was very warm; he still kept his on and talked in the same kind of voice he practised at the masquerade. He paid me most profuse compliments on the beauty of my dress and, throwing his arms round my waist, congratulated himself on possessing such an angel, at the same time kissing my face and bosom with such a strange kind of eagerness as made me suppose he was intoxicated; and, under that idea, being very desirous of disengaging myself from his arms, I struggled to get away from him. He pressed me to go to bed; and, in short, his behaviour was unaccountable: at last, on my persisting to entreat him to let me go, he blew out one of the candles. I then used all my force and burst from him, and at that instant his mask gave way; and in the dress of my husband (Oh, Louisa! Judge, if you can, of my terror), I beheld that villain Lord Biddulph.

"Curse on my folly!" cried he. "That I could not restrain my raptures till I had you secure."

"Thou most insolent of wretches!" said I, throwing the most contemptuous looks at him. "How dared you assume the dress of my husband, to treat me with such indignity?" While I spoke, I rang the bell with some violence.

He attempted to make some apology for his indiscretion, urging the force of his passion, the power of my charms, and such stuff.

I stopped him short by telling him the only apology I should accept would be his instantly quitting the house and never insulting me again with his presence. With a most malignant sneer on his countenance, he said, "I might indeed have supposed my caresses were disagreeable, when offered under the character of a husband; I had been more blest, at least better received, had I worn the dress of the baron. All men, Lady Stanley, are not so blind as Sir William." I felt myself ready to expire with confusion and anger at his base insinuation.

"Your hint," said I, "is as void of truth as you are of honour; I despise both equally, but would advise you to be cautious how you dare traduce characters so opposite to your own."

By this time a servant came in; and the hateful wretch walked off, insolently wishing me a good repose, and humming an Italian air, though it was visible what chagrin was painted on his face. Preston came into the room to assist me in undressing:—she is by no means a favourite of mine; and, as I was extremely fatigued and unable to sit up, I did not choose to leave my door open till Sir William came home, nor did I care to trust her with the key. I asked for Winifred. She told me she had been in bed some hours.

"Let her be called then," said I.

"Can't I do what your ladyship wants?"

"No; I choose to have Win sit with me."

"I will attend your ladyship, if you please."

"It would give me more pleasure if you would obey, than dispute my orders." I was vexed to the soul and spoke with a peevishness unusual to me. She went out of the room, muttering to herself. I locked the door, terrified lest that monster had concealed himself somewhere in the house; nor would I open it till I heard Win speak. Poor girl! She got up with all the cheerfulness in the world and sat by my bedside till morning, Sir William not returning the whole night. My fatigue, and the perturbation of mind I laboured under, together with the total deprivation of sleep contributed to make me extremely ill. But how shall I describe to you, my dear Louisa, the horror which the reflexion of this adventure excited in me?

Though I had, by the mercy of heaven, escaped the danger, yet the apprehension it left on my mind is not to be told; and then the tacit aspersion which the base wretch threw on my character, by daring to say he had been more *welcome* under another appearance, struck so forcibly on my heart that I thought I should expire from the fears of his traducing my fame; for what might I not expect from such a consummate villain, who had so recently proved to what enormous lengths he could go to accomplish his purposes? The blessing of having frustrated his evil design could hardly calm my terrors; I thought I heard him each moment, and the agitation of my mind operated so violently on my frame that my bed actually shook under me. Win suffered extremely from her fears of my being dangerously ill and wanted to have my leave to send for a physician: but I too well knew it was not in the power of medicine to administer relief to my feelings, and, after telling her I was much better, begged her not to quit my room at any rate.

About eleven I rose, so weak and dispirited that I could hardly support myself. Soon after, I heard Sir William's voice; I had scarce strength left to speak to him; he looked pale and forlorn. I had had a conflict within myself, whether I should relate the behaviour of Lord Biddulph to my husband, lest the consequences should be fatal; but my spirits were so totally exhausted that I could not articulate a sentence without tears. "What is the matter, Julia, with you?" said he, taking my hand. "You seem fatigued to death. What a poor rake you are!"

"I have had something more than *fatigue* to discompose me," answered I, sobbing, "and I think I have some reproaches to make you for not attending me home as you promised."

"Why, Lord Biddulph promised to see you home. I saw him afterwards; and he told me he left you at your own house."

"Lord Biddulph!" said I, with the most scornful air. "And did he tell you likewise of the insolence of his behaviour? Perhaps he promised you too, that he would insult me in my own house."

"Heyday, Julia! What's in the wind now? Lord Biddulph insult you! Pray let me into the whole of this affair?"

I then related the particulars of his imprudent conduct, and what I conceived his design to be, together with the repulse I had given him.

Sir William seemed extremely *chagrined;* and said he should talk in a serious manner on the occasion to Lord Biddulph; and, if his answers were not satisfactory, he should lie under the necessity of calling him to account in the field. Terrified lest death should be the consequence of a quarrel between this infamous lord and my husband, I conjured Sir William not to take any notice of the affair, any otherwise than to give up his acquaintance: a circumstance much wished for by me, as I have great reason to believe, Sir William's passion for play was excited by his intimacy with him, and, perhaps, may have led him to all the enormities he has too readily, and too rapidly, plunged himself into. He made no scruple to assure me that he should find no difficulty in relinquishing the acquaintance and joined with me that a silent contempt would be the most cutting reproof to a man of his cast. On my part, I am resolved my doors shall never grant him access again; and, if Sir William should entirely break with him (which, after this atrocious behaviour, I think he must), I may be very happy that I have been the instrument, since I have had such an escape.

But still, Louisa, the innuendo of Lord Biddulph disturbs my peace. How shall I quiet my apprehensions? Does he dare scrutinize my conduct, and harbour suspicions of my predilection for a certain unfortunate? Base as is his soul, he cannot entertain an idea of the purity of a virtuous attachment! Ah! That speech of his has sunk deep in my memory; no time will efface it. When I have been struggling too—yes, Louisa, when I have been combating this fatal—but what am I doing? Why do I use these interdicted expressions? I have done. Alas! What is become of my boasting? If I cannot prescribe rules to a pen, which I can, in one moment, throw into the fire, how shall I restrain the secret murmurings of my mind, whose thoughts I can with difficulty silence, or even control? Adieu!

Yours, more than her own,

Julia Stanley

� � � � � � � � � �

LETTER 35

� � � � � � � � � �

To Miss Grenville

Alas! Louisa, fresh difficulties arise every day; and every day I find an exertion of my spirits more necessary, and myself less able to exert them. Sir William told me this morning that he had lost frequent sums to Lord Biddulph (it wounds my soul to write his detested name); and since it was prudent to give up the acquaintance, it became highly incumbent on him to discharge these play debts, for which purpose he must have recourse to me, and apprehended he should find no difficulty, as I had expressed my wish of his breaking immediately with his lordship. This was only the prelude to a proposal of my resignation of my marriage articles. My ready compliance with his former demands emboldened him to be urgent with me on this occasion. At first, I made some scruples, alleging the necessity there was of keeping something by us for a future day, as I had too much reason to apprehend that what I could call my own would be all we should have to support us. This remonstrance of mine, however just, threw Sir William into a violent rage; he paced about the room like a madman, swore that his difficulties proceeded from my damned prudery and that I should extricate him, or abide by the consequences. In short, Louisa, he appeared in a light entirely new to me; I was almost petrified with terror and absolutely thought once he would beat me, for he came up to me with such fierce looks and seized me by the arm, which he actually bruised with his grasp, and bade me, at my peril, refuse to surrender the writings to him. After giving me a violent shake, he pushed me from him with such force that I fell down, unable to support myself from the trembling with which my whole frame was possessed.

"Don't think to practise any of the cursed arts of your sex upon me; don't pretend to throw yourself into fits."

"I scorn your imputation, Sir William," said I, half fainting and breathless. "Nor shall I make any resistance or opposition to your leaving me a beggar. I have now reason to believe I shall not live to want what you are determined to force from me, as these violent methods will soon deprive me of my existence, even if *you* would withold the murderous knife."

"Come, none of your damned whining; let me have the papers; and let us not think anymore about it." He offered to raise me.

"I want not your assistance," said I.

"Oh! You are sulky, are you? But I shall let you know, madame, these airs will not do with me." I had seated myself on a chair and leaned my elbow on a table, supporting my head with my hand; he snatched my hand away from my face while he was making the last speech.

"What the devil! Am I to wait all day for the papers? Where are the keys?"

"Take them," said I, drawing them from my pocket. "Do what you will, provided you leave me to myself."

"Damned sex!" cried he. "Wives or mistresses, by heaven! You are all alike." So saying, he went out of the room and, opening my bureau, possessed himself of the parchment so much desired by him. I have not seen him since, and now it is past eleven. What a fate is mine! However, I have no more to give up; so he cannot storm at or threaten me again, since I am now a beggar as well as himself. I shall sit about an hour longer, and then I shall fasten my door for the night; and I hope he will not insist on my opening it for him. I make Win lie in a little bed in a closet within my room. She is the only domestic I can place the least confidence in. She sees my eyes red with weeping; she sheds tears, but asks no questions. Farewell, my dearest Louisa: pity the sufferings of thy sister, who feels every woe augmented by the grief she causes in your sympathizing breast.

Adieu! Adieu!

J.S.

⚜ ⚜ ⚜ ⚜ ⚜ ⚜ ⚜ ⚜ ⚜
LETTER 36
⚜ ⚜ ⚜ ⚜ ⚜ ⚜ ⚜ ⚜ ⚜

From the Sylph

I find my admonitions have failed, and my Julia has relinquished all her future dependance. Did you not promise an implicit obedience to my advice?

How comes it then, that your husband triumphs in having the power of still visiting the gaming tables and betting with the utmost *éclat*? Settlements, as the late Lord Hardwicke used to say, are the foolishest bonds in nature, since there never was yet a woman who might not be kissed or kicked out of it: which of those methods Sir William has adopted, I know not; but it is plain it was a successful one. I pity you, my Julia; I grieve for you, and much fear, now Sir William has lost all restraint, he will lose the appearance of it likewise. What resource will he pursue next? Be on your guard, my most amiable friend; my foresight deceives me, or your danger is great. For when a man can once lose his humanity so far to deprive his wife of the means of subsisting herself, I much, very much fear he will so effectually lose his honour likewise, as to make a property of hers. May I judge too feverishly! May Sir William be an exception to my rule! And oh! May you, the fairest work of heaven, be equally its care!

Adieu!

LETTER 37

To the Sylph

Alas! I look for comfort when I open my Sylph's letters; yet in this before me you only point out the shoals and quicksands—but hold not out your sustaining hand to guide me through the devious path. I have disobeyed your behest; but you know not how I have been urged, and my pained soul cannot support the repetition. I will ever be implicit in my obedience to you, as far as *I* am concerned only; as to this particular point, you would not have me disobey my husband, I am sure. Indeed I could do no other than I did. If he should make an ill-use of the sums raised, I am not answerable for it; but, if he had been driven to any fatal exigence through my refusal, my wretchedness would have been more exquisite than it now is, which I think would have exceeded what I could have supported. Something is in agitation now; but what I am totally a stranger to. I have just heard from one of my servants that Mr. Stanley, an uncle of Sir William's, is expected in town. Would to heaven he may have the will and power to extricate us! But I hear he is of a most morose temper and was never on good terms with his nephew. The dangers you hint at, I hope, and pray without ceasing to heaven, to be delivered from. Oh! That Sir William would permit me to return to my dear father and sister! In their kind embraces I should lose the remembrance of the tempests I have undergone; like the poor shipwrecked mariner, I should hail the friendly port, and never, never trust the deceitful ocean more. But ah! How fruitless this wish! Here I am doomed to stay a wretch undone.

Adieu!

ᵜ ᵜ ᵜ ᵜ ᵜ ᵜ ᵜ ᵜ ᵜ ᵜ

LETTER 38

ᵜ ᵜ ᵜ ᵜ ᵜ ᵜ ᵜ ᵜ ᵜ ᵜ

To Miss Grenville

The baron called here this morning. Don't be angry with me, my dearest Louisa, for mentioning *his* name; this will indeed be the last time. He is gone; yes, Louisa, I shall never see him again. But will his looks, his sighs, and tears be forgotten? Oh! Never, never! He came to bid me adieu. "Could I but leave you happy," he cried in scarce articulate accents—"Was I but blest with the remote hope of your having your merit rewarded in this world, I should quit you with less regret and anguish. Oh! Lady Stanley! Best of women! I mean not to lay claim to your gratitude; far be such an idea from my soul! But for your sake I leave the kingdom."

"For mine!" I exclaimed, clasping my hands wildly together, hardly knowing what I said or did. "What! Leave me! Leave the kingdom for my sake! Oh! My God! What advantage can accrue to me by losing"—I could not proceed; my voice failed me, and I remained the petrified statue of despair.

"Lady Stanley," said he with an assumed calmness, "be composed, and hear me. In an age like this, where the examples of vice are so many and so prevalent, though a woman is chaste as the icicle that hangs on Dian's temple, still she will be suspected; and, was the sun never to look upon her, yet she would be tainted by the envenomed breath of slander. Lady Anne Parker has dared in a public company to say that the most virtuous and lovely of her sex will speedily find consolation for the infidelity of her husband by making reprisals; her malevolence has farther induced her to point her finger to one who adores all the virtues with which heaven first endued woman in your form. A voluntary banishment on my side may wipe off this transient eclipse of the fairest and most amiable character in the world, and the beauties of it shine forth with greater lustre, like the diamond, which can only be sullied by the breath, and which evaporates in an instant and beams with fresh brilliancy. I would not wish you to look into my heart," added he with a softened voice, "lest your compassion might affect you too much; yet you know not, you never can know, what I have suffered, and must forever suffer.

> Condemn'd, alas! Whole ages to deplore,
> And image charms I must behold no more.

I sat motionless during his speech; but, finding him silent and, I believe, from his emotions, unable to proceed, "Behold," I cried, "with what a composed resignation I submit to my fate. I hoped I had been too inconsiderable to have excited the tongue of slander, or fix its sting in my bosom. But may you, my friend, regain your peace and happiness in your native country!"

"My native country!" exclaimed he. "What is my native country, what the whole globe itself, to that spot which contains all? But I will say no more. I dare not trust myself, I must not. Oh Julia! Forgive me! Adieu, forever!" I had no voice to detain him; I suffered him to quit the room, and my eyes lost sight of him—forever!

I remained with my eyes stupidly fixed on the door. Oh! Louisa, dare I tell you? My soul seemed to follow him; and all my sufferings have been trivial to this. To be esteemed by him, to be worthy his regard and read his approbation in his speaking eyes; this was my support, this sustained me, nor suffered my feet to strike against a stone in this disfigured path of destruction. He was my polar star. But he is gone, and knows not how much I loved him. I knew it not myself; else how could I promise never to speak, never to think of him again? But whence these wild expressions? Oh! Pardon the effusions of frenetic fancy. I know not what I have said. I am lost, lost!

J.S.

To Colonel Montague

Congratulate me, my dear Jack, on having beat the baron out of the pit. He is off, my boy! And now I may play a safer game, for, between ourselves, I have as much inclination to sleep in a whole skin as somebody else you and I know of. I have really been more successful than I could have flattered myself I should be; but the devil still stands my friend, which is grateful to be sure, as the devil is in it if one good turn does not deserve another; and I have helped his fable divinity to many a good job in my day. The summit of my wishes was to remove this troublesome fellow; but he has taken himself clean out of the kingdom, lest the fame of his Dulcinea should suffer in the *Morning Post*. He, if any man could, would not scruple drubbing that Hydra of scandal; but then the stain would still remain where the blot had been made. I think you will be glad that he is punished at any rate for his impertinent interference in your late affair with the recruit's sweetheart. These delicate minds are ever contriving their own misery, and, from their exquisite sensibility, find out the method of refining on torture. Thus, in a fit of heroics, he has banished himself from the only woman he loves, and who in a short time, unless my ammunition fails, or my mine springs, too soon he might have a chance of being happy with was he cast in mortal mould.—But I take it he is one of that sort which Madame Sevigné calls "a pumpkin fried in snow," or engendered between a Lapland sailor and a mermaid on the icy plains of Greenland. Even the charms of Julia can but just warm him. He does not burn like me. The consuming fire of Etna riots not in his veins, or he would have lost all consideration but that of the completion of his wishes. Mine have become ten times more eager from the resistance I have met with. Fool that I was! Not to be able to keep a rein over my transports till I had extinguished the lights! But to see her before me, my pulse beating with tumultous passion, and my villainous fancy anticipating the tempting scene, all conspired to give such spirit to my caresses as ill-suited with the character I assumed of an indifferent husband. Like Calista of old, she soon discovered the God under the semblance of Diana. Heavens! How she fired up, and like the leopard appeared more beauteous when heightened by anger? But in vain, my pretty trembler, in vain you struggle in the toils; thy price is paid, and thou wilt soon be mine. Stanley has lost everything to me but his property in his wife's person; and though perhaps he may make a few wry faces, he must digest that bitter pill. He has obliged her to give up all her jointure, so she has now no dependence. What a fool he is! But he has ever been so; the most palpable cheat passes on him; and though he is morally certain that to *play* and to *lose* is one and the same thing, yet nothing can cure his cursed itch of gaming. Notwithstanding all the *remonstrances* I have made, and the *dissuasives* I have daily used, he is bent upon his own destruction; and, since that is plainly the case, why may not I, and a few clever fellows like myself, take advantage of his egregious folly?

It was but yesterday I met him. "I am most consumedly in the flat key, Biddulph," said he. "I know not what to do with myself. For God's sake! Let us have a little touch at billiards, picquet, or something, to drive the devil melancholy out of my citadel (touching his bosom), for, by my soul, I believe I shall make away with myself if left to my own *agreeable* meditations." As usual, I advised him to reflect how much luck had run against him and begged him to be cautious, that I positively had no pleasure in playing with one who never turned a game, that I should look out for someone who understood billiards well enough to be my conqueror.

"What the devil!" cried he. "You think me a novice; come, come, I will convince you, to your sorrow, I know something of the game; I'll bet you five hundred, Biddulph, that I pocket your ball in five minutes."

"You can't beat me," said I, "and I will give you three."

"I'll be damned if I accept three; no, no, let us play on the square." So to it we went; and as usual it ended. The more he loses, the more impetuous and eager he is to play.

There will be a confounded bustle soon; his uncle, old Stanley, is coming up to town. In disposing of his wife's jointure, part of which was connected to an estate of Squaretoes, the affair has consequently reached his ears, and he is all fury upon the occasion. I believe there has been a little chicanery practised between Sir William and his lawyer, which will prove but an ugly business. However, thanks to my foresight in these matters, I am out of the scrape; but I can see the baronet is cursedly off the hooks from the idea of its transpiring, and had rather see the Devil than the Don. He has burnt his fingers, and smarts till he roars again.

Adieu! Jack:

Remember thy old friend,

Biddulph

♀ ♀ ♀ ♀ ♀ ♀ ♀ ♀ ♀ ♀

LETTER 40

♀ ♀ ♀ ♀ ♀ ♀ ♀ ♀ ♀ ♀

To Miss Grenville

My storm of grief is now little appeased; and I think I ought to apologize to my dearest Louisa for making her so free a participator of my frenzy; yet I doubt not of your forgiveness on this, as well as many occasions, reflecting with the liveliest gratitude on the extreme tenderness you have ever shown me.

The morning after I had written that incoherent letter to you, Miss Finch paid me a visit. She took no notice of the dejection of my countenance, which I am convinced was but too visible; but, putting on a cheerful air, though I thought she too looked melancholy when she first came in, "I am come to tell you, my dear Lady Stanley," said she, "that you must go to the Lady D——'s route this evening; you know you are engaged, and I design you for my *chaperone*."

"Excuse me, my dear," returned I, "I cannot think of going thither, and was just going to send a card to that purpose."

"Lady Stanley," she replied, "you must go indeed. I have a very particular reason for urging you to make your appearance there."

"And I have as particular a reason," said I, turning away my head to conceal a tear that would unbidden start in my eye, "to prevent my going there or anywhere else at present."

Her eyes were moistened; when, taking my hand in hers and looking up in my face with the utmost friendliness, "My amiable Lady Stanley, it grieves my soul to think any of the licentious wretches in this town should dare asperse such excellence as yours; but that infamous creature, Lady Anne, said last night in the coffee room at the opera that she had heard Lady Stanley took to heart (was her expression) the departure of Baron Ton-hausen, and that she and Miss Finch had quarrelled about their gallant. Believe me, I could sooner have lost the power of speech than have communicated so disagreeable a piece of intelligence to you, but that I think it highly incumbent on you, by appearing with cheerfulness in public with me, to frustrate the malevolence of that spiteful woman as much as we both can."

"What have I done to that vile woman?" said I, giving loose to my tears. "In what have I injured her, that she should thus seek to blacken my fame?"

"Dared to be virtuous, while she is infamous," answered Miss Finch;— "but, however, my dear Lady Stanley, you perceive the necessity of contradicting her assertion of our having quarrelled on any account; and nothing can so effectually do it as our appearing together in good spirits."

"Mine," cried I, "are broken entirely. I have no wish to wear the semblance of pleasure, while my heart is bowed down with woe."

"But we must do disagreeable things sometimes to keep up appearances. That vile woman, as you justly call her, would be happy to have it in her power to spread her calumny; we may in part prevent it: besides, I promised the baron I would not let you sit moping at home, but draw you out into company, at the same time giving you as much of mine as I could, and as I found agreeable to you."

"I beg you to be assured, my dear, that the company of no one can be more so than yours. And, as I have no doubts of your sincere wish for my welfare, I will readily submit myself to your discretion. But how shall I be able to confront that infamous Lady Anne, who will probably be there?"

"Never mind her; let conscious merit support you. Reflect on your own worth, nor cast one thought on such a wretch. I will dine with you; and in the evening we will prepare for this visit."

I made no enquiry why the baron recommended me so strongly to Miss Finch. I thought such enquiry might lead us farther than was prudent; besides, I knew Miss Finch had a *tendre* for him, and therefore, through the course of the day, I never mentioned his name. Miss Finch was equally delicate as myself; our discourse then naturally fell on indifferent subjects; and I found I grew towards the evening much more composed than I had been for some time. The party was large; but, to avoid conversation as much as possible, I sat down to a quadrille table with Miss Finch; and, encouraged by her looks and smiles, which I believe the good girl forced into her countenance to give me spirits, I got through the evening tolerably well. The next morning, I walked with my friend into the park. I never dine out, as I would wish always to be at home at mealtimes, lest Sir William should choose to give me his company, but that is very seldom the case; and as to the evenings, I never see him, as he does not come home till three or four in the morning, and often stays out the whole night. We have of course separate apartments. Adieu, my beloved! Would to God I could fly to your arms, and there forget my sorrows!

Yours, most affectionately,

J.S.

ψ ψ ψ ψ ψ ψ ψ ψ ψ ψ
LETTER 41
ψ ψ ψ ψ ψ ψ ψ ψ ψ ψ

To Lord Biddulph

For heaven's sake, my dear lord, let me see you instantly; or on second thoughts (though I am too much perplexed to be able to arrange them properly) I will lay before you the cursed difficulties with which I am surrounded, and then I shall beg the favour of you to go to Sir Brudenel and see what you can do with him. Sure the devil owes me some heavy grudge; everything goes against me. Old Stanley has rubbed through a damned fit of the gout. Oh! That I could kill him with a wish! I then should be a free man again.

You see I make no scruple of applying to you, relying firmly on your professions of friendship; and assure yourself I shall be most happy in subscribing to any terms that you may propose for your own security, for fourteen thousand six hundred pounds I must have by Friday, if I pawn my soul twenty times for the sum. If you don't assist me, I have but one other method (you understand me), though I should be unwilling to be driven to such a procedure. But I am (except in my hopes in you) all despair.

Adieu!

W. Stanley

LETTER 42

To Sir William Stanley

[*Enclosed in the foregoing.*]

Sir,

I am extremely concerned, and as equally surprised, to find by my lawyer that the Pemberton estate was not yours to dispose of. He tells me it is, after the death of your wife, the sole property of your uncle, Mr. Dawson (who is Mr. Stanley's lawyer), having clearly provided it to him by the deeds, which he swears he is possessed of. How then, Sir William, am I to reconcile this intelligence with the transactions between us? I have paid into your hands the sum of fourteen thousand six hundred pounds and (I am sorry to write so harshly) have received a forged deed of conveyance. Mr. Dawson has assured Stevens, my lawyer, that his client never signed the conveyance. I should be very unwilling to bring you, or any gentleman, into such a dilemma; but you may suppose I should be as sorry to lose such a sum for nothing; nor, indeed, could I consent to injure my heirs by such a negligence. I hope it will suit you to replace the above sum in the hands of my banker, and I will not hesitate to conceal the writings now in my possession; but the money must be paid by Friday next. You will reflect on this maturely, as you must know in what a predicament you at present stand, and what must be the consequence of such an affair coming under the cognizance of the law.

I remain, sir,

Your humble servant,

George Brudenel

✠ ✠ ✠ ✠ ✠ ✠ ✠ ✠ ✠ ✠
LETTER 43
✠ ✠ ✠ ✠ ✠ ✠ ✠ ✠ ✠ ✠

To Miss Grenville

I write to you, my dearest Louisa, under the greatest agitation of spirits and know no other method of quieting them than communicating my griefs to you. But alas! How can you remedy the evils of which I complain? Or how shall I describe them to you? How many times I have repeated, *how hard is my fate!* Yes, Louisa! And I must still repeat the same. In short, what have I to trust to? I see nothing before me but the effects of deep despair. I tremble at every sound, and every footstep seems to be the harbinger of some disaster.

Sir William breakfasted with me this morning, the first time these three weeks I believe; a letter was brought him. He changed countenance on the perusal of it and, starting up, traversed the room in great disorder. "Any ill news, Sir William?" I asked. He heeded me not, but rang the bell with violence.

"Get the chariot ready directly—no, give me my hat and sword." Before they could be brought, he again changed his mind. He would then write a note. He took the standish, folded some paper, wrote, blotted, and tore many sheets, bit his lips, struck his forehead, and acted a thousand extravagances. I could contain myself no longer.

"Whatever may be the consequence of your anger, Sir William," said I, "I must insist on knowing what sudden turn of affairs has occasioned this present distress. For heaven's sake! Do not refuse to communicate your trouble. I cannot support the agony your agitation has thrown me into."

"And you would be less able to support it were I to communicate it."

"If you have any pity for me," cried I, rising and going up to him, "I conjure you by that pity to disclose the cause of your disorder. Were I certain of being unable to bear the shock, yet I would meet it with calmness rather than be thus kept in the most dreadful suspense."

"Suffice it then," cried he, throwing out his arm, "I am ruined forever."

"Ruined!" I repeated with faint voice.

"Yes!" he answered, starting on his feet and muttering curses between his teeth. Then, after a fearful pause, "There is but one way, but one way to escape this impending evil."

"Oh!" cried I. "May you fall on the right way! but, perhaps, things may not be so bad as you apprehend; you know I have valuable jewels; let me fetch them for you; the sale of them will produce a great deal of money."

"Jewels! O God! They are gone, you have no jewels."

"Indeed, my dear Sir William," I replied, shocked to death at seeing the deplorable way he was in and fearing, from his saying they were gone, that his head was hurt—"Indeed, my dear Sir William, I have them in my own cabinet," and immediately fetched them to him.

He snatched them out of my hand and, dashing them on the floor, "Why do you bring me these damned baubles; your diamonds are gone; these are only paste."

"What do you mean?" I cried, all astonishment, "I am sure they are such, as I received them from you."

"I know it very well; but I sold them when you thought them new-set; and now I am more pushed than ever."

"They were yours, Sir William," said I, stifling my resentment, as I thought he was now sufficiently punished, "you had therefore a right to dispose of them whenever you chose; and, had you made me the *confidante* of your intention, I should not have opposed it; I am only sorry you should have been so distressed as to have yielded to such a necessity, for tho' my confidence in you, and my ignorance in jewels, might prevent *my* knowing them to be counterfeits, yet, no doubt, everybody who has seen me in them must have discovered their fallacy. How contemptible then have you made us appear!"

"Oh! For God's sake, let me hear no more about them; let them all go to the devil; I have things of more consequence to attend to."

At this moment a Mr. Brooksbank was announced. "By heaven," cried Sir William, "we are all undone! Brooksbank! Blown to the devil! Lady Stanley, you may retire to your own room; I have some business of a private nature with this gentleman."

I obeyed, leaving my husband with this *gentleman,* whom I think the worst-looking fellow I ever saw in my life, and retired to my own apartment to give vent to the sorrow which flowed in on every side. "Oh! Good God!" I cried, bursting into floods of tears. "What a change eighteen months has made! A princely fortune dissipated, and a man of honour, at least one who has appeared as such, reduced to the poor subterfuge of stealing his wife's jewels, to pay gaming debts, and support kept mistresses." These were my sad and solitary reflexions. What a wretched hand has he made of it! And how deplorable is my situation! Alas! To what resource can he next fly? What is to become of us? I have no claim to any farther bounty from my own family; like the prodigal son, I have received my portion; and although I have not been the squanderer, yet it is all gone, and I may be reduced to feed on the husks of acorns; at least, I am sure I eat bitter herbs. Surely, I am visited with these calamities for the sins of my grandfather! May they soon be expiated!

That wretch Lord Biddulph has been here, and, after some conversation, he has taken Sir William out in his chariot. Thank heaven, I saw him not; but Win brought me this intelligence. I would send for Miss Finch to afford me a little consolation, but she is confined at home by a feverish complaint. I cannot think of going out while things are in this state; so I literally seem a prisoner in my own house. Oh! That I had never, never seen it! Adieu! Adieu!

J.S.

LETTER 44

To Colonel Montague

I acquainted you sometime since of Stanley's affairs being quite *dérangé*, and that he had practised an unsuccessful manoeuvre on the Brudenel. A pretty piece of business he has made of it, and his worship stands a fair chance of swinging for forgery, unless I contribute my assistance to extricate him, by enabling him to replace the money. As to raising any in the ordinary way, it is not in his power, as all his estates are settled on old Stanley, he (Sir William) having no children; and he is inexorable. There may be something to be said in the old fellow's favour too; he has advanced thousand after thousand, till he is tired out, for giving him money is really only throwing water into a sieve.

In consequence of a hasty letter written by the baronet, begging me to use all my interest with Brudenel, I thought it the better way to wait on Stanley myself and talk the affair over with him and, as he promised to subscribe to any terms for security, to make these terms most pleasing to myself. Besides, I confess, I was unwilling to meet Sir George about such a black piece of business, not choosing likewise to subject myself to the censures of that puritanic mortal for having drawn Stanley into a love of play. I found Sir William under the greatest disorder of spirits; Brooksbank was with him; that fellow carries his conscience in his face; he is the portrait of villainy and turpitude. "For God's sake! My lord," cried Sir William (this you know being his usual exclamation). "What is to be done in this cursed affair? All my hopes are fixed on the assistance you have promised me."

"Why, faith, Sir William," I answered. "It is as you say, a most cursed unlucky affair. I think Brooksbank has not acted with his accustomed caution. As to what assistance I can afford you, you may firmly rely on, but I had a confounded tumble last night after you left us; by the by, you was out of luck absenting yourself; there was a great deal done; I lost upwards of seventeen thousand to the young cub in less than an hour, and nine to the count, so that I am a little out of elbows, which happens very unfortunate at this critical time."

"Then I am ruined forever!"

"No, no, not so bad neither, I dare say. What say you to Lady Stanley's diamonds? They are valuable."

"O Christ, they are gone long ago. I told her I thought they wanted new-setting and supplied her with paste, which she knew nothing of till this morning when she offered them to me." (All this I knew very well, for D. the jeweller told me so, but I did not choose to inform his worship so much.)

"You have a large quantity of plate."

"All melted, my lord, but one service, and that I have borrowed money on."

"Well, I have something more to offer; but, if you please, we will dismiss Mr. Brooksbank. I dare say he has other business." He took the hint and left us to ourselves.

When we were alone, I drew my chair close to him; he was leaning his head on his hand, which rested on the table in a most melancholy posture. "Stanley," said I, "what I am now going to say is a matter entirely between ourselves. You are no stranger to the passion I have long entertained for your wife, and from your showing no resentment for what I termed a frolic on the night of the masquerade, I have reason to believe you will not be mortally offended at this my open avowal of my attachment. Hear me" (for he changed his position, and seemed going to speak): "I adore Lady Stanley; I have repeatedly assured her of the violence of my flame, but have ever met with the utmost coldness on her side; let me, however, have your permission, I will yet ensure myself success."

"What, Biddulph! Consent to my own dishonour! What do you take me for?"

"What do I take you for?" cried I with a smile in which I infused a proper degree of contempt. "What will Sir George Brudenel take you for, you mean."

"Curses, everlasting curses, blast me for my damned love of play! That has been my bane."

"And I offer you your cure."

"The remedy is worse than the disease."

"Then submit to the disease, and sink under it. Sir William, your humble servant," cried I, rising as if to go.

"Biddulph, my dear Biddulph," cried he, catching my hand and grasping it with dying energy, "what are you about to do? You surely will not leave me in this damned exigency? Think of my situation! I have parted with every means of raising more money, and eternal infamy will be the consequence of this last cursed subterfuge of mine transpiring. Oh, my God! How sunk am I! And will you not hold out your friendly arm?"

"I have already offered you proposals," I replied with an affected coldness, "which you do not think proper to accede to."

"Will you consign me to everlasting perdition?"

"Will you make no sacrifice to extricate yourself?"

"Yes; my life."

"What, at Tyburn?"

"Damn on the thought! Oh! Biddulph, are there no means? Reflect—the honour of my injured wife!"

"Will not *that* suffer by your undergoing ignominious death?"

"Ah! Why do you thus stretch my heartstrings? Julia is virtuous and deserves a better fate than she has met with in me. What a wretch must that man be who will consign his wife to infamy! No; sunk, lost, and ruined as I am, I cannot yield to such baseness; I should be doubly damned."

"You know your own conscience best, and how much it will bear; I did not use to think you so scrupulous; what I offer is as much for your advantage as my own; nay, faith, for your advantage solely, as I may have a very good chance of succeeding with her by and by, when you can reap no benefit from it. All I ask of you is your permission to give you an opportunity of suing for divorce. Lay your damages as high as you please, I will agree to anything and, as an earnest, will raise this sum which distresses you so much; I am not tied down as you are; I can mortgage any part of my estate. What do you say? Will you sign a paper, making over all right and title to your wife in my favour? There is no time to be lost, I can assure you. Your uncle Stanley's lawyer has been with Brudenel; you know what hopes you have from that quarter, for the sooner you are out of the way, the better for the next heir."

You never saw a poor devil so distressed and agitated as Stanley was; he shook like one under a fit of the tertianague. I used every argument I could muster up and conjured all the horrible ideas which were likely to terrify a man of his cast; threatened, soothed, sneered: in short, I at last gained my point, and he signed a commission for his own cuckoldom; which that I may be able to achieve soon, dear Venus grant! I took him with me to consult with our broker about raising the money. In the evening I intend my visit to the lovely Julia. Oh! That I may be endued with sufficient eloquence to soften her gentle heart and tune it to the sweetest notes of love! But she is virtuous, as Stanley says; that she is most truly: yet who knows how far resentment against her brutal husband may induce her to go? If ever woman had provocation, she certainly has. O that she may be inclined to revenge herself on him for his baseness to her! And that I may be the happy instrument of effecting it!

Gods! What a thought is there!

Adieu!

Biddulph

☥ ☥ ☥ ☥ ☥ ☥ ☥ ☥ ☥ ☥

LETTER 45

☥ ☥ ☥ ☥ ☥ ☥ ☥ ☥ ☥ ☥

To Miss Grenville

Oh! My Louisa, what will now become of your wretched sister? Surely the wide world contains not so forlorn a wretch who has not been guilty of any crime! But let me not keep you in suspense. In the afternoon of the day I wrote you last (I told you Miss Finch was ill)—Oh! Good God! I know not what I write. I thought I would go and see her for an hour or two. I ordered the coach and was just stepping into it when an ill-looking man (Lord bless me! I have seen none else lately) laid hold of my arm, saying, "Madame, you must not go into that carriage."

"What do you mean?" I asked with a voice of terror, thinking he was a madman.

"Nothing, my lady," he answered, "but an execution on Sir William."

"An execution! Oh! Heavens! What execution?" I was breathless, and just fainting.

"They are bailiffs, my lady," said one of our servants. "My master is arrested for debt, and these men will seize everything in the house; but you need not be terrified, your ladyship is safe, they cannot touch you."

I ran back into the house with the utmost precipitation; all the servants seemed in commotion. I saw Preston; she was running upstairs with a bundle in her hand.

"Preston," said I, "what are you about?"

"Oh! The bailiffs, my lady!"

"They won't hurt you; I want you here."

"I can't come, indeed, my lady, till I have disposed of these things; I must throw them out of the window, or the bailiffs will seize them."

I could not get a servant near me but my faithful Win, who hung weeping round me; as for myself, I was too much agitated to shed a tear, or appear sensible of my misfortune.

Two of these horrid men came into the room. I demanded what they wanted. To see that none of the goods were carried out of the house, they answered. I asked them if they knew where Sir William Stanley was. "Oh! He is safe enough," said one of them. "We can't touch him; he pleads privilege, as being a member of Parliament; we can only take care of his furniture for him."

"And am I not allowed the same privilege? If so, how have you dared detain me?"

"Detain you? Why, I hope your ladyship will not say as how we have offered to detain you! You may go where you please, provided you take nothing away with you."

"My lady was going out," said Win, sobbing, "and you would not suffer it."

"Not in the coach, mistress, to be sure; but don't go for to say we stopped your lady. She may go when she will."

"Will one of you order me a chair or hackney coach? I have no business here." The last word melted me; and I sunk into a chair, giving way to a copious flood of tears. At that instant almost the detestable Biddulph entered the room. I started up—"Whence this intrusion, my lord?" I asked with a haughty tone. "Are you come to join your *insults* with the misfortunes you have in great measure effected?"

"I take heaven to witness," answered he, "how much I was shocked to find an executor in your house; I had not the least idea of such a circumstance happening. I, indeed, knew that Sir William was very strained for money."

"Accursed be those," interrupted I, "ever accursed be those whose pernicious counsels and baseful examples have brought him into these exigencies. I look on you, my lord, as one cruel cause of the ruin of our house."

"Rather, Lady Stanley, call me the prop of your sinking house. View, in me, one who would die to render you service."

"Would to heaven you had done so long—long before I had seen you!"

"How unkind is that wish! I came, madame, with the intention of being serviceable to you. Do not then put such hard constructions on my words. I wished to consult with you on the most efficacious means to be used for Sir William's emolument. You know not what power you have!"

"Power! Alas! What power have I?"

"The most unlimited," he replied, fixing his odious eyes on my face, which I returned by a look of the utmost scorn. "O Lady Stanley," he continued, "do not—do not, I entreat you, use me so hardly. Will you allow me to speak to you alone?"

"By no means."

"For God's sake do! Your servant shall remain in the next room, within your call. Let me beseech you to place some confidence in me. I have that to relate concerning Sir William which you would not choose a domestic should hear. Dearest Lady Stanley, be not inexorable."

"You may go into that room, Win," said I, not deigning to answer this importunate man. "My lord," addressing myself to him, "you can have nothing to tell me to which I am stranger; I know Sir William is totally ruined. This is known to every servant in the house."

"Believe me," said he, "the execution is the least part of the evil. That event happens daily among the great people: but there is an affair of another nature, the stain of which can never be wiped off. Sir William, by his necessities, has been plunged into the utmost difficulties and to extricate himself has used some unlawful means; in a word, he has committed a forgery."

"Impossible!" cried I, clasping my hands together in agony.

"It is too true; Sir George Brudenel has the forged deed now in his hands, and nothing can save him from an ignominious death but the raising a large sum of money, which is quite out of his power. Indeed, I might with some difficulty assist him."

"And will you not step forth to save him?" I asked with precipitation.

"What would *you* do to save him?" he asked in his turn, attempting to take my hand.

"Can you ask me such a question? To save his life, what would I not do?"

"You have the means in your power."

"Oh! Name them quickly, and ease my heart of this load of distraction! It is more—much more than I can bear."

"Oh! My lovely angel!" cried the horrid wretch. "Would you show some tenderness to me? Would you but listen to the most faithful, most enamoured of men, much might be done. You would, by your sweet condescension, bind me forever to your interest, might I but flatter myself I should share your affection. Would you but give me the slightest mark of it, oh!—how blest I should be! Say, my adorable Julia, can I ever hope to touch your heart?"

"Wretch!" cried I. "Unhand me. How dare you have the insolence to affront me again with the mention of your hateful passion? I believe all you have uttered to be a base falsehood against my Sir William. You have taken an opportunity to insult his wife at a time when you think him too much engaged to seek vengeance; otherwise your coward soul would shrink from the just resentment you ought to expect!"

"I am no coward, madame," he replied, "but in my fears of offending the only woman on whom my soul dotes, and the only one whose scorn would wound me. I am not afraid of Sir William's resentment—I act but by his consent."

"By his consent!"

"Yes, my dear creature, by his. Come, I know you to be a woman of sense; you are acquainted with your husband's handwriting, I presume. *I* have not committed *forgery*, I assure you. Look, madame, on this paper; I will see how much you need dread the just vengeance of an injured husband, when I have his especial mandate to take possession as soon as I can gain my lovely charmer's consent; and, oh!—may just revenge inspire you to reward my labours!" He held a paper towards me; I attempted to snatch it out of his hand. "Not so, my sweet angel, I cannot part with it; but you shall see the contents of it with all my heart."

Oh! Louisa, do I live to tell you what were those contents!—

I resign right and title to my wife, Julia Stanley, to Lord Biddulph, on condition that he pays into my hands the sum of fourteen thousand six hundred pounds, which he enters into an engagement to perform. Witness my hand,

William Stanley

Grief, resentment, and amazement struck me dumb.

"What say you to this, Lady Stanley? Should you not pique yourself on your fidelity to such a good husband who takes so much care of you? You see how much he prizes his life."

"Peace, monster! Peace!" cried I. "You have taken a base, most base advantage of the wretch you have undone!"

"The fault is all yours; the cruelty with which you have treated me has driven me to the only course left of obtaining you. You have it in your power to save or condemn your husband."

"What, should I barter my soul to save *one* so profligate as his? But there are other resources yet left, and we yet may triumph over thee, thou cruel, worst of wretches!"

"Perhaps, you may think there are hopes from old Stanley; there can be none, as he has caused his execution. It would half ruin your family to raise this sum, as there are many more debts which they would be called upon to pay. Why then will you put it out of your power to extricate him? Let me have some influence over you! I swear by the great God that made me, I will marry you as soon as a divorce can be obtained. I have sworn the same to Sir William."

Think, my dearest Louisa, what a situation this was for me! I was constrained to rein in my resentment, lest I should irritate this wretch to some act of violence—for I had but too much reason to believe I was wholly in his power. I had my senses sufficiently collected (for which I owe my thanks to heaven) to make a clear retrospect of my forlorn condition—eight or ten strange fellows in the house who, from the nature of their profession, must be hardened gainst every distress and, perhaps, ready to join the hand of oppression in injuring the unfortunate—my servants (in none of whom I could confide), most of them employed in protecting what they styled their own property, and either totally regardless of me, or, what I more feared, might unite with this my chief enemy in my destruction. As to the forgery, though the bare surmise threw me into agonies, I rather thought it a proof how far the vile Biddulph would proceed to terrify me than reality;

but the fatal paper signed by Sir William—that was too evident to be disputed. This conflict of thought employed every faculty and left me speechless—Biddulph was still on his knees, "For heaven's sake," cried he, "do not treat me with this scorn; make me not desperate! Ardent as my passion is, I would not lose sight of my respect for you."

"That you have already done," I answered, "in thus openly avowing a passion to me so highly disagreeable. Prove your respect, my lord, by quitting so unbecoming a posture, and leave the most unfortunate of women to her destiny."

"Take care, take care, madame," cried he. "How much you drive me to despair; I have long, long adored you. My perseverance, notwithstanding your frowns, calls for some reward; and unless you assure me that in a future day you will not be thus unkind, I shall not easily forgo the opportunity which now offers."

"For mercy's sake!" exclaimed I, starting up. "What do you mean? Lord Biddulph! How dare—I insist, sir—leave me." I burst into tears and, throwing myself again in my chair, gave free vent to all the anguish of my soul.

He seemed moved. Again he knelt, and implored pardon—"Forgive me—Oh! Forgive me, thou sweet excellence! I will not hereafter offend, if it is in nature to suppress the extreme violence of my love. You know not how extensive your sway is over my soul! Indeed you do not!"

"On the condition of your leaving me directly, I will endeavour to forgive and forget what has passed," I sobbed out, for my heart was too full of grief to articulate clearly.

"Urge me not to leave you, my angelic creature. Ah! Seek not to drive the man from your presence who dotes, dotes on you to distraction. Think what a villain your husband is; think into what accumulated distress he has plunged you. Behold, in me, one who will extricate you from all your difficulties; who will raise you to rank, title, and honour; one whom you may make a convert. Oh! That I had met with you before this cursed engagement, I should have been the most blest of men. No vile passion would have interfered to sever my heart from my beauteous wife; in her soft arms I should have found a balm for the disquietudes of the world, and learnt to despise all its empty delusive joys in the solid bliss of being good and happy!"

This fine harangue had no weight with me, though I thought it convenient he should think I was moved by it. "Alas! My lord," said I, "it is now too late to indulge these ideas. I am doomed to be wretched; and my wretchedness feels increase if I am the cause of making any earthly being so; yet, if you have the tenderness for me you express, you must participate of my deep affliction. Ask your own heart if a breast, torn with anguish and sorrow as mine is, can at present admit a thought of any other sentiment than the grief so melancholy a situation excites? In pity, therefore, to the woman you profess to love, leave me for this time. I said I would forgive and forget; your compliance with my request may do more; it certainly will make me grateful."

"Dearest of all creatures," cried he, seizing my hand and pressing it with rapture to his bosom. "Dearest, best of women! What is there that I could refuse you? Oh nothing, nothing; my soul is devoted to you. But why leave you? Why may I not this moment reap the advantage of your yielding heart?"

"Away! Away, my lord," cried I, pushing him from me. "You promised to restrain your passion; why then is it thus boundless? Entitle yourself to my consideration before you thus demand returns."

"I make no demands. I have done. But I flattered myself I read your soft wishes in your lovely eyes." (Detestable wretch! How my soul rose up against him! But fear restrained my tongue.) "But tell me, my adorable angel, if I tear myself from you now, when shall I be so happy as to behold you again?"

"Tomorrow," I answered. "I shall be in more composed spirits tomorrow, and then I will see you here; but do not expect too much. And now leave me this moment, as I have said more than I ought."

"I obey, dearest Julia," cried the insolent creature. "I obey." And, blessed be heaven! He left the room. I sprung to the door and double locked it, then called Win into the room, who had heard the whole of this conversation. The poor soul was as pale as ashes; her looks were contagious; I caught the infection; and, forgetting the distance betwixt us (but misery makes us all equal), I threw my arms round her and shed floods of tears into her faithful bosom. When my storms of grief had a little subsided, or indeed when nature had exhausted her store, I became more calm and had it in my power to consider what steps I should take, as you may believe I had nothing further from my intention than meeting this vile man again. I soon came to the determination to send to Miss Finch, as there was no one to whom I could apply for an asylum; I mean, for the present, as I am convinced I shall find the properest and most welcome in yours and my dear father's arms by and by. I rang the bell; one of the horrid bailiffs came for my orders. I desired to have Griffith called to me. I wrote a note to Miss Finch, telling her in a few words the situation of my affairs and that my dread was so great of receiving further insult from Lord Biddulph that I could not support the idea of passing the night surrounded by such wretches, therefore entreated her to send someone in whom she could confide, in her carriage, to convey me to her for a little time till I could hear from my friends. In a quarter of an hour Griffith returned with a billet containing only three lines—but, oh, how much comfort.

> My dearest creature, my heart bleeds for your distresses; there is no one so proper as your true friend to convey you hither. I will be with you in an instant; yours, forever, Maria Finch.

I made Win bundle up a few nightclothes and trifles that we both might want, and in a short time I found myself pressed to the bosom of my dear Maria. She had risen from her bed, where she had lain two days, to fly to my succour. Ah! How much am I indebted to her! By Miss Finch's advice, I wrote a few words to—oh! What shall I call him?—the man, my Louisa, who tore me from the fostering bosom of my beloved father to abandon me to the miseries and infamy of the world! I wrote thus:

> Abandoned and forsaken by him to whom I alone ought to look up for protection, I am (though, alas!—unable) obliged to be the guardian of my own honour. I have left your house; happy, happy had it been for me, never to have entered it! I seek that asylum from strangers, I can no longer meet with from my husband. I have suffered too much from my fatal connexion with you to feel disposed to consign myself to everlasting infamy (notwithstanding I have your permission) to extricate you from a trivial inconvenience. Remember, this is the first instance in which I ever disobeyed your will. May you see your error, reform, and be happy! So prays your much injured but still faithful wife,
> Julia Stanley

Miss Finch, with the goodness of an angel, took me home with her; nor would she leave me a moment to myself. She has indulged me with permission to write this account, to save me the trouble of repeating it to her. And now, my Louisa, and you, my dear honoured father, will you receive your poor wanderer? Will you heal her heartrending sorrows and suffer her to seek for happiness, at least a restoration of ease, in your tender bosoms? Will you hush her cares and teach her to kiss the hand which chastises her? Oh! How I long to pour forth my soul into the breast from whence I expect to derive all my earthly comfort!

Adieu!

J.S.

LETTER 46

To Colonel Montague

Well, Jack, we are all *entrain*. I believe we shall do in time. But old Square-toes has stole a march on us and took out an extent against his nephew. Did you ever hear of so unnatural a dog? It is true he has done a great deal for Sir William and saw plainly, the more money he paid, the more extravagant his nephew grew; but still it was a damned affair too after all. I have been with my dear bewitching charmer. I have her promise to admit me as a visitor tomorrow. I was a fool not to finish the business tonight, as I could have bribed everyone in the house to assist me. Your bailiffs are proper fellows for the purpose, but I love to have my adorables meet me—*almost* half way. I shall, I hope, gain her at last; and my victory will be a reward for all my pains and labours.

I am interrupted. A messenger from Sir William. I must go instantly to the Thatched House tavern. What is in the wind now, I wonder?

❧ ❧ ❧

Great God! Montague, what a sight have I been witness to! Stanley, the ill-fated Stanley, has shot himself. The horror of the scene will never be worn from my memory. I see his mangled corpse staring ghastly upon me. I tremble. Every nerve is affected. I cannot at present give you the horrid particulars. I am more shocked than it is possible to conceive. Would to heaven I had no connexion with him! Oh! Could I have foreseen this unhappy event! But it is too, too late. The undone self-destroyed wretch is gone to answer for his crimes; and you and I are left to deplore the part we have had in corrupting his morals and leading him on, step by step, to destruction.

My mind is a hell—I cannot reflect—I felt all despair and self-abasement. I now thank God, I have not the weight of Lady Stanley's seduction on my already overburdened conscience.

In what a different style I began this letter—with a pulse beating with anticipated evil, and my blood rioting in the idea of my fancied triumph over the virtue of the best and most injured of women. On the summons, I flew to the Thatched House. The waiter begged me to go upstairs. "Here has a most unfortunate accident happened, my lord. Poor Sir William Stanley has committed a rash action; I fear his life is in danger."

I thought he alluded to the affair of forgery, and in that persuasion made answer, "It is an ugly affair, to be sure; but, as to his life, that will be in no danger."

"Oh! My lord, I must not flatter you; the surgeon declares he can live but a few hours."

"Live! What do you say?"

"He has shot himself, my lord." I hardly know how I got upstairs; but how great was my horror at the scene which presented itself to my affrighted view! Sir George Brudenel and Mr. Stanley were supporting him. He was not quite dead, but his last moments were on the close. Oh! The occurrences of life will never for one instant obliterate from my recollection the look which he gave me. He was speechless; but his eloquent silence conveyed, in one glance of agony and despair, sentiments that sunk deep on my wounded conscience. His eyes were turned on *me* when the hand of death sealed them forever. I had thrown myself on my knees by him and was pressing his hand. I did not utter a word, indeed I was incapable of articulating a syllable. He had just sense remaining to know me, and I thought strove to withdraw his hand from mine. I let it go; and, seeing it fall almost lifeless,

Mr. Stanley took it in his, as well as he could; the expiring man grasped his uncle's hand and sunk into the shades of everlasting night. When we were convinced that all was over with the unhappy creature, we left the room. Neither Sir George nor Mr. Stanley seemed inclined to enter into conversation; and my heart ran over plentifully at my eyes. I gave myself up to my agonizing sorrow for some time. When I was a little recovered, I enquired of the people of the house how this fatal event happened. Tom said Sir William came there about seven o'clock and went upstairs in the room we usually played in, that he looked very dejected but called for coffee and drank two dishes. He went from thence in an hour and returned again about ten. He walked about the room in great disorder. In a short space, Sir George Brudenel and Mr. Stanley came and asked for him. On carrying up their message, Sir William desired to be excused seeing them for half an hour. Within that time, a note was brought him from his own house by Griffith, Lady Stanley's servant. His countenance changed on the perusal of it. "This then decides it," he exclaimed aloud. "I am now determined." He bade the waiter leave the room and bring him no more messages. In obedience to his commands, Tom was going downstairs. Sir William shut the door after him hastily and locked it; and before Tom had got to the passage, he heard the report of a pistol. Alarmed at the sound, and the previous disorder of Sir William, he ran into the room where were Brudenel and Stanley, entreating them for God's sake to go up, as he feared Sir William meant to do some desperate act. They ran up with the utmost precipitation, and Brudenel burst open the door. The self-devoted victim was in an arm chair, hanging over on one side, his right cheek and ear torn almost off, and speechless. He expressed great horror and, they think, contrition, in his looks; and once clasped his hands together and turned up his eyes to heaven. He knew both the gentlemen. His uncle was in the utmost agitation. "Oh! My dear Will," said he, "had you been less precipitate, we might have remedied all these evils." Poor Stanley fixed his eyes on him and faintly shook his head. Sir George too pressed his hand, saying, "My dear Stanley, you have been deceived, if you thought me your enemy. God forgive those who have brought you to this distress!" This (with the truest remorse of conscience, I say) bears hard on my character. I did all in my power to prevent poor Stanley's meeting with Sir George and his uncle and laboured, with the utmost celerity, to confirm him in the idea that they were both inexorable, to further my schemes on his wife. As I found my company was not acceptable to the gentlemen, I returned home under the most violent dejection of spirits. Would to heaven you were here! Yet, what consolation could you afford me? I rather fear you would add to the weight instead of lightening it, as you could not speak peace to my mind, which is inconceivably hurt.

I am yours,

Biddulph

ᵚ ᵚ ᵚ ᵚ ᵚ ᵚ ᵚ ᵚ ᵚ ᵚ
LETTER 47
ᵚ ᵚ ᵚ ᵚ ᵚ ᵚ ᵚ ᵚ ᵚ ᵚ

To Miss Grenville

Dear Madame,

A letter from Mr. Stanley, which accompanies this, will inform you of the fatal catastrophe of the unfortunate Sir William Stanley. Do me the justice to believe I shall with pleasure contribute all in my power to the ease and convenience of Lady Stanley, for whom I have the tenderest friendship.

We have concealed the whole of the shocking particulars of her husband's fate from her ladyship, but her apprehensions lead her to surmise the worst. She is at present too much indisposed to undertake a journey into Wales; but, as soon as she is able to travel, I shall do myself the honour of conveying her to the arms of relations so deservedly dear to her.

Mr. Stanley is not a man who deals in professions; he therefore may have been silent as to his intentions in favour of his niece, which I know to be very noble.

Lady Stanley tells me she has done the honour of mentioning my name frequently in her correspondence with you. As a sister of so amiable a woman, I feel myself attached to Miss Grenville and beg leave to subscribe myself her obliged humble servant,

Maria Finch

LETTER 48

From the Sylph

The vicissitudes which you, my Julia, have experienced in your short life must teach you how little dependence is to be placed in sublunary enjoyments. By an inevitable stroke, you are again cast under the protection of your first friends. If, in the vortex of folly where late you resided, my counsels preserved you from falling into any of his snares, the reflexion of being so happy an instrument will shorten the dreary path of life and smooth the pillow of death. But my task, my happy task, of superintending your footsteps is now over.

In the peaceful vale of innocence, no guide is necessary, for there all is virtuous, all beneficent, as yourself. You have passed many distressing and trying scenes. But, however, never let despair take place in your bosom. To hope to be happy in this world may be presumptuous; to despair of being so is certainly impious; and, though the sun may rise and see us unblest and setting leave us in misery, yet, on its return, it may behold us changed, and the face which yesterday was clouded with tears may tomorrow brighten into smiles. Ignorant as we are of the events of tomorrow, let us not arrogantly suppose there will be no end to the trouble which now surrounds us; and, by murmuring, arraign the hand of Providence.

There may be, to us finite beings, many seeming contradictions of the assertion that *to be good is to be happy*, but an infinite Being knows it to be true in the enlarged view of things, and therefore implanted in our breasts the love of virtue. Our merit may not, indeed, meet with the reward which we seem to claim in this life; but we are morally ascertained of reaping a plentiful harvest in the next. Persevere then, my amiable pupil, in the path you were formed to tread in, and rest assured, though a slow, a lasting recompense will succeed. May you meet with all the happiness you deserve in this world! And may those most dear to you be the dispensers of it to you! Should any future occasion of your life make it necessary to consult me, you know how a letter will reach me; till then adieu!

Ever your faithful

Sylph

LETTER 49

To Sir George Brudenel
Woodley Vale

My dear Sir George,

It is with the utmost pleasure I assure you of my niece having borne her journey with less fatigue than we even could have hoped for. The pleasing expectation of meeting with her beloved relations contributed towards her support and combated the afflictions she had tasted during her separation from them and her native place. As we approached the last stage, her conflict increased, and both Miss Finch and myself used every method to recompose her fluttered spirits; but, just as we were driving into the inn yard where we were to change horses for the last time, she clasped her hands together, exclaiming, "Oh my God! My father's chaise!" and sunk back, very near fainting. I tried to laugh her out of her extreme agitation. She had hardly power to get out of the coach; and hobbling, as you know me to be with the gout, an extraordinary exertion was necessary on my part to support her, tottering as she was, into a parlour. I shall never be able to do justice to the scene which presented itself. Miss Grenville flew to meet her trembling sister. The mute expression of their features, the joy of meeting, the recollection of past sorrows, oh!—it is more than my pen can paint; it was more than human nature could support; at least, it was with the utmost difficulty it could be supported till the venerable father approached to welcome his lovely daughter. She sunk on her knees before him and looked like a dying victim at the shrine of a much-loved saint. What agonies possessed Mr. Grenville! He called for assistance; none of the party were able, from their own emotions, to afford him any. At last the dear creature recovered and became tolerably calm; but this only lasted a few minutes. She was seated between her father and sister; she gazed fondly first on one, and then the other, and would attempt to speak; but her full heart could not find vent at her lips; her eyes were rivers through which her sorrows flowed. I rose to retire for a little time, being overcome by the affecting view. She saw my intentions, and rising likewise, took my hand—"Don't leave us—I will be more myself—don't leave us, my second father! Oh! Sir," turning to Mr. Grenville, "help me to repay this generous, best of men a small part of what my grateful heart tells me is his due."

"I receive him, my Julia," cried her father, "I receive him to my bosom as my brother." He embraced me, and Lady Stanley threw an arm over each of our shoulders. Our spirits, after some time, a little subsided, and we proceeded to this place. I was happy this meeting was over, as I all along dreaded the delicate sensibility of my niece.

Oh! Sir George! How could my unhappy nephew be blind to such estimable qualities as Julia possesses? Blind!—I recall the word: he was not blind to them; he could not, but he was misled by the cursed follies of the world, and entangled by its snares, till he lost all relish for whatever was lovely and virtuous. Ill-fated young man! How deplorable was thy end! Oh! May the mercy of heaven be extended towards thee! May it forget its justice, *nor be extreme to mark what was done amiss*!

I find Julia was convinced he was hurried out of this life by his own desperate act, but she forbears to enquire into what she says she dreads to be informed. She appears to me (who knew her not in her happier days) like a beautiful plant that had been chilled with a nipping frost which congealed, but could not destroy, its loveliness; the tenderness of her parent, like the sun, has chased away the winter, and she daily expands and discovers fresh charms. Her sister too—indeed we should see such women now and then to reconcile us to the trifling sex, who have laboured with the utmost celerity, and with too much success, to bring an odium on that most beautiful part of the creation. You say you are tired of the women of your world. Their caprices, their follies, to soften the expression, have caused this distaste in you. Come to Woodley Vale, and behold beauty ever attended by— what should ever attend beauty—native innocence. The lovely widow is out of the question. I am in love with her myself, that is, as much as an old fellow of sixty-four ought to be with a young girl of nineteen; but her charming sister, I must bring you acquainted with her; yet, unless I was perfectly convinced that you possess the best of hearts, you should not even have a glance from her pretty blue eyes. Indeed, I believe I shall turn monopolizer in my dotage and keep them all to myself. Julia is my child. Louisa has the merit with me (exclusive of her own superlative one) of being *her* sister. And my little Finch is a worthy girl; I adore her for her friendship to my darling. Surely your hearts must be impenetrable, if so much merit, and so much beauty, does not assert their sway over you.

Do you think that infamous fellow (I am sorry to express myself thus while speaking of a peer of our realm) Lord Biddulph is sincere in his reformation? Perhaps returning health may renew in him vices which are become habitual from long practice. If he reflects at all, he has much, very much, to answer for throughout this unhappy affair. Indeed, he did not spare himself in his conversation with me. If he sees his errors in time, he ought to be thankful to heaven for allowing that *time* to him, which, by his pernicious counsels, he prevented the man he called *friend* from availing himself of. Adieu! My dear Sir George. May you never feel the want of *that peace which goodness bosoms ever*!

Edward Stanley

♈︎♈︎♈︎♈︎♈︎♈︎♈︎♈︎♈︎♈︎

LETTER 50

♈︎♈︎♈︎♈︎♈︎♈︎♈︎♈︎♈︎♈︎

To Miss Finch

You are very sly, my dear Maria. Mr. Stanley assures me you went to Lady Barton's purposely to give her nephew, Sir George, the meeting. Is it so? And am I in danger of losing my friend? Or is it only the jocularity of my uncle on the occasion? Pray be communicative on this affair. I am sure I need not urge you on that head, as you have never used any reserve to me. A mind of such integrity as yours requires no disguises. What little I saw of Sir George Brudenel shows him to be a man worthy of my Maria. What an encomium I have paid him in one word! But, joking apart (for I do not believe you entertained an idea of a *rencontre* with the young baronet at Barton house), Mr. Stanley says, with the utmost seriousness, that his friend Brudenel made him the *confidant* of a *penchant* for our sweet Maria, sometime since, on his inviting him down hither to pick up a wife *unhackneyed in the ways of the world*. However, don't be talked into a partiality for the swain, for none of us here have a wish to become matchmakers.

179

And now I have done with the young man, permit me to add a word or two concerning the old one; I mean Mr. Stanley. He has, in the tenderest and most friendly manner, settled on me two thousand a year (the sum fixed on another occasion) while I continue the widow of his unfortunate nephew; and if hereafter I should be induced to enter into other engagements, I am to have fifteen thousand pounds at my own disposal. This, he says, justice prompts him to do, but adds, "I will not tell you how far my affection would carry me, because the world would perhaps call me an *old fool.*"

He leaves us next week to make some preparation there for our reception in a short time. I am to be mistress of his house; and he has made a bargain with my father that I shall spend half the year with him, either at Stanley Park or Pemberton Lodge. You may believe all the happiness of my future life is centred in the hope of contributing to the comfort of my father, and this my second parent. My views are very circumscribed; however, I am more calm than I expected to have been, considering how much I have been tossed about in the stormy ocean. It is no wonder that I am sometimes under the deepest dejection of spirits when I sit, as I often do, and reflect on past events. But I am convinced I ought not to enquire too minutely into some fatal circumstances. May the poor deluded victim meet with mercy! I draw a veil over his frailties. Ah! What errors are they which death cannot cancel? Who shall say, *I will walk upright, my foot shall not slide or go astray?* Who knows how long he shall be upheld by the powerful hand of God? The most presumptuous of us, if left to ourselves, may be guilty of a lapse. Oh! May *my* trespasses be forgiven, as I forgive and forget *his!*

My dear Maria will excuse my proceeding; the last apostrophe will convince you of the impossibility of my continuing to use my pen.

Adieu!

Julia Stanley

[*The correspondence, for obvious reasons, is discontinued for some months. During the interval, it appears that a union took place between Sir George Brudenel and Miss Finch.—While Lady Stanley was on her accustomed visit to her uncle, she received the following letter from Miss Grenville.*]

ѱѱѱѱѱѱѱѱѱѱ
LETTER 51
ѱѱѱѱѱѱѱѱѱѱ

To Lady Stanley
Melford Abbey

This last week has been so much taken up that I could not find one day to tell my beloved Julia that *she* has not been *one day* out of my thoughts, tho' you have heard from me but once since I obeyed the summons of our friend Jenny Melford, to be witness of her renunciation of that name. We are a large party here, and very brilliant.

I think I never was accounted vain; but, I assure you, I am almost induced to be so from the attention of a very agreeable man, who is an intimate acquaintance of Mr. Wynne's, a man of fortune and, what will have more weight with me, a man of strict principles. He has already made himself some little interest in my heart by some very benevolent actions, which we have by accident discovered. I don't know what will come of it, but, if he should be importunate, I doubt I should not have power to refuse him. My father is prodigiously taken with him; yet men are such deceitful mortals—well, time will show—in the meantime, adieu!

Yours most sincerely,

Louisa Grenville

ѱѱѱѱѱѱѱѱѱѱ
LETTER 52
ѱѱѱѱѱѱѱѱѱѱ

To Lady Stanley

I cannot resist writing to you, in consequence of a piece of intelligence I received this morning from Mr. Spencer, the hero of my last letter.

At breakfast Mr. Spencer said to Mr. Wynne—"You will have an addition to your party tomorrow; I have just had a letter from my friend Harry Woodley, informing me that he will pay his *devoir* to you and your fair bride before his journey to London."

The name instantly struck me—"Harry Woodley!" I repeated.

"Why, do you know Harry Woodley?" asked Mr. Spencer.

"I once knew a gentleman of that name," I answered, "whose father owned that estate *my* father now possesses. I remember him a boy, when he was under the tuition of Mr. Jones, a worthy clergyman in our neighbourhood."

"The very same," replied Mr. Spencer. "Harry is my most particular friend; I have long known him, and as long loved him with the tenderest affection—an affection," whispered he, "which reigned unrivaled till I saw you; he *was* the *first,* but *now* is *second* in my heart." I blushed, but felt no anger at his boldness.

I shall not finish my letter till I have seen my old acquaintance; I wish for tomorrow; I expressed my impatience to Mr. Spencer. "I should be uneasy at your earnestness," said he, "did I not know that curiosity is incident to your sex; but I will let you into a secret: Harry's heart is engaged, and has long been so; therefore, throw not away your fire upon him, but preserve it, to cherish one who lives but in your smiles."

He is arrived (Mr. Woodley, I mean); we are all charmed with him. I knew him instantly, tho' the beautiful boy is now flushed with manliness. It is five years since we saw him last—he did not meet us without the utmost emotion, which we attributed to the recollection that we now owned those lands which ought in right to have been his. He has, however, by Mr. Spencer's account, been very successful in life and is master of a plentiful fortune. He seems to merit the favour of all the world.

Adieu!

Yours most truly,

Louisa Grenville

LETTER 53

To Lady Stanley
Melford Abbey

Mr. Spencer tells me it is a proof I have great ascendancy over him since he has made me the *confidante* of his friend Woodley's attachment. And who do you think is the object of it? To whom has the constant youth paid his vows in secret, and worn away a series of years in hopeless, pining love? Ah! My Julia, who can inspire so tender, so lasting a flame as yourself? Yes! You are the saint before whose shrine the faithful Woodley has bent his knee and sworn eternal truth.

You must remember the many instances of esteem we have repeatedly received from him. To me it was friendship; to my sister it was love—and *love* of the purest, noblest kind.

He left Woodley Vale, you recollect, about five years ago. He left all he held dear, all the soft hope which cherished life in the flattering idea of raising himself, by some fortunate stroke, to such an eminence that he might boldly declare how much, how fondly, he adored his Julia. In the first instance, he was not mistaken—he has acquired a noble fortune. Flushed with hope and eager expectation, he flew to Woodley Vale, and the first sound that met his ear was—that object of his tenderest wishes was, a few weeks before his arrival, married. My Julia! Will not your tender sympathizing heart feel, in some degree, the cruel anxiety that must take place in the bosom which had been, during a long journey, indulging itself in the fond hope of being happy—and just at that point of time, and at that place where the happiness was to commence, to be dashed at once from the scene of bliss, with the account of his beloved's being married to another? What then remained for the ill-fated youth but to fly from those scenes where he had sustained so keen a disappointment and, without casting one glance on the plains the extravagance of his father had wrested from him, seek in the bosom of his friends an asylum?

He determined not to return till he was able to support the sight of such interesting objects with composure. He proposed leaving England: he traveled, but never one moment, in idea, wandered from the spot which contained all his soul held dear. Some months since, he became acquainted with the event which has once more left you free. His delicacy would not allow him to appear before you till the year was near expired. And now, if such unexampled constancy may plead for him, what competitor need Harry Woodley fear?

I told you my father was much pleased with Mr. Spencer, but he is more than pleased with his old acquaintance. You cannot imagine how much he interests himself in the hope that his invariable attachment to you may meet its due reward, by making, as he says, a proper impression on your heart. He will return with us to Woodley Vale. My father's partiality is so great that I believe should you be inclined to favour the faithful Harry, he will be induced to make you the eldest and settle Woodley on you, that it may be transmitted to Harry's heirs, a step which, I give you my honour, I shall have no objection to. Besides, it will be proving the sincerity of Mr. Spencer's attachment to me—a proof I should not be averse to making, for, you know, *a burnt child dreads the fire.*

These young men take up all our attention; but I will not write a word more till I have enquired after my dear old one. How does the worthy soul do? I doubt you have not sung to him lately, as the gout has returned with so much violence. You know, he said your voice banished all pain. Pray continue singing, or anything which indicates returning cheerfulness, a blessing I so much wish you. I have had a letter from Lady Brudenel; she calls on me for my promised visit, but I begin to suspect I shall have engagements enough on my hands by and by. I doubt my father is tired of us both, as he is planning a scheme to get rid of us at once. But does not this seeming eagerness proceed from that motive which guides all his actions towards us—his extreme tenderness—the apprehension of leaving us unconnected, and the infirmities of life hastening with large strides on himself? Oh! My Julia! He is the best of fathers!

Adieu! I am dressed *en cavalier* and just going to mount my horse, accompanied by my two beaux. I wish you was here, as I own I should have no objection to a *tête-à-tête* with Spencer; nor would Harry with you. But *here*—he is in the way.

Yours,

L. Grenville

LETTER 54

To Miss Grenville
Stanley Park

Alas! My dearest Louisa, is it to me your last letter was addressed? To me, the sad victim of a fatal attachment? Torn as has been my heart by the strange vicissitudes of life, am I an object fit to admit the bright ray of joy? Unhappy Woodley, if thy destiny is to be decided by my voice! It is—it must be ever against thee. Talk not to me, Louisa, of love—of joy and happiness! Ever, ever, will they be strangers to my care-worn breast. A little calm (Oh! How deceitful!) had taken possession of my mind and seemed to chase away the dull melancholy which habitual griefs had planted there. Ah! Seek not to rob me of the small share allotted me. Speak not—write not of Woodley; my future peace depends upon it. The name of *love* has awakened a thousand, thousand pangs, which sorrow had hushed to rest; at least, I kept them to myself. I look on the evils of my life as a punishment for having too freely indulged myself in a most reprehensible attachment. Never has my hand traced the fatal name! Never have I sighed it forth in the most retired privacy! Never then, my Louisa, oh!—never mention the destructive passion to me more!

I remember the ill-fated youth—ill-fated, indeed, if cursed with so much constancy! The first predilection I felt in favour of one too dear— was a faint similitude I thought I discovered between him and Woodley. But if I entertained a partiality at first for him, because he reminded me of a former companion, too soon he made such an interest in my bosom as left him superior there to all others. It is your fault, Louisa, that I have adverted to this painful, this forbidden subject. Why have you mentioned the pernicious theme?

Why should my father be so earnest to have me again enter into the pale of matrimony? If your prospects are flattering— indulge them, and be happy. I have tasted of the fruit—have found it bitter to the palate, and corroding to the heart. Urge me not then to run any more hazards; I have suffered sufficiently. Do not, in pity to Mr. Woodley, encourage in him a hope that perseverance may subdue my resolves. Fate is not more inexorable. I should despise myself if I was capable, for one moment, of wishing to give pain to any mortal. He cannot complain of me—he may of *Destiny;* and, oh!—what complaints have I not to make of *her*!

I have again perused your letter; I am not free, Louisa, even if my heart was not devoted to the unfortunate exile. Have I not sworn to my attendant Sylph? He who preserved me in the day of trial? My vows are registered in heaven! I will not recede from them! I believe he knows my heart, with all its weaknesses. Oh! My Louisa, do not distress me more.

Adieu!

Julia Stanley

❦❦❦❦❦❦❦❦❦❦

LETTER 55

❦❦❦❦❦❦❦❦❦❦

To Lady Stanley

Where has my Julia learnt this inflexibility of mind? Or what virtue so rigid as to say she is not free to enter into other engagements? Are your affections to lie forever buried in the grave of your unfortunate husband? Heaven, who has given us renewable affections, will not condemn us for making a transfer of them when the continuance of that affection can be of no farther advantage to the object. But your case is different; you have attached yourself to a visionary idea! The man, whose memory you cherish, perhaps thinks no longer of you; or would he not have sought you out before this? Are you to pass your life in mourning his absence, and not endeavour to do justice to the fidelity of one of the most amiable of men?

Surely, my Julia, these sacrifices are not required of you! You condemn my father for being so interested in the fate of his friend Woodley!—He only requests you to see him. Why not see him as an acquaintance? You cannot form the idea of my father's wishing to constrain you to accept him! All he thinks of at present is that you would not suffer prejudices to blind your reason. Woodley seeks not to subdue you by perseverance; only give him leave to try to please you; only allow him to pay you a visit. Surely, if you are as fixed as fate, you cannot apprehend the bare sight of him will overturn your resolves! You fear more danger than there really is. Still we say—*see him*. My dearest Julia did not use to be inexorable! My father allows he has now no power over you, even if he could form the idea of using it. What then have you to dread? Surely you have a negative voice!

I am called upon—but will end with the strain I began. See him, and then refuse him your esteem, nay more, your tender affection, if you can.

Adieu!

Yours most sincerely,

Louisa Grenville

LETTER 56

To Miss Grenville

Oh, my Louisa! How is the style of your letters altered! Is this change (not improvement) owing to your attachment to Mr. Spencer? Can *love* have wrought this difference? If it has, may it be a stranger to my bosom!—for it has ceased to make my Louisa amiable!—She, who was once all tenderness—all softness!—who fondly soothed my distresses, *and felt for weakness which she never knew*—

> It is not friendly, 'tis not maidenly;
> Our sex, as well as I, may chide you for it,
> Though I alone do feel the injury—

you, to whom I have freely exposed all the failings of my wayward heart! in whose bosom I have reposed all its tumultuous beatings!—All its anxieties!—Oh, Louisa! Can you forget my *confidence* in you, which would not permit me to conceal even my errors? Why do you then join with men in scorning your friend? You say, *my father has now no power over me, even if he could form the idea of using power.* Alas! You have all too much power over me! You have the power of rendering me forever miserable, either by your persuasions to consign myself to eternal wretchedness or by my *inexorableness,* as you call it, in flying in the face of persons so dear to me!

How cruel it is in you to arraign the conduct of one to whose character you are a *stranger*! What has the man who, unfortunately both for himself and me, has been too much in my thoughts; what has he done that you should so decisively pronounce him to be inconstant and forgetful of those who seemed so dear to him? Why is the delicacy of *your favourite* to be so much commended for his forbearance till the year of mourning was near expired? And what proof that another may not be actuated by the same delicate motive?

But I will have done with these painful interrogatories; they only help to wound my bosom, even more than you have done.

My good uncle is better; you have wrung my heart—and, harsh and unbecoming as it may seem in your eyes, I will not return to Woodley Vale till I am assured I shall not receive anymore persecutions on his account. Would he be content with my esteem, he may easily entitle himself to it by his still further *forbearance.*

My resolution is fixed—no matter what that is—there is no danger of making anyone a participator of my sorrows.

Adieu!

Julia Stanley

⚜⚜⚜⚜⚜⚜⚜⚜⚜⚜
LETTER 57
⚜⚜⚜⚜⚜⚜⚜⚜⚜⚜

To Miss Grenville
Stanley Park

Louisa! Why was this scheme laid? I cannot compose my thoughts even to ask you the most simple question! Can you judge of my astonishment? The emotions with which I was seized? Oh! No, you cannot—you cannot, because you was never sunk so low in the depths of affliction as I have been; you never have experienced the extremes of joy and despair as I have done. Oh! You know nothing of what I feel!—of what I cannot find words to express! Why don't you come hither?—I doubt whether I shall retain my senses till your arrival.

Adieu!

Yours forever,

Julia Stanley

⚜⚜⚜⚜⚜⚜⚜⚜⚜⚜
LETTER 58
⚜⚜⚜⚜⚜⚜⚜⚜⚜⚜

To Lady Brudenel
Stanley Park

Yes! My dear Maria, you shall be made acquainted with the extraordinary change in your friend! You had all the mournful particulars of my past life before you. I was convinced of your worth, nor could refuse you my confidence. But what is all this? I cannot spend my time, my precious time, in prefacing the scenes which now surround me.

You know how depressed my mind was with sorrow at the earnestness with which my father and sister espoused the cause of Mr. Woodley.

I was ready to sink under the dejection their perseverance occasioned, aggravated too by my tender, long-cherished attachment to the unfortunate baron. (This is the first time my pen has traced that word.)

I was sitting yesterday morning in an alcove in the garden, ruminating on the various scenes which I had experienced and giving myself up to the most melancholy presages, when I perceived a paper fall at my feet. I apprehended it had dropped from my pocket in taking out my handkerchief, which a trickling tear had just before demanded. I stooped to pick it up and, to my surprise, found it sealed and addressed to myself. I hastily broke it open, and my wonder increased when I read these words:

I have been witness to the perturbation of your mind. How will you atone to your Sylph for not availing yourself of the privilege of making application to him in any emergency? If you have lost your confidence in him, he is the most wretched of beings. He flatters himself he may be instrumental to your future felicity. If you are inclined to be indebted to him for any share of it, you may have the opportunity of seeing him in five minutes. Arm yourself with resolution, most lovely, most adored of women, for he will appear under a semblance not expected by you. You will see in him the most faithful and constant of human beings.

I was seized with such a trepidation that I could hardly support myself; but, summoning all the strength of mind I could assume, I said aloud, though in a tremulous voice, "Let me view my amiable Sylph!"—But oh! What became of me when at my feet I beheld the most wished-for, the most dreaded, *Ton-hausen*! I clasped my hands together and shrieked back half insensible on the seat.

"Curse on my precipitance!" he cried, throwing his arms round me. "My angel! My Julia! Look on the most forlorn of his sex, unless you pity me."

"Pity you!" I exclaimed, with a faint accent—"Oh! from whence, and how came you here?"

"Did not my Julia expect me?" he asked, in the softest voice and sweetest manner.

"I expect you! How should I? Alas! What intimation could I have of your arrival?"

"From this," he replied, taking up the billet written by the Sylph.

"What do you mean? For heaven's sake! Rise, and unravel this mystery. My brain will burst with the torture of suspense."

"If the loveliest of women will pardon the stratagems I have practised on her unsuspecting mind, I will rise the happiest of mortals. Yes, my beloved Julia, I am that invisible guide that has so often led you through the wilds of life. I am that blissful thing, whom you supposed something supernatural."

"It is impossible," I cried, interrupting him. "It cannot be!"

"Will not my Julia recollect this poor pledge of her former confidence?" drawing from a ribbon a locket of hair I had once sent to the Sylph. "Is this, to me inestimable, gift no longer acknowledged by you? This dear part of yourself, whose enchantment gave to my wounded soul all the nourishment she drew, which supported me when exiled from all that the world had worth living for? Have you forgot the vows of lasting fidelity, with which the value of the present was enhanced? Oh! Sure you do not. And yet you are silent. May I not have one word, one look?"

"Alas!" cried I, hiding my face from his glances. "What can I say? What can I do? Oh! Too well I remember all. The consciousness that every secret of my heart has been laid bare to your inspection covers me with the deepest confusion."

"Bear witness for me," cried he, "that I never made an ill-use of that knowledge. Have I ever presumed upon it? Could you ever discover, by the arrogance of Ton-hausen's conduct, that he had been the happy *confidant* of your retired sentiments? Believe me, Lady Stanley, that man will ever admire you most, who knows most your worth; and oh!—who knows it more, who adores it more than I?"

"Still," said I, "I cannot compose my scattered senses. All appears a dream; but, trust me, I dote on the illusion. I would not be undeceived, if I am in an error. I would feign persuade myself that but one man on earth is acquainted with the softness, I will not call it weakness, of my soul; and he the only man who could inspire that softness."

"Oh! Be persuaded, most angelic of women," said he, pressing my hand to his lips. "Be persuaded of the truth of my assertion that the Sylph and I are one. You know how you were circumstanced."

"Yes! I was married before I had the happiness of being seen by you."

"No; you was not."

"Not married, before I was seen by you?"

"Most surely not. Years, years before that event, I knew, and, knowing, loved you—loved you with all the fondness of man while my age was that of a boy. Has Julia quite forgot her juvenile companions? Is the time worn from her memory when Harry Woodley used to weave the fancied garland for her?"

"Protect me, Heaven!" cried I. "Sure I am in the land of shadows!"

"No," cried he, clasping me in his arms and smiling at my apostrophe, "you shall find substance and substantial joys too here."

"Thou Proteus!" said I, withdrawing myself from his embrace. "What do you mean by thus shifting characters, and each so potent?"

"To gain my charming Nymph," he answered. "But why should we thus waste our time? Let me lead you to your father."

"My father! Is my father here?"

"Yes, he brought me hither; perhaps, as Woodley, an unwelcome visitant. But will you have the cruelty to reject him?" added he, looking slyly.

"Don't presume too much," I returned with a smile. "You have convinced me you are capable of great artifice; but I shall insist on your explaining your whole plan of operations as an atonement for your double, nay treble dealing, for I think you are three in one. But I am impatient to behold my father, whom, the moment before I saw you, I was accusing of cruelty in seeking to urge me in the favour of one I was determined never to see."

"But now you have seen him (it was all your sister required of you, you know), will you be inexorable to his vows?"

"I am determined to be guided by my Sylph," cried I, "in this momentous instance. That was my resolution, and still shall remain the same."

"Suppose thy Sylph had recommended you to bestow your hand on Woodley? What would have become of poor *Ton-hausen?*"

"My confidence in the Sylph was established on the conviction of his being my safest guide; as such, he would never have urged me to bestow my hand where my heart was refractory; but, admitting the possibility of the Sylph's pursuing such a measure, a negative voice would have been allowed me; and no power, human or divine, should have constrained that voice to breathe out a vow of fidelity to any other than him to whom the secrets of my heart have been so long known."

By this time we had nearly reached the house, from whence my father sprung with the utmost alacrity to meet me. As he pressed me to his venerable bosom, "Can my Julia refuse the request of her father, to receive, as the best pledge of his affection, this valuable present? And will she forgive the innocent trial we made of her fidelity to the most amiable of men?"

"Ah! I know not what to say," cried I. "Here has been sad management amongst you. But I shall soon forget the heartaches I have experienced, if they have removed from this gentleman any suspicions that I did not regard him for himself alone. He has, I think, adopted the character of Prior's Henry; and I hope he is convinced that the faithful Emma is not a fiction of the poet's brain. I know not," I continued, "by what name to call him."

"Call me *yours,*" cried he, "and that will be the highest title I shall ever aspire to. But you shall know all, as indeed you have a right to do. *Your* sister, and soon, I hope, *mine,* related to you the attachment which I had formed for you in my tenderest years, which, like the incision on the infant bark, *grew with my growth, and strengthened with my strength.* She likewise told you (but oh!—how faint, how inadequate to my feelings!) the extreme anguish that seized me when I found you was married. Distraction surrounded me; I cannot give words to my grief and despair. I fled from a place which had lost its only attractive power. In the first paroxysm of affliction, I knew not what resolutions I formed. I wrote to Spencer—not to give rest or ease to my overburdened heart, for that—alas!—could receive no diminution; nor to complain, for surely I could not complain of you. My form was not imprinted on your mind, though yours had worn itself so deep a trace in mine. Spencer opposed my resolution of returning to Germany, where I had formed some connexions (only friendly ones, my Julia, but, as such, infinitely tender). *He* it was that urged me to take the name of Ton-hausen, as that title belonged to an estate which devolved to me from the death of one of the most valuable men in the world, who had sunk into his grave, as the only asylum from a combination of woes. As some years had elapsed, in which I had increased in bulk and stature, joined to my having had the smallpox since I had been seen by you, he thought it more than probable you would not recollect my person. I hardly know what I proposed to myself, from closing with him in this scheme, only that I take heaven to witness, I never meant to injure you; and I hope the whole tenor of my conduct has convinced you how sincere I was in that profession.

From the great irregularity of your late husband's life, I had a *presenti-ment* that you would at one time or other be free from your engagements. I revered you as one to whom I hoped to be united; if not in this world, I might be a kindred-angel with you in the next. Your virtuous soul could not find its congenial friend in the riot and confusion in which you lived. I dared not trust myself to offer to become your guide. I knew the extreme hazard I should run and that, with all the innocent intentions in the world, we might both be undone by our *passions* before *reason* could come to our assistance. I soon saw I had the happiness to be distinguished by you! And that distinction, while it raised my admiration of you, excited in me the desire of rendering myself still more worthy of your esteem, but even that esteem I refused myself the dear privilege of soliciting for. I acted with the utmost caution; and if, under the character of the Sylph, I dived into the recesses of your soul and drew from thence the secret attachment you professed for the happy baron, it was not so much to gratify the vanity of my heart as to put you on your guard, lest some of the invidious wretches about you should propagate any reports to your prejudice; and, dear as the sacrifice cost me, I tore myself from your loved presence on a sarcasm which Lady Anne Parker threw out concerning us. I withdrew some miles from London and left Spencer there to apprize me of any change in your circumstances. I gave you to understand I had quitted the kingdom; but that was a severity I could not impose upon myself: however, I constrained myself to take a resolution of never again appearing in your presence till I should have the liberty of indulging my passion without restraint. Nine parts of ten in the world may condemn my procedure as altogether roman-tic. I believe few will find it imitable; but I have nice feelings, and I could act not other than I did. I could not, you see, bear to be the rival of myself. *That* I have proved under both the characters I assumed; and had I found you had forgotten Ton-hausen, Woodley would have been deprived of one of the most delicate pleasures a refined taste can experience. And now all that remains is to entreat the forgiveness of my amiable Julia, for these *pious frauds,* and to reassure her she shall, if *the heart of man is not deceit-ful above all things,* never repent the confidence she placed in her faithful Sylph, the affection she honoured the happy Ton-hausen with, nor the esteem, notwithstanding his obstinate perseverance, which she charitably bestowed on that unfortunate knight-errant, Harry Woodley."

"Heaven send I never may!" said I. But really I shall be half afraid to venture the remainder of my life with such a variable being. However, my father undertakes to answer for him in future.

I assure you, my dear Maria, you are much indebted to me for this recital, for I have borrowed the time out of the night, as the whole day has been taken up in a manner you may more easily guess than I can describe.

Say everything that is civil to Sir George on my part, as you are conscious I have no time to bestow on any other men than those by whom I am surrounded. I expect my sister and her swain tomorrow.

Adieu!

I am yours ever,

Julia Stanley

ψ ψ ψ ψ ψ ψ ψ ψ ψ ψ
LETTER 59
ψ ψ ψ ψ ψ ψ ψ ψ ψ ψ

To Lady Brudenel

You would hardly know your old acquaintance again, he is so totally altered; you remember his pensive air, and gentle unassuming manner, which seemed to bespeak the protection of everyone. Instead of all this, he is so alert, so brisk, and has such a saucy assurance in his whole deportment as really amazes; and, I freely own, delights me, as I am happily convinced that it is owing to myself that he is thus different from what he was. Let him be what he will, he will ever be dear to me.

I wanted him to relate to me all the particulars of his friend Frederick's, the late baron's, misfortunes. He says the recital would fill a volume, but that I shall peruse some papers on the subject sometime or other when we are tired of being cheerful, but that now we have better employment; I therefore submit for the present.

I admire my sister's choice very much; he is an agreeable man, and extremely lively: much more so naturally, notwithstanding the airs some folks give themselves, than my Proteus. Louisa too is quite alive; Mr. Stanley has forgot the gout; and my father is ready to dance at the wedding of his eldest daughter, which, I suppose, will take place soon.

Pray how do you go on? Are you near your *accouchement*? Or dare you venture to travel as far as Stanley Park? For my uncle will not part with any of us yet.

Ah! I can write no longer; they threaten to snatch the pen from my hand; that I may prevent such a solecism in politeness, I will conclude, by assuring you of my tenderest wishes.

Adieu!

Julia Stanley

ᵼ ᵼ ᵼ ᵼ ᵼ ᵼ ᵼ ᵼ ᵼ ᵼ

LETTER 60

ᵼ ᵼ ᵼ ᵼ ᵼ ᵼ ᵼ ᵼ ᵼ ᵼ

To Lady Stanley

Upon my word, a pretty kind of a romantic adventure you have made of it, and the conclusion of the business just as it should be, and quite in the line of *poetical justice.* Virtue triumphant, and Vice dragged at her chariot wheels:—for I heard yesterday that Lord Biddulph was selling off all his movables and had moved himself out of the kingdom. Now my old friend Montague should be sent on board the *Justitia*, and *all's well that ends well.* As to your Proteus, with all his *aliases,* I think he must be quite a Machiavel in artifice. Heaven send he may never change again! I should be half afraid of such a Will-of-the-wisp lover. First this, then that, now the other, and always the same. But bind him, bind him, Julia, in adamantine chains; make sure of him, while he is yet in your power; and follow, with all convenient speed, the dance your sister is going to lead off. Oh! She is in a mighty hurry! Let me hear what she will say when she has been married ten months, as poor I have been! And here must be kept prisoner with all the dispositions in the world for freedom!

What an acquisition your two husbands will be! I bespeak them both for godfathers; pray tell them so. Do you know I wanted to persuade Sir George to take a trip, just to see how you proceed in this affair; but, I blush to tell you, he would not hear of any such thing, because he is in expectation of a little impertinent visitor, and would not be from home for the world. *Tell it not in Gath.* Thank heaven, the dissolute tribe in London know nothing of it. But, I believe, none of our set will be anxious about their sentiments. While we feel ourselves happy, we shall think it no sacrifice to give up all the nonsense and hurry of the *beau monde.*

Adieu!

Maria Brudenel

APPENDIX

The Sylph, a comic piece by
Germain François Poullain de Saint-Foix

DRAMATIC PERSONAE

Finetta, housekeeper to Julia

The Marquis, disguised as Ziblis, a sylph

Julia

SCENE

Julia's seat in the country.

❦ ❦ ❦ ❦ ❦ ❦ ❦ ❦ ❦ ❦

Scene 1

[FINETTA, THE MARQUIS *(in a woman's habit).*]

FINETTA [*running up in a fright*]: Oh sir, sir.

MARQUIS: What's the matter? Why all this trembling?

FINETTA: 'Tis all over with us.

MARQUIS: The devil it is!—How so, pray?

FINETTA: Poor I shall pay dear enough for my stupid complaisance.

MARQUIS: What the mischief is it that has happened?

FINETTA: Why, sir, you know well enough how I met you, a week ago, in the avenue.—You told me what your name and rank was—and you added that you had heard such wonders of our Miss Julia that your curiosity to see and to converse with her was insurmountable.—'Twas in vain that I represented to you that our young lady lived the life of a hermit in this mansion and that for the three months that she has been in possession of it, by the death of her old aunt, she has neither paid nor received a single visit but has pored away her hours over a cursed pack of Kabbalistic (I think that's the name of 'em) books.—You still pursued your point—you drew out a purse of gold, you offered it to me, I had not the heart to refuse it; and, unfortunately joining in with your whole scheme, I introduced you that very evening to my mistress, in a woman's habit as a niece of mine who was just arrived at Paris from Gascony. I hopes of bettering herself in point of service.

MARQUIS: Very well.

FINETTA: Very well, with a mischief! I wish to heaven that you had but appeared such a splatter-mouth'd, awkward, two-fisted wench . . .

MARQUIS: Much obliged for your good wishes.

FINETTA: My dear sir, it would have been the luckiest thing in the world, for then our young lady would never have thought of taking you into her service, and then we should never have been in such a cursed scrape . . .

MARQUIS: What scrape is it that you are talking of? Explain yourself.

FINETTA: Lord! Sir, my mistress has been relating so many particular circumstances of her conversation with a spirit that I am convinced of its reality and am terrified out of my senses! Why, sir, she has been actually visited by one every night for this week past.—He has made her the most zealous professions of love and has even promised to make himself, this very evening, visible to her eyes.—You laugh, sir.—A pretty joke, indeed, when perhaps the next news may be that this plaguey sylph has twisted both our necks off—yours as his rival and mine as your most unfortunate go-between.

MARQUIS: So, Finetta, you have still the terrors of Raw-head and Bloody-bones before your eyes!

FINETTA: I was always afraid of ghosties, may it please your honour, but now that I have such evidence . . .

MARQUIS: Well, well, child, set your heart at rest; this is a spirit which will do thee no harm, take my word for it.

FINETTA: Aye, aye, sir, that's fine talking, but I shall take care to get far enough out of the reach of it, without trusting to fair words.

MARQUIS: Upon my soul, Finetta, you amaze me!—Why, has it never entered into your imagination that this same Buggaboe and your adopted niece Florina are one and the same person?

FINETTA: The deuce they are!—What! And has not my mistress recollected Florina, if it was only by her voice?

MARQUIS: How should she, Finetta, when you must remember that when you introduced me as your niece Florina, I affected a strong provincial accent? This I still keep up as the chambermaid, but when I present myself in the night as a sylph, I speak in my own natural voice and tone.—Thus have I easily . . .

FINETTA: I take you, sir, I take you; I have already got the better of my fright, and I comprehend well enough that you have passed yourself on her for one of those aerial beings which she is so very desirous of getting acquainted with.—But I cannot help admiring, in the meanwhile, your inimitable prudence and self-denial.—A young lover with a downright substantial body to have resolution enough to maintain the character of a pure spirit though admitted to his mistress's chamber at every hour of the night!—And then again, all the day long, to attend her, fiddle about her, and perform a thousand offices, which fall to the share of ladies' women, and, in spite of thousands of temptations, to be still the mere, unfeeling Abigail!—Excuse me, sir, but it is an effort which I should not have believed you capable of.

MARQUIS: And yet, Finetta, you see, 'tis a mask I have worn these eight days.—'Tis a strange whim of hers, this partiality towards the sylphs.

FINETTA: I have told you before, sir, that she has been ever since her infancy plunged over head and ears in the mysteries of the Kabbalah.— That old aunt to whom she owes this estate was her tutoress, and all these prejudices considered, perhaps her idea of the air being filled with little inhabitants, amiable and gallant, is by no means so ridiculous as the freaks of those who, without any system at all, start at their own shadow and cannot give half so ingenious a reason.

[FINETTA *sees a rich dress hanging on the back of a sofa.*]

But what have we here?—How elegant! How light!—'Tis a robe for a fairy.—If these pretty fellows, these same sylphs, were ever to visit this globe, this is the very habit they would wish to appear in.

[THE MARQUIS *stamps, and a splendid girandole appears. He stamps again, and it disappears.*]

Aha!—And all this machinery too!—Well, sir, you have managed cleverly to do all this under the Rose.—Do, sir, explain to me a little this scheme.

MARQUIS: Time enough.—In the meanwhile, help me on with this dress, for 'tis now dark, and I expect Julia every instant to return from her evening walk in the garden—we must be in order for her.

[JULIA *is heard without singing an air.*]

The devil!—Here she comes.—This is your doing, with your chattering.—What the deuce shall I do now?—I don't know.—Quick! Out with the lights!

[*The candles are put out.*]

Here, take this dress, and slip out as softly as you can, and put it in my room.

[*Exit* FINETTA, *feeling her way out, as in the dark.*]

Scene 2

[JULIA, THE MARQUIS *as her woman.*]

JULIA: Methinks I hear somewhat.—Is it you, celestial spirit?
MARQUIS: No; 'tis your ladyship's most terrestrial chambermaid.
JULIA: What! All alone, and in the dark!—Are you not afraid?
MARQUIS: I begin, madame, to take a little courage; and I really cannot help thinking this sylph of your ladyship's but a very silly kind of being.—He spends whole nights at your bedside, without any sensation but what is purely spiritual, and never makes himself felt, except in playing me some jade's trick or another.
JULIA: I must own, I should not be sorry if, to cure thee of thy way of treating everything I relate to thee as chimeras, thou wer't to be . . .
MARQUIS: To be haunted a little, I presume you mean, madame—but, faith and troth, I have not much fear about that matter—these hobgoblins, these sylphs, gnomes, and salamanders, are such a new race of beings that I shan't be easily brought to credit them.
JULIA: Foolish wench! A new race of beings!—Why these very ideas, which seem so new to thee, were known in the earliest ages of the world—but thou hast never heard of Neroides, which reign beneath the waters—of

Aeolus and his children, who govern the waves.—The forests too have their inhabitants, the fauns and satyrs.—According to the systems of our forefathers, there was neither grove nor fountain unprovided with its nymph or its naiad—they thought each element peopled with a race of intelligent beings, who, having the power of making themselves visible when they chose it, participated with mankind in their passions and were frequently engaged in intrigues with simple mortals.—These were their sylphs.—Ah, girl, were but your eyes enlightened by the knowledge of the Kabbalah!

MARQUIS: Aye, madame, then I should see wonders . . .

JULIA: You would see how from the first instant in which we attain to the knowledge of what love is the sylph, to whom we may happen to appear amiable, attaching himself to his mistress alone, flutters and flits around her, like a bee 'round the newly opening blossom. During the night, in dreams, which he contrives to excite, he takes care to be the principal object of her ideas—in the morn, he renews the pleasing illusion—in the gayest hours of the spring, 'tis her sylph who perpetually causes those pleasing reveries, in which the mind is employed in meditating on that reciprocal tenderness which gives new graces to all the works of nature.—'Tis amazing, Florina, how many artful methods the sylph has recourse to, that, by little and little, he may search to the bottom the heart which he wishes to find worthy of a sincere attachment.

MARQUIS: Very well, madame, you may say what you please, but you can never persuade me that there is any method so likely to gain the heart of a young lady as the presenting an agreeable figure before her eyes.— Why now, madame, here you have had five or six of these evening conversations with this same bodiless lover of yours . . .

JULIA: Ah! Heavens! What conversations! What enchanting vivacity! What affecting tenderness!

MARQUIS: Be it so, madame; yet if tonight his figure should not have the luck to hit your taste, you will be astonished at your ever having these tender sensations for him . . .

JULIA: This, child, is a reflexion adapted to a grovelling, sensual mind.— To such an imagination 'tis in vain to attempt an explanation of that sublime purity which alone can fit us for commerce with such aerial beings.—We have talked enough on this point—go, fetch a light.

MARQUIS: I am gone, madame, but my mind misgives me plaguily that this same aerial being of yours is only some shabby . . .

[*Groping out,* THE MARQUIS *screams as if in a fright, then departs as if to his room, but returns privately in the dark.*]

JULIA: What's the matter with the girl? What does she squall about!

MARQUIS [*disguising his voice as Ziblis's, still in the dark*]: I have only pluck'd her ears a little to teach her to call names; that's all, madame.

JULIA: Ah! I recollect in an instant that voice, so dear to my heart; 'tis you, my Ziblis—'tis my sylph—'tis my lover.

MARQUIS: Yes, my enchanting Julia, and the happiest of lovers, as I find myself received with such delicious kindness.

JULIA: I am on the wing to get a light.—You remember your yesterday's promise, of becoming visible the next time I saw you—I will not defer, for one instant, the joy I expect from the sight of my lover.

MARQUIS: I am ready to keep my word.—But tell me under what form you would wish me to appear.

JULIA: In your own—undoubtedly.

MARQUIS: My own! Alas! My fairest, the bodies of the inhabitants of the air—fluid, transparent, and always dissolved at the approach of day— can never be rendered visible to the eyes of mere mortals.

JULIA: How is this?—Why—upon my word—to be sure, you know, I love you only for yourself; but however, nevertheless . . .

MARQUIS [*smiling*]: But however, nevertheless—so I find that you love me only for myself; yet you must acknowledge that there is still something material wanting.—'Tis on this account that I would propose to your consideration, my Julia, that method which we sylphs make use of in our commerce with mortals—that of taking upon ourselves the figures which they think most agreeable to their taste.

JULIA: But 'tis your own shape which I would wish to see. Alas! I must acknowledge, I had formed an idea . . .

MARQUIS: That idea, my lovely Julia, you formed of my love, of which you can never have too high a notion.—How often have you reproach'd me for quitting you during the day?—But with how much injustice!—Eager to be the object of all your thoughts, of all your wishes, it has been my utmost endeavour to be everywhere where you were pleased and to be everything which gave you pleasure.—I was the zephyr which fanned your lovely face—when you admired the fragrancy of the flowers which formed your nosegay, my breath cooled your ruby lips.—It animated too the song of that bird which gave you so much entertainment in your evening's walk. These metamorphoses, as they flattered my passion, enabled me to wait with patience that happy moment when, certain of the affection of my Julia, I have no more to do than to render myself visible under whatever figure you shall approve of.—Shall I take that of your neighbour, that little senator to whom your family so much wish you united?

JULIA: No! For the love of heaven, think not of it!—Be your soul possessed of ever so much power, I would defy it to correct the vanity, the self-sufficiency, the phlegm, and the fatuity of that conceited body. When one has such a figure, one must e'en make the best on't; but 'tis not the figure in the world to pick out for a tête-à-tête party.

MARQUIS: Well then, let us consider—name another.

JULIA: Another!—I name another?

MARQUIS: Would you have me take the form of . . .

JULIA: I would have you take none at all.

MARQUIS: But, madame . . .

JULIA: But, sir—your scheme seems to me a very strange one.—What is become of the warmth of your love, if, without feeling the stings of jealousy, you can hear me name one whose figure I approve?—Would you not think such a one a rival?

MARQUIS: I see, my fair one, the delicacy of that sentiment.—Well—then—suppose I take the figure of Florina, your attendant.—She shall no longer perform the cold unanimated part of a confidante; she shall be, my lovely Julia, my very self—the most tender, the most passionate of lovers.—'Tis but the work of a few minutes just to dispose of her soul—that is, to place it in some other body while I take its place in hers . . .

JULIA: But Ziblis . . .

MARQUIS: One moment's patience, and I am with you again.

[THE MARQUIS *goes off the stage.*]

Scene 3

JULIA: He is gone and will not hear me.—Nay, perhaps, he fancies that the scruples I would raise are only the caprices of my sex—and that, in my heart, I am delighted at the power which he enjoys of changing, at will, his person; and, by that means, of affording his mistress the perpetual charms of novelty.—Alas! Such is the indelicacy of mankind that such a thought is but too natural.—But 'tis far otherwise with me—the idea is disgusting to my imagination, and were it not for a curiosity which I am not, at present, able to restrain . . . Ah!

Scene 4

[*The stage is at once enlightened.*]

[THE MARQUIS *(in the dress of a sylph) kneels at the feet of* JULIA.]

MARQUIS: Julia! Adorable Julia! Am I at length permitted to kneel before you? It is no longer by my voice alone that I can describe my transports!—This enchanting hand is now in my possession—I feel I have it—I convince myself of it by thousands of kisses.

JULIA: Be quiet.

MARQUIS: How, madame! Do you fly me!—Can you be displeased at the warmth of . . .

JULIA: Why . . .

MARQUIS: If so, madame, to how little purpose have I taken a mortal body!—But it can never be my Julia's intent to refuse these innocent favours to my love; 'tis to the unlucky figure I have taken that I owe this cruel repulse.

JULIA: Believe me, you are mistaken.

MARQUIS: Mistaken?

JULIA: Yes, I repeat, you are mistaken—for whether it be from that nameless something which love adorns his votaries with, or whether from the partiality of my sentiments for you, 'tis certain that under the appear-

ance you appear to my eyes infinitely more pleasing than she ever did.—
You laugh.

MARQUIS: I do, indeed, my charmer, for I must acknowledge that this is not
the first time that you have beheld me in this same figure.

JULIA: You surprise me.

MARQUIS: This morning, at your toilette . . .

JULIA: Ah! I understand you—poor Florina's soul was sent a wandering,
whilst you . . .

MARQUIS: Whilst I adjusted the curls and placed flowers in that lovely
hair—whilst I—but you blush . . .

JULIA: Ah, Ziblis!—This is by no means fair play.—When one thinks
one's self with a companion of one's own sex, one is so unguarded—so
thoughtless of decorums.—And then, to find that all the while one's
lover has been of the party . . .

MARQUIS: And could you then imagine that the soul of your lover, hovering perpetually 'round the spot which contains everything which is dear
to him, has not often gazed on you, when . . .

JULIA: Pardon me—that is quite another affair.—Your soul, indeed, may
gaze—but now you have a body.

MARQUIS: 'Tis another affair, indeed; and I am so sensible of the difference, that I intend, with my fair one's permission, to appropriate the
person of Florina entirely to myself and to attend upon her from this
instant.

JULIA: You joke with me.

MARQUIS: 'Tis a settled point—the lover and the attendant now will be one
and the same person.—'Tis an opportunity . . .

JULIA: Which, with your permission, good sir, I must decline to make use
of.—No, no—'tis too difficult a task always to be certain of separating
one's ideas from the power of the senses.—How do I know but that
my affection may be engaged, in spite of myself, by features which,
though you condescend to wear them, are yet actually foreign to your
own?—You must drop your scheme—'tis little else than placing a rival
about your mistress's person.

MARQUIS: 'Tis a rival of whom, depend upon it, I shall never be in the
least jealous.

JULIA: You have very little delicacy then.

MARQUIS: Pardon me, it is you that have too much—for after all, these scruples will have the same force, let me take what form I will. Yet some form I must have.—You, my Julia, have eyes, have lips, have hands—I must provide myself with the like, else we shall be at a sad loss.

JULIA: Ah! Ziblis! Ziblis!

MARQUIS: Well, madame!

JULIA: I begin to doubt whether the sylphs have not amongst them characters as much depraved as are amongst us mortals.

MARQUIS: And why these unkind suspicions?

JULIA: Do you imagine that I am ignorant that there are other methods . . .

MARQUIS: What methods do you hint at?

JULIA: Had I not read the works of the Kabbalistic philosophers, love alone would have taught me that when a sylph is truly enamoured of a mortal, he can if he sincerely wishes for her company raise her to his own sphere of immortality, instead of debasing himself down to her level.— 'Tis then that the attractive power of his passion, joined to that of his mistress's, increasing the aerial and weakening the substantial particles which compose her being, she becomes, at his wish, a pure atherial spirit and is in every respect a sylphid—you seem thunderstruck!

MARQUIS [aside]: And who the plague would be otherwise.—[Aloud.] What, madame, do you imagine it to be my duty as your lover to set you floating about in the air, unbodied, like a boy's paper kite?

JULIA [disdainfully]: By the manner in which you treat my wish, I see plainly enough what I have to expect from your love.—But since I find you think me unworthy your alliance, you must excuse me if I too deprive myself of the honour of your addresses—and if, as I am satisfied of the nature of your ideas of me, I think the present hour rather too late a one for any longer conversation between us.

MARQUIS: But, madame . . .

JULIA [going and shutting the door after her]: I know too well that I can find no asylum from the persecutions of a sylph—I know that an aerial being can penetrate into the most retired places.—But I flatter myself that as you are not willing to be the author of my happiness you have too much benevolence to wish to become my tyrant.

Scene 5

[THE MARQUIS, FINETTA.]

MARQUIS: Was there ever such a conceit?—Well, faith, this last frolic has turned all my schemes upside down.

FINETTA: 'Tis true, the proposal is a little puzzling.—And, my dear sir, I wish you had it in your power to oblige her by complying with her request and at the same time to fit me up in her cast person.—I should like very well to figure about in the world in the character of a young, handsome, rich . . .

MARQUIS: And, in spite of my passion, I see I must give up all thoughts of this fantastic beauty.

FINETTA: No! No! Sir—'tis not come to that yet.—I took notice from my lurking place of her actions.—Be assured, she is struck with your figure; she was enchanted with it.

MARQUIS: Let her be never so much enchanted with it; you may yet be certain that the attachment which her heart may have been surprised into will never triumph over the caprices of her imagination.

FINETTA: Just the way of all lovers.—Ever eager, ever in a hurry, yet discouraged in a moment at the first obstacle which presents itself.

MARQUIS: Why, what wouldst have me do?

FINETTA: Nothing in the world, sir. Go—drop the scheme—I wish you a pleasant ride back to Paris.

MARQUIS: Dost think, child, that I should have any chance for success if I was at once to leave my disguise, to throw myself at her feet, and discovering who I really am, honestly to display my passion.—Ah! No! 'Tis all in vain —'twould never do.

FINETTA: I am silent.

MARQUIS: 'Twould be a better plan for me to resume the person of Florina.

FINETTA: As you please.

MARQUIS: 'Twill at least give some relief to my imagination, which her confounded proposal has quite disjoined.—Who knows what project may come into my head?

FINETTA: Very true, as you say, who knows . . .

MARQUIS: But then, what kind of project can it be?

FINETTA: Aye! That's a puzzling question.

MARQUIS: She is determined to become a sylphid . . .

FINETTA: That's the devil!

MARQUIS: I am, to be sure, the most unlucky dog . . .

FINETTA: You are, to be sure, a good deal discomposed at present.

MARQUIS: My dear, dear Finetta . . .

FINETTA: My dear, dear sir!

MARQUIS: A little advice, for heaven's sake!

FINETTA: Well then, sir, I advise you to begin by going immediately in again—since, as I doubt not but the mind of your mistress is little less uneasy than your own, you may depend upon it that she will come back again in a minute or two.—She should not see us together.

MARQUIS: You are in the right.

FINETTA: I will be in her way when she returns.

MARQUIS: Well—and what will you have to say to her?

FINETTA: Oh, never fear—let me alone for that—I shall have something at my tongue's end.—I shall examine her, interrogate her, persecute her, teaze her till I shall be able to prove to you how thoroughly nature will triumph over all those cursed volumes of Kabbalistical nonsense.—And you must, by no means, be idle—by listening, and by attending, you may find means—faith, 'tis enough to set one a swearing, to think of a man's despairing to subdue the folly of a woman, when you may see, every day, their wisdom perpetually put to the rout.

MARQUIS: Well, do you stay where you are then—I will go in.—But stop, hearken a moment—I fancy . . .

FINETTA: Hearken a moment yourself, and you will find that the door is just on the point of opening.—Go, fancy away in your own room—get you gone, in an instant.

Scene 6

[JULIA *(a casket in her hand, which she places on her toilette)*.]

JULIA: No! No! I can never, surely repent of my behaviour.—His ironical manner of answering my proposal was the more provoking, as the proposal itself was the strongest proof which I could give that I loved him for himself alone.—But what shall I do about poor Florina—the girl is so attached to me—how shall I part with her?—It hurts me to think of it.

Scene 7

[JULIA, FINETTA *(pretending to laugh heartily).*]

JULIA: Why so very merry, Finetta?

FINETTA: Merry, madame!—Excuse me, madame, I did not see your lady-ship—but poor Florina is in such a chase . . .

JULIA: Why so? What has anger'd her?

FINETTA [*seeming to hesitate*]: Because, madame—why, if I must own the truth, I had, you must know, so much curiosity to hear what your sylph had to say that I listened and heard the whole conversation.—After you had left him abruptly, he disappeared in a few moments—while I, being uneasy on poor Florina's account, went directly to her room.—I found her rubbing her eyes like one just awake—I made my excuses to her, for disturbing her from probably an agreeable dream.—She smiled—I insisted on hearing what it was.—She told me that I was certainly a con-jurer—that she had actually been dreaming, that she was on a sudden become a gay and a richly dress'd young bride, that her spouse had ap-peared astonished at the sprightliness of her behaviour, and that he had rallied her upon that happy freedom of air which matrimony had con-ferred upon her.—At last, however, the gentleman grew so very fond of her and began to take such freedoms that she waked in a fright.—This, madame, was her story.—But when I told her that she had not been in a dream and that your ladyship's sylph had, to facilitate his access to you, done her the honour to borrow her person, she flew into a terrible rage.

"What," said she, "and has my lady consented to this cruel trick?"

"Very cruel, indeed," said I. "Were you not very well off?"

"Mighty well, indeed," replied she. "The soul of a poor girl, like me, given over to deal with such a boisterous fellow of a husband—heaven knows what might have happened in another minute or two!—'Tis a fine affair, truly, that one is to deprive one's self of a thousand pleasures—resist all temptations, do everything, and avoid everything necessary to

be done and avoided by a girl that wishes to preserve her character.—
And after all, how can she answer for her person, if such doings are
suffered?—Who can tell what sort of company this devil of a sylph may
keep?—Or to what kind of places he may introduce my poor body while
my soul is gone a wool-gathering?"

JULIA [*sighing*]: He shall have no more to say to her soul or body either.—It
was only on my account, Finetta, that he ever made so free with them;
and I am determined on that account to part with her.

FINETTA: To part with her, madame!

JULIA: Alas, Finetta, in the garb of thy niece, my sylph was but too lovely
in my eyes.—It was a severe struggle between my honour and my love;
and I cannot now name it without emotion.—Would you then wish me
to nourish in my bosom a hopeless absurd passion by keeping ever before my eyes an object which I shall often imagine to be my lover; nay,
perhaps, may sometimes wish to be him?—No, my girl, she must go—
'tis determined—and I will console myself for her loss by representing
to myself that the presents which I intend to bestow on her may help to
place her in a situation above that which seems to have been allotted to
her. You shall give her this casket . . .

FINETTA [*opening the casket*]: Why, my dear, dear madame, here is the Lord
knows how much gold!—And jewels too!—Ah! madame! Was poor Florina, instead of being a girl and my niece, was she but a young fellow of
rank and fortune equal to your own—would you then part with this terrific
object?—Would you not, madame, willingly give up your whole system?

JULIA: Nonsense! I to prefer a mortal to a spirit! Let me hear no more of
this species of folly which your discourse is perpetually running into
and which always puts me out of humour.—Go take this casket to your
niece.—Tell her (for I cannot bear to take my leave of her in person,
'twould affect me too much)—tell her my reasons for parting with
her—she must confess that they are but just ones.—Tell her, besides,
that she will be ever near my heart. But stay—I should imagine—aye,
aye, I will add one more present to those you have got for her.—She
shall have the miniature picture of me.—Poor dear girl, I know she will
not think that the least valuable gift I have made her.

[*Exit* JULIA.]

Scene 8

[THE MARQUIS *(as a sylph)*, FINETTA.]

MARQUIS: Finetta!

FINETTA: 'Tis true, sir, you are in the right in your idea of our whimsical lady—let her passion for you be ever so violent, 'twill make no odds in your favour.—In short—you have heard the whole affair—you must be packing.

MARQUIS: Excuse me, my dear Finetta, I shall keep my ground—and I have even hopes, from this *éclaircissement*, of a favourable event to my love.—I have thought of an almost certain method of making her give up her ridiculous notions about immateriality . . .

FINETTA: That would be the very thing, sir, but . . .

MARQUIS: But you may wait a little, and you shall see—here she comes; and you have nothing to do but to acquaint her that you think her sylph is come back again—and, d'ye hear, seem to be in a fright about it.

Scene 9

[JULIA *(musing and holding in her hand a picture)*, FINETTA.]

JULIA: With what uneasiness, with what trouble, is my heart at present agitated!

FINETTA: Believe me, madame, mine is in no easier situation.—Do, madame, make your presents and your farewells in your own person.

JULIA: I will, Finetta, I will.—It would look unkind to part with the poor girl without speaking to her—I was just thinking so.

FINETTA: Indeed, madame, that did not enter into my head—I only beg leave to decline having any concern in the affair; for I think your ladyship's sylph is returned again—and I choose to keep out of his clutches.

JULIA: Returned!—Let us examine into this . . .

Scene the Last

[FINETTA, JULIA, THE MARQUIS *(as a sylph)*.]

[FINETTA *retires screaming.*]

JULIA: How! Ziblis!—What still in the shape of that girl!

MARQUIS: Deign, madame, but one instant's attention . . .

JULIA: Excuse me—I cannot listen to one who undervalues me . . .

MARQUIS: How, madame! How can you say that of me?—Me, who adore you!

JULIA: I am and ever shall remain firmly persuaded that you can make me become a sylphid—that you will not do it—and that, in consequence, 'tis affronting my understanding, to think that I will hearken to your love.

MARQUIS: But, my fairest . . .

JULIA: All you can say will be in vain.

MARQUIS: Consider a little . . .

JULIA: I have considered.

MARQUIS: Well, madame, well, since you are determined, I love you too well not to wish to satisfy your wishes, even at the expense of my fondest hopes.—You shall become a sylphid.—But how very cruel is your request!

JULIA: Cruel, indeed! To be content to change my species for the sake of sharing in your tenderness!

MARQUIS [*leading* JULIA *to her glass*]: See, my fair one—see once more, and take leave of those charms of which you are resolved to deprive yourself and your lover.—Alas! 'Tis in vain that our sylphids attempt to depreciate the charms of their mortal rivals—I feel but too plain a conviction in my heart that envy alone causes their contemptuous manner of treating what they style a little red and white and a set of regular features.

JULIA: Envy! Impossible! Do not all our Kabbalistic writers paint them in the loveliest colours?

MARQUIS [*sighing*]: Have patience, my Julia, you shall soon resemble them.

JULIA: You speak most dismally.

MARQUIS: I feel so at present.

JULIA: Do explain yourself.—Are they not handsome?

MARQUIS: They are inimitable as to wit, as to sentiment, and as to the infinity of their knowledge, but you must consider that to form that beauty, that elegance, which causes the brilliancy of mortal charmers, there must be a mixture of all the elements.

JULIA: Without doubt there must.

MARQUIS: And that, in consequence, we must not expect to find in a sylphid, which is a being purely aerial, a shape, a mouth, a complexion—no, 'tis quite otherwise.

JULIA: How! Is it not so then?

MARQUIS: Certainly not.—The instant you become a sylphid, these graces will exist no longer, except in the heart of your lover—confined, as well as yourself, to charms merely philosophical, there will no longer remain that eager ardour, which the sight of those graces always inspires—those delicious transports, that soft attraction of desire, which almost alone would constitute the most enchanting joys of love, will then be no more.

JULIA [in confusion]: Very extraordinary, I must confess!—Why then, after all—but Ziblis, suppose, at your request, I should now and then revisit the earth.

MARQUIS: Revisit the earth!—A sylphid!—Ah! No! 'Tis impossible.

JULIA: And why, pray? Are not you here upon earth?

MARQUIS: Our sex has some allowances granted which yours has not. Besides, when you quit your new element and borrow the appearance of some person totally a stranger to you, should you be much flattered with the homage . . .

JULIA [interrupting him]: But I shall take my own person.

MARQUIS: Your own!—No—when once the purer particles of your body are separated and have formed for you a person merely aerial, consider then that like a fair flower torn from its stalk and withered, all the terrestrial part of my now lovely Julia will love that spirit, that brilliancy, that vivacity which render her at present the most lovely of her sex.

JULIA [terrified]: What! Shall I become a fright, then?

MARQUIS: What, my fair one, would you have? Why this terror?—It is not until after you have deprived yourself of this enchanting form that this change will happen.—How then can it affect you?

JULIA [sighing]: Affect me! Alas, but too much!

MARQUIS: Come then—let us immediately begin those ceremonies which will annihilate my Julia's connexions with this part of the universe.

JULIA [hastily]: Oh! For heaven's sake! Stop, Ziblis!

MARQUIS: You amaze me! And can you feel, then, any reluctance at quitting graces which otherwise a little time must destroy.—Will not the immortality which awaits you make amends for that sacrifice?—Recall then your firmness, and lift your eyes with joy to the regions which you are now to inhabit.

JULIA: Stop, I entreat you—I cannot thus rob myself of myself.—I own my weakness, Ziblis.—I was born with these features, I have watched their daily progress, I am used to them, and what is still more, I owe to them the conquest of your heart.—It is that which renders them dear to me—and I will not be thus deprived of them.

MARQUIS: And will you then permit me to keep this figure?

JULIA: What! A figure which you have no right to assume?

MARQUIS: And will my charmer still oppose to my happiness a delicacy so ill-founded?

JULIA: Alas! How can I do otherwise?

MARQUIS: Are you not a little capricious?—You refuse to become a sylphid for fear of losing your own form—you refuse to permit me to retain this form because it is not my own.

JULIA: Ah! Ziblis! And why is it not your own?

MARQUIS: Suppose it was.—I should then be a man—and you think so ill of all that race . . .

JULIA: Would to heaven you were!—This wish is unworthy me—unworthy you—but 'tis the effusion of my heart.

MARQUIS [*throwing himself at her feet*]: Crown then my passion, lovely Julia!—Behold, at your feet, the Marquis de S———: the most tender, the most ardent of lovers.

JULIA: How!

FINETTA [*advancing from behind the scenes*]: Yes, madame, this is no lover fallen from the clouds—he is downright flesh and blood.—'Twas I that introduced him—*the sylph, Florina, and the marquis* are one and the same person.

MARQUIS [*still on his knees before* JULIA]: It was, my fairest, the notions in which you had been educated respecting the Kabbalah and your prejudice against mankind which reduced a lover, who adored you, to these disguises.—Recollect, I entreat you, notwithstanding the eagerness of his passion, yet he never permitted it, tempting as his opportunities were, to exceed the bounds of the most scrupulous delicacy.—Alas! When every, every instant increased my love, it at the same time augmented my anxiety for its success!—For pity's sake, my lovely Julia, look on me— confirm my happiness.

JULIA [*presenting him with her hand and looking at him tenderly*]: Ah! Traitor! You are too well acquainted with my heart to doubt me.

FINETTA: Huzza! Down with sylphs and hobgoblins—'tis all over with them, by the Lord Harry, we have got something now worth a million of them.—Well—Paris forever!—Thank heaven, we shall now have done with this old humdrum castle—Paris, Paris is the only element for a fine woman to breathe in.

[*Exit all.*]

NOTES

Letter 1

5   *"smiling mischief"*   Lord Stanley uses these words as a somewhat sinister metonymy (substitute naming) for love. Lady
Georgiana was friendly with Samuel Johnson and may have
borrowed the phrase from his drama *Irene* (1754):

> MAHOMET: Where's this *smiling mischief,* Whom neither
> vows could fix, nor favours bind?
> HASAN: Thine orders, mighty Sultan! are perform'd, And
> all Irene now is

> (Samuel Johnson, Irene, act 5)

The phrase also appears in Psalm 119:165 (Book of Common
Prayer):

> Secure substantial peace have they,
> No smiling mischief them can tempt.

And, finally, it is used as a metonymy to characterize Belvidera
in Thomas Otway's *Venice Preserved* (act 4.2):

> Where's my friend, my friend, thou smiling mischief!
> Nay, shrink not, now 'tis too late, for dire revenge
> Is up and raging for my friend.

5   *"adamantine everlasting chains"*   This quotation blends a biblical passage from Jude 1:6–7 (Authorized [King James] Version
[AV]) ("And the angels which kept not their first estate, but left
their own habitation, he hath reserved in everlasting chains under darkness unto judgment of the great day") with a description of Satan in *Paradise Lost:*

Him the Almighty power
Hurl'd headlong flaming from th' Ethereal sky
With hideous ruin and combustion down
To bottomless perdition, there to dwell
In Adamantine Chains, and penal Fire.

(John Milton, *Paradise Lost*, 1.44–48)

7   *like Patience on a monument*

She sat like patience on a monument,
Smiling at grief.

(Shakespeare, *Twelfth Night*, act 2.4)

In Shakespeare's play, these lines are spoken by Viola to Orsino. Lady Georgiana used the same passage in *Emma; or, The Unfortunate Attachment*, so it must have been a favorite. It works dramatically in this novel because Stanley inadvertently effeminizes himself by comparing himself to a woman, though this is quite in keeping with his pose as a dandy or macaroni. Stanley reveals himself to be a coxcomb, fresh from Italy, with only a handful of foreign phrases.

8   *Mr. Grenville*   Julia's father's name, Grenville, recalls Thomas Grenville, a close friend of Lady Georgiana's.

12   *the devil a bit*   The passion was too great to resist; Stanley is tempted to think of seducing Julia. It is a "strong temptation" when *devil* precedes a verb (*OED*). See also Thomas Urquhart and Peter Motteux's 1708 translation of Rabelais's *Gargantua and Pantagruel* 5.221: "The Devil-a-Bit he'll see the better."

13   *my wife, like Caesar's, should not be suspected*   Caesar said this of his second wife, Pompeia Sulla (fl. first century B.C.), whom he married for political reasons. Publius Clodius's flirtation with her, combined with the social circle in which she moved,

led Caesar to divorce her, stating, "Caesar's wife must be above suspicion."

13   *"settle soberly and raise a brood"*   This phrase appears in "The Goldfinches," *Elegy* 22, by the Reverend Richard Jago, M.A.:

> Through Nature's spacious walks at large they ranged
> No settled haunts, no fix'd abode their aim;
> As chance or fancy led, their path they changed,
> Themselves, in every vary'd scene, the same
>
> Till on a day to weighty cares resign'd,
> With mutual choice, alternate they agree'd,
> On rambling thoughts no more to turn their mind,
> But settle soberly, and raise a breed.
>
> (Richard Jago, "The Goldfinches," lines 13–20 [Bell, p. 100])

The poem recounts the mating of two goldfinches but adds an ominous note about a truant schoolboy, which Lord Biddulph (the very recipient of Lord Stanley's letter) will play:

> but ah! What earthly happiness can last
> How does the fairest purpose often fail?
> A truant schoolboy's wantonness could blast
> And leave them both to wail.
>
> (Richard Jago, "The Goldfinches," lines 29–32
> [Bell, p. 100])

13   *publish it not in the streets of Askalon*   "Tell it not in Gath, publish it not in the streets of Askelon" (11 Samuel 1:20 [AV]).

Letter 2

14   *Even in Paradise unblest.*   Stanley proves himself unable to enjoy the Eden-like countryside of Wales, as he explains in his first letter. Though he gains Julia's hand in marriage, he is un-

able to appreciate her merit, other than her beauty. As Pope explains in the following poem, woman is "the last, the best reserv'd of God."

> Our grandsire, Adam, ere of Eve possesst,
> Alone, and e'en in Paradise unblest,
> With mournful looks the blissful scenes survey's,
> And wander'd in the solitary shade.
> The Maker say, took pity, and bestow'd
> Woman, the last, the best reserv'd of God.
>
> (Alexander Pope, "January and May," L.63)

14   *sin and sea-coal*   Sea-coal was used to heat rooms, presumably where sinful seductions could take place. Sea-coal was more expensive to transport than other types of coal, as in Byron's "I like a seacoal fire, when not too dear" (Byron, *Beppo* [1817], 4:144), line 378.

14   *And days of peace do still succeed / To nights of calm repose.*   These lines appear in Fanny Greville's "Prayer for Indifference." The same poem is quoted in *Emma; or, The Unfortunate Attachment*, thus linking the author of *Emma* (pp. 303, 309) to *The Sylph*.

15   *And when I am weary of wandering all day, / To thee my delight in the evening I come.*   Matthew Prior's poem "A Better Answer" captures Lord Stanley's effort to win Julia's love, though it is not clear that Stanley (or Prior's speaker) has forsworn his other mistresses in favor of her. Prior's speaker suggests that his love is so real it is beyond rhetorical embellishment. Yet Prior's poem, like Stanley's literary embellishments in his letter, tells a different story.

> So when I'm wearied with wand'ring all day,
> To thee my delight in the evening I come:
>
> (Matthew Prior, "A Better Answer," lines 21–22)

Letter 3

18   *doubt*   *Doubt* here means suspect; see also, for example, pp. 23, 38, and 64.

Letter 4

22   *as Lord Chesterfield justly observes*   Lord Chesterfield's letters to his son emphasized the importance of *les bienseances*. Samuel Johnson found Chesterfield morally superficial, and Lady Georgiana, a friend of Johnson's, writes against male fops and the education that produces them.

Letter 6

24   *James Spencer, Esq.*   The use of the name Spencer alludes to Georgiana's family name (she was born Georgiana Spencer).

25   *My dear-lov'd Julia! from my youth began / The tender flame, and ripen'd in the man; / My dear-lov'd Julia! to my latest age, / No other vows shall e'er my heart engage.*   The lines here quoted by Woodley were addressed to Laura in "An Epistle, Written in 1764," by F. N. C. Munday, Esq., p. 261, lines 120–23. The poem depicts a young man, a rustic like Julia and Henry Woodley, who refuses to marry solely for money. Instead, he invokes the name of his lover, Laura, to remind him what true love is:

> Mix with the world, the polish'd world you cry,
> Nor waste thy prime in dull obscurity
> . . . .
> 'Twere strange to see a horse with human head;
> As strange that I, a rustic born and bred,
> My life half spent shou'd now embrace the town.
>
> (F. N. C. Munday, Esq., "An Epistle, Written in 1764,"
> lines 1–2, 15–17)

The male speaker, like Julia, hates French manners and French wine: "to routs, to Ranelagh, to cards a foe, / Who on my dress but little care bestow" (lines 70–71). He states:

> My choice was early, I approve it still
> These school-boy rimes may testify the truth,
> Writ in the plain simplicity of youth.
>
> (F. N. C. Munday, Esq., "An Epistle, Written
> in 1764," lines 129–31)

He is "without one pride, except an honest name" (line 141).

Letter 7

29   *innate virtue of her mind*   J. Spencer's comment, with its focus on innate virtue, reflects Rousseau's ideas. The name of *The Sylph*'s heroine, as well as the belief in innate virtue, reflect Georgiana's underscoring in Rousseau's novel *Julie, ou la nouvelle Héloïse,* her copy of which can still be seen at Chatsworth.

Letter 8

30   *Pont sang*   Bloody bridge.

31   *au dernier goût*   According to the latest style.

32   *like poor Actaeon when he had suffered the displeasure of Diana* Actaeon viewed Diana bathing nude and was punished by being transformed into a stag and then hunted and killed by his own hounds (Ovid, *Metamorphoses,* 3.138–253).

32   *nut-brown maid*   The phrase is from an anonymous fifteenth-century poem with the refrain "for in her heart she loved but him alone." Matthew Prior modernized the folk legend of the nut-brown maid:

No longer shall the Nut-brown Maid be old;
Tho' since her Youth three hundred Years have roll'd.
At Thy Desire, She shall again be rais'd;
And her reviving Charms in lasting Verse be prais'd.

(Matthew Prior, "Henry and Emma," lines 9–12)

See entry for Prior's *Henry*, letter 58, p. 193.

32   *pommade de Venus*   Blue violet leaves with a particular scent that are used as a cure for insomnia. Violets were used by Athenians to moderate anger, procure sleep, and soften the heart. See E. Cobham Brewer, *Brewer's Dictionary of Phrase and Fable*.

32   *vous êtes fini, madame, au dernier goût*   Your hair is made up according to the latest taste.

32   *ell*   A former English unit of length often used to measure cloth and equal to forty-five inches.

33   *six enormous large feathers—black, white, and pink—that reminded me of the plumes which nodded on the immense casque in the castle of Otranto*   In Horace Walpole's *Castle of Otranto* (1764), the plumes on an enchanted helmet (or casque) quiver in such a way as to indicate moral approval or disapproval about an action Manfred is about to take (p. 61). In Walpole's novel, the heroine tries to escape the unwanted attentions of an older man, much as Julia Stanley, Nancy Johnson, and Maria Maynard must fend off assaults by Lord Biddulph, Colonel Montague, and Edward Grenville's commanding officer, which they do with varying degrees of success.

33   *Duchess of D——*   The name Duchess of D—— alludes to Lady Georgiana.

33   *ruelle*   "A bedroom where ladies of fashion in the seventeenth and eighteenth centuries, especially in France, held a morning reception of persons" (*OED*).

Letter 9

45   *grace act*   A "formal pardon; specifically, a free and general pardon granted by Act of Parliament" (*OED*).

48   *But when will spring visit the mouldering urn? Ah! When will it dawn on the gloom of the grave?*   These lines are from James Beattie's "The Hermit" (1776, chap. 5, lines 31–32). They show that Edward Grenville has joined the army primarily to end his life, since he is in a state of despair over the death of his wife and his disinheritance. He quotes Beattie's lines to his commanding officer after volunteering to engage in a dangerous military maneuver.

57   *Seeks thee still in many a former scene . . .*   The lines Grenville quotes here to express his feelings for his dead wife Maria are from "Summer," one of the *Seasons* poems by James Thomson:

> And art thou Stanley, of that sacred Band?
> Alas, for us too soon!—Though rais'd above
> The reach of human pain, above the flight
> Of human joy, yet, with a mingled ray
> Of sadly pleased remembrance, must thou feel
> A mother's love, a mother's tender woe;
> Who seeks thee still in many a former scene,
> Seeks thy fair form, thy lovely beaming eyes,
> Thy pleasing commerce, by gay lively sense
> Inspir'd—where moral wisdom mildly shone
> Without the toil of art; and virtue glow'd
> In all her smiles, without forbidding pride
>
> (James Thomson, "Summer," lines 564–75)

Letter 11

66   *Clowns as well can act the rake, / As those in a higher sphere.*   With this line, Louisa requests that Julia send Winifred home to Wales

before her morals become corrupted. The line comes from Isaac Bickerstaffe's *Love in a Village* and shows that seducers come from every social class:

> Cease gay seducers, pride to take
> In triumphs o'er the fair;
> Since clowns as well can act the rake,
> As those in higher sphere
>
> Where then to shun a shameful fate
> Shall helpless beauty go;
> In ev'ry rank, in ev'ry state,
> Poor woman finds a foe.
>
> (Isaac Bickerstaffe, *Love in a Village*,
> 2.3.95–112)

Letter 12

69   *Cambro-Briton*   The Cambro-Britain is a Welsh folk dance. Julia uses the term *Cambro-Briton* to describe her servant Griffith's rural manners and accent, which the London servants of Lord Stanley ridicule.

69   *"Conscience makes cowards of us all"*   The line "Conscience does make cowards of us all" appears in Shakespeare's *Hamlet*, 3.1.56.

Letter 13

71   *the heart of man naturally loves variety*   One of many examples in which a virtuous character, here Lady Melford, echoes the words of a disreputable one. Lady Besford made the following comment about Julia's husband. "He is of a gay disposition, and his taste must be fed with variety." In *The Sylph*, the verbal doubling of Lady Besford and Lady Melford shows how women can accept man's fickle nature or condemn him

for it. Julia chooses a middle course, passively accepting Lord Stanley's behavior as part of man's nature, as Lady Besford might do, but not expressing her moral disapproval, as Lady Melford does. See pages 63 and 83.

72   *orgeat*   Orgeat is a syrup or cooling drink made from barley or almonds and orange-flower water (*OED*).

72   *Rauzzini*   Venanzio Rauzzini (1746–1810) was a singer and music teacher who performed in Bath (1777), Dublin (1778), and London (1778 and 1781). A young castrato who studied singing and dancing at Rome, he participated in entertainments given by William Beckford at Fonthill (Baldwin and Wilson).

73   *tout la mode de François*   In the fashionable French style.

73   *"For man the lawless libertine may rove."*   This phrase refers to Julia's husband, Lord Stanley, and to the double standard that marked upper-class marriage in the period. The quote is from Jane Shore's speech in Nicholas Rowe's *Tragedy of Jane Shore* (1714). Shore was seduced by and became mistress to Edward IV; she later became William Hastings's mistress and was a pawn in the struggle with Richard III.

81   *Is everything by starts, and nothing long.*   This line is taken from John Dryden's *Absalom and Achitophel*, line 547.

Letter 14

82   *the busy haunts of men*   The phrase recalls Pausanias's *Description of Greece*, an account of Greece in the second century A.D. Pausanias writes, "The Taragrans seem to me to have paid attention above all the Greeks to the gods, for their houses were apart, and the sacred edifices were by themselves in an open space away from the busy haunts of men" (Pausanias 9.22.2).

82   *that peace which goodness bosoms ever*   Louisa worries that her
      sister, Julia, will lose the peaceful state of mind that comes from
      innocence. The line comes from Milton's *Comus: A Mask:*
      "The sweete peace that goodness bosoms ever" (1.371).

Letter 15

83   *"The heart of man is deceitful above all things."*

> The heart is deceitful above all things, and desperately
> wicked: who can know it? I the LORD search the heart, I
> try the reins, even to give every man according to his ways,
> and according to the fruit of his doings.

(Jeremiah 17:9–10 [AV])

See also notes for letter 13, p. 71 and letter 34, p. 142.

A key phrase in the novel, this line shows how difficult it is for
characters to determine the motives of others as well as their
own. Many of the characters fail to achieve self-understanding,
or use stratagems to fool their prey. Biddulph is a libertine who
falls in love with Julia enough to pay an exorbitant amount of
money to possess her. He does so as much to thwart Stanley as
to gain her hand. Stanley professes his love but is a hardened
roué; Julia pretends to be in love with her husband but secretly
covets Ton-hausen; Ton-hausen plays the gentleman but desires Julia as his wife. The novel offers many examples of the
deceitful heart of both men and women, thereby illustrating
the biblical passage.

Letter 16

86   *I am a Rosicrucian by principle*   Rosicrucianism is a sect of Free-
      masonry popularized by Christian Rosenkreutz (1378–1484).

Letter 19

93   *bragg*   Bragg was a game of cards in which bluffing opponents played an important role. This fashionable English card game was a precursor to the American version of poker that became popular in the nineteenth century.

95   *picquet*   Sometimes spelled *piquet;* a game for two players using thirty-six cards (sixes through aces). Each hand of piquet is divided into five parts: blanks and discards, ruffs, sequences, sets, and tricks.

Letter 20

102   *Riches make to themselves wings, and fly away*   See Proverbs 23:5 (AV). This passage underscores how ephemeral Lord Stanley's fortune is; or, to answer a proverb with a proverb, a fool and his fortune are soon parted.

103   *Which, selfish joy disdaining, seeks alone / to bless the dearer object of its soul.*   Julia uses Thomson's lines to describe her husband as being incapable of self-sacrificing love:

> Even Love itself is Bitterness of Soul,
> A pensive Anguish pining at the heart:
> Or, sunk to sordid interest, feels no more
> That restless Wish, that infinite Desire,
> Which, selfish Joy disdaining, seeks, alone,
> To bless the dearer object of its Flame.

(James Thomson, "Spring," lines 288–93)

Thomson added these lines in his expanded version of the poem. In the 1735 edition of the poem, they appear in a footnote to lines 338–43 (Zippel, p. 20).

Letter 22

107   *vice-gerents*   A vicegerent is "a person appointed by a king or other ruler to act in his place or exercise certain of his administrative functions"; more generally, one who acts in place of another (*OED*).

Letter 23

108   *Jew brokers*   Julia shows a crass anti–Semitism in this passage, not unlike the same unfortunate stereotypes that inform *The Merchant of Venice*. In England, as elsewhere in the eighteenth century, Jews were confined to certain professions, one of them money lending.

Letter 24

112   *Anderton's Coffee House*   Anderton's Coffee House on Fleet Street served as a location for posting anonymous letters to the *Morning Post* and other publications (Carretta, p. 105).

Letter 26

113   In the 1779 edition of *The Sylph,* the second volume began with letter 26.

115   *Lord Chesterfield*   See note for letter 4, p. 22.

122   *Pamela Andrews*   Nancy's father, who receives money from Baron Ton-hausen, tells the story of how a neighbor put Samuel Richardson's *Pamela* in the hands of his daughter in order to give her the illusion that she could marry above her station and enjoy a comfortable life. The full title of this novel is *Pamela; or, Virtue Rewarded* (1740), which Nancy's father (who does not seem well-read) quotes incorrectly. In Richardson's novel, Pamela resists Mr. B.'s efforts to take advantage of her

231

position as a servant girl; she is rewarded when he marries her. Nancy, by contrast, is reunited with William, a man of her own social class.

126 *halberts*   A place of punishment where soldiers were flogged (*OED*).

Letter 34

141 *cast one longing lingering look behind*   This line comes from Thomas Gray's "Elegy Written in a Country Churchyard" (1751), line 88.

142 *the heart of man is deceitful above all things*   See notes for letter 13, p. 71 and letter 15, p. 83. Lady Georgiana makes use of dramatic irony when she employs this quotation for the third time. In other words, the Sylph asks Julia if she will regret leaving a certain person (the baron) behind. She practically confesses that she will. The Sylph says that the baron's motives are obscure to him. In posing as a sylph, the baron exhibits the very deceitfulness that he bemoans. This passage is perhaps closest to Poullain de Saint-Foix's dramatic adaptation of Crébillon Fils' story.

Letter 38

151 *chaste as the icicle that hangs on Dian's temple*   The insinuation is that virgins are cold: Diana is compared to an icicle because of her legendary virginity. Biddulph's slang (*Dian's* not *Diana's*) indicates his insolent attitude toward the chaste goddess and Julia. Baron Ton-hausen, by contrast, leaves England in order to save Julia from Lady Anne Parker's insinuation that they are spending too much time together. Due to the prevalence of vice in London, women are assumed to be unchaste unless proven otherwise. The baron's concern for Julia's reputation is one more sign of his virtue.

151   *Condemn'd, alas! Whole ages to deplore, / And image charms I must behold no more.*   This line comes from Alexander Pope's "Eloise to Abelard" (lines 361–62). Baron Ton-hausen confesses, somewhat melodramatically, how difficult he will find it to leave Julia, even if he does so to preserve her reputation as a married woman. He can "image" (or imagine) her charms but cannot see her in person anymore.

Letter 39

152   *"a pumpkin fried in snow"*   "His mind is like porridge, his body is like wet paper, and his heart is like a pumpkin fried in snow" (Madame de Sévigné, *Letters from Madame la Marquise de Sévigné*, p. 56). Biddulph uses this vivid image of emotional coldness to explain Baron Ton-hausen's willingness to give up Julia in order to preserve her reputation.

153   *Calista*   Zeus rapes one of Diana's nymphs, Calista, by disguising himself as Artemis. To punish her, Hera turns her into a she-bear.

        Calista is also the religious heroine of Nicholas Rowe's *Fair Penitent.*

154   *had rather see the Devil than the Don*   In Tirso de Molina's *El Burlador de Sevilla,* Don Juan's amorous adventures end when he is invited to dinner by a guest of stone who turns out to be Satan.

Letter 44

163   *Tyburn*   Tyburn was a village known for its gallows, where most of London's public executions by hanging took place. Forgery was a capital crime.

163   *tertianague*   A particularly strong form of the flu.

Letter 46

173   *My mind is a hell*   This line echoes one from Satan's speech in Milton's *Paradise Lost:* "Which way I fly is Hell; myself am Hell" (2.187).

174   *a note was brought him from his own house*   The note brought is the billet which Lady Stanley wrote before quitting her husband's house. (This editor's note appeared in the 1779 edition.)

Letter 47

175   *A letter from Mr. Stanley*   Mr. Stanley's letter is omitted.

Letter 49

178   *nor be extreme to mark what was done amiss!*   "If thou, Lord, wilt be extreme to mark what is done amiss, O Lord, who may abide it?" (Psalm 120 [AV]). Lord Stanley's uncle wonders how Lord Stanley could fail to appreciate Julia's gifts but stops himself. He realizes that no one can "abide" to have his sins enumerated without mercy.

Letter 50

179   *unhackneyed in the ways of the world*   This phrase appears in Bishop Warburton's "Letter on Dr. Law" (September 22, 1751), p. 71. Warburton was an editor of Alexander Pope's and an eminent scholar.

180   *I will walk upright, my foot shall not slide or go astray*   See Psalm 18:23 (AV): "I was also upright before him, and I kept myself from mine iniquity"; see also Psalm 26:1–3 (AV): "I have trusted also in the Lord; therefore I shall not slide."

184   *a burnt child dreads the fire*   "The burnt child dreads the fire;
they do not know to entertain the devil," (Ben Jonson, "The
Devil Is an Ass," 1.2). Also an English proverb; see Marvin,
p. 46. Those who give way to dangerous curiosity at a young
age learn to avoid it. Louisa is willing to have her father's fortune settled on Julia's husband (Woodley) rather than on hers
(Spencer) in order to test Spencer's devotion to her. By testing
Spencer, she hopes to avoid repeating the "fire" of her previous
romantic history, which left her disillusioned and "burnt."

Letter 56

187   *It is not friendly, 'tis not maidenly; / Our sex, as well as I, may
chide you for it, / Though I alone do feel the injury*   This passage is taken from Shakespeare's *A Midsummer Night's Dream*
(3.2.217–19). In Shakespeare's play all the lovers are at cross-
purposes, and Helena assumes Hermia and others have betrayed their female friendship. Julia uses these words for the
same purpose. She faults her sister, Louisa, for betraying their
female bond by taking the side of her father, who is urging her
to marry Woodley.

Letter 58

192   *Thou Proteus!*   Proteus was the eldest son of the Titans Oceanus
and Tethys and able to change shape at will. Menelaus, leaving
Troy, held Proteus down, despite his many frightening transformations, to learn his fate. In *The Sylph*, Julia suggests that Woodley's nature may be no more reliable than that of her husband,
Stanley, since he so frequently changes his shape and form.

193   *Prior's Henry*   This is a reference to a poem by Matthew Prior
titled "Henry and Emma," which was modeled on "The Nut-

Brown Maid" (see entry for letter 8, p. 32). The poem emphasizes the patience of Emma, whose behavior resembles that of Griselda, a figure in German legend and Chaucer's "Clerk's Tale."

194   *the heart of man is not deceitful above all things*   This line is repeated three times previous to this allusion (see letters 13, 15, and 34). By letter 58, Julia Stanley has begun to repudiate her dark view of human nature, altering the quote from Jeremiah to state that man's heart is *not* deceitful, just confusing. Like Proteus (see note for letter 58, p. 192), Woodley appears in three forms: as himself, Baron Ton-hausen, and the Sylph. Other configurations of three include symbolic allusions to the Father, Son, and Holy Ghost. The tripartite structure of the novel in which the heroine is born (Wales), lost (London), and born again (return to Wales) also deserves mention insofar as it reinforces the three-in-one symbolism.

Letter 60

196   *adamantine chains*   See note for letter 1, p. 5. The novel ends by revising Lord Stanley's cynical perspective on marriage, which he confided to Lord Biddulph in the first letter of the novel.

197   *Tell it not in Gath.*   This phrase comes from 11 Samuel 1:20 (AV): "Tell it not in Gath, Publish it not in the streets of Askelon." Maria Brudenel informs Julia that she is pregnant but does not want the dissolute crowd in London to know. Where Maria has the good news of her own pregnancy which she wishes to keep secret, in the biblical passage David hopes to conceal the untimely deaths of Saul and Jonathan lest the Philistines rejoice in his misfortune and the "daughters of the uncircumcised" celebrate (11 Samuel 1:20 [AV]):

> The beauty of Israel is slain upon thy high places: how are the mighty fallen! Tell it not in Gath, publish it not in the

streets of Askelon; lest the daughters of the Philistines rejoice, lest the daughters of the uncircumcised triumph.

(11 Samuel 1:19–20 [AV]).

Maria's reference to Gath echoes Lord Stanley's in letter 1. He does not want it published that he almost prefers the moral tranquility of Wales to the unsettling bustle of London. Similarly, Maria wishes to conceal the good news of her pregnancy from Londoners who, like David's Philistines in Samuel, do not wish her well.

BIBLIOGRAPHY

Editions of The Sylph
by Georgiana, Duchess of Devonshire

The Sylph. 1st ed. London: Printed for T. Lowndes, No. 77, Fleet-Street, 1779. Harvard University copy. [Also at Newberry Library.]

The Sylph. 2nd ed. London: T. Lowndes, 1779. University of Chicago Special Collections.

The Sylph. 1st ed. Dublin: Printed for S. Price, J. Williams, W. Colles, W. Wilson, T. Walker, C. Jenkin, R. Moncrieffe, W. Gilbert, E. Cross, W. Spotswood, G. Burnet, J. Exshaw, R. Beatty, and R. Burton, 1779.

The Sylph. 2nd ed. Dublin: Printed by P. Higly for S. Price, J. Williams, W. Colles, W. Wilson, T. Walker, C. Jenkin, R. Moncrieffe, W. Gilbert, E. Cross, W. Spotswood, G. Burnet, J. Exshaw, J. Beatty, and R. Burton, 1780.

The Sylph. 3rd ed. London: Printed for T. Lowndes, No. 77, Fleet-Street, 1783.

The Sylph. 3rd ed. Dublin: Printed for W. Wilson, T. Walker, C. Jenkin, R. Moncrieffe, W. Gilbert, G. Burnet, J. Exshaw, R. Burton, J. Cash, and W. Wilkinson, 1784.

The Sylph. 4th ed. London: Delaloy, 1796. [Not listed in *The English Novel, 1770–1829: A Bibliographical Survey of Prose Fiction Published in the British Isles.* 2 vols. Oxford: Oxford University Press, 2000.]

The Sylph. Edited by Amanda Foreman. Yorkshire: Henry Parker, 2001.

Other Works of the Same Title: The Sylph

Fagan, James Pettit Andrews, and M. de Saint-Foix. *Three Comedies: The Uneasy Man, The Financier, and The Sylph.* London: J. Walter, 1771.

New York: Readex Microprint, 1967; courtesy of New York Public Library; Microprint TCD E4.9 S984; Indiana State University microprints, pp. 114–61. [A play that anticipates the plot device in *The Sylph;* n.b. Germain François Poullain de Saint-Foix is the full name for M. de Saint-Foix.]

London, P. P. *The Sylph.* London: T. Longman and J. Debrett, 1796. [A prose tract, consisting mainly of advice.]

The New Sylph, or, Guardian Angel. A Story. London: W. Lane, 1788.

Thomson, Charles West. *The Sylph and Other Poems.* Philadelphia: Carey, Lea, & Carey, 1828. [A work by an American poet having little relation to Georgiana's novel.]

Primary Sources

Baldwin, Olive, and Thelma Wilson. "Rauzzini, Venanzio (1746–1810)." In *Oxford Dictionary of National Biography*, ed. H. C. G. Matthew and Brian Harrison. Oxford: Oxford University Press, 2004.

Beattie, James. "The Hermit." In *The Poetical Works of James Beattie, with a Memoir by Rev. Alexander Dyck*, 94–96. London: George Bell & Sons, 1894.

Bickerstaffe, Isaac. *Love in a Village: A Comic Opera.* London: J. Bell, 1791.

Boswell, James. *Life of Johnson.* Edited by Pat Rogers. Oxford: Oxford University Press, 1998.

Burney, Fanny. *Journals and Letters.* Edited by Peter Sabor and Lars Troide. London: Penguin, 2001.

———. *Evelina, or, The History of a Young Lady's Entrance into the World: Authoritative Text, Contexts, and Contemporary Reactions, Criticism.* Edited by Stewart J. Cooke. New York: W.W. Norton, 1998.

Byron, George Gordon, Lord. *Beppo.* In *The Complete Poetical Works*, edited by Jerome McGann, vol. 4, 129–60. Oxford: Oxford University Press, 1986.

———. *Byron's Letters and Journals.* Edited by Leslie Marchand. 12 vols. Cambridge: Belknap Press, 1982–92.

Chaucer, Geoffrey. "The Clerk's Tale." In *The Text of the Canterbury Tales*, edited by John M. Manly and Edith Rickert, vol. 3, 327–416. Chicago: University of Chicago Press, 1940.

Chesterfield, Lord. *Lord Chesterfield's Letters.* Edited by David Roberts. Oxford: Oxford's World Classics, 1998.

de Crébillon, Claude Prosper Jolyot (Crébillon Fils). *Le sylphe ou songe de Madame de R***. Écrit par elle-même à Madame de S***.* In *Œuvres complètes,* edited Jean Sgard. 4 vols. 1730. Paris: Gallimard, Classiques Garnier, 1999–2003.

Devonshire, Georgiana, Duchess of. "The Duchess's Diary." In *Sheridan: A Life. Sheridan: From New and Original Material; Including a Manuscript Diary by Georgiana, Duchess of Devonshire,* edited by Walter Sichel, vol. 2, 399–426. London: Constable, 1909.

————. *Emma; or, The Unfortunate Attachment.* Edited by Jonathan David Gross. New York: State University of New York Press, 2004.

————. "A Negro Song." In *Travels in the Interior Districts of Africa,* by Mungo Park, xxi–xxv. London: W. Bulmer, 1799. Hypertext by Stephanie D. Storrs, October 27, 1999. http://www2.bc.edu/~richarad/asp/gcns.html.

————. "A Negro Song." In *Amazing Grace: An Anthology of Poems About Slavery, 1660–1810,* edited by James G. Basker, 500–501. New Haven: Yale University Press, 2002.

Dolan, Brian. *Ladies of the Grand Tour: British Women in Pursuit of Enlightenment and Adventure in Eighteenth-Century Europe.* New York: HarperCollins, 2001.

Dryden, John. *Poetry, Prose, and Plays.* Edited by Douglas Grant. London: Hart-Davis, 1952.

Gabalis, Comte de [Abbe N. de Montfaucon de Villars]. *Discourses on the Secret Sciences and Mysteries, in Accordance with the Principles of the Ancient Magi and the Wisdom of the Kabalistic Philosophers,* by the Abbe N. de Montfaucon de Villars, newly rendered into English with commentary and annotations. London: William Rider, 1922.

Garrick, David. *Bon Ton; or, High Life Above Stairs. A Comedy, in Two Acts as It Is Performed at the Theatre Royal, in Drury-lane.* London: T. Becket, 1775.

————. *Poetical Works of David Garrick.* Edited by Benjamin Blom. New York: Ayer, 1968.

Gray, Thomas. "Elegy Written in a Country Churchyard." In *Selected Poems of Thomas Gray and William Collins,* edited by Arthur Johnston, 38–49. London: Edward Arnold, 1967.

Greville, Fanny. "Prayer for Indifference." In *The Oxford Book of English Verse, 1250–1918*, edited by Sir Arthur Quiller-Couch, 566. New York: Oxford University Press, 1940.

Jago, Richard, Rev. "The Goldfinches," *Elegy* 22. In *Bell's Classical Arrangement of Fugitive Poetry*, edited by John Bell. 7 vols. London: John Bell, 1789.

Johnson, Samuel. *Irene*. Menston, U.K.: Scolar Press, 1973.

Jonson, Ben. "The Devil Is an Ass." In *The Complete Plays of Ben Jonson*, edited by G. A. Wilkes, vol. 4, 127–241. Oxford: Clarendon Press, 1981–95.

Melbourne, Lady Elizabeth. *Byron's "Corbeau Blanc": The Life and Letters of Lady Melbourne, 1751–1818*. Edited by Jonathan David Gross. Houston: Rice University Press, 1997.

Milton, John. *Complete Poems and Major Prose*. Edited by Merritt Hughes. Indianapolis: Hackett, 2003.

———. *Paradise Lost*. Edited by Merritt Y. Hughes. New York: Odyssey Press, 1962.

Molina, Tirso de. *El Burlador de Sevilla*. Edited by Andreas de Claramonte. Kassel, Ger.: Edition Reichenberger, 1987.

Moore, Edward. *The Foundling: A Comedy* and *The Gamester: A Tragedy*. Edited by Anthony Amberg. Newark: University of Delaware Press, 1996.

Munday, F. N. C., Esq. "An Epistle, Written in 1764." In *The Poetical Register, and Repository of Fugitive Poetry for 1806–7*. London: F. C. and J. Rivington, 1811.

Otway, Thomas. *Venice Preserved*. Edited by Malcolm Kelsall. Lincoln: University of Nebraska Press, 1969.

Ovid. *Ovid: Metamorphoses*. Translated by Rolfe Humphries. Bloomington: Indiana University Press, 1955.

Pausanias. *Description of Greece*. Edited by R. E. Wycherley. Cambridge: Loeb Classical Library, 1935.

Pope, Alexander. *Pope: Poetical Works*. Edited by Herbert Davis with a new introduction by Pat Rogers. 1st ed. reprint. London: Oxford University Press, 1990.

———. *The Rape of the Lock and Other Poems*. Edited by Geoffrey Tillotson. New Haven: Yale University Press, 1940.

Prior, Matthew. "A Better Answer." In *The Literary Works of Matthew Prior*, edited by H. Bunker Wright and Monroe K. Spears, vol. 1, 450–51. Oxford: Clarendon, 1971.

———. "Henry and Emma." In *The Literary Works of Matthew Prior*, edited by H. Bunker Wright and Monroe K. Spears. vol. 1, 278–300. Oxford: Clarendon, 1971.

Rabelais, Francois. *Gargantua and Pantagruel.* Edited by Thomas Urquhart and Peter Motteux. New York: Harcourt Brace, 1931.

Richardson, Samuel. *Pamela; or, Virtue Rewarded.* Edited by Peter Sabor, with an introduction by Margaret Doody, 1740. New York: Penguin, 1980.

Rowe, Nicholas. *The Tragedy of Jane Shore.* Menston, U.K.: Scolar Press, 1973.

Sévigné, Madame de. *Letters from Madame la Marquise de Sévigné.* Edited by Violet Hammersley. London: Secker & Warburg, 1955.

Shakespeare, William. *Hamlet.* In *The Complete Works of Shakespeare*, edited by David Bevington. 4th ed. 1060–1116. New York: HarperCollins, 1992.

———. *A Midsummer Night's Dream.* In *The Complete Works of Shakespeare*, edited by David Bevington. 4th ed. 150–77. New York: HarperCollins, 1992.

———. *Twelfth Night.* In *The Complete Works of Shakespeare*, edited by David Bevington. 4th ed. 326–61. New York: HarperCollins, 1992.

Sheridan, Frances. *Memoirs of Miss Sidney Biddulph.* Edited by Sue Townsend. New York: Pandora, 1987.

Thomson, James. *The Poetical Works of James Thomson.* Port Washington, N.Y.: Kessinger Press, 2003.

———. "Spring" and "Summer." In *Thomson's Seasons: Critical Edition*, edited by Otto Zippel, 1–54 and 55–182. Berlin: Mayer and Muller, 1908.

Walpole, Horace. *The Castle of Otranto.* New York: Dover, 2004.

Warburton, William, Bishop of Gloucester. "Letter on Dr. Law." (September 22, 1751). *Letter of Bishop Warburton.* In *Literary Anecdotes of the Eighteenth Century*, edited by John Nichols, vol. 2, 71. London: W. Bowyer, 1812.

Secondary Sources

Andrew, Donna T., and Randall MacGowen. *The Perreaus and Mrs. Rudd: Forgery and Betrayal in Eighteenth-Century London.* Berkeley: University of California Press, 2001.

Benedetti, Jean. *David Garrick and the Birth of Modern Theatre.* London: Metheun, 2001.

Bloom, Harold. *Fanny Burney's* Evelina. New York: Chelsea Books, 1988.

Brewer, E. Cobham. *Brewer's Concise Dictionary of Phrase and Fable.* 16th ed. Edited by Betsy Kirkpatrick. London: Cassell, 1992.

Campbell, Colin. *The Romantic Ethic and the Spirit of Modern Consumerism.* Oxford: Oxford University Press, 1987.

Carretta, Vincent. "Possible Gustavus Vassa/Olaudah Equiano Attributions." In *The Faces of Anonymity: Anonymous and Pseudonymous Publication from the Sixteenth to the Twentieth Century,* edited by Robert John Griffin, 103–39. New York: Palgrave Macmillan, 2003.

Castle, Terry. *Masquerade and Civilization: The Carnivalesque in Eighteenth-Century English Culture and Fiction.* Stanford: Stanford University Press, 1986.

Cecil, Lord David. *Lord M., or The Later Life of Lord Melbourne.* New York: Bobbs-Merrill, 1939.

Chancellor, E. Beresford, ed. *The Annals of Fleet Street: Its Traditions and Associations.* Port Washington, N.Y.: Kessinger Press, 2005.

Dolan, Brian. *Ladies of the Grand Tour: British Women in Pursuit of Enlightenment and Adventure in Eighteenth-Century Europe.* London: HarperCollins, 2001.

Doody, Margaret. *Frances Burney: The Life in the Works.* New Brunswick: Rutgers University Press, 1988.

Foreman, Amanda. *Georgiana.* New York: HarperCollins, 1998.

Griffin, Robert John, ed. *The Faces of Anonymity: Anonymous and Pseudonymous Publications from the Sixteenth to the Twentieth Century.* New York: Palgrave Macmillan, 2003.

Hall, James A. *Hall's Dictionary of Subjects and Symbols in Art.* Introduction by Kenneth Clark. London: John Murray, 1974.

Harman, Claire. *Fanny Burney: A Biography.* New York: Alfred Knopf, 2001.

Kendall, Alan. *David Garrick: A Biography.* London: Harrap, 1985.

Mack, Maynard. *Alexander Pope: A Life.* New Haven: Yale University Press, 1986.

Marvin, Dwight Edwards, ed. *Antiquity of Proverbs.* New York: Putnam, 1926.

Masters, Brian. *Georgiana.* London: Hamish Hamilton, 1981.

Poovey, Mary. *The Proper Lady and the Woman Writer: Ideology as Style in the Works of Mary Wollstonecraft, Mary Shelley, and Jane Austen.* Chicago: University of Chicago Press, 1984.

Prola, Diana J. "The Sylph in Pope's *Rape of the Lock.*" Master's thesis, California State University, Hayward, 1974.

Raven, James, and Antonia Forster, with the assistance of Stephen Bending. *The English Novel, 1770–1829: A Bibliographical Survey of Prose Fiction Published in the British Isles.* vol. 1. Oxford: Oxford University Press, 2000.

Schrodter, Willy. *A Rosicrucian Notebook: The Secret Sciences Used by Members of the Order.* New York: Weiser Books, 1992.

Seeber, Edward D. "Sylphs and Other Elemental Beings in French Literature Since Le Comte de Gabalis (1670)." *PMLA* 59, no. 1 (1944): 243–55.

Shelley, Percy. *Letters of Percy Shelley.* Edited by Frederick Lafayette Jones. Oxford: Clarendon Press, 1964.

Stone, George Winchester. *David Garrick: A Critical Biography.* Carbondale: Southern Illinois Press, 1979.

Woods, Leigh. *Garrick Claims the Stage: Acting as Social Emblem in Eighteenth-Century England.* Westport, Conn.: Greenwood Press, 1984.